I0630630

Hinchliff.

*Catullus.*

# EROTICA.

## THE POEMS OF

# CATULLUS AND TIBULLUS,

### AND

## THE VIGIL OF VENUS.

A LITERAL PROSE TRANSLATION WITH NOTES,

BY

### WALTER K. KELLY.

TO WHICH ARE ADDED
#### THE METRICAL VERSIONS OF LAMB AND GRAINGER,
##### AND A SELECTION OF VERSIONS BY OTHER WRITERS.

## Fredonia Books
## Amsterdam, The Netherlands

Erotica:

The Poems of Catullus and Tibullus, and the Vigil of Venus

by
Valerius Catullus
Albius Tibullus

Translated by Walter K. Kelly

ISBN: 1-4101-0431-1

Copyright © 2004 by Fredonia Books

Reprinted from the 1880 edition

Fredonia Books
Amsterdam, The Netherlands
http://www.fredoniabooks.com

# CONTENTS.

# THE ELEGIES OF TIBULLUS.

## BOOK I.

# BIOGRAPHICAL INTRODUCTION.

## CATULLUS.

A MEAGRE array of facts more or less controverted, and a few critical remarks, are all we can offer towards a biography of Valerius Catullus. We learn from the testimony of many ancient writers, that he was a native of Verona or its immediate neighbourhood; and the Marquis Scipio Maffei, himself a Veronese, asserts that in his day there were still traits of the language of Catullus in the dialect of his countrymen. Whether the poet's prænomen was Caius or Quintus is uncertain, the former being assigned to him by Apuleius, the latter by Pliny. A more important question is that which concerns the dates of his birth and death. According to Hieronymus, in the Eusebian chronicle, he was born B. C. 87, and died in his thirtieth year, B. C. 57. The second date is undoubtedly erroneous, for we have positive evidence from his own works that he was alive in the consulship of Vatinius, B. C. 47. It is evident too that he must have survived at least till B. C. 45, for Cicero, in his Letters, talks of the verses of Catullus against Cæsar and Mamurra (xxix.) as newly written, and first seen by Cæsar in that year. The chronologer's mistake as to the time of the poet's death, throws some doubt also on that which he assigns to his birth. We shall however be exact enough for all literary purposes, if we conclude with Dunlop that Catullus " was nearly contemporary with Lucretius, having come into the world a few years after him, and having survived him but a short period."

It is not certain that the poet belonged to the patrician family of the Valerii, but his father must have been a person of some consideration, for he was the friend and habitual entertainer of Julius Cæsar. The son took up his abode in Rome in the very spring of youth (lxviii. 15) and plunged without restraint into all the expensive pleasures of the best—that is to say, the most debauched—society. This is sufficient to account for the jocular complaints of poverty interspersed through his writings. It is easy to conceive that one whose only business was to enjoy life in an age and in a city of unbounded luxury, and who was a liberal purchaser of such commodities as were dealt in by the worthy Silo (ciii.), should have been often " hard up " for cash ; and that he should have had occasion for frequent intercourse with lawyers and orators, such as Alphenus Varus,

B

Licinius Calvus, and M. Tullius Cicero. Yet his fortune was by no means small, for he possessed a noble villa on the beautiful promontory of Sirmio, another near Tibur, and he made a voyage from the Pontus in his own yacht. To improve his pecuniary circumstances, he adopted the usual Roman expedient for quickly filling a lank purse, and accompanied Caius Memmius, the celebrated patron of Lucretius, to Bithynia, when he was appointed Prætor of that province. But it is plain from his direct testimony, as well as from the bitterness of his invectives against his chief, that he derived little profit from that expedition.

Catullus repeatedly deplores with every mark of heartfelt grief the loss of a brother who died in the Troad. This event is generally supposed to have happened whilst the poet was in Bithynia; but, as Professor Ramsay has well remarked, "any evidence we possess leads to a different conclusion. When railing against the evil fortune which attended the journey to the East, he makes no allusion to any such misfortune as this; we find no notice of the event in the pieces written immediately before quitting Asia and immediately after his return to Italy; nor does the language of those passages in which he gives vent to his sorrow, in any way confirm the conjecture."

Gifted with a fine person, a vigorous constitution, and rare genius, Catullus was meant by nature for better things: it was the curse of his times that made him an idler and a voluptuary:

> O blame not the bard if he fly to the bowers
> Where Pleasure sits carelessly smiling at Fame;
> He was born for much more, and in happier hours
> His soul might have glowed with a holier flame.

That he was not indifferent to public wrongs is proved by the vehemence with which he assailed Cæsar in the plenitude of his power. A man of fine sensibility and delicate fancy, he was no less remarkable for the strength and depth of his feelings. Regarded as indications of character, his poems to Lesbia are unique in Roman literature for the intensity and self-oblivion of the passion they portray. Some of them breathe the delicious frenzy of desire; or the sweet sadness that ever mingles with the best of joy, and is so like it that we scarce know whether to call it pain or pleasure; the rest are heavy with the grief for which there is no cure, the anguish of a heart that dotes, yet more than doubts; that cannot cease to love what it loathes and scorns.

Clodia, as we learn from Apuleius, was the real name of Lesbia, "but this bare fact"—we again quote Ramsay—"by no means entitles us to jump to the conclusion at which many have arrived, that she was the sister of the celebrated Clodius slain by Milo. Indeed the presumption is strong against such an inference. The tribute of high-flown praise paid to Cicero would have been but a bad recommendation to the favour of one whom the orator makes the subject of scurrilous jests, and who is said to have cherished against him all the vindictive animosity of a woman first slighted, and then openly insulted." Of other women with whom he may have amused himself, Catullus names only Hypsithilla and Aufilina, ladies of Verona; but the language in which he writes of them denotes an intercourse in which the senses were vividly interested, the affections not at all. Some of his poems are hideous from the traces of a turpitude to which we cannot without a painful effort make even a passing allusion. But so are portions of almost every Roman poet; and amidst our natural disgust at these abominations, and at the filthy ribaldry of many of the short pieces of Catullus, it is right to remember that these things were the vices of the age rather than of the individual. " The filth of Catullus seldom springs from a prurient imagination revelling in voluptuous images ; it rather proceeds from habitual impurity of expression, and probably gives a fair representation of the manners and conversation of the gay society of Rome at that period."

In the contents of a very small book, Catullus has given proof of extraordinary versatility, and consummate skill in the most dissimilar moods of his art. His compass is a wide one, and he is master of all within it. His peculiar characteristics are neatness, racy simplicity, graceful turns of thought, and exquisite happiness of expression. In these qualities he has never been surpassed ; and they are apparent alike in his most playful trifles, and when he ascends to the mountain-heights of passion and imagination. Of him it may be affirmed with absolute truth, that he adorned all he touched ; hence the appropriateness of the epithet *doctus* which was bestowed upon him by his poetic brethren, not, as many have supposed, because of his proficiency in Greek literature, but because of his mastery in the art he professed. *Doctus* does not always mean book-learned ; it is often used to signify skill in any art —as in that of archery for instance, when Tibullus calls Cupid's hands *doctas*, after they had learned the use of the bow. *Doctus* means " taught," and as one who is well taught is accomplished in his speciality, the epithet came naturally to bear that secondary signification. That the English epithet "learned" is restricted to one particular kind of proficiency, is merely the result of arbitrary custom. The wider import of the Latin word is better expressed in such obsolete phrases as " cunning of fence," "cunning in music, in mathematics," &c. In this sense Horace applies it to the great actor Roscius ; and in this sense it was applied by courtesy to poets in general, and distinctively and emphatically to Catullus.

Horace unjustly assumes to himself (Epist. 19, lib. i.) the credit of having been the first to enrich the literature of his country with imitations of the Greek lyric poets; Catullus had preceded him in that field, and with the more essential advantage which genius possesses over talent. "Catullus," says Dunlop, "translated many of the shorter and more delicate pieces of the Greeks; an attempt which hitherto had been thought impossible, though the broad humour of their comedies, the vehement pathos of their tragedies, and the romantic interest of the Odyssey, had stood the transformation. His stay in Bithynia, though little advantageous to his fortune, rendered him better acquainted than he might otherwise have been with the productions of Greece ; and he was therefore in a great degree indebted to this expedition (on which he always appears to have looked back with mortification and disappointment) for those felicitous turns of expression, that grace, simplicity, and purity, which are the characteristics of his poems, and of which hitherto Greece alone had afforded models. Indeed in all his verses, whether elegiac or heroic, we perceive his imitation of the Greeks, and it must be admitted that he has drawn from them his choicest stores. His Hellenisms are frequent ; his images, similes, metaphors, and addresses to himself, are all Greek ; and even in the versification of his odes we see visible traces of their origin. Nevertheless he was the inventor of a new species of *Latin* poetry ; and as he was the first who used such variety of measures, and perhaps invented some that were new, he was amply entitled to call the poetical volume which he presented to Cornelius Nepos *Lepidum Novum Libellum.* The beautiful expressions, too, and idioms of the Greek language, which he has so carefully selected, are woven with such art into the texture of his composition, and so aptly figure the impassioned ideas of his amorous muse, that they have all the fresh and untarnished hues of originality." It is certain that some, and probable that many, of the poems of Catullus have perished. Pliny makes mention of verses upon love-charms of which no trace remains, and Terentianus Maurus mentions some *Ithyphallica.* The scholiasts Servius and Nonius refer to passages which are not to be found in the existing collection of the works of Catullus. On the other hand, the *Ciris* and the *Pervigilium Veneris* have been erroneously ascribed to him. We should have lost him wholly but for the fortuitous discovery of a single manuscript in bad condition, which was found in France in the year 1425. From this source were derived all the MSS. on which the old editions were founded, and hence, as might be expected, the text is very corrupt, and presents a greater number of various and contradictory readings than that of almost any other classic. It is certain too that it has been repeatedly interpolated.

The present prose translation of Catullus, the first, we believe, that has appeared in English, has been framed upon the principle of adhering as closely to the letter of the original as is consistent with the genius of the respective languages. For a faithful rendering of the letter, prose is the best medium ; but there its powers end ; for all beyond we must have recourse to verse. The poetical versions that follow have been carefully selected from many writers, and comprise all the best specimens of their kind that have yet been published.

---

# TIBULLUS.

ALBIUS TIBULLUS (his prænomen is unknown) was a Roman knight, contemporary with Horace and Virgil. The date of his birth is uncertain, but must be placed somewhere about B. C. 59, the year in which Livy came into the world. A spurious distich in the fifth Elegy of book iii. was long accepted as proof that Tibullus was born in the same year as Ovid, who, on the contrary, invariably speaks of him as a more ancient writer and an older man than himself, and particularly in a passage of the Tristia, (IV. x.,) in which he fixes the order of succession of the Elegiac poets :—

> Virgil I but beheld ; and greedy fate
> Denied Tibullus' friendship, wish'd too late :
> He followed Gallus, next Propertius came ;
> The last was I. the fourth successive name. ELTON.

It appears from an epigram of Domitius Marsus, another contemporary of Tibullus, that he died soon after Virgil, that is to say, in or about B. C. 19, while he was yet in the prime of life, or, as the epigram says, while he was still *juvenis*, for by that term the Romans meant one who had not passed his forty-sixth year.

> Te quoque, Virgilio comitem, non æqua, Tibulle,
> Mors juvenem campos misit ad Elysios :
> Ne foret, aut elegis molles qui fleret amores,
> Aut caneret forti regia bella pede.

> Thee, young Tibullus, to th' Elysian plain
> Death bade accompany great Maro's shade ;
> Determined that no poet should remain,
> Or to sing wars, or weep the cruel maid. GRAINGER.

Tibullus was descended from an ancient and wealthy equestrian family; but we learn from himself that he possessed only a small portion of the estates of his forefathers. The cause of this decline of fortune has been warmly debated among the learned ; some alleging, rightly, as it seems to us, that we need not look further for it than to the confiscations of the tri-umviri, in which so many Italian estates were involved ; others, that he was ruined by his own extravagance. The father of Tibullus had been en-gaged on the side of Pompey in the civil wars, and died soon after Cæsar had finally triumphed over the liberties of Rome. It is not to be doubted that the patrimony of the son should have been involved in the subsequent partition of the lands of Italy ; and though he saved something from the wreck, probably through the interest of his patron, Messala, we do not find in his Elegies a single expression of gratitude or compliment from which it might be conjectured that Augustus had atoned to him for the wrongs done by Octavius. It is certainly remarkable, in reference to this question, and it raises our respect for the man, that the name of Augustus, celebrated with such persevering and fulsome adulation by the other great poets of the day, is nowhere to be found in the writings of Tibullus. The notion that he wasted his large fortune in dissipation is little more than a gratuitous assumption, the only evidence offered in support of it being a poetical hyperbole. In the fourth Elegy of the second book he declares himself ready to sacrifice all that was left of his hereditary possessions to gratify the demands of his covetous mistress : whence some would have us infer, that the man who could deliberately talk thus, in a good hex-ameter and pentameter distich, must certainly have made ducks and drakes of his property. We rather think that the general tenour of his writings, as well as the direct testimony of his friend Horace, leads to the opposite conclusion. That discreet Epicurean would not have complimented a reckless spendthrift on his knowledge of the art of enjoyment.

Tibullus acquired at an early period the friendship of his great patron, Messala, and retained it to the end of his life. He declined that com-mander's invitation to accompany him in the naval war which was des-tined to close with the decisive battle of Actium, doubtless because he remained stedfast in his attachment to the cause for which his father had suffered. Immediately after that victory, Messala was detached by Cæsar to suppress a formidable insurrection which had broken out in Aquitaine ; and Tibullus accompanied him in the honourable post of *contubernalis*,

corresponding nearly to that of aid-de-camp. Part of the glory of the
Aquitanian campaign, for which Messala, four years later, obtained a triumph, and which Tibullus celebrates in language of unwonted loftiness,
redounds, according to the poet, to his own fame (book I. vii. 9—11).
In the following year, (B. C. 30,) Messala was sent to Asia, and again
Tibullus went with him, but was taken ill and obliged to remain in Corcyra, an incident which forms the theme of another beautiful poem
(book I. iii.).

After his recovery he seems to have returned home, and to have spent
the rest of his days, excepting occasional visits to the capital, at his country seat near Pedum, a small town of Latium on the skirts of the Apennines, between Præneste and Tibur. That he lived there in the enjoyment of a liberal competence is clear enough, and also that when he speaks
of his poverty, that term is only to be understood by contrast with the
overgrown fortunes of many of his noble countrymen. This is apparent
from many of his own expressions (e. g. book I. i. 5) ; as a Roman knight
he must have been worth upwards of three thousand pounds ; and Horace
even speaks of him as wealthy. According to him, Tibullus possessed all
the blessings of life : he was beautiful in person (Horace on this point
confirms the strong language of the old biographers) ; he had a competent
fortune, favour with the great, fame, health ; and knew how to enjoy all
those blessings. Epist. iv. book i.

> Albius ! the candid critic of my strains,
> What shall I say thou dost on Pedum's plains ?
> Say, dost thou verses write that shall outvie
> Cassius of Parma's darling poesy ?
> Dost thou steal silent through some healthful wood,
> And muse thoughts worthy of the wise and good ?
> Thou wert not born a body void of mind ;
> Yet heaven to thee a graceful form assigned.
> Heaven gave thee riches, and it gave thee more,
> The art to use and to enjoy thy store.
> What beyond this could some fond nurse devise
> To bless her foster-son ? whose thoughts are wise,
> And graced with fluent speech ; whom favours crown
> From the high great, and, from his muse, renown ;
> Abundant health ; a style of life and board
> Genteel with decency, and purse well stored. ELTON.

Notwithstanding all his personal and mental graces, and his singularly
amiable disposition, Tibullus was not happy in love. The object of that
attachment, which we have Ovid's authority for considering as his first, is
celebrated under the poetic name of Delia, a Greek equivalent for her real
name, which Apuleius tells us was Plania. It is evident (see book I. vi.)
that she was not of gentle blood (not *ingenua*, but *libertinæ conditionis*).
She belonged, says Milman, " to that class of females of the middle order,
not of good family, but above poverty, which answered to the Greek
hetairai." Tibullus became attached to her before his expedition to
Aquitaine, and thought of retiring to the country with her as his mistress.
But Delia was faithless during his absence. On his return from Corcyra
he found her ill, and attended her with affectionate solicitude, again hoping

to realize his favourite project. But first a richer rival supplanted him; next there appears a husband in the way; and after the seventh Elegy of the first book we hear no more of Delia. His last love was the mercenary Nemesis, to whom the second book and the last two years of the poet's life were devoted, apparently without any return. The third book —if this indeed is the composition of Tibullus—is chiefly occupied with his unfortunate passion for Neæra. Her, it would appear, he wished to marry, he had indeed been actually betrothed to her, but she forsook him on the eve of the nuptials. Lastly, there was Glycera, who gave him great pain by forsaking him for a younger man, and whom we have no reason for confounding with any of the other three, though she is not known to us from his own writings, but only from the Ode in which Horace attempts to console him for her inconstancy.

Tibullus belongs eminently to that class of poets whose works reflect the form and colour of their own history. His lot fell upon the evil days of his country, in which the remnant of its virtues perished with its rights. A long series of civil wars and proscriptions had produced that general dissoluteness of manners which invariably attends uncertainty of life and property; Eastern conquests had filled Rome with the accumulated wealth, and polluted her with the vices, of enslaved nations. Had her freedom survived, the old Roman spirit might yet have rallied; but the one died out when the other was crushed under the despotism of Augustus. The empire grew in might and majesty; but its men and women became daily viler; and the refinement gained by imitation of foreign examples, though in itself a good thing, was a poor exchange for the honour and honesty of the rough old republican days; for the racy freshness of home-grown habits, thoughts, feelings, and affections; for every native grace of life, lost for ever. Imagine a man like Tibullus cast upon such times as those, —a man of instinctive elegance of mind, of extreme sensibility and warm affections, more given to contemplation than to action,—and you may go near to anticipate much of the general tone of those effusions in which his inward nature spontaneously reveals itself. Add to this, that he was unhappy in love—how could he have been otherwise?—less prosperous in fortune than in early youth he had reason to expect, a member of a defeated party, and faithful to the memory of a ruined cause; and we shall more clearly discern the sources of that tender melancholy which is his habitual mood, and of those changeful and often impulsive emotions that break its even flow, but always subside into it and leave it as before. Ill at ease among the realities of the life that surrounded him, he flew to nature, the perpetual nurse of wounded spirits, and animating his solitude with the traditions of the past, he lived in an ideal world. A relish for the delights of the country was a national characteristic of the Romans; in him it had the force of a passion. Hence all those exquisite pictures of rural scenes and habits, which so strongly impress us with the idea of the poet's kindly nature.

The Latin elegy, like the Greek epigram or inscription, had a latitude beyond its title. Practically the name implies nothing more definite than a poem not exceeding a certain length, and written in alternate hexameter and pentameter lines. Of that species which turns on love, Tibullus is confessedly the master. He is also the most original Latin poet of the Augustan age, by which we do not mean that he is distinguished for extraordinary powers of invention, but that he owed nothing to Greek models. His subjects, method, diction, and tone, are all his own. His thoughts are natural; he abounds with delicate strokes of sentiment and expression; his language is pure from conceit, and his style, though highly finished, has a perfectly easy and flowing simplicity. His range, however, as may be supposed from what we have already said, is not a wide one; and it must be admitted that he recurs to one set of themes and imagery with something of a monotonous frequency. But this defect belongs only to his elegies taken collectively. Separately considered, each piece is remarkable for the copious variety of its thoughts and images, as well as for the subtlety of the links by which it is made to cohere in the smoothest and most unconstrained manner.

The poems which bear the name of Tibullus are comprised in four books. The authenticity of the first two has never been questioned; but a controversy was raised by I. H. Voss, towards the close of the last century, respecting the authorship of the third book, which is addressed to Neæra, nominally by one Lygdamus. Who was he? According to the common opinion, he was either a fictitious personage, or, much more probably, Tibullus himself under an assumed name. Voss however contended that Lygdamus, or whoever wrote under that name, was not Tibullus, but another and very inferior poet. This opinion found some adherents in Germany; but Milman, so far as we are aware, is the only scholar of note by whom it has been adopted in this country.[1] Bach, who at one time inclined to the Vossian theory, has pronounced what we think a sounder critical opinion in his edition of 1819. He says it appears that Tibullus addressed the book in question to Neæra when he was very young, and that this circumstance sufficiently explains the faults here and there observable in a work which bears strong marks of resemblance to the manner of Tibullus, and is on the whole not unworthy of his genius. As for the fourth book, we see no reason to dissent from the judgment pronounced upon it by Milman, in common with many of the best critics. "The hexameter poem on Messala," he says, "which opens the fourth book, is so bad, that although a successful Elegiac poet may have failed when he attempted Epic verse, it cannot well be ascribed to a writer of the exquisite taste of Tibullus. The smaller Elegies of the fourth book have all the inimitable grace and simplicity of Tibullus. With the exception of the thirteenth, (of which some lines are hardly surpassed by Tibullus himself,) these poems relate to the love of Sulpicia, a woman of noble birth, for Cerinthus, the real or fictitious name of a beautiful youth. Sulpicia seems to have belonged to the intimate society of Messala (El. iv. 8). Nor is there any improbability in supposing that Tibullus may have written Elegies in the name or by the desire of Sulpicia. If Sulpicia was herself the poetess, she approached nearer to Tibullus than any other writer of Elegies."

[1] Smith's Dict. of Greek and Rom. Biog. *art.* Tibullus.

# THE POEMS

### OF

# VALERIUS CATULLUS.

---

## I. DEDICATION.

To whom do I give this sprightly little book, new, and just polished with dry pumice?[1] To you, Cornelius;[2] for you were wont to think my trifles of some account, and that even at the time when you alone among Italian *scholars* dared to expound the history of every age in three treatises, Jupiter! how erudite and elaborate! Accept therefore this little book, such as it is; and, O protecting Virgin,[3] may it endure for many a century.

## II. TO LESBIA'S SPARROW.[4]

SPARROW, delight of my girl, which she plays with, which

---

[1] *Dry pumice.*] The Romans wrote on parchment, and used pumice stone, as the moderns do, to smooth the face of the sheet that it might the better receive the ink. When the writing was finished they smoothed the outside of the sheet also; hence any highly finished composition was said figuratively to be *pumice expolitum.*

[2] *Cornelius.*] That this was Cornelius Nepos, the historian, is sufficiently established by a poem of Ausonius.

[3] *Protecting Virgin.*] Minerva, the patroness of literature. Several editions read *patrima Virgo*, an allusion to the birth of the goddess from the brain of Jove without a mother. But probably the whole passage is spurious, as Handius argues; nor is it likely that Catullus would have invoked the austere Minerva's patronage for his light and sportive effusions, though she might not have disdained a few of his poems, such as the "Nuptials of Peleus and Thetis."

[4] *To Lesbia's Sparrow.*] The learned Politian, Lampridius, Turnebus, and Vossius will have it, that Lesbia's sparrow is an indecent allegory, typifying the same thing as the "grey duck" in Pope's imitation of Chaucer. Politian has been smartly castigated for this by Sannazarius,

she keeps in her bosom, to whose eager beak she offers the tip
of her finger, and provokes its sharp peckings, when my brightly fair darling has a mind to indulge in some little endearing
sport, as a solace, I believe, for the grief *of absence*, that the
painful smarting *of her bosom* may be still : to be able to
play with thee, as she does, and allay my grief and anxiety of
mind, were as welcome to me, as they say was to the swift-
footed girl[1] that golden apple, which loosed her long-bound
zone.[2]

in some witty lines, which end with something to the effect that the critic
would like to devour the bird :

Meus hic Pulicianus
Tam bellum sibi passerem Catulli
Intra viscera habere concupiscit.

"I agree with Sannazarius," says Noel. "Take this piece in its natural
and obvious sense, and it is a model of grace and good taste : adopt the
licentious allegory, and nothing can be more forced and frigid." Martial,
the professed imitator of Catullus, and for that very reason to be dis-
trusted as his interpreter, set the first example of this perverse refinement
on the simple meaning of the poem. "Kiss me," he says, "and then
*Donabo tibi passerem Catulli*, I will give you Catullus's sparrow,"—by
which he does not mean a poem. Again, in the Apophoreta there is the
following passage about putting a bird in a cage.

Si tibi talis erit, qualem dilecta Catullo
Lesbia ploravit, hic habitare potest.

"If you have such a sparrow as Catullus's Lesbia deplored, it may lodge
here." Chaulieu has an epigram to the same purport :

Autant et plus que sa vie
Phyllis aime un passereau ;
Ainsi la jeune Lesbie
Jadis aima son moineau.
Mais de celui de Catulle
Se laissant aussi charmer,
Dans sa cage, sans scrupule,
Elle eut soin de l' enfermer.

[1] *The swift-footed girl.*] Atalanta would accept no one as a husband
who could not excel her in the race. After baffling many suitors by her
extraordinary speed, she was won by Hippomenes by means of a strata-
gem suggested by Venus. The goddess gave him three golden apples,
which he threw down before Atalanta at critical moments in the race ;
she stopped to pick them up, and was beaten.

[2] *Loosed her zone.*] Virgins wore a girdle which was unbound by the
bridegroom's own hands on the wedding night. The custom was common
both to Greece and Italy, and, in the language of both, the phrase *to undo
the zone*, was currently used to signify the loss of virginity. In Greece
the same significance was attached to the "mitra," the band, or "snood,"
as the Scotch call it, with which maidens bound up their hair ; and in

## III. LAMENT FOR THE DEATH OF THE SPARROW.[1]

LAMENT, O Loves and Desires, and every man of refinement! My girl's sparrow is dead, my girl's pet sparrow, which she loved more than her own eyes; for it was a honeyed *darling*, and knew its mistress as well as my girl herself knew her mother; nor did it ever depart from her breast, but hopping about now hither, now thither, would chirp ever more to its mistress only. Now does it go along the gloomy path to that region whence no one can return. Malediction to you! cruel glooms of Orcus, that devour all fair things; such a pretty sparrow you have taken from me. Unhappy event! poor little sparrow! On your account my girl's eyes are now red and swollen with weeping.

## IV. THE PRAISE OF THE PINNACE.[2]

THAT pinnace you see, my friends, avers that it was once the swiftest of vessels, and never failed to outstrip the speed of any craft that swam, whether the course was to be run with oars or canvass. And this, it says, the coast[3] of the threatening Adriatic, and the Cyclades[4] deny not, nor noble Rhodes, nor rugged Thrace,[5] Propontis,[6] nor the angry Pontic Gulf;[7] where that pinnace, *as it* afterwards *became*, was formerly a leafy wood; for often hath it uttered a rustling sound with its vocal foliage on the Cytorian range.

Scotland formerly, the lassie who had *lost her snood* without permission of the kirk, was in danger of the cutty stool.

[1] *The Death of the Sparrow.*] This exquisite little poem was in high repute among the ancients. Juvenal alludes to it in his sixth Satire, and Martial in several places. It has been imitated, but far from equalled, by Ovid, in his elegy on the death of a parrot, and by Stella, Martial's contemporary, in a lost poem on a dove. Noel, the French translator of Catullus, has enumerated fifteen modern Latin imitations.

[2] *The Praise of the Pinnace.*] Catullus appears to have written this poem on the occasion of his return from Bithynia. It contains a geographical summary of his voyage in inverted order.

[3] *Coast.*] There is a peculiar propriety in this word; because the ancient navigators usually coasted along and seldom ventured on the open sea.

[4] *Cyclades.*] A round cluster of islands in the Archipelago.

[5] *Thrace.*] Now called Romania or Roumelia.

[6] *Propontis.*] Sea of Marmora.

[7] *Pontic Bay.*] The Euxine, now the Black Sea.

To you also, Pontic Amastris,[1] and box-clad Cytorus,[2] my
pinnace says that these facts were well known,—says that from
its earliest origin it stood upon your summit, that it first
dipped its oars in your waters, and bore its master thence
through so many raging seas, whether the wind piped from
larboard or from starboard, or whether favouring Jove[3] fell
on both sheets[4] together ; and that it made no vows *under
distress* to the gods of the coast, when it came from the extremity of the sea and reached this limpid lake.[5]

But these things belong to the past ; it is now growing old
in secluded repose, and dedicates itself to thee, Castor, and to
thy twin brother.[6]

## V. TO LESBIA.

Let us live and love, my Lesbia, and a farthing for all the
talk of morose old sages ! Suns may set and rise again ; but
we, when once our brief light has set, must sleep through a
perpetual night. Give me a thousand kisses, then a hundred,
then another thousand, then a second hundred, then still[7]
another thousand, then a hundred. Then when we shall have
made up many thousands, we will confuse the reckoning, so
that we ourselves may not know their amount, nor any spite-

---

[1] *Amastris.*]   A town near Cytorus, now called Famastro.
[2] *Cytorus.*]   A mountain in Paphlagonia in Asia Minor. Evelyn calls
Box-hill in Surrey, " The Cytorus of England."
[3] *Favouring Jove.*]   The god of the air, put by synecdoche for the
wind.
[4] *Both sheets.*]   *Utrumque pedem.* The lower corners of the sail, and
the ropes by which they were made fast, were called *pedes.* " Sheets "
is the corresponding technical term in English.
[5] *This limpid lake.*]   Lake Benacus, now the Lago di Garda.
[6] *Dedicates itself,* &c.]   This little poem, which was probably suspended as an *exvoto* in the temple of Castor and Pollux, has compara-
tively slight interest for modern readers, yet it has been the theme of
countless imitations and parodies, the earliest of which is extant in the
*Catalecta Virgilii.* It is a squib upon the famous Ventidius, who began
life as a muleteer, and afterwards rose to be prætor and consul. The
modern parodies are very numerous. A collection of ten, edited with
notes by Sextus Octavianus, was published at York in 1579. The most
notable of them is one by Julius Cæsar Scaliger ; it is a fine sample of
the mutual amenity of the learned of the sixteenth century. The subject
of the lampoon is Doletus, who is shown up as a pimp, a thief, an
assassin, and a drunkard, &c.
[7] *Still another,* &c.]   *Usque :* without intermission ; in a breath.

ful person have it in his power to envy us[1] when he knows
that our kisses were so many.

## VI. TO FLAVIUS.

FLAVIUS, you would freely tell Catullus of your charmer,
nor could you keep silence *on that subject*, were it not that
she has neither sprightliness nor grace. Surely you love
some hot-blooded jade or another, and you are ashamed to
confess it. Your couch, scented with garlands and Syrian
oil, *is* by no means silent, *but* tells a clamorous tale; so too
does the cushion equally indented in this place and in that,
and the creaking and stamping of the quivering bed; for
unless *you can hush up* these *evidences*, silence is of no avail.
Who is there to whom your lank, enfeebled flanks do not
reveal what follies you commit by night? Tell me therefore
what you have got, whether fair or foul; I wish to cry up
you and your beloved to the skies in gay verse.

## VII. TO LESBIA.

YOU ask how many kisses of yours, Lesbia, may be enough
for me, and more ? As the numerous sands that lie on the spicy
shores[2] of Cyrene, between the oracle of sultry Jove[3] and the
sacred tomb of old Battus;[4] or as the many stars that in the
silence of night behold men's furtive amours;[5] to kiss you with
so many kisses is enough and more for madly fond Catullus;

[1] *Envy us.*] *Invidere;* i. e. to hurt us by his envy; for Roman superstition recognised an occult and mischievous potency in the very sentiment of envy. See the last note on Poem vii.

[2] *Spicy shores.*] Literally, productive of Laserpitium. This Laserpitium appears to have been a gum-resin, but what was its precise nature
is unknown to the moderns. In an old translation of three plays of
Plautus, a note on the words of Sirpe and Laserpitium says: " This
Sirpe is a species of Benjamin, from whence sprung an odoriferous
liquor, called Laserpitium, quasi Lac Serpitium."

[3] *The oracle,* &c.] The oracle of Jupiter Ammon on the confines of
Egypt. The epithet *æstuosi,* here translated *sultry,* is literally *surging,*
and applies to the heaps of burning sand, like waves, amidst which stood
the oases of Jupiter Ammon.

[4] *Old Battus.*] Battus was the royal founder of the city of Cyrene in
Libya. His tomb was four hundred miles from Ammon's temple.

[5] *As the many stars,* &c.] Thus imitated by Ariosto, canto 4,
   E per quanti occhi il ciel le furtive opre
   Degli amatori a mezza notte scopre.

such a multitude as prying gossips can neither count, nor be-witch[1] with their evil tongues.

### VIII.  TO HIMSELF.

WRETCHED Catullus, cease your folly, and look upon that as lost which you see has perished.  Fair days shone once for you, when you bent your constant steps whither that girl drew them, who was loved by us as none ever will be loved.  There all these merry things were done which you desired, and to which she was nothing loth.  Fair days indeed shone for you *then*.  Now she is not willing, be you too self-possessed, and follow not one who shuns you, nor lead a miserable life, but bear all with obstinacy, be obdurate.  Farewell, girl; Catullus is now obdurate: he will neither seek you more, nor solicit your unwilling favours.  But you will grieve, false one, when you shall not be entreated for a single night.  What manner of life now remains for you?  Who will visit you?  Who will think you charming?  Whom will you love now?  Whose will you be called?  Whom will you kiss?  Whose lips will you bite?[2]  But you, Catullus, be stubbornly obdurate.

### IX.  TO VERANNIUS.[3]

VERANNIUS, foremost in my eyes of all my friends, *had I* three hundred thousand of them, are you come home to your household gods, to your affectionate brothers, and your aged

---

[1] *Bewitch.*]  The Romans thought it unlucky to let the exact count of any of their possessions be known.  So far did they carry this super-stition, that when they stored their wine, they would never write "one" on the first jar, but "many" as being an indefinite number.  The French have an old adage which seems to arise from the same source.  "Brebis comptée, le loup la mange:"  Count your sheep and the wolf will eat them.

[2] *Whose lips will you bite?*]  Plautus speaks of Teneris labellis molles morsiunculæ.  Thus too Horace:

> Sive puer furens
> Impressit memorem dente labris notam.

> Or on thy lips the fierce fond boy
> Marks with his teeth the furious joy.  *Francis.*

Plutarch tells us that Flora, the mistress of Cn. Pompey, used to say in commendation of her lover, that she could never quit his arms without giving him a bite.

[3] *Verannius.*]  He had followed Cneius Calpurnius Piso into Spain, whether he went as questor with pretorian power.  See Poem xxv.

mother? Are you come? O happy news for me! I shall see you safe and well, and hear you tell of the regions, acts, and tribes of the Iberians, as your custom is; and, neck to neck, I shall kiss your pleasant mouth and eyes. O all ye happy men, what gladness or happiness exceeds mine?

## X. ON VARUS' MISTRESS.

VARUS[1] took me to see his mistress, as I was returning leisurely from the Forum: a wench, as it struck me at a glance, by no means deficient in sprightliness or beauty. When we came in, various subjects of conversation occurred to us: among them, what sort of a country was Bithynia,[2] what was the state of things there, and how much money had I made in it. I answered as was the fact, that neither myself, nor the prætors, nor their followers had made wherewith any one of us should show a better scented head[3] on his return, especially as we had a blackguard prætor, who did not care a rush for his followers. "But surely," said she, "you at least got bearers for your litter, for the custom is said to have originated there."[4] "Nay," said I, that I might pass myself off to the girl as one of the prosperous, "it did not go so hardly with me, bad as I found the province, that I could not procure eight straight-backed fellows." But not one had I either here or there who could lay the broken leg of my old truckle-bed on his neck. Thereupon, as became a wanton, she said, "Lend me those fellows for a little, I entreat you, my Catullus, for I want to be carried to the temple of Sera-

[1] *Varus.*] Probably Alphenus Varus, for whom see Poem xxvii.
[2] *Bithynia.*] Catullus held some office under C. Memmius Gemellus, the provincial prætor of Bithynia.
[3] *Show a better scented head.*] A common metaphor for becoming rich.
[4] *Originated there.*] We have followed, but with some misgiving, the common interpretation, which is based upon the questionable assertion that the litter or palanquin was first introduced at Rome from Bithynia. But Handius maintains the true reading to be:

quod illic
Natum dicitur, ære comparasti,

that is to say, "But surely—for money (metal) is said to grow there—you bought, &c." Bithynia was a sort of Australia in old times, as appears from many passages in classical writers, as well as from the names of some of its cities, such as Chrysopolis, Chalcedon, &c.

pis."[1]  "Stop," said I to the girl; "what I just said I had
—I made a mistake—Cinna is my comrade—Caius Cinna—
he bought them.  But whether his or mine, what matters it
to me?  I use them as freely as though I had bought them.
But you are plaguily absurd and vexatious, who will not
allow one to be careless."

## XI.  TO FURIUS AND AURELIUS.[2]

FURIUS and Aurelius, comrades of Catullus, whether he
shall make his way among the farthest Indians, where the
shore is beaten by the far-resounding eastern wave; or among
the Hyrcani, and the soft Arabs, or the Sacæ and the Par-
thian archers, or where the seven-mouthed Nile colours the
sea; or whether he shall march across the lofty Alps, visiting
the monuments of the great Cæsar, the Gallic Rhine and the
horrible and remotest Britons; you who are ready to venture
with him upon all enterprises whatever, which the will of
the gods shall impose, bear these few unwelcome words to my
girl: let her live and be happy with her paramours, three
hundred of whom she embraces, loving not one of them truly,
but wearing them all out alike.[3]  Let her not regard my love [4]
as before, a love which has fallen like a flower on the verge
of the meadow, after it has been touched by the passing
ploughshare.[5]

[1] *Serapis.*]  The temple of this Egyptian deity stood in the suburbs in
Catullus's time.  It was a favourite resort of loose women.
[2] *Furius and Aurelius.*]  This Furius is supposed to have been F. Bi-
baculus, whom Quintilian ranks high among the Iambic poets; and Aurelius may have been L. Aurelius Cotta, the Prætor.  Catullus soon quarrelled
with these dear friends, as we shall see presently.
[3] *Wearing them all out alike.*]  *Ilia rumpens.*  More exactly rendered
by Biacca :

E sol di tutti

Tenta l' iniqua ad isnervar i fianchi.

Guarini says of a coquette, that she likes to do with lovers as with gowns,
have plenty of them, use one after another, and change them often.
[4] *Regard my love.*]  Noel discerns a peculiar grace in the word *respectet,*
which seems to portray the coquette *looking back* to see if she is still
followed by the lover she affects to shun.
[5] *Like a flower,* &c.]  Very like this is a passage in Virgil, which has
been imitated by Ariosto :

Purpureus veluti cum flos, succisus aratro

Languesci moriens . . .

## XII. TO ASINIUS.

MARRUCINUS Asinius,[1] you use your left hand[2] in no credit-able manner in hours of mirth and wine. You filch the napkins of those who are at all heedless. Do you think this witty? You do not perceive, silly fellow, how low and un-becoming a thing it is. You do not believe me? Believe your brother Pollio,[3] who would be.glad if your thefts could be got rid of even at the cost of a talent: for he is a youth ac-complished in pleasantries.[4] Wherefore expect either three hundred lampoons, or send me back my napkin, which I regard not for its intrinsic value, but as a souvenir of my comrade. For Fabullus and Verannius sent me napkins as a present from Iberian Setabis,[5] which of course I must prize as I do my Verannius and Fabullus.

Come purpureo fior languendo more
Che 'l vomere al passar tagliato lassa.

Noel's remarks on this poem are ingenious. Catullus, he says, appears by no means cured of his passion, though he talks so boldly. He is jealous and piqued : he vents his resentment in no gentle terms, but dares not address his faithless mistress directly. He imposes that painful task on his friends, and implies that in so doing he puts their friendship to as severe a test as though he asked them to accompany him upon one of those formidable journeys he has enumerated. This explanation justifies the geographical exordium, which would otherwise seem cold and out of place.

[1] *Marrucinus Asinius.*] Whether Marrucinus is a name or an epithet, and if the latter, what is to be understood by it, are questions much dis-puted. The Marrucini were a people of Campania, situate between the Vestini and the Peligini : their chief town was Teate, now Chieti. They were distinguished for their fidelity to the Romans ; therefore Vulpius and Doering suppose the epithet Marrucinian is meant to reproach Asinius with his degeneracy from the high character of his countrymen. Scaliger says, the Marrucini stood in equal repute with Bœotians for stupidity, and accuses Avantius of proposing to read " Inter cœnam," in-stead of " Marrucine," merely because he was himself a Marrucinian by birth, and wished to destroy the record of the hebetude of his countrymen. Many conceive that Asinius is merely styled of the country he belonged to, without any reproach implied. Lastly, Marrucinus may be a proper name.

[2] *Left hand.*] *Thievish* hand is implied.

[3] *Pollio.*] Supposed to be Asinius Pollio, the poet, orator, and states-man, the friend of Horace and Virgil, who played so important a part under the reign of Augustus.

[4] *Pleasantries.*] *Facetiarum :* the word has a larger meaning than its English derivative "facetiousness." *Facetus* comes from *facere*; and signifies, as Noel well says, " un homme qui a l' heureux don de l' àpropos dans tout ce qu'il dit et tout ce qu'il fait."

[5] *Setabis.*] A city of Spain, on the river Tarracon.

c

### XIII. TO FABULLUS.

You will sup well at my house in a few days, my Fabullus, if the gods favour you, provided you bring with you a good and copious supper, not forgetting a fair girl, and wine, and wit, and all manner of laughter. These things I say if you bring with you, my bonny man, you shall sup well; for the purse of your Catullus is full of cobwebs. But in return you shall have *what you may call* a very love,[1] or if there be anything else sweeter or more elegant, *you may call it by that name*. For I will give you an unguent[2] which the Loves and Desires bestowed on my girl; and when you smell it, you will beseech the gods, Fabullus, to make you all nose.

### XIV. TO LICINIUS CALVUS.[3]

Did I not love you more than my eyes, most pleasant Calvus, I should hate you with Vatinian hatred[4] for that present of yours. For what have I done, or what have I said, that you should cruelly plague me with so many poets? May the gods heap many evils on that client who sent you such a lot of villains. But if, as I suspect, Sulla, the commentator,

[1] *A very love.*] *Accipies meros amores.* Doering and others take this to mean: You shall have whatever I can offer in token of the love I bear you, in other words, a hearty welcome. Achilles Statius explains the phrase as a promise that nothing shall be talked of at the supper but love, either love in general, or "my love," i. e. Catullus's, if the reading be *meos amores;* and he quotes several passages in point, e. g. *Vineta crepat mera,* Hor., "He prates of nothing but vineyards." Our interpretation is supported by the authority of Muretus.

[2] *An unguent.*] Both Greeks and Romans used perfumes and chaplets of flowers at their entertainments. "Longepierre, to give an idea of the luxurious estimation in which garlands were held by the ancients, relates an anecdote of a courtesan, who in order to gratify three lovers without leaving cause of jealousy with any of them, gave a kiss to one, let the other drink after her, and put a garland on the brow of the third; so that each was satisfied with his favour and flattered himself with the preference."—*Moore, Anacr.* lxx.

[3] *Calvus.*] Cornelius Licinius Calvus, a celebrated lawyer, orator, and poet. See Poems l. liii.

[4] *Vatinian hatred.*] Calvus had prosecuted Vatinius for bribery, and the man's general character for malignity made Vatinian hate proverbial. See Poem l.

has given you this new and choice present, I am not vexed, but delighted that your labours were not spent in vain.[1] Great gods, what a horrible and accursed book! And this forsooth you have sent to your Catullus, that he might be bored to death all day long in the Saturnalia,[2] the best of our festivals. No, no, wag, this shall not pass with you so; for as soon as it dawns I will run to the booksellers' stalls; I will collect your Cæsii, your Aquinii, Suffenus, and all sorts of poisonous trash, and pay you back with these torments.

Fare you well, meanwhile, hence with you, begone to whence you came in evil hour, pests of the age, you execrable poets.

## XV. TO AURELIUS.

I commend myself and my love to you, Aurelius, with this modest request; if ever your heart was set upon an object and longed to find it chaste and unsullied, watch over the chastity of this ward I commit to your care, and keep it safe ;— not from the general public: I have no fear of men who hurry here and there through the streets, engrossed with business; but I fear you and your everlasting priapism, that spares neither fair nor foul. Expend it abroad, how you please and on whom you please; I except this one object alone, and not unreasonably, as I think. But if in natural depravity and the delirium of concupiscence, you proceed to the unpardonable crime of inveigling one who is dear to me as my own life, oh then merciless will be your fate: feet bound—doors open— radishes and mullets![3]

---

[1] *Labours not spent in vain.*] That is, I am glad that you have received so appropriate an honorarium for advocating the cause of that wretched pedant.

[2] *Saturnalia.*] At the festival of the Saturnalia held in December, friends exchanged presents; slaves took mirthful liberties with their masters; all business was suspended; and in short, people endeavoured to revive for the time the famed golden age of the reign of Saturn.

[3] *Radishes, mullets.*] He threatens Aurelius with the atrocious punishment, which law or custom allowed the injured person to inflict on the spot upon the adulterer who was caught in the fact. It is thus described by Parthenius: Deprehensos quadrupedes constituebant, ac partibus posterioribus violenter expilatis, grandiores raphanos, aut mugiles, summo cum cruciatu immittebant.

## XVI. TO AURELIUS AND FURIUS.

I WILL trim you and trounce you,[1] Aurelius and Furius,
you infamous libertines, who judge from my verses that I am
myself indecent because they are a little voluptuous; for it
becomes the true poet[2] to be himself chaste; but it is not at
all necessary that his verses should be so.[3] On the contrary,

[1] *I will trim you and trounce you.*] *Pædicabo et irrumabo.* These
detestable words are used here only as coarse forms of threatening, with
no very definite meaning. It is certain that they were very commonly
employed in this way, with no more distinct reference to their original
import than the corresponding phrases of the modern Italians, *T' ho in
culo* and *becco fottuto,* or certain brutal exclamations common in the
mouths of the English vulgar.

[2] *The true poet.*] *Pium poetam;* the idea which these words conveyed
to the mind of a Roman corresponded very closely with that which is
expressed in the words, "the poet who is true to his vocation." In Poem
xiv. the epithet *impiorum* is applied to bad poets.

[3] *To be chaste,* &c.] Ovid has a distich to the same effect:

Crede mihi, distant mores a carmine nostri;
Vita verecunda est, musa jocosa mihi.

"Believe me there is a wide difference between my morals and my song;
my life is decorous, my muse is wanton." And Martial says:

Lasciva est nobis pagina, vita proba est.

Which is thus translated by Maynard:

Si ma plume est une putain,
Ma vie est une sainte.

Pliny quotes this poem of Catullus to excuse the wantonness of his
own verses, which he is sending to his friend Paternus; and Apuleius
cites the passage in his Apology for the same purpose. "Whoever," says
Lambe, "would see the subject fully discussed, should turn to the Essay
on the Literary Character by Mr. Disraeli." He enumerates as instances
of free writers who have led pure lives, La Motte le Vayer, Bayle, La
Fontaine, Smollet, and Cowley. 'The imagination,' he adds, 'may be a
volcano, while the heart is an Alp of ice.' It would, however, be difficult to enlarge this list, while on the other hand the catalogue of those
who really practised the licentiousness they celebrated, would be very
numerous. One period alone, the reign of Charles the Second, would
furnish more than enough to outnumber the above small phalanx of
purity. Muretus, whose poems clearly gave him every right to knowledge on the subject, but whose known debauchery would certainly have
forbidden any credit to accrue to himself from establishing the general
purity of lascivious poets, at once rejects the probability of such a contrast, saying:

Quisquis versibus exprimit Catullum
Raro moribus exprimit Catonem.

"One who is a Catullus in verse, is rarely a Cato in morals."

the very thing to give them zest and charm, is that they be a little voluptuous and indecent, and able to excite prurience, I do not say in beardless boys, but in the hardened fibres of veterans in debauchery. You, because you have read of many thousand kisses in my lines, think me effeminate; but do not presume upon my written follies; hands off! or I will give you awkward proof of my manhood.

## XVII. TO A TOWN.

O TOWN, that wishest to exhibit games on a long bridge,[1] and art ready to dance, but fearest the crazy legs of the little bridge standing on piles, lest it fall flat beyond recovery, and sink in the deep pool; may a good bridge be made for thee after thy own heart, one on which even the Salian rites[2] may be undertaken; but then, O town, grant me this most laughter-moving boon.

I want a certain townsman of mine to be pitched neck and heels from the bridge into the water; and just in that part where the boggy slime is the bluest and deepest in the whole lake and fetid marsh. The man is utterly witless; he has not as much sense as a child of two years old, rocked to sleep on his father's arm. Though he has to wife a girl in her earliest bloom, and though this girl, more delicate than a tender kid, should be watched more carefully than the ripest grapes, he lets her play as she will, and never cares a rush; nor does he bestir himself on his own part, but lies like the felled alder in a Ligurian ditch,[3] as wholly insensible as though he had no wife at all. Just so this dolt of mine sees nothing, hears nothing; he does not even know who he is, or whether he exists or not.

Now I want to send him head foremost from the bridge, *in order to see* if it be possible suddenly to rouse the stolid

---

[1] *Exhibit games on a long bridge.*] Public spectacles were usually exhibited on the town bridge; and the practice continued in modern Italy in the times of Volpi and Corradini.

[2] *The Salian rites.*] Salisubsulus was a name of Mars, whose priests, the Salii, used in their rites to dance wildly through the streets, carrying the sacred ancilia in procession.

[3] *Ligurian ditch.*] The Ligurians carried on a considerable traffic in timber which they felled in the forests of the Apennines.

numskull, and leave his inert soul behind in the heavy mud, as the mule leaves her iron shoe[1] in the stiff slough.

### XVIII. TO THE GARDEN GOD.[2]

THIS grove I dedicate and consecrate to thee, Priapus,[3] who hast thy dwelling and thy woodlands at Lampsacus; for the coast of the Hellespont, abounding above all others in oysters, especially worships thee in its cities.

### XIX. THE GARDEN GOD.

SHAPED out of a dry oak[4] by a rustic hatchet, I, lads, have fostered this place, and the marsh-land cot thatched with rushes and bundles of reeds, so that they have thriven more and more every year. For the masters of the place worship me and salute me as a god, both the father of the cottage and his son; the one taking care with diligent husbandry to keep my fane clear from brambles and rough weeds, the other continually bringing me little offerings with liberal hand. I am crowned with a garland of bright flowers, the firstlings of the blossoming spring, and with the soft green blade and ear of the tender corn. Yellow violets are offered to me, and the yellow poppy, pale gourds and fragrant apples, and the red grape reared under its shady vine. Sometimes (but you will keep it secret)[5] even the bearded he-goat and the horny-footed she-goat stain my altar with blood; in return for which

[1] *Iron shoe.*] The shoes of beasts, among the ancients, were not nailed to the hoof, but tied on with leather; consequently they were very liable to slip off.

[2] *To the Garden God.*] This fragment, and the two following poems, are found in the Catalecta of Virgil, but they are assigned to Catullus by many of the best critics, chiefly on the authority of Terentianus Maurus.

[3] *Priapus.*] This lusty god, born at Lampsacus, a city of Asia Minor, near the Hellespont, was the son of Bacchus and Venus, and his temperament was such as became his parentage. Hence the appropriateness of that peculiarly Catullian epithet *ostreosior*, "more abounding in oysters," as applied to the coasts most favoured by the lascivious deity.

[4] *A dry oak.*] The bust of Priapus was commonly cut out of the standing trunk of a tree, and was armed with a sickle, as well as with a *phallus* of most formidable dimensions.

[5] *Keep it secret.*] Some understand by this that Priapus was afraid of the anger of the Celestials if they heard of his receiving honours due to

honours Priapus is bound to do all those things *which are expected of him,* and to watch the master's garden and vineyard. Forbear therefore, boys, from pilfering here. Our next neighbour is rich and his Priapus is negligent. Take from him; this path will lead you to his grounds.

## XX. THE GARDEN GOD.

I, TRAVELLER, I, fashioned by rustic art out of a dry poplar, watch the little field you see on the left, and the cottage and the little garden of the poor owner, and repel the thief's rapacious hands. I am crowned in spring with a wreath of many colours; in the heat of summer with reddening corn; *in autumn* with sweet grapes and green shoots of the vine, and with the pale green olive. The delicate goat carries to the town from my pasture udders distended with milk; and the fat lamb from my folds sends its owner home with a handful of money; and the tender calf, in spite of its mother's lowings, pours out its blood before the temples of the gods. Therefore, traveller, you shall revere this god, *who addresses you,* and keep your hands off. It will be better for you; for an instrument of punishment, a rude *phallus,* is in readiness. "I should like to see it, egad," say you: then, egad, here comes the farmer, and that same *phallus,* plucked from its place by his sturdy arm, will become a handy cudgel in his fist.

## XXI. TO AURELIUS.

AURELIUS, chief furnisher of famine-spread boards,[1] past, present, and to come, you are bent on debauching my young friend; and you make no secret of it; for you never quit the poor thing's side, nor lose an opportunity of toying and trying all the arts of seduction. But all in vain; for my vengeance will anticipate your insidious purposes. Now if you did all this upon a full stomach, I might have patience; but

them alone; for he was one of that lower order of deities, to which Faunus, Hippona, and others belonged, who were not admitted into heaven, or entitled to blood offerings.

[1] *Furnisher of famine-spread boards.*] *Pater esuritionum :* literally "father of starvations." It was usual in the banquets of the Romans to appoint a president, not necessarily the master of the house, who was called master, lord, or father of the feast. In allusion to th.s custom, Catullus humorously calls Aurelius a father of fasts.

what vexes me is, that under your tuition the poor child must learn to bear hunger and thirst. Desist, now, I warn you, whilst you can do so with honour, lest——

## XXII. TO VARUS.

THAT Suffenus, whom you, Varus, know well, is a nice fellow, a pleasant talker, and a wit;[1] moreover he makes no end of verses. I believe he has written ten thousand or more, nor are they scribbled as usual on palimpsest.[2] *O no!* royal paper, new covers, new bosses, red bands, the sheets ruled with lead, and the whole smoothed with pumice. When you read these books, then that graceful and witty Suffenus seems to you again a downright goatherd[3] or a ditcher, so extreme is the change. What are we to think of this? He who but now seemed a professed jester, or whatever else is more glib and flippant, becomes stupider than a stupid country clown as soon as he puts his hand to poetry; and this same man is never so happy as when he is writing poetry, he so delights in himself, so admires himself.[4] Doubtless we are all likewise fallible, nor is there any one whom you may not perceive to be a Suffenus in some particular. Each has his own assign-

[1] *A wit.*] *Urbanus.* Muretus, in a note on this word, adduces passages from Horace and Plautus, in which it is applied in this sense to "diners out."

[2] *Palimpsest.*] Parchment used a second time to write on, after erasing the characters previously inscribed on it, was called a palimpsest. The Romans called their best kinds of paper, royal, hieratic, Augustan, &c. The word *liber*, which commonly signifies a book, is here understood to mean the wrapper. The Romans had very few books of the modern form, *libri quadrati;* their volumes (*volumen*, from *volvere*, to roll) were generally scrolls consisting of sheets of parchment cemented together and rolled round a piece of wood. The scroll had an ornamental boss, *umbilicus*, attached to its lower end; and it was tied up with thongs of stained leather, *lora.*

[3] *A downright goatherd.*] *Unus caprimulgus*, h. e. plane et quantus quantus est. DOERING.

[4] *Is never so happy*, &c.] So Horace, Epist. ii. 2, 107:
Gaudent scribentes, et se venerantur, et ultro,
Si taceas, laudant, quicquid scripsere beati.
and Boileau in his second satire:
Un sot en écrivant fait tout avec plaisir;
Il n'a pas dans ses vers l'embarras de choisir;
Et toujours amoureux de ce qu' il vient d'écrire,
Ravi d'étonnement, en soi-même il s'admire.

ed failing; but we do not see what is in the wallet on our back.[1]

## XXIII. TO FURIUS.

You, Furius, who possess neither slave nor coffer, nor a bug nor a spider, nor a fire,[2] have yet a father and a step-mother whose teeth can chew up even flint. A pretty life you lead with your father and your father's wooden spouse;[3] and no wonder; for you are all in good health, you digest well, you fear nothing, neither fires, nor heavy losses, nor impious deeds, nor treacherous poison, nor any perilous chances. Moreover you have bodies more dried than horn, or if anything else there is more arid, by heat, and by cold, and hunger. Wherefore should you not be comfortable and happy? You are free from sweat, from spittle, from mucus, and unpleasant snivel at the nose. To this cleanliness add the still cleanlier fact that your posteriors are neater than a salt cellar, nor do you void anything from them ten times in a year, and *when you do*, it is harder than a bean or than pebbles, so that if you rub and crumble it in your hands you can never dirty a finger. Despise not these precious advantages, Furius, nor think little of them, and cease to pray, as you are wont, for a hundred thousand sesterces; for you are blest enough.

## XXIV. TO JUVENTIUS.

O FAIREST bud of the Juventian race, past, present, and to come, I had rather you had given my wealth to that fellow who has neither slave nor coffer, than suffer yourself to be loved by him.—What! is he not handsome? you will say.— He is; but this handsome man has neither slave nor coffer. Disdain my words, and make light of them as you will; still, I say, he has neither slave nor coffer.

---

[1] *The wallet*, &c.] An allusion to Æsop's fable, that Jove has hung two wallets on every man, one in front, stuffed with his neighbour's faults, the other behind, containing his own.

[2] *Neither slave*, &c.] To have neither slave nor coffer, was a proverbial phrase to express extreme poverty. The house that could not maintain a bug must have been a poor one indeed.

[3] *Wooden spouse*.] Dry and meagre as wood; like the woman of whom Scarron says, that she never snuffed the candle with her fingers for fear of setting them on fire.

## XXV. TO THALLUS.

LASCIVIOUS Thallus, softer than rabbit's fur, or goose down, or the tip of the ear, or spider's web, yet more rapacious than the driving storm, when the dire wintry sea forces the boding birds ashore: send me back my cloak which you stole, and my Setabian napkin, and my Thynian tablets, which you, fool, exhibit openly as if they were heir-looms. Unglue them now from your nails,[1] and send them back to me, lest the smarting whip inscribe ugly marks on your delicate flanks and soft buttocks, and you toss about in a way you are not used to, like a tiny bark caught by the raging wind on the vast sea.

## XXVI. TO FURIUS.

YOUR villa, Furius, is set[2] not against the south wind, nor the west, nor the keen north, nor the east; but against fifteen thousand two hundred sesterces.[3] O horrible and pestilent wind!

## XXVII. TO HIS YOUNG CUP-BEARER.

YOUNG server of old Falernian, pour out for me stronger cups,[4] for so orders the law imposed by our president Posthumia, more drunken than a drunken grape-seed. But you, spring water, bane of wine,[5] begone hence whither yon

---

[1] *Unglue them*, &c.] *Reglutina.* The Italians say, "Appicarsi la roba alle mani," and the Italian translator of Catullus thus renders this line: Sciogli adunque dalla pece l' unghia infame.

[2] *Is set.*] Catullus puns upon the word *opposita*, which besides its ordinary meaning, *opposed to*, signifies also *pawned for*—

[3] *15,200 sesterces.*] A sum nominally equivalent to about £95, according to the calculation of Vossius, but in reality to more than ten times that amount.

[4] *Stronger cups.*] Literally *more bitter, amariores,* that is, draughts of *drier* wine, the original sweetness of which has been converted into spirit by the slow fermentation of years.

[5] *Bane of wine.*] This scorn of water implies an uncompromising determination to get drunk as soon as possible, for it was the general practice of the ancients to dilute their wine. Anacreon, like a sage tippler as he was, exclaims,

> Fill me, boy, as deep a draught,
> As e'er was fill'd, as e'er was quaff'd;

will, and migrate to the sober: here is nothing but pure
Thyonian juice.[1]

### XXVIII. TO VERANNIUS AND FABULLUS.

YE followers of Piso, empty-handed train, with knapsacks
well-packed and light of burthen, excellent Verannius and
you my Fabullus, what are you doing? Have you endured
cold and hunger enough with that scamp?[2] How much of
your profits figures in your account-books as expended? As
happened to myself, who, when I followed my prætor, was out
of pocket instead of gaining. O Memmius, finely you cheated
and abused me in all that business.[3] But as far as I see,
you, my friends, have been in the same case; for you have
had to do with just such another scoundrel. Court noble
friends *after this!* But may gods and goddesses shower many
curses on you, disgraces to Romulus and Remus!

> But let the water amply flow,
> To cool the grape's intemperate glow:
> Let not the fiery god be single,
> But with the nymphs in union mingle.
> For though the bowl's the grave of sadness,
> Oh! be it ne'er the birth of madness!

There is an ingenious epigram on this subject in the Greek Anthology,
which has been imitated in Latin by Pierius Valerianus. Bacchus, be
it remembered, "was from his mother's womb untimely snatched,"
when she was consumed by the effulgence of Jove, her lover, whom she
had rashly insisted on beholding in his native majesty.

> Ardentem ex utero Semeles lavère Lyæum
>     Naiades, extincto fulminis igne sacri;
> Cum nymphis igitur tractabilis, at sine nymphis
>     Candente rursus fulmine corripitur.

> While heavenly fire consumed his Theban dame,
> A Naiad caught young Bacchus from the flame,
> And dipp'd him burning in her purest lymph;
> Still, still he loves the sea-maid's crystal urn,
> And when his native fires infuriate burn,
> He bathes him in the fountain of the nymph.   MOORE.

[1] *Thyonian juice.*] Thyoneus was one of the names of Bacchus.
[2] *That scamp.*] *Vappa.* The word means primitively wine that is
grown flat and good for nothing. Vulpius remarks with much probability,
that Catullus chose this common term of contempt for the sake of the contrast with Frugi (thrifty), the surname of the Piso family.
[3] *O Memmius*, &c.] The original of this passage will not bear to be
translated literally. Catullus vents his indignation against Memmius in
the most obscene invective. See the last note on Poem xxxv.ii.

## XXIX. TO CÆSAR ON MAMURRA.[1]

WHO can behold this, who can endure it, save a lewd reprobate, and an extortioner, and a reckless squanderer, that Mamurra should have all the fulness of long-haired Gaul[2] and farthest Britain? Vicious Cæsar,[3] wilt thou behold and tolerate such things? Thou art a lewd reprobate, and an extortioner, and a reckless squanderer. And shall he now, proud and profuse, perambulate all men's beds, like the white dove *of Venus*, or Adonis? Vicious Cæsar, wilt thou behold and tolerate such things? Thou art a lewd reprobate, and an extortioner, and a reckless squanderer. Is it for this, sole and unrivalled emperor, that thou hast been to the extremest island of the west, that this worn-out lecher of thine should riot in boundless extravagance? "What matters it?" says thy ill-placed liberality. Has he *then* made away with little? Has he devoured little? First his patrimony was spent; next the spoil of Pontus; then thirdly that of Iberia, which the auriferous Tagus knows. He is the terror of Gaul, the terror of Britain. Why dost thou cherish this wretch? Or what

[1] *Mamurra.*] Mamurra Formianus was a Roman knight, and commander of the artillery, *præfectum fabrûm*, to Cæsar during his wars in Gaul. From the fruits of that and other expeditions he amassed an immense fortune, and is said by Pliny to have been the first in Rome who adorned his house with pillars of solid marble. When Cæsar was on a visit at Cicero's villa, this poem, or that numbered lvii., which appears to have been written before it, was read to him by one of his suite as he was bathing. He heard it without even changing countenance, and with a moderation which has been highly extolled, accepted the submission of Catullus, and invited him on the same evening to supper. But the nature of this submission, as implied by the word *satisfacientem* in the passage in which Suetonius relates this anecdote, was abject enough, for it was a penitent retractation made before witnesses.

[2] *Long-haired Gaul.*] *Gallia comata.* All Transalpine Gaul was so called.

[3] *Vicious Cæsar.*] *Cinæde Romule.* The epithet is here applied in its grossest sense, which again is implied in the allusion to the spoil of Pontus; for this, as Vossius proves, can only be understood to mean the wealth obtained by Cæsar, when a young man, through his infamous relations with Nicomedes, king of Pontus—as witness two lines sung by Cæsar's own soldiers on the occasion of his triumph:

Ecce Cæsar nunc triumphat, qui subegit Galliam;
Nicomedes non triumphat, qui subegit Cæsarem.

can he do but devour fat inheritances? Was it for this, sole
and unrivalled emperor, that both of you, father-in-law and
son-in-law,[1] ruined the world?

## XXX. TO ALPHENUS.

ALPHENUS,[2] unmindful, and false to your affectionate companions, you have no pity now, hard-hearted man, for your
dear friend. You do not hesitate to beguile and betray me,
perfidious wretch! The impious deeds of deceitful men please
not the celestials; but this you heed not, and you desert me
in misfortune. Alas, what can men do henceforth, or in
whom can they have confidence? Surely you bade me yield
my soul to you implicitly, unjust one, luring me to love you
as though I had nothing to fear. And now you retract, and
let the winds and the airy clouds carry away all your idle
words and acts. If you have forgotten, yet the gods remember. Faith[3] remembers and will make you by and by repent
your conduct.

## XXXI. TO THE PENINSULA OF SIRMIO.[4]

SIRMIO, thou precious little eye of all peninsulas and
islands which either Neptune owns in calm lakes and in the

---

[1] *Father-in-law and son-in-law.*] Pompey married Cæsar's daughter,
Julia, and is commonly supposed to be the "son-in-law" here meant;
but Vossius argues with some force, that *socer* and *gener* apply, not to
Cæsar and Pompey, but to Cæsar and Mamurra. Those words, and the
corresponding terms in Greek, were often used in an unnatural sense, as
for instance in an epigram on Noctuinus, attributed to Calvus, in which
occurs this very line, *Gener socerque perdidistis omnia.*

[2] *Alphenus.*] The circumstances which provoked this complaint are
not known to us. The person to whom it is addressed is presumed to
have been that Alfenus Varus of Cremona, mentioned by Horace, (*Sat.* 4,
lib. i.,) who was originally a barber, and afterwards turned lawyer.

[3] Faith had a temple at Rome and was treated with divine honours.

[4] *The Peninsula of Sirmio.*] Vulpius infers from the expression "your
master," near the end of the poem, that the whole peninsula belonged to
Catullus. It is a beautiful spot, finely wooded, and about two miles in
circumference. At its extreme point on the Lago di Garda, the founda-
tions of a very extensive edifice have been discovered—the villa, as some
suppose, of Catullus. After the siege of Peschiera by the French, General
Lacombe Saint Michel surveyed the site, and drew a ground-plan of the
building, which is printed in Noel's notes. It indicates the existence of

vast sea; how willingly, how joyfully do I revisit thee, scarcely
believing myself that I have left Thynia and the Bithynian
plains, and behold thee in safety! Oh, what is more blessed
than cares dismissed; when the mind lays down all its burthen, and, weary with foreign toil, we come to our own home,
and rest in the longed-for bed! This is what alone repays
me for so many toils. Hail, beautiful Sirmio, and rejoice in
thy master. Rejoice too, ye waves of the Lydian lake.[1] Peal
out every laugh that is in my home.

### XXXII. TO HYPSITHILLA.

My sweet Hypsithilla, my delight, my merry soul; bid me,
like a dear girl, come to you to pass the noon.[2] And if you bid
me, add this, that no one bar the gate, that no fancy take you
to go abroad, but that you remain at home, and prepare for
us no end of amorous delights.[3] But if you agree, summon
me immediately, for I am lying on my back after dinner, full,
and pampered, and am bursting my tunic and my very cloak.[4]

a noble palace in former days, and if this was the villa of Catullus, he
must have possessed no inconsiderable fortune. The same general gave a
brilliant fête on the spot in honour of its ancient owner, whose praises
were said and sung on the occasion by the Italian poet Anelli. Appropriate toasts were drunk, and such was the enthusiasm of the moment, that
the inhabitants of Sermione (the modern name of the town of Sirmio)
luckily just then arriving with a petition of some troops quartered upon
them, obtained their request! Bonaparte himself, when going to ne-
gotiate the treaty of Campo Formio, turned out of his road between
Brescia and Peschiera to visit the poet's residence.

[1] Lydian lake.] Why Benacus should be so called is not very clear;
Vulpius says it is because the territory of Verona, in which the lake lies,
belonged to the Rhœti; the Rhœti sprang from the Tuscans, and the
Tuscans from the Lydians.

[2] To pass the noon.] That is, to take my siesta with you. See Ovid,
Amor. i. Eleg. v.

[3] Prepare for us, &c.] We have substituted a vague phrase for a singularly plain and precise one. Noel, the French translator, approaches
the original more nearly, but still in a covert manner: "Prépare neuf
couronnes au front de ton vainqueur." The Abbé Marolle, he says,
"traduit ce passage scabreux d'une manière assez plaisante : ' Et de neuf
facons qu' il y a de caresser quand on est de bonne humeur, n'en oublie
pas une.' Il est gai, le cher abbé!"

[4] Am bursting, &c.] Pezay, a French translator, strangely mistakes the
meaning of the passage, as if it amounted to this, "I have gorged till I
am ready to burst;" and he quotes the remark of "une femme charmante," who said that her only reply to such a billet-doux would have

XXXIII. ON THE VIBENNII.[1] [*See Metrical Version.*]

XXXIV. HYMN TO DIANA.[2]

WE, virgins and unblemished youths, are under the protection of Diana. Unblemished youths and virgins, let us sing Diana.

O great Latonian progeny of mightiest Jove, whom thy mother laid down near the Delian olive;

That thou mightest be mistress of mountains, and verdant woods, and secluded groves, and sounding rivers;

Thou art called Juno Lucina by women in the pains of childbed; thou art the mighty Trivia, and art called Luna with the borrowed light.[3]

Thou, goddess, measuring the annual period with thy monthly round, fillest the rustic roofs of the husbandman with good harvests.

Be sacred under whatever name it pleases thee,[4] and pre-

been to send the writer an emetic. But the lady might have prescribed a different remedy if she had been acquainted with Martial's line:

O quoties rigidâ pulsabis pallia venâ!

or with this quatrain of an old French poet:

Ainsi depuis une semaine
La longue roideur de ma veine,
Pour néant rouge et bien en point,
Bat ma chemise et mon pourpoint.

[1.] *On the Vibennii.*] Instead of a literal translation of this, and of some other pieces, which would be insufferable in English, the reader will please to accept Noel's free version in French prose: Effroi des bains publics, filou consommé dans ton art, Vibennius aux mains armées de glu, et toi digne fils d' un tel père, dégoutant Ganymède, fuyez, l' exil est votre seule ressource. Que feriez-vous ici? Le père est trop illustre par ses rapines, et les charmes du fils, quoique mis au rabais, ne trouvent plus de chalands.

[2] *Hymn to Diana.*] This was probably composed for some festival of Diana, but chronology establishes that it was not a secular ode. Addresses to this goddess were sung by youths and girls of noble families. Horace has three odes on the same subject.

[3] *Luna with the borrowed light.*] "Bastard light" would be a more literal translation. The ancients knew that the moon derived her light from the sun. The fact is mentioned both by Lucian and Pliny; and Luna's car was fabled to be drawn by mules, as emblematic of her spurious splendour.

[4] *Whatever name it pleases thee.*] Diana, as well as Isis, was "Dea

serve by thy good aid, as thou art wont, the race of Romulus and Ancus.

### XXXV. INVITATION TO CÆCILIUS.

SAY, paper, to the tender poet, my companion Cæcilius, that he must come to Verona, forsaking the walls of New Comum and the Larian shore,[1] for I wish him to hear certain reflections of his friends and mine. Wherefore, if he be wise, he will devour the way, though a girl a thousand times fair call him back, and throwing both her arms round his neck entreat him to delay; a girl who now, if I am truly informed, yearns for him with uncontrollable love. For ever since he read *to her* his story of the mistress of Dindymus,[2] fires have been consuming the inward marrow of the poor girl. I can excuse thee, girl, more learned than the Muse of Sappho; for beautifully has the Mighty Mother been sung by Cæcilius.

### XXXVI. ON THE ANNALS OF VOLUSIUS.

ANNALS of Volusius, most execrable book,[3] fulfil a vow for my girl; for she pledged herself to sacred Venus and to Cupid that if I were restored to her, and ceased to brandish my truculent iambics,[4] she would give the choicest productions

Myrionoma," a goddess of ten thousaud names. Callimachus, in a hymn to Diana, represents her as asking Jove for perpetual chastity and many names; attributes which seem rather discordant to us, who are not taught to esteem an alias as connected with any virtue. However, she thought the distinction of value, for she preserved it more carefully than Jove's other gift. Minerva is, I believe, of all heathen goddesses, the only one of quite unimpeached chastity, except the Furies. This passage, begging Diana to choose the name she liked, was to avoid a tedious enumeration; it was usual in invocations to the deities to call upon them by all their names, lest the most agreeable might be missed. Why was there no chance of offence from some nickname or disrelished title ?—*Lambe.*

[1] *Larian shore.*] The Larius Lacus is now the Lake of Como.

[2] *The mistress of Dindymus.*] The goddess Cybele.

[3] *Annals of Volusius,* &c.] These annals were an historical poem by Volusius of Padua, written, as the author hoped, after the manner of Ennius. "Most execrable" is a strong epithet, but not half so strong as the original : *cacata charta;* "rhapsodie digne du cabinet," says Noel, borrowing a phrase of Molière's.

[4] *Truculent iambics.*] The Iambic verse was held to be peculiarly adapted to invective and sarcasm.

of the worst poet to the limping god,[1] to be burnt with unlucky wood.[2] So it is plain to my girl that by her merry
and facetious oath she has devoted these worst of poems to the
gods.[3] Now, O offspring of the azure deep, who dwellest in
the sacred Idalium, and the open plains of Syria, in Ancona,
the reedy Cnidus, Amathus and Golgos, and Dyrrachium,[4]
the hostelry of the Adriatic, accept and recognise the fulfilment of the vow, if it is not devoid of piquancy and pretti-
ness. Into the fire with you, meanwhile, full as you are of
boorishness and stupidity, Annals of Volusius, most execrable
book.

### XXXVII. TO CORNIFICIUS.

ALL goes ill, Cornificius, with your Catullus, ill indeed and
distressingly, and more and more so every day and hour. I
am angry with you. Is it thus you return my love? Have
you—it would have been the slightest and easiest task for
you—have you comforted me by any line of yours? some
little line or other *would be welcome to me*, though sadder than
the tearful strains of Simonides.[5]

### XXXVIII. TO THE FREQUENTERS OF A CERTAIN TAVERN.

LEWD tavern, the ninth sign-post from the temple of the
capped brothers,[6] and you its frequenters, do you think that

---

[1] *The limping god.*] Vulcan, who was thrown down from heaven to
earth by Jupiter, and had his thigh broken by the fall.

[2] *Unlucky wood.*] Roman superstition classified even firewood as
lucky and unlucky. To the former belonged in general the wood of such
trees as bore fruit, to the latter the rest; but this rule was not without
exceptions.

[3] *So it is plain, &c.*] Other meanings have been given to this passage,
but all of them appear forced and insipid in comparison with that which
we have adopted. The text itself is variously given; we follow Doering's
reading:

Et hæc pessima so puella vidit
Jocoso et lepide vovere Divis.

[4] *Idalium, &c.*] Catullus here enumerates the places where Venus was
chiefly worshipped. Ascalon, in the southern lowlands of Syria, was the
first city which had a public building in honour of the goddess. Amathus
and Golgos were cities, Idalium a forest and city, of Cyprus. Dyrrachium,
formerly Epidamnum, is now Durazzo.

[5] *Simonides.*] An exquisite elegiac poet of the island of Ceos.

[6] *The capped brothers.*] Castor and Pollux, who were represented as

D

you alone have the attributes of manhood? that you alone are
licensed to kiss the girls, all and sundry, [and to scorn other
men as if they were rank goats]?[1] Is it because you sit there
night and day, a hundred boobies or two, that you do not
think I will venture to tackle the whole two hundred of you
at once? Ay, but you may think it; and I will write all
over the front of your tavern with burnt sticks.[2] For my girl,
who has fled from my bosom, my girl whom I loved with a love
that will never be equalled, for whom I have waged great
wars, has sat herself down there; and now you all make love
to her, pleasant, comfortable fellows, and—what is really too
bad—all of you pitiful knaves, gallants of the by-streets, and
you above all, Egnatius, one of the long-haired race from the
rabbit-warrens of Celtiberia, you whose merit consists in a
bushy beard, and teeth scrubbed with Spanish urine.[3]

### XXXIX. UPON EGNATIUS.

BECAUSE Egnatius has white teeth he grins incessantly.
Whether he be present at a criminal prosecution when the

wearing a sort of Phrygian cap, in shape like half an egg-shell,—an allusion to their birth from Leda's eggs.

[1] *Rank goats.*] The line corresponding to the passage enclosed between brackets, appears in all the editions, but is certainly spurious, as
Handius has shown.

[2] *Burnt sticks.*] *Scipionibus*, which is the reading of all the MSS., is
shrewdly suspected by Handius to be a transcriber's mistake for *inscrip-
tionibus*, a word which is here doubly appropriate, whilst the "burnt
stick" is a common-place detail, the mention of which is superfluous.
*Inscriptio* is the Latin equivalent for the Greek word *epigram*. Moreover
it was customary to display on the fronts of brothels the names of the
inmates, just as shopkeepers' names were inscribed over places of more
reputable trade: this was called *inscriptio* or *titulus*. The passage thus
amended would mean, "I will scribble the front of your tavern all over
with epigrams and inscriptions of your names."

[3] *Spanish urine.*] This is not a malicious invention of the angry poet's.
Strabo and Diodorus state positively that the Spaniards were in the
habit of beautifying their teeth and skin with this singular cosmetic.
It has been necessary greatly to mitigate the obscene ribaldry of this
poem in the translation; but this perhaps has not induced any great
sacrifice of fidelity. There is often an immense difference between the
conventional and the etymological meaning of words, and a translator
who regards only the latter must often grossly misrepresent his original.
A perfectly literal version of this poem would not be more repugnant to
the taste of the English reader than to the spirit of the original, which is
that of coarse, half-angry jocularity, rather than of serious menace.

orator moves the audience to tears, he grins; or whether at the scene of woe round the funeral pile of a dutiful son, when the bereaved mother weeps for her only child, he grins. Whatever is in hand, wherever he is, whatever he does, he grins. He has this disease upon him, a thing neither elegant, in my opinion, nor genteel. Wherefore I must admonish you, good Egnatius, if you were a native of Rome, or a Tiburtine, or an Umbrian hog, or a fat Etruscan, or a swarthy and huge-toothed Lanuvian, or a Transpadane—that I may touch upon my own countrymen also—or were you a native of any country where they wash their teeth in clean water, still I would not have you grin incessantly; for nothing is sillier than silly laughter. But every Celtiberian in the Celtiberian land is in the habit of scrubbing his teeth and his red gums in the morning with his last night's urine, so that the more finely polished your teeth are, the more the fact declares you to have drunk of chamber-lye.

### XL. TO RAVIDUS.

WHAT infatuation, wretched Ravidus, drives you headlong upon my iambics? What god, an evil counsellor for you, urges you to an insane strife? Is it that you may become the common talk? What would you have? Do you wish to be notorious on any terms? You shall be so, since you have sought to supplant me in my love at the cost of lasting punishment.

### XLI. ON MAMURRA'S MISTRESS.

Is that battered strumpet in her senses, who asks me ten thousand sesterces?[1] That girl with the nasty nose, the mistress of the desperate spendthrift Formianus? Ye kinsmen, to whom the care of the girl belongs, call together friends and physicians: the girl is insane. Do not ask what is her malady: she is labouring under visionary delirium.[2]

[1] *Ten thousand sesterces.*] Nominally about £60, but equivalent to more than ten times that amount in coin of the present day.

[2] *She is labouring,* &c.] Such is the best explanation given of the dubious text *solet hæc imaginosum; solet* being construed as a neuter transitive verb. But we strongly incline to Doering's conjectural emendation: ———— nec rogare
Qualis sit, solet; en imaginosam!
"The girl is mad, and never thinks of asking what sort of a looking person she is; what a fanciful wench!"

### XLII. ON A HARLOT.

HITHER, Phalæcian verses![1] hither all of you from every quarter; hither one and all! A vile harlot thinks me a fit laughing-stock, and refuses to return me your tablets,[2] if you can bear this. Let us pursue her and beset her with our demands. Who is she, do you ask? That jade whom you see moving with ugly affected gait, and grinning disgustingly with a mouth like a Gallic beagle. Plant yourselves round her and beset her with your demands; "Filthy harlot, give back the tablets; give back the tablets, filthy harlot. You care not a farthing? O lump of mud, O common strumpet, or more infamous still if anything can be so?"

But you must not think even this enough; if, however, it can do nothing more, at least let us force a blush upon her iron dog's-face.[3] Shout again with louder voice: "Filthy harlot, give back the tablets; give back the tablets, filthy harlot."

But we can do no good; she is not moved a jot. You must change your plan and method, and try if you can succeed any better. "Chaste and virtuous maid, return the tablets."

### XLIII. TO THE MISTRESS OF FORMIANUS.

HAIL, girl, with not over-much of a nose, with no pretty foot, nor black eyes, nor long fingers, nor dry mouth, nor particularly pleasing tongue, hail, spendthrift Formian's mistress! Does the province[4] tell that you are beautiful? Does it compare you with my Lesbia? O senseless and stupid age!

---

[1] *Phalæcian verses.*] The hendecasyllabic metre, so called from Phalæcus, who perfected, if he did not invent it.

[2] *Tablets.*] *Pugillaria.* These were tables of ivory or wood, thinly coated with wax, the writing upon which could be erased, or scratched in again at pleasure. Upon these Catullus set down the rough draft of the verses he apostrophises in this poem; therefore he calls the lost property "*your* tablets."

[3] *Iron dog's-face.*] The Latins said *os ferreum*, "iron face," as we now say "brazen face."

[4] *The province.*] The Transpadanian province.

## XLIV. TO HIS FARM.

O MY farm, whether Sabine or Tiburtine [1]—for those who have no wish to vex Catullus, aver that you belong to the territory of Tibur; but those who do so wish, will lay any bet that you are Sabine—but whether you are Sabine or rather Tiburtine, gladly did I find myself in your suburban villa, and get rid of a bad cough which my stomach bestowed upon me not undeservedly, whilst I indulged in sumptuous feasting. For Sextianus, whilst I had a mind to be a partaker of his good cheer, read me an oration delivered in opposition to Antius, the prosecutor, full of poisonous and pestilent stuff; thereupon a cold rheum and frequent cough shook me [2] until I fled to your bosom, and doctored myself with basil and nettle. Wherefore, now restored to health, I return you my best thanks for that you have not punished my fault. Nor do I now object, if again I listen to Sextian's infernal writings, but that their frigidity may inflict rheum and cough, not on me, but on Sextius himself, who only invites me when he has a bad book of his to read.

## XLV. ON ACME AND SEPTIMIUS.

THUS said Septimius, as he held his beloved Acme on his bosom : " If I do not love thee to perdition, my Acme, and am not bent on still loving thee constantly through all coming years, as much and as consumingly as possible, [3] may I be ex-

---

[1] *Sabine or Tiburtine.*] The farm was situated on the confines of both territories. Why Catullus preferred Tibur does not appear.

[2] *A cold rheum*, &c.] Modern compositions have had the same influence on their readers. Swift tells us, in his verses on burning a dull poem :

> " The cold conceits, the chilling thoughts,
> Went down like stupifying draughts ;
> I found my head begin to swim ;
> A numbness crept through every limb."

[3] *If I do not love thee*, &c.] Granville, Lord Lansdown, has imitated this passage, in an inscription on a drinking glass, written under the name of the Lady Mary Villiers, whom he afterwards married :

> " If I not love thee, Villiers, more
> Than ever mortal loved before :

posed alone to a grim-eyed lion[1] in Libya or in scorching India." When he said this, Love, who had looked upon him before from the left, now sneezed approvingly from the right.

But Acme gently bending back her head, and kissing the love-drunken eyes of her sweet boy with that rosy mouth of hers, said, "My own life, Septimillus, let us ever serve this one lord alone, so surely as the fire in my soft marrow burns fuller far and more fiercely *than ever*."[2] When she said this, Love, who had looked upon her before from the left, now sneezed approvingly from the right.

Now sped upon their course with a good omen, they love and are loved with mutual affection. Love-lorn Septimius prefers Acme before Syria and Britain:[3] faithful Acme centres all her pleasure and delight in Septimius alone. Who ever saw happier mortals? Who ever saw a more auspicious passion!

## XLVI. HIS FAREWELL TO BITHYNIA.

Now spring brings back tepid gales, now the fury of the equinoctial sky is hushed before the pleasant breath of zephyr.

> With such a passion, fix'd and sure,
> As e'en possession could not cure,
> Never to cease but with my breath,
> May then this bumper be my death!"

[1] *A grim-eyed lion.*] *Cæsio leoni.* This epithet, says Dr. Nott, here implies having eyes of a greenish brightness, as cats, tigers, lions, and the generality of beasts of prey: *cæsius* is much the same with the Greek *glaucus;* whence Minerva, who had such eyes, is called *glaucopis.*

[2] *My own life*, &c.] Both Nott and Lambe appear to have mistaken the meaning of this passage, making Acme institute a comparison between the force of her own passion and her lover's, of which we can discover no indication in the original here subjoined:

> Sic, inquit, mea vita, Septimille,
> Huic uni domino usque serviemus,
> Ut multo mihi major acriorque
> Ignis mollibus ardet in medullis.

Acme's meaning is, Let our exclusive devotion to this god increase evermore, as does the fervour of my passion.

[3] *Syria and Britain.*] The Romans supposed Syria to be the centre of the world, and Britain the extremity. Hence there is a peculiar force in the use of these two words in this place; they imply that Acme was dearer to Septimius than all between the world's centre and its remotest verge.

Left be the Phrygian fields, Catullus, and the fertile soil of sultry Nicæa; let us fly to the illustrious cities of Asia.[1] Now my mind, in a flutter of anticipation, longs to roam; now my feet grow strong in joyful eagerness. Farewell, sweet circle of companions, who left your distant home together, and who depart by various ways.

### XLVII. TO PORCIUS AND SOCRATION.

PORCIUS and Socration, two unlucky, scurvy knaves of Piso, and famished underlings of Memmius, has that circumcised Priapus preferred you to my Verannulus and Fabullus? Do you fare sumptuously every day; and are my comrades forced to look for invitations in the street?[2]

### XLVIII. TO HIS LOVE.

WERE I allowed to kiss your sweet eyes without stint, I would kiss on and on up to three hundred thousand times; nor even then should I ever have enough, not though our crop of kissing were thicker than the dry ears of the corn-field.

### XLIX. TO MARCUS TULLIUS CICERO.

MARCUS Tullius, most eloquent of the race of Romulus, of all that are, that have been, and that shall be in future years, Catullus thanks you heartily, Catullus the worst of poets—as much the worst of poets as you are the best of all advocates.

### L. TO LICINIUS.

YESTERDAY, Licinius, we spent our leisure in writing many sportive things on my tablets, as became *men like us.* Each of us writing verses of refined wit frolicked now in this measure now in that, interchanging sallies amid mirth and wine. I left the place so fired by your wit and fun, that food had no relish for poor me, nor could sleep veil my eyes in quiet, but

---

[1] *Phrygian fields . . . Asia.*] Achilles Statius says, As Phrygia is in Asia, how could Catullus leave Phrygia to go into Asia? The answer is: Phrygia is in Asia Minor, not in Asia Proper.

[2] *Look for invitations,* &c.] This hunting for invitations does not, according to modern notions, place the two friends of Catullus in a respectable light; but it was a common and avowed practice at Rome.

I tossed all about the bed in unconquerable excitement, longing to see the light, that I might talk to you and be with you.

But after my wearied limbs lay half dead upon my bed, I wrote these lines to you, pleasant friend, that you might perceive from them my grief *at your absence.* Now be not overweening, and despise not my prayers I entreat you, apple of my eye, lest Nemesis exact penalties from you. She is a vehement goddess; beware of offending her.

## LI. TO LESBIA.[1]

He seems to me to be equal to a god, he seems to me, if it be meet, to surpass the gods, who, sitting opposite to thee, at

[1] *To Lesbia.*] The first three stanzas of this poem are translated from Sappho's celebrated ode, preserved by Longinus. Ambrose Phillips's well-known version of it will be found in a subsequent page; here follows one in meagre prose:

"That man seems to me to be equal to the gods, who sits opposite thee, and hearkens to thee near him sweetly speaking and laughing. This flutters the heart in my breast; for when I see thee, no voice comes from my throat, but my tongue is silent; a subtle fire immediately suffuses my skin; I have no sight in my eyes; my ears boom; a cold sweat overspreads me; trembling seizes me all over; I am greener than grass, and breathless, I seem all but dead."

The reader will perceive that Catullus has not translated Sappho's last stanza, but has substituted for it (or some one else has done so) one of a very common-place and inapposite character. It is scarcely credible indeed that Catullus can have written such a piece of bathos at all; it is more probably the patchwork of some stupid and conceited pedant. Three attempts have been made to supply the missing stanza. One is by Achilles Statius:

> Sudor it latè gelidus trementi
> Artubus totis, violamque vincit
> Insidens pallor, moriens nec auras
> Ducere possum.

Another is by Jans Van der Does or Douza:

> Frigidus sudor fluit; horror artus
> Pallidos herbâ magis it per omnes,
> Et pati mortem videor morans in
> Limine mortis.

The third is by Henry Stephens:

> Manat et sudor gelidus, tremorque
> Occupat totam; velut herba pallent
> Ora; sperandi neque compos, orco
> Proxima credo.

It is also to be remarked, that Catullus has injudiciously omitted to once beholds thee and hears thy sweet laughter; but this takes away all my senses, wretch that I am; for, as soon as I have looked upon thee, Lesbia, there remains to me [*no voice*], but my tongue is paralysed; a subtle flame flows down through my limbs; my ears ring with their own sound; both my eyes are veiled in night.

Ease is baneful to thee, Catullus; thou revellest and delightest to excess in ease; *love of* ease has ere now destroyed kings and prosperous cities.

## LII. TO HIMSELF.

WHEREFORE, Catullus, wherefore dost thou delay to die? Struma Nonius sits in the curule chair; Vatinius perjures himself in the consulship. Wherefore, Catullus, wherefore dost thou delay to die?

## LIII. ON CALVUS.

I LAUGHED at some one in the crowd at the Forum, who, when my friend Calvus had marvellously well set forth the crimes of Vatinius, exclaimed in admiration, lifting up his hands: "Great gods, what an eloquent little hop-on-a-stool!"[1]

translate the phrase signifying "sweetly speaking." Horace has caught the spirit of it more faithfully:

> Dulce ridentem Lalagen amabo,
> Dulce loquentem.

[1] *Hop-on-a-stool.*] The word which contains the point of this epigram has been the subject of much debate among the learned. Some read *solopachium*, meaning "a mannikin eighteen inches high;" Saumasius proposes salopygium, a "wagtail;" several editors have *salaputium*, an indelicate word nurses used to children when they fondled them, so that the exclamation would mean, "what a learned little puppet!" Thus Augustus called Horace *purissimum penem*. The reading to which we have adhered is *salicippium*, implying that little Calvus perched himself upon a stool. This reading is confirmed by a passage in Seneca, which mentions the oration against Vatinius, and particularly records the fact that on one occasion at least Calvus *imponi se supra cippum jussit*, and that his friend Catullus called him *salicippium disertum*.

### LIV.  TO CÆSAR.[1]

COARSE-MINDED Cæsar, I would that, if not everything, *at least* Otho's very puny head, Vettius's half-washed legs, and Libo's nasty stinking habit, were disliked by you, and by that double-dyed old rogue[2] Fuffitius.  You shall again be angered by my honest iambics, unique captain !

### LV.  TO CAMERIUS.

I BEG you will tell me, if it is not an impertinent question, where is your hiding-place.  I looked for you in the Lesser Campus, in the Circus, in all the book-shops, in the consecrated temple of supreme Jove, and likewise in Pompey's promenade.  I stopped all the girls I met, those more especially whom I saw looking serenely,[3] and demanded you of them, cry-

---

[1] *To Cæsar.*]  Muretus declared these lines to be utterly unintelligible to any but a sibyl ; and so they are in the form in which they appear in most editions ; but the sense of the amended text, as given by Doering, is clear and pointed.  He reads,

> Othonis caput oppido pusillum,
> Vetti, rustice, semilauta crura,
> Subtile et leve peditum Libonis,
> Si non omnia, displicere vellem
> Tibi, et Fuffitio seni recocto.
> Irascere iterum meis iambis
> Immerentibus, unice imperator.

[2] *Double-dyed old rogue.*]  *Seni recocto.*  Horace applies this epithet to one who had often served the office of *quinquevir,* or proconsul's notary, and who was therefore master of all the arts of chicanery.  These are his words, Sat. v. lib. 2 :

> *Plerumque recoctus*
> *Scriba ex quinqueviro corvum deludit hiantem.*

A seasoned scrivener, bred in office low,
Full often dupes and mocks the gaping crow.  FRANCIS.

The modern Italians say of a man of this stamp, *Egli ha cotto il culo ne' ceci rossi.*  The phrase *seni recocto* may also imply one who enjoys a green and vigorous old age, as if made young again, as the old woman was by wine, of whom Petronius speaks, *Anus recocta vino ;* or Æson, who was re-cooked by Medæa.  That witch, says Valerius Flaccus, *Recoquit fessos ætate parentes.*

[3] *Looking serenely.*]  "Meaning," says Dr. Nott, " that the lovely tranquillity of every female countenance convinced me you were safe ; for if any accident had happened to you, all the women in the city must have had grief pictured in their faces."  " Rather," says Lambe, " supposing

ing, "Give me up my Camerius, wicked wantons !" One of them, baring her bosom, says, "Lo, here he lies hid in these rosy nipples." Now it would be a labour of Hercules to seek you, *if that be true,* for in such a proud lodging as that you *are sure to be* "not at home," my friend. Tell me where you are likely to be; out with it boldly, give it to the light of day. Do the milk-white girls detain you? If you keep a close tongue, you will throw away all the fruits of love; Venus delights in tattling. Or if you will, you may keep your mouth shut, provided I have a share in your friendship. Not if I were that famed guardian of Crete;[1] not if I were borne by the flying Pegasus; not if I were Ladas,[2] or the wing-footed Perseus;[3] not if Rhesus'[4] swift, snow-white team *were mine,*—add to these the feather-footed flying *sons of Boreas,*[5] take too the speed of the winds, and though you should bestow upon me all these put together, still I should be wearied in the marrow of every limb, and eaten up with fatigue upon fatigue in hunting after you, my friend.

LVI.   TO CATO.[6]   [*See Metrical Version.*]

it probable that any female who looked peculiarly smiling, was rejoicing in the possession of your love, and the knowledge of your place of concealment." The choice between these two interpretations turns upon the meaning to be given to *tamen* in the line *Quas vultu vidi tamen sereno.* If the force of the word *tamen* (however) be thrown on the relative pronoun, it will give us Nott's view of the passage; but if it be made to bear upon the antecedent, it will give us Lambe's. Doering adopts the latter construction, and exhibits it in this paraphrase : illas tamen præcipue, quas vultum serenum præ se ferre videbam, vel his verbis, ut te mihi redderent, impensius rogabam.

[1] *Guardian of Crete.*]   Talus, a giant with a brazen body, employed by Jove to guard Crete while Europa resided there as his mistress.   He went round the whole island every day.

[2] *Ladas.*]   One of Alexander the Great's couriers, who ran so swiftly as to leave no foot-marks in the sand.

[3] *Perseus.*]   Son of Jupiter and Danae.   Mercury lent him his winged sandals to enable him to attack the Gorgons.

[4] *Rhesus.*]   King of Thrace, possessed of very swift horses, on which the fate of Troy depended.

[5] *Sons of Boreas.*]   Calais and Zethus.

[6] *To Cato.*]   L' aventure est trop plaisante !   Tu vas rire mon cher Caton ; toi qui aimes les bons contes, tu vas en rire pour l' amour de moi.   Je viens de surprendre un joli enfant, que ma nymphe initiait complaisamment aux plus doux mystères.   J' ai percé le petit drôle d' un trait vengeur, et Venus a souri de ma vengeance.   NOEL.

## LVII.  ON MAMURRA AND CÆSAR.

WELL matched are the infamous reprobates,[1] the pathic
Mamurra and Cæsar, and no wonder; for on both foul marks,
contracted by the one at Rome, by the other at Formiæ, are
deeply and indelibly impressed.   Both libidinous[2] alike, a
twin pair, sharing one bed, both dabblers in erudition,[3] the
one not a more insatiable lecher than the other, rival allies of
the girls—well-matched are these infamous reprobates.

## LVIII.  TO CÆLIUS[4] ON LESBIA.

O CÆLIUS, our Lesbia, Lesbia, that Lesbia whom Catullus
loved more than himself and all his kin, now in the public
streets and in alleys makes herself a common trull to the
magnanimous descendants of Remus.[5]

[1] *Infamous reprobates.*]  *Improbis cinædis.*   There is scarcely a phrase
in this most atrocious lampoon which we dare reproduce in its loathsome
nudity.

[2] *Libidinous.*]  *Morbosi,* say the commentators, has the same meaning
as *pathici.*   Herodotus says that angry Venus smote the Scythians *morbo
muliebri.*   Perhaps the epithet may be elucidated by this line of Juvenal:
Cæduntur tumidæ, medico ridente, mariscæ.

[3] *Dabblers in erudition.*]  *Erudituli.*   We are content, with the ma-
jority of commentators, to understand this in a contemptuous, but at least
a decent sense.   Some, however, will have it that the accomplishments
alluded to are not literary, but Priapeian.   It is in this sense Petronius
calls Gito *doctissimus puer.*   Œzema, a grave German jurist, parodied a
part of this piece.   His epigram can be read without danger of having
one's stomach turned.

> Belle convenit inter elegantes
> Dione's famulas, et eruditos
> Antiquæ Themidis meos sodales.
> Nos jus justitiamque profitemur:
> Illæ semper amant coluntque rectum.

"There is a charming coincidence of sentiment between the fair votaries
of Venus and my learned brethren: we profess law and justice; they
dearly love the thing that is upright.

[4] *Cælius.*]   This is conjectured to have been Cælius Rufus, Catullus's
rival in the affection of Lesbia, supposing—which is again conjectural—
that she was the sister of Clodius.

[5] *O Cælius,* &c.]   Nothing can exceed the sad sweetness of the first
three of these five verses; but that villanous *glubit* in the last line is
enough to poison all the waters of Aganippe.

### LIX. ON RUFA.

*Can it be that* Rufa of Bononia, the wife of Menius, cajoles *the consequential* Rufulus? That Rufa whom you have seen in the burial-grounds snatching a meal from the funeral pile, and who, when she prowled for the bread that rolled down out of the fire, was beaten by the half-shaved body-burner?

### LX. FRAGMENT.

DID a lioness on the Libyan mountains, or Scylla barking with the part below her groins, bring thee forth of so hard and savage a mind that thou shouldst hold in contempt the voice of a suppliant in extremity? O too savage-hearted!

### LXI. EPITHALAMIUM.

#### ON THE MARRIAGE OF MANLIUS AND JULIA.[1]

DWELLER on the hill of Helicon, offspring of Urania, who snatchest away the tender virgin to the bridegroom, Hymen! O Hymen!

Bind thy brows with blossoms of the fragrant marjoram; take thy flame-coloured veil;[2] hither, hither come, joyous, wearing the yellow sandal[3] on thy snow-white foot;

And roused by this glad day, carolling nuptial songs with silvery voice, beat the ground with thy feet, shake the pine torch in thy hand.

For Julia—lovely as Idalian Venus when she came before

---

[1] *Epithalamium, &c.*] The Epithalamium was a poem sung by youths or virgins, or both, when the bride was brought to the bridegroom and placed in the *thalamus* or bridal bed; hence the name, from ἐπὶ and θάλαμος. Of Julia no more is known than that her cognomen Aurunculeia was that of the Cotta family; but Manlius of tho illustrious line of the Torquati, is a well-known character. Catullus commemorates his friendship in another poem.

[2] *Flame-coloured veil.*] The Flammeum, which the bride put on before she proceeded to her husband's house. It covered her from head to foot, and its bright saffron or flame colour is supposed to have been intended as another means of concealing her blushes.

[3] *Yellow sandal.*] This has always been given to Hymen by the poets. It is more usual to crown him with roses than with marjoram.

the Phrygian judge—*Julia*, a virgin good, with good omen weds Manlius,[1]—

*Julia*, shining forth as the myrtle on Asian ground[2] with its blossomed branches, which the Hamadryads nourish with dewy moisture to be the scene of their sports.

Come then; wending hither, forsake the Aonian grottoes of the Thespian rock, over which flows the cool water of Aganippe.

And call home the lady yearning for her bridegroom, binding her mind with love, as the clinging ivy enfolds the tree,[3] spreading its sprays all over it.

And you too, joining with us, chaste virgins for whom a like day approaches, come, repeat in measure, Hymen, O Hymen!

That so much the more willingly hearing himself summoned to his office, the conductor of chaste Venus, the conjoiner of true love, may wend his way hither.

What god, oh what god, is more worthy to be invoked by lovers? Which of the celestials should men worship more? Hymen, O Hymen!

Thee the anxious parent invokes for his children; for thee virgins loose the zone from their bosoms;[4] thee the agitated bridegroom listens for with craving ear.

Thou givest to the arms of the fiery youth the blooming maid, snatched from her mother's bosom. Hymen, O Hymen!

No indulgence can Venus take without thee which fair fame approves; but with thy consent she may. What power may be compared with this god?

No house can have heirs without thee, no parent race be

---

[1] *Julia, a virgin,* &c.] Julia will her Manlius wed,
　　　　　　Good with good, a blessed bed. LEIGH HUNT.

[2] *Asian ground.*] A marshy tract of land, with a town on it of the same name, between the river Cayster and Mount Tmolus.

[3] *As the clinging ivy,* &c.] This natural simile is constantly recurring in the poets; and their fondness for it is fully justified by its beauty. In Shakspeare, Titania thus addresses her monstrous idol, Bottom:

　　Sleep thou, and I will wind thee in my arms;
　　Fairies, begone, and be all ways away!
　　So doth the woodbine the sweet honeysuckle
　　Gently entwist; the female ivy so
　　Enrings the barky fingers of the elm.

[4] *Loose the zone,* &c.] See the last note to Poem viii.

prolonged in its progeny; but with thy consent it may. What power may be compared with this god?

The land that lacks thy rites cannot give itself magistrates;[1] but with thy consent it may. What power may be compared with this god?

Gates, unfold your wings! The virgin is at hand. See you how the torches shake their gleaming hair? But thou tarriest; the day is waning; come, bride, come!

Ingenuous shame retards her, and she weeps more and more, hearing that she must needs advance. But thou tarriest; the day is waning; come, bride, come!

Cease to weep; there is no danger for thee, Aurunculeia, that any fairer woman shall see the bright day coming up from the ocean.

So stands the hyacinth amidst the varied bloom of a rich owner's garden. But thou tarriest; the day is waning; come, bride, come!

Come, bride, come, (now she is in sight,) and hear our words. See you how the torches shake their golden hair? Come, bride, come!

Not like a profligate sunk in vile adultery, not in pursuit of base pleasures, will thy husband wish to rest apart from thy tender breast.

As the clinging vine entwines its companion tree, will he be entwined in thy embrace. But the day is waning; come, bride, come!

O white-footed bed, . . . . . . . .[2]

What joys await thy master, what joys in the rayless night and in the noon-day. But the day is waning; come, bride, come!

Lift up your torches, boys, I see the flame-coloured veil approaching. Come, carol in measure, Hymen, O Hymen!

\*　　\*　　\*　　\*　　\*[3]

---

[1] *Magistrates.*] Before the time of the Cæsars those of illegitimate birth were excluded from all magisterial offices.

[2] Three lines are wanting here.

[3] Here we omit some lines which foully disfigure this beautiful poem. They are thus rendered by Noel:

Que les airs retentissent de vos chansons folâtres; la fête permet un peu de licence; et toi, favori d' hier, délaissé aujourdhui, jette à ces enfans les noix que l' usage leur abandonne.

It is said of thee, essenced bridegroom, that thou canst
hardly abstain from thy illicit joys; but abstain.  Hymen,
O Hymen!

We know that only those delights have been known to thee
which are allowed; but those same delights are not allowable
for a married man.  Hymen, O Hymen!

And thou too, bride, beware of refusing what thy husband
craves, lest he go and seek it elsewhere.  Hymen, O Hymen!

Lo, what a potent and prosperous house thou hast in thy
husband's, which shall obey thee for ever; Hymen, O Hymen!

Until white-haired age nods perpetual assent with thy
tremulous head.  Hymen, O Hymen!

Bear thy golden feet with a good omen over the threshold,[1]
and enter the polished gates.  Hymen, O Hymen!

Look how thy husband, reclining within on the purple
couch, expects thee with his whole soul.  Hymen, O Hymen!

A flame glows in his inmost breast, no less than in thine,
but with deeper searching fire.  Hymen, O Hymen!

Ce jeu de leur age ne convient plus au tien.  L' Hymen dont Manlius
suit les loix, rend désormais ton ministère inutile.

Hier encore, fier de la faveur du maître, tu dédaignais les avances des
jeunes filles.  Aujourdhui tes beaux cheveux vont tomber sous le fer;
favori disgracié, donne à ces enfans les noix qu' ils attendent.

"This coarse imitation of the Fescennine poems," says Dunlop, (History of Roman Literature,) "leaves on our minds a stronger impression
of the prevalence and extent of Roman vices, than any other passage in
the Latin classics.  Martial, and Catullus himself elsewhere, have branded
their enemies; and Juvenal, in bursts of satiric indignation, has re-
proached his countrymen with the blackest crimes.  But here in a com-
plimentary poem to a patron and intimate friend, these are jocularly
alluded to as the venial indulgence of his earliest youth."

[1] *Over the threshold.*]  The bride entering her husband's house was
lifted over the threshold, that she might not touch it.  Various reasons
have been assigned for this, among others, that the threshold was sacred
to Vesta, the goddess of chastity, who might be offended at the nuptials;
or that the bride should avoid touching any spell which some jealous
rival might have secretly laid there.  Perhaps the true reason is less
recondite.  Cicero speaks of the *offensio pedis*, (striking the threshold with
the foot,) generally as an ill omen; and Ovid and Tibullus both mention
it as to be avoided at the outset of any undertaking.  Shakspeare, Henry
VI., part 3, makes Gloucester say, on finding the gates of York closed
against him and Edward IV.,

"The gates made fast!  Brother, I like not this;
For many men, that stumble at the threshold,
Are well foretold that danger lurks within."

Let go the maiden's arm, smooth, purple-robed boy,[1] and let her now go to her husband's bed. Hymen, O Hymen!

You, worthy matrons, known for your faithfulness to your aged husbands, place the maiden.[2] Hymen, O Hymen!

Now, bridegroom, thou mayest come; thy wife is in the bridal chamber, her blooming face shining like the white camomile and the yellow poppy.[3]

But, so help me the celestials, thou bridegroom art no less handsome, nor does Venus neglect thee. But the day is waning; forward! make no delay.

Thou hast not long delayed; thou comest now; may kind Venus aid thee, since thou takest openly what thou desirest, nor dost thou make a secret of thy virtuous love.

Let him first compute the number of the Red Sea's sands, or of the glittering stars, who would count your many thousand sports and joys.

Sport to your hearts' content, and soon produce children:

[1] *Purple-robed boy.*] This was the *paranymphus*, whose province it was to escort the bride home; he was chosen of noble birth, and therefore wore the *prætexta* or garb bordered with purple.

[2] *Place the maiden.*] Widows, and matrons who had contracted a second marriage, were disqualified for this office.

[3] *White camomile,* &c.] Commentators have expended a world of labour in endeavouring to identify the *parthenice*, which we have rendered "camomile," in accordance with what seems to us the most plausible conjecture. The "yellow poppy," *luteum papaver,* suggests to the English reader an unfortunate image which was certainly not contemplated by Catullus. According to Parthenias, the poet's meaning is, that the fair complexion of the bride looks as beautiful through her yellow marriage veil, as the white blossom of the parthenice does beside the yellow poppy. Dr. Nott thinks this interpretation ingenious, but unsound, for, he says, "When the bride is in bed (*uxor in thalamo est*) we must suppose the *flammeum* or veil thrown aside: there is then no aptness in the comparison, which evidently relates to her blooming countenance (*os floridulum*): I should rather think *luteus* was meant to express a colour bordering on red. We are very ignorant of the true meaning of Latin words that have a reference to colours." Admitted: but *luteus* is one of the least ambiguous words of its class, and is decidedly more suggestive of jaundice than of the roseate hue of youthful beauty. And why must we suppose that the act of removing the bride's veil was not a pleasure and a privilege reserved for the bridegroom himself, as is the custom among some oriental nations to this day? In the celebrated Aldobrandini fresco-painting, found in the baths of Titus, the bride is seated veiled on a bed, with the *pronuba* or bridesmatron near her, whilst the bridegroom sits at the foot of the bed.

E

it is not meet that so ancient a name should be without children, but that heirs to it should be engendered evermore.[1]

I long to see a little Torquatus,[2] stretching out his tender
hands from his mother's bosom, smile sweetly at his father
with little lips half-opened.

May he be like his father Manlius, and easily recognised by
every stranger, so that he shall attest his mother's chastity
with his face.

And may a fair repute approve his birth from his good
mother, such a rare fame as devolved from his excellent
mother on Telemachus, the son of Penelope.

Close the doors, virgins;[3] we have sported enough. And

---

[1] *Engendered.*] *Indidem semper ingenerari.* The word *indidem* is not
superfluous; it emphasizes the wish that the heirs should be of the same
race, not adopted from other families.

[2] *A little Torquatus.*] *Parvulus Torquatus.*

> Si quis mihi parvulus aulâ
> Luderet Æneas, qui te tantum ore referret;

says Virgil's Dido: but there the parallel necessarily ceased; the charming image which accompanies the same wish in Catullus, could not be
expressed by the forsaken queen. Biacca, the Italian translator, has been
happy in his version of this passage:

> M' auguro de' Torquati un figlio erede
> Veder scherzando della madre in seno,
> Con la tenera man cercar le poppe;
> E con la bocca ridente e mezza aperta,
> Quasi voglia parlar, volgersi al padre.

It has been thus imitated by Sir William Jones:

> And soon, to be completely blest,
> Soon may a young Torquatus rise,
> Who, hanging on his mother's breast,
> To his known sire shall turn his eyes,
> Outstretch his infant arms awhile,
> Half ope his little lips and smile.

[3] *Close the doors, virgins.*] The virgins addressed are those who accompanied the bride in the procession. Some suppose, however, that the
Muses are meant, and cite in favour of that opinion Ovid's distich,

> Conscius ecce duos accepit lectus amantes;
> Ad thalami clausas, Musa, resiste fores.

" The conscious bed has received the loving pair; halt, Muse, before the
closed door of the bridal chamber."

This epithalamium, says Noel, is incontestably the paragon of all
poems of its kind. Those who would compare it with others, may
refer to Seneca's tragedy of Medea for the epithalamium of Jason
and Creusa, chanted by the chorus; to Statius, for that of Stella and

now live happily, well-matched pair, and exercise unceasingly the functions of your lusty youth.

## LXII. NUPTIAL SONG.[1]

### YOUTHS.

HESPERUS is here, arise, youths, together; Hesperus[2] is just now lifting his long-expected light in the heavens. It is now time to rise, and leave the rich tables. Now will the virgin come; now let the hymenæal song be raised. Hymen, Hymen, hither, Hymen!

### VIRGINS.

Virgins, do you see the youths? Rise up against them. Doubtless the evening star shows its Œtæan fires.[3] It is so indeed. Do you see how swiftly they have rushed forth? They have not rushed forth for nothing; they will sing what it is for you to surpass. Hymen, Hymen, hither, Hymen!

### YOUTHS.

No easy triumph awaits us, comrades. Look how the virgins muse and meditate together; nor do they meditate in vain; they have found something worthy of memory. We have divided *our attention, giving* our minds to one thing, our ears to another;[4] justly therefore shall we be defeated; vic

Violantella; and to Claudian, for that of Honorius and Marca, the daughter of Stilicho. The modern Latin poets have frequently employed themselves upon this subject. A great number of specimens will be found in the *Deliciæ.* I will only mention two: Buchanan's epithalamium on Francis II. and the unfortunate Mary Stuart, and one by another Scot, Thom. Rhœdus. The former is remarkable for grandeur of thought and pomp of style; the other for the elaborate oddity of its libertine allusions.

[1] *Nuptial Song.*] This is an epithalamium as well as the preceding poem, but there is no evidence to support the conjecture of Achilles Statius that it was made on the same marriage.

[2] *Hesperus.*] The evening star. Its rising was the signal for conducting the bride in procession to the bridegroom's house.

[3] *Œtæan fires.*] Rising from Mount Œta in Thessaly.

[4] *We have divided,* &c.] Nos alio mentes, alio divisimus aures. Dr. Nott understands this to mean, We have suffered our attention to be diverted from the matter in hand, by the beauty and the sweet voices of the virgins. But the words cannot possibly admit of such a construction. The Delphin editor's interpretation is, We direct our minds to one thing, our ears to another; and this brings us half-way to the clearer explana-

tory favours diligence. Wherefore, now at least apply your
minds *to your task*; the virgins will presently begin their
strain; you will presently have to reply. Hymen, Hymen,
hither, Hymen!

### VIRGINS.

Hesperus, what more cruel light does heaven bear than
thine? who canst tear the child from her mother's embrace,
tear from her mother's embrace the child that clings fast to
it,[1] and bestow the chaste girl on a hot youth. What worse
than this could enemies do in a captured city? Hymen, Hymen, hither, Hymen!

### YOUTHS.

Hesperus, what more cheerful light shines in heaven than
thine? who ratifiest with thy beams the compacts of wedlock which lovers and parents have previously made, but
which they never fulfil before thy fires have risen. What is
there in the gift of the gods more desirable than that blissful
hour? Hymen, Hymen, hither, Hymen!

### VIRGINS.

Hesperus has taken from us one of our companions.[2] * * * *
At thy appearance the wakeful guard is set, spoilers[3] always
prowl by night, and often, Hesperus, returning with an altered
name,[4] thou catchest them still in the fact. Hymen, Hymen,
hither, Hymen!

tion given by Vulpius, namely, that the young men, having to improvise
their responses, must attend to what the virgins sing, and think at the
same time of what they shall reply.

[1] *Clings to it.*] This is not merely a metaphorical expression. It was
a part of the established etiquette of the marriage procession, that it
should begin with forcing away the daughter, whilst she pretended to
cling to her mother with all her might. This custom is said to have been
instituted in commemoration of the rape of the Sabines.

[2] There is here a line lost of the original: its import must have been
to charge Hesperus with furtive propensities, proof of which is offered in
the lines that follow. Another hiatus at the end of the virgins' part, probably involves no more than the burden.

[3] *Spoilers.*] *Fures*, thieves, meaning lovers; for by almost every
Latin poet, lovers are called *fures*, and amours *furta*.

[4] *Altered name.*] The same planet that at night is called Hesperus,
is in the morning called Phosphorus or Lucifer. It is the first star to
rise. and the last to set.

### YOUTHS.

The virgins are pleased to attack thee with feigned reproaches. What if they attack whom they in their secret
hearts desire? Hymen, Hymen, hither, Hymen!

### VIRGINS.

As a flower grows sequestered in a fenced garden, unknown
to the cattle, bruised by no ploughshare, whilst the breezes
freshen it, the sun gives it strength, and the shower nourishes
it; many a youth, many a girl covets it. But when plucked
from its tender stem and faded, no youths, no girls covet it.
So whilst the virgin remains untouched, she is dear to her
kindred; but when she has lost her chaste flower from her
polluted body, she remains no longer pleasing to youths, nor
dear to maids.[1] Hymen, Hymen, hither, Hymen!

---

[1] *As a flower*, &c.] This exquisite passage has been imitated times
without number, but by no poet so closely as by Ariosto, cant. i. 42.

> La verginella è simile alla rosa,
> Che 'n bel giardin su la nativa spina,
> Mentre sola, e sicura si riposa,
> Nè gregge, nè pastor se le avvicina;
> L' aura soave, e l' alba rugiadosa,
> L' acqua, la terra al suo favor s' inchina
> Giovini vaghi, e donne innamorate
> Amano averne e seni, e tempie ornate.
>
> Ma non sì tosto dal materno stelo
> Rimossa viene, e dal suo ceppe verde,
> Che, quanto avea da gli uomini, el dal cielo,
> Favor, grazia, e bellezza, tutto perde.
> La vergine, che 'l fior, di che più zelo
> Che de' begli occhi, e della vita, aver dè,
> Lascia altrui corre, il pregio, ch' avea innanti,
> Perde nel cor di tutti gli altri amanti.

Tasso has certainly had Catullus in view, while drawing a different moral
from the same subject:

> Deh! mira (egli cantò) spuntar la rosa
> Dal verde suo modesta, e verginella,
> Che mezzo aperta ancora, e mezzo ascosa,
> Quanto si mostra men tanto è più bella
> Ecco poi nudo it sen gia baldanzosa
> Dispiega, ecco poi langue, e non par quella,
> Quella non par, che desiata avanti
> Fu da mille donzelle. e mille **amanti**

### YOUTHS.

As the unwedded vine which grows in a naked field, never lifts its head, never matures a mellow grape, but bending prone its tender body under its own weight, touches its topmost shoot with its root; no hinds, no herdsmen cherish it; but if perchance it be united with a husband elm, many hinds, many herdsmen cherish it: so the virgin, whilst she remains untouched, grows old, uncared for; when she has secured a fit union in due season, she is dearer to her spouse, and less irksome to her parent.

### YOUTHS AND VIRGINS.

Then offer no resistance, virgin, to such a spouse *as thine*. It is not right to resist one to whom thy father has given thee, thy father himself with thy mother whom thou must obey. Thy virginity is not wholly thine own; it is partly thy parents'. One third of it belongs to thy father, another to thy

> Cosi trapassa al trapassar d' un giorno
> Della vita mortale il fiore, e 'l verde,
> Ne perche faccia in dietro april ritorno
> Si rinfiori ella mai, ne si renverde.
> Cogliam la rosa in sù 'l mattino adorno
> Di questo dì, che tosto il seren perde,
> Cogliam d' amor la rosa: amiamo or, quando
> Esser si puote riamato amando.

Thus exquisitely rendered by Spencer, Faery Queen, b. ii. c. 12:

> The whiles some one did chaunt this lovely lay:
>    "Ah! see, whoso fayre thing doest faine to see,
> In springing flowre the image of thy day!
>    Ah! see the virgin rose, how sweetly she
>    Doth first peepe foorth with bashfull modestie,
> That fairer seemes the lesse ye see her may!
>    Lo see soone after how more bold and free
>    Her bared bosome she doth broad display;
> Lo! see soone after how she fades and falls away!
>
> "So passeth, in the passing of a day,
>    Of mortal life the leafe, the bud, the flowre;
> Ne more doth flourish after first decay,
>    That erst was sought to deck both bed and bowre
>    Of many a lady, and many a paramoure!
> Gather therefore the rose whilest yet is prime,
>    For soone comes age that will her pride deflowre;
> Gather the rose of love whilest yet is time,
> Whilest loving thou mayst loved be with equal crime."

mother, the remaining third alone is thine : do not strive against two *parents* who have bestowed their own rights along with thy dower on their son-in-law.  Hymen, Hymen, hither Hymen !

## LXIII.  ON ATYS.

BORNE over the deep seas in a swift bark, Atys eagerly touched the Phrygian forest with hurried foot, and went to the gloomy, wood-covered grounds of the goddess ; where, goaded by raging madness, he emasculated himself with a sharp flint.

So when he found his limbs bereft of manhood, and while still spotting the ground with fresh blood, *this new-made woman*[2] hurriedly took in her snowy hands the light timbrel, the timbrel and the trumpet[3] proper to thy initiatory rites, *mighty* mother Cybele, and, shaking the hollow bull's hide in her tender fingers, she began, quivering with excitement, to sing thus to her followers:

"Come, speed ye together, Gallæ,[4] to Cybele's deep forests ;

---

[1] *Atys.*]  This poem, unique in subject and in metre, is spoken of by Gibbon with enthusiasm.  "Perhaps," says Ramsay, "the greatest of all our poet's works is the Atys, one of the most remarkable poems in the whole range of Latin literature.  Rolling impetuously along in a flood of wild passion, bodied forth in the grandest imagery and the noblest diction, it breathes in every line the frantic spirit of orgiastic worship, the fiery vehemence of the Greek dithyramb."  It is the only specimen we have in Latin of the Galliambic measure; so called because sung by the Galli, the emasculated votaries of Cybele.  The Romans under the republic, being a more sober and severe people than the Greeks, gave less encouragement than they to the celebration of orgiastic rites, such as those of Bacchus and Cybele, and have left few examples of dithyrambic poetry.

[2] *This new-made woman.*]  These words are a prosaic substitute for the abrupt transition to the feminine gender, which is so striking in the original.

[3] *Timbrel.*]  *Tympanum.*  An instrument like the modern tambourine, but without its jingling metallic appendages.  The *Cymbalum* was a small cup-like brazen instrument with a handle.  Vossius reads *tympanum tubam*, without a comma interposed, and understands the passage to mean, "the tympanum which serves in lieu of a trumpet in the mysteries of Cybele."  This reading is authorized by Suidas, who says expressly, that the only instruments used in those rites were the *tympanum* and *flagellum.*

[4] *Gallæ.*]  Catullus substitutes the feminine form *Gallæ* for the mascu-

speed ye together, roving cattle of the mistress of Dindymus ; [1]
who seeking foreign lands, like exiles, following my sect, led
by me, have borne as my comrades the rapid salt-sea wave,
the fierceness of the deep, and have unmanned your bodies
in intense hatred of Venus ; gladden your souls with frenzied
excitement ; let dull delay begone from your minds ; speed
ye together ; follow to the Phrygian home of Cybele, to the
goddess's Phrygian forests, where the cymbals resound, where
the timbrels roar aloud, where the Phrygian flutist drones on
the curved pipe, where the ivy-crowned Mænades [2] wildly
toss their heads, where they ply their hallowed mysteries
with piercing yells ; where that roving train of the goddesses
is wont to run to and fro, thither it befits us to hasten in
quick-step dancing measure."

When Atys, the new-made woman, thus sang to her mates,
the whole rout [3] forthwith yelled with quivering tongues, the
light timbrel booms, the hollow cymbals clash, and up to
Ida goes the impetuous rout with hurried steps ; with them
goes Atys with her timbrel, raving, panting, like one lost
and demented, and leads the way through the murky forests,
like an unbroke heifer shunning the burthen of the yoke.
Swiftly the Gallæ follow their hasty-footed leader. [4] So when
they reach the home of Cybele, wearied with excessive exer-
tion, they fall asleep fasting. Heavy sleep covers their drooping eyes with languor, and their raving phrensy subsides in
soft repose.

line *Galli*, the ordinary name of the emasculated priests of Cybele. They
were so called from Gallus, a river of Phrygia, the water of which mad-
dened those who drank it.

[1] *Dindymus.*]  A part of Mount Ida, sacred to Cybele.

[2] *Mænades.*]  Women devoted to the service of Bacchus or of Cybele ;
for many things were common to the rites of both deities. The name is
derived from μαίνεσθαι, to rave.

[3] *The whole rout.*]  *Thiasus* is properly a chorus of sacred singers and
dancers, living in community, like a college of dervishes, who, indeed,
are an exact counterpart of the Galli as regards their howling and dancing
ritual, but have the advantage of their predecessors in one important
particular.

[4] *Hasty-footed leader.*]  We adopt the suggestion of Vossius, who objects to the tautology of the common reading, *Rapidæ ducem sequuntur
Gallæ propero pede.* For *propero pede* he substitutes *properipedem*, which,
as he further observes, is more conformable to the style of this poem, in
which Catullus affects the use of compound words, such as *hederigeræ,
sonipedibus, herifugæ, sylvicultrix, nemorivagus,* &c.

But when the sun surveyed with the radiant eyes of his golden face the æther, and the firm land, and the wild sea, and chased the shades of night with his sonorous-footed steeds, then Sleep swiftly fled from awakened Atys, and the divine Pasithea[1] received the fugitive to her bosom. So when, her madness allayed by soothing rest, Atys reflected on her own acts, and saw with lucid mind what she had lost, and where she was, again with surging soul she retraced her way to the shore. There, gazing on the vast sea with streaming eyes, the sorrowing wretch thus piteously apostrophized her native land.

"My country! O creatress, parent country! which I, wretch, forsaking, as fugitive slaves forsake their masters, fled to the forests of Ida, to dwell amid snow and the chill dens of wild beasts, and to roam frantically among all their lairs! Where, in what quarter, shall I now deem thee placed, my country? My very eyeball longs to turn its rays to thee, whilst my mind is for a brief while free from fierce delirium. Must I roam these woods remote from my own home? Must I dwell far away from my country, from all I possess, from my friends, my parents; far from the forum, the palæstra, the stadium, and the gymnasia?[2] O wretched, wretched soul! for ever and for ever must I wail. For what kind of form is there that I have not worn? I have been man,[3] youth, stripling, boy. I was the flower of the gymnasium and the pride of the wrestling ground. My gate, my hospitable threshold was thronged, my home was hung with flowery chaplets,[4] when

---

[1] *Pasithea*.] One of the three Graces, whom Juno bestowed in marriage on the god of sleep for exerting his power over Jupiter, while Juno was assisting the Trojans.

[2] *The forum*, &c.] Atys enumerates the recreations of his manhood: the public spectacles of the forum; the wrestling ground (*palæstra*); the race course (*stadium*); and the schools for gymnastic exercises.

[3] *A man*.] *Puber*. We adopt without hesitation this amended reading of Scaliger's instead of *mulier*, which is irreconcilable with the general tenor of the passage.

[4] *Hung with flowery chaplets*.] It was customary with lovers to hang garlands before the doors of the beloved. See Tibullus, book i. El. ii. There are some beautiful lines on this subject by a modern poet, Angerianus, translated by Moore:

> Ante fores madidæ sic sic pendete corollæ,
>   Mane orto imponet Cælia vos capiti;
> At quum per niveam cervicem influxerit humor,
>   Dicite, non roris sed pluvia hæc lacrymæ.

I had to leave my couch at sunrise. Must I rank as a votaress of the gods, as Cybele's bondsmaid? Must I be a Mænas,
a part of myself, a sterile man? Must I dwell in green Ida's
snow-clad regions, and pass my life under the lofty peaks of
Phrygia, where dwell the sylvan stag, and the forest-ranging
boar? Now do I grieve, now do I repent what I have done."

When these sounds escaped her rosy lips,[1] then Cybele, unyoking the lions *from her chariot*, and pricking the left hand
foe of the herd, thus speaks: "Up, fierce beast, up, she says;
go, hence with him, in madness, make him return hence, smitten with madness, into the forest, who audaciously desires to
fly from my sway. Up! beat thy flanks with thy tail; lash
thyself; make the whole region resound with thy roaring.
Toss fiercely thy tawny mane on thy brawny neck."—So said
terrific Cybele, and unfastened the yokes with her hand. The
beast, inciting himself, pricks up his impetuous spirit, runs,
roars, and breaks down the bushes in his headlong course.
But when he reached the verge of the foam-whitened shore,
and saw soft Atys near the breakers, he made a rush. The
bewildered wretch fled into the wild forest, and there he remained all his life long a bondsmaid[2] *to Cybele*.

Goddess, mighty goddess, goddess lady of Dindymus, far
from my house be all thy fury, *dread* mistress: goad others
*to such rage;* madden others; *but leave me free.*

## LXIV. THE MARRIAGE OF PELEUS AND THETIS.[3]

PINES that grew on Mount Pelion are said to have swum
through Neptune's liquid waves to the banks of the river

> By Cælia's arbour all the night
>   Hang, humid wreath, the lover's vow;
> And haply, at the morning light,
>   My love shall twine thee round her brow.
>
> Then, if upon her bosom bright
>   Some drops of dew shall fall from thee,
> Tell her, they are not drops of night,
>   But tears of sorrow shed by me.

[1] *Rosy lips.*] The line beginning *Geminas Deorum* is condemned as
spurious by the best commentators. We have not translated it.

[2] *A bondsmaid.*] *Famula.* This mingling of two genders in the same
sentence exists in the original.

[3] *The Marriage of Peleus and Thetis.*] This longest and most elaborate

Phasis[1] and the Æetæan confines; when chosen young men, the flower of the stout Argive youth, desiring to carry off the Golden Fleece[2] from Colchis, dared to traverse the salt seas in a fleet ship, sweeping the azure plains with oars of fir. The goddess who holds the citadels in the high places of towns,[3] herself made for them the chariot that flew with a light breath of wind, connecting the knitted pine timbers[4] with the curved keel. That ship first acquainted inexperienced Amphitrite[5] with navigation. As soon as it clove the windy sea with its prow, and the oar-tortured wave grew white with foam, wild faces emerged out of the whitening deep, *namely*, the marine Nereids, wondering at the prodigy;[6] on that day, and no other, mortal eyes saw sea-nymphs with naked bodies exposed to the breasts from out the hoary waters. Then Peleus is said to have been inflamed with love for Thetis; then Thetis did not despise human nuptials; then father Jove himself consented that Peleus should be united to Thetis.[7]

O heroes born in that happier age, hail, progeny of gods !

of the poems of Catullus has been erroneously styled an Epithalamium, for no other reason than because it treats of a marriage. We might be content to reject the misnomer in silence, were it not that it has been made the pretext for some very silly criticism, according to which we are to regard the poem as altogether void of method and symmetry, a mere tissue of splendid faults ; and this because its structure does not conform to that of the epithalamium, a species of composition with which it has no affinity. It is wonderful how much there is in a name. Call the poem, with Gurlitt, a small Epos, which it really is, and you take away all ground for objection, especially as to the length of the episode of Ariadne, which no man of taste would wish to shorten by a single line.

[1] *Phasis.*] A river of Colchis, up which the Argonauts sailed to the capital of king Æetes, the father of Medea.

[2] *Golden Fleece.*] The expedition of the Argonauts to rob Æetas, king of Colchis, of the golden fleece, is narrated by Ovid, and is the subject of a Greek poem by Apollonius Rhodius, and of a Latin poem by Valerius Flaccus.

[3] *The goddess*, &c.] Minerva.

[4] *Knitted pine timbers.*] *Pinea texta.* To build ships is in Latin *texere naves;* and the shipbuilder's yard is *textrinum.*

[5] *Amphitrite.*] The wife of Neptune, here put for the sea.

[6] *Wondering at the prodigy.*] The reader of the original will not fail to note the fine effect produced by making *admirantes* the ending of a spondaic hexameter.

[7] *Jove consented*, &c.] Jupiter had himself intended to marry Thetis, but, learning from Prometheus that she was fated to bear a son who should eclipse the glory of his father, he bestowed her on his grandson Peleus.

O good mother[1] *of the brave!* Often will I invoke thee in my song ; and thee too so surpassingly honoured by thy happy marriage, Thessalia's bulwark, Peleus, to whom Jupiter himself, the father of the gods himself, resigned his love. Did Thetis, fairest daughter of Neptune, accept thee? Did Tethys grant thee to wed her grandchild, and did Oceanus consent, who embraces the whole globe with the sea?

Now when in due time the longed-for day was come, all Thessaly thronged to the abode *of Peleus;* the palace is filled by the joyous assemblage ; they bring presents ; and declare with their faces the gladness *of their hearts.* Scyros is deserted ; they leave Phthian Tempe, and Cranon's homes and the walls of Larissa ; they flock to Pharsalia,[2] and throng the Pharsalian halls. No one tills the lands ; the callous necks of the steers are left to soften ; the low vine is not cleared from weeds with rakes ; no bull tears up the glebe with the prone plough ; no pruner's hook thins the trees' shady boughs ; squalid rust overspreads the deserted ploughshares.

But the mansion, in every part of its opulent interior, glitters with shining gold and silver ; white are the ivory seats ; goblets gleam on the tables ; the whole dwelling rejoices in the splendour of regal wealth. In the midst of the mansion is placed the genial couch of the goddess, inlaid with polished Indian tooth, and covered with purple dyed with the shell's rosy juice. This coverlet, diversified with figures of the men of yore, portrays the virtues of heroes with wondrous art.[3]

[1] *Good mother.*] The ship Argo, poetically called the mother of her valiant crew.

[2] *Scyros,* &c.] An island in the Ægean, off the coast of Thessaly. The celebrated vale of Tempe in Thessaly is called Phthiotica from the neighbouring city of Phthia, or from Phthiotis, the region to which the city belongs. Cranon and Larissa were towns of Thessaly. Pharsalus, where stood the palace of Peleus, is well known as the scene of the battle between Cæsar and Pompey.

[3] *This coverlet, diversified,* &c.] The tapestry comprised two pictures, each of which represented a scene in the history of Ariadne, which the poet now proceeds to expound. We are to imagine him standing by the picture, and explaining to the admiring crowd not only the incidents actually portrayed, but also their causes and consequences ; and hence we account for the words *ferunt, perhibent,* and so forth, which occur throughout the narrative. In the first compartment Ariadne is seen just at the moment when she has discovered her lover's perfidy, and stands petrified by the shock, *saxea ut effigies bacchantis.*

For, gazing from the wave-sounding shore of Dia,[1] Ariadne,[2] her heart filled with unconquered rages, beholds Theseus departing with his swift ship;[3] nor does she yet believe that she sees what she does see,[4] as but just awakened from her treacherous sleep she finds herself wretched and deserted on the lonely sands.  But the ungrateful youth, flying from her, smites the sea with his oars, abandoning his vain promises to the stormy winds.  With sad eyes the daughter of Minos, like a stone image of a Mænad yelling Evoë, gazes on him speeding far from the weedy strand, and she heaves with great waves of sorrow.  No more she retains the slender fillet on her yellow hair ; no more the light veil conceals her bosom ; no more the smooth cincture[5] binds her struggling

[1] *Dia.*]  Naxos, the divine island, δία, sacred to Bacchus, is generally held to have been the scene of Ariadne's desertion; but Vossius contends that the Dia in question was an islet near Crete, now called Standia.  His arguments, however, have very little weight.

[2] *Ariadne.*]  For the sake of brevity we will here compress together the leading facts connected with the story of Theseus and Ariadne.  The Athenians having joined in the murder of Androgeus, son of Minos, king of Crete, the latter made war on them, and compelled them to send every year to Crete seven youths and as many virgins to be devoured by the Minotaur.  This monster was the fruit of an unnatural passion which Pasiphaë, the daughter of the Sun, and the wife of Minos, had conceived for a bull.  Dædalus, who had lent his mechanical skill to the fulfilment of the queen's desires, built the famous labyrinth to conceal her half-human, half-brute offspring.  Theseus, son of Ægeus, king of Athens, slew the monster, and made his way out of the labyrinth by means of a clue supplied to him by Ariadne, one of the two daughters of Minos and Pasiphaë.  Theseus then departed for his home, taking with him Ariadne, who was accompanied by her sister Phædra ; but he deserted the former at Naxos, and took the latter to Athens as his bride.  Catullus, however, omits this part of the story, and says expressly that Ariadne left her sister behind when she fled from Crete.

[3] *Swift ship.*]  *Classis* must here stand for a single ship, for a fleet was not requisite to convey to Crete the tribute of fourteen human victims.

[4] *Nor does she yet believe,* &c.]  The true reading of this line is very uncertain ; we have adopted that proposed by Vossius.  Achilles Statius would read *Necdum etiam sese quæ sit tum credidit esse,* " Nor does she yet believe that she is herself."

[5] *Cincture.*]  The strophium was a band which confined the breasts and restrained the exuberance of their growth.  Martial apostrophizes it thus :

Fascia, crescentes dominæ compesce papillas,
Ut sit quod capiat nostra tegatque manus.

" Confine the growth of my fair one's breasts, that they may be just large enough for my hand to enclose them."

breasts; the salt wave sports with them all, dropped from her body, and scattered at her feet. But thinking neither of fillet, nor of floating veil, lost and undone, she was intent on thee, Theseus, with her whole heart, and soul, and mind. Ah wretched Ariadne, whom Venus doomed to distracting sorrows,[1] implanting thorny cares in thy bosom, what time cruel Theseus, issuing from the curved shores of the Piræus,[2] reached the Gortynian[3] abode of the unjust king.

For ancient legends tell that, compelled by a dire pestilence to atone for the murder of Androgeos, the Cecropian city[4] was wont to present choice youths and fairest virgins as food for the Minotaur. Seeing that the little city was thus afflicted, Theseus desired to sacrifice his own body for his dear Athens, rather than that such unfuneralled funerals[5] of Athens should be carried to Crete. Borne therefore in a fleet ship by gentle winds, he came to the arrogant[6] Minos and his superb abode. There as soon as the royal virgin beheld him with desiring eye, she whom the chaste bed, breathing sweet odours, cherished in her mother's soft embrace, lovely as the myrtles which the waters of Eurotas[7] rear, or the various-coloured flowers which the breath of spring brings forth; she did not take her glistening eyes off him until her whole bosom was thoroughly on fire, and she burned to her inmost marrow. Alas! divine boy, who confoundest together human joys and sorrows, with ruthless heart exciting wretched mortals to frenzy, and thou who rulest Golgos, and the evergreen Idalium,[8] on what billows ye tossed that soul-kindled maiden,

[1] *Doomed to distracting sorrows.*] *Externavit,* put beside thyself.

[2] *Piræus.*] The harbour of Athens, but mentioned here with poetic independence of historical fact, for it was not made a naval station until the time of Themistocles.

[3] *Gortynian.*] Gortyna, a city of Crete.

[4] *Cecropian city.*] Athens, founded by Cecrops.

[5] *Unfuneralled funerals.*] *Funera nefunera:* a Greek form of expression, frequently imitated in Latin.

[6] *Arrogant.*] *Magnanimum.* Doering justly observes that this epithet must here be understood in a bad sense.

[7] *Eurotas.*] The river of Sparta.

[8] *Idalium.*] Lambe's note on this passage is judicious. "Venus," he says, " is not mentioned merely as the goddess of love, as seems to have been conceived by most commentators. Pasiphaë, Ariadne's mother, was the daughter of the Sun and Perseis, one of the Oceanides; and Venus persecuted all the descendants of Apollo, because that god discovered her amour with Mars. This is finely alluded to in the Phèdre of Racine:

often sighing for the yellow-haired stranger ! What fears she endured in her fainting heart ! How often did she grow wanner than the sheen of gold ! When Theseus, eager to contend with the dread monster, was about to encounter death or the glory of victory, then did she timidly frame vows with silent lip,[1] promising gifts to the gods, *gifts* not unacceptable *to them*, but offered unprofitably *for herself*. For as an irresistible whirlwind tears up an oak that shakes its branches on the summit of Taurus, or a cone-bearing pine with oozing stem, twisting the trunk with its blast; uprooted it falls prone, covering a wide space, and breaking all beneath it far and near; so Theseus prostrated the carcase of the vanquished monster, vainly tossing its horns to the empty air. Thence he returned safely with great renown, directing his wandering steps by a slender thread, that the indistinguishable maze might not baffle his attempt to issue from its labyrinthine windings.

But why, digressing from my first subject, need I tell more ? How the daughter, forsaking her father's face, forsaking the embrace of her sister, and even of her mother, who wept in despair for her child, gladly preferred the sweet love of Theseus to them all ? Or how their ship was borne to the foamy shores of Dia ? Or how her husband, departing with ungrateful breast, left her with her eyes closed in calamitous sleep ? Often, 'tis said, with a heart on fire with rage, she sent out shrill shrieks in gushes[2] from the bottom of her breast ; then sadly climbed the precipitous mountains, whence she could stretch forth her gaze over the wide billows ; then ran into the opposing waves of the agitated sea, lifting up the soft coverings from her bared leg,[3] and with streaming face and shivering sobs, uttered these words in the extremity of her woe :

> ' O haine de Venus ! O fatale colère !
> Dans quels égaremens l' amour jeta ma mère !
> Ariane, ma sœur ! De quel amour blessée,' &c."

[1] *Timidly frame vows*, &c.] *Tacito suspendit vota labello.* This is an uncommon and beautiful use of the word *suspendit*, the meaning of whioh may be deduced from the familiar phrase *podem suspendere*, to tread cautiously, as if one feared to set one foot before the other. Ariadne durst not breathe a syllable of the wishes of her heart.

[2] *In gushes.*] *Fudisse.*

[3] *Lifting*, &c.] Nott quotes with approval the remark made on this passage by an English annotator on Tibullus, who notes as " a fine stroke

"Is it thus, perfidious! thou hast left me, borne away from my native shores, left me, perfidious Theseus! on the desert strand? Is it thus thou departest, in contempt of the gods, ingrate! and carriest home thy perjuries and the curses that cling to them ?[1] Could nothing change the purpose of thy cruel mind? Was there no mercy about thee, that thy ruthless breast might have pity on me? But not such were the promises thou gavest me formerly; this was not what thou badest me, miserable girl, to expect, but joyful union, happy rites of wedlock;—all idle words scattered by the winds! Henceforth let no woman believe man's oaths; let none hope that a man's words are trusty; for whilst their lusting minds are bent on obtaining, they shrink from no oaths, they spare no promises; but as soon as their lustful desire is satiated, they have no fear *to break* their words, they care nothing for perjury. Surely I rescued thee when thou wast in the midst of the vortex of death, and resolved rather to lose my brother than to fail thee, treacherous as thou art, in that supreme moment. For this I shall be given as a prey to be torn asunder by wild beasts and birds, and when dead, I shall remain unentombed, with no earth cast upon my body. What lioness gave thee birth under some lonely rock? What sea conceived and spat thee forth from her foaming waves? What Syrtis, what greedy Scylla, what vast Charybdis, bore thee, who returnest such rewards for sweet life? If thou wast averse to wedlock with me because thou didst abhor the cruel edicts of my stern father,[2] yet thou mightest have taken me to thy dwelling, and I would have served thee as a handmaid[3] with cheerful labour, bathing thy

of genius" this picture of "Ariadne running into the sea, as though to catch Theseus, who was sailing off." And then in the very next sentence he tells us that the "coverings" of which she bared her legs were her buskins! Instead of instinctively catching up the robe that impeded her movements, an act which would have been consistent with the most impetuous emotion, she stopped, like a thrifty girl, to take off her best buskins, lest the salt water should spoil them!

[1] *Perjuries and the curses*, &c.] *Devota perjuria*, perjuries that are *diris obnoxia*, that infer the wrath of the gods.

[2] *Stern father.*] *Prisci*; one whose cast of mind retains the primitive harshness of earlier times.

[3] *Served thee as a handmaid.*] Lambe quotes from the old ballad of Childe Waters, in Percy's collection, a simple but pathetic parallel to this touching passage:

"To-morrow, Ellen, I must forth ride
Farr into the north countrie:

white feet with limpid water, or spreading the purple coverlet on thy bed.

"But why, beside myself *with woe*, do I complain in vain to the ignorant winds, which being endowed with no senses, can neither hear uttered words, nor return any? He is now nearly mid-way on the sea, and no mortal appears on the vacant beach. Thus cruel fortune, too much insulting me in my last moments, grudges even ears to hear my lamentations. Almighty Jove, would that neither in the beginning the Cecropian ships had touched the Gnossian shores; nor that the perfidious mariner had ever unmoored for Crete, bringing dire tribute to the unconquered bull; nor that yon bad man, concealing cruel purposes under a winning form, had rested as a guest in our abode! For whither shall I betake myself? On what hope shall I, undone, rely? Shall I seek the Cretan mountains? But the fierce severing sea divides me from them with its wide expanse. Can I hope for aid from my father, whom I left of my own accord to follow the youth stained with my brother's gore? Can I console myself with the trusty love of a husband who flees from me, bending his pliant oars in the deep? If I pass from the shore, the lonely island is without a roof; nor is there any exit open from it, encompassed as it is by the waves. There is no means of escape, no hope; all around is silence and desolation; all around is death. Not however shall my eyes languish in death, nor shall my senses depart from my weary body, before I implore from the gods a just penalty for my betrayal, and invoke the faith of the celestials in my last hour. Wherefore, ye who visit the deeds of men with avenging chastisement, Eumenides, whose brows, covered with serpents for hairs, bespeak the wrath that exhales from your breasts,[1] hither,

> The fairest lady that I can find,
>   Ellen, must goe with me."
>
> "Though I am not that lady fayre,
>   Yet let me goe with thee;
> And ever, I pray you, Childe Waters,
>   Your foot-page let me bee."

[1] *Wrath that exhales.*] *Expirantis pectoris iras:* literally, "the wrath of . . . . expiring breast." That is, as we understand it, of "your" breasts, or, according to Elton, "my" breast, i. e. Ariadne's. The Delphin editor absurdly interprets the passage as meaning "Whose brows covered, &c., typify the anguish of the dying man."

F

hither speed ye, hear my wailings, which I, how wretched! am forced, helpless, with burning brain, blind with raving madness, to pour out from my inmost vitals. And since they truly spring from the bottom of my heart, suffer not my cries of agony to pass idly away; but through that spirit which prompted Theseus to leave me forlorn, through that same spirit, goddesses, let him bring destruction on him and his."

After the anguished girl, imprecating punishment on the cruel deeds of her betrayer, sent forth these words from her sad bosom, the ruler of the celestial gods assented with his potent nod, whereat the earth and the rough sea trembled, and the firmament shook its glittering stars. But Theseus himself, seized with thick mental darkness, lost from his oblivious bosom all those injunctions which he before held fast in mind, and hoisted no glad signals for his sad father, to show that he was in sight of harbour safe and rescued. For they say that previously, when Ægeus intrusted his son to the winds, as he was leaving the city of the goddess *Pallas* with his fleet, embracing *his son*, he gave the young man these injunctions:

" My only son, dearer to me than long life, my son, lately restored to me at the end of an extreme old age,[1] and whom I am compelled to send away to dangerous adventures, since my ill fortune and thy hot valour tear thee away from me so loth to part with thee, for not yet have my dim eyes had enough of my son's dear face: not in joy and gladness of heart will I send thee away, nor will I let thee show tokens of prosperous fortune; but first I will send forth many a lamentation from my heart, defiling my white hairs with earth and dust; and then I will hang dyed sails upon the flitting mast, that so the Iberian canvass with its dark dye may declare my grief, and the burning anguish of my mind. But if the dweller on sacred Itone[2] (who has promised us, her trusting votaries, to defend our race and these abodes) grants thee to stain thy right hand with the blood of the bull, then be sure that these injunctions have force, stored up in thy heart, and that no lapse of time obliterate them. As soon as thine eyes behold our hills, let the yards drop every where their funereal clothing, and let

---

[1] *Lately restored to me.*] Theseus was born in Trœzene, and brought up by his maternal grandfather Pittheus.

[2] *Itone.*] A town in Bœotia, in which Pallas was especially worshipped.

the twisted ropes hoist white sails, so that discerning them as soon as possible, I may recognise their glad tidings with joy, when a prosperous time puts thee, returned, before me."

As clouds driven by the breath of the winds leave a snowy mountain's airy crest, so these injunctions departed from the memory of Theseus, who had previously retained them with constant mind. But his father, as he looked out from the top of the fortress, wasting his anxious eyes in ceaseless tears, when first he beheld the canvass of the inflated sail, threw himself headlong from the top of the rocks, believing that Theseus was lost by a cruel fate. Thus exulting Theseus, entering a house woe-stricken by his father's death,[1] himself encountered such sorrow as he had inflicted by his forgetfulness on the daughter of Minos; while she, wholly rapt, still gazed upon his departing ship, and heart-stricken, was agitated with manifold woes.[2]

But on another part *of the coverlet* the blooming Iacchus was hastening with his crew of Satyrs and the Nysa-reared Sileni, seeking thee, Ariadne, and burning with love for thee. In wild joy they raved all around him, yelling Evoë, Evoe, and rolling their heads about. Some of them brandished thyrsi with ivy-covered points ; some snatched away the limbs of oxen torn to pieces; some girt themselves with twisted serpents ; some celebrated mysterious orgies with *implements contained in* wicker-baskets, orgies which the uninitiated vainly desire to hear. Others beat timbrels with extended hands, or produced fine tinklings with the smooth brass. Horns yielded hoarse blasts to many, and the barbarian pipe droned with horrible notes.[3]

[1] *Thus exulting Theseus*, &c.] We follow Vossius and Doering in their interpretation of this passage. Others understand it thus : Theseus, exulting in the death of the monster, entered his woe-stricken paternal dwelling, &c.

[2] *While she, wholly rapt*, &c.] The common reading is,

Quæ tum prospectans cedentem mæsta carinam.

We prefer that given by Vossius on manuscript authority,

Quæ tamen aspectans oedentem cuncta carinam.

Theseus had reached home, but though his ship was no longer in sight, she still remained with her gaze fixed on vacancy, and wholly absorbed in gazing, as though the ship was still before her eyes.

[3] *Horrible notes.*] The introduction of Bacchus closes the episode with an animated picture, and forms a pleasing contrast to the melancholy

Magnificently adorned with such figures, the coverlet concealed the bed, enfolding it with its drapery.  After the young men of Thessaly had satisfied themselves with eagerly inspecting it, they began to make room for the holy gods.  As Zephyr with his morning breath crisping the calm sea, when Aurora rises, just at the dawn of the journeying sun, stirs up the slanting waves, which first move slowly, urged by a mild breath, and sound with a gentle noise of laughter, but afterwards as the wind increases, grow more and more frequent, and gleam afar as they float away from the purple light : so then leaving the royal vestibule they departed, each to his own home, with steps diverging in all directions.

After they were gone, foremost from the summit of Pelion, came Chiron,[1] bringing sylvan gifts.  For all kinds of flowers which the fields produce, which the Thessalian land engenders on its broad mountains, and which the pregnant breath of warm Favonius brings forth beside the running waters, these he brought interwoven in promiscuous garlands, and the house laughed, impregnated with their pleasant odour.

Presently comes Peneus, leaving green Tempe, girt with over-hanging woods, leaving Tempe to be frequented by the

scenes that precede it.  At the same time the poet, delicately breaking off without ever hinting at the fair one's ready acceptance of her new lover, leaves the pity we feel for her abandonment unweakened on the mind.—*Dunlop.*

[1] *Chiron.*]  The mortals having departed, the demigods next arrive ; who neither inhabited Olympus with Jupiter, nor were of rank enough to join his train.  Catullus has with peculiar propriety selected those who had promoted or were interested in the nuptials, or were connected by some tie with the bride or bridegroom.  The centaur Chiron, the inhabitant of Mount Pelion in Thessaly, the kingdom of Peleus, and afterwards tutor of Achilles, the predestined offspring of the marriage, first bears his offerings.  Next Peneus, the offspring of Oceanus and Tethys, is selected from the water deities as the most celebrated river of Thessaly, and as a kinsman of the bride.  He bears an appropriate offering of the trees that grow on his banks, and with Chiron decks the palace with flowers and boughs ; with which it was usual to decorate every part of the bridegroom's abode, and particularly the door, as we learn from Ovid, Fast. 4, Juvenal, Sat. 6, and Plutarch in Erotico.  To these are added Prometheus, who, by his prophecy of the powerful offspring to spring from Thetis, had induced Jupiter to sanction her union with Peleus, and might regard the wedding as his own work.  These three are the fitting forerunners of the celestial host, who, with Jupiter, descend from Olympus to honour the bridal which he had sanctioned.—*Lambe.*

Dorian choirs of the Nessonides;[1] nor does he come empty-handed, for he has brought tall beeches, roots and all, and stately bay-trees with straight stems, with the nodding plane-tree, and lightning-stricken Phaethon's flexible sister,[2] and the airy cypress. These, grouped together, he planted widely round the mansion, that the vestibule might look verdant with its pleasant leafy screen.

After him follows ingenious Prometheus, bearing partly effaced traces of his old punishment, which he once endured, chained to a rock, and suspended from the precipitous peaks of *Caucasus*.[3]

Then the father of the gods came from heaven with his divine spouse and his children, leaving only thee, Phœbus,[4] and thy twin sister, dweller on the mountains of Ida; for like thee she scorned Peleus, and would not celebrate the nuptials of Thetis.

After the gods bent their snowy limbs on the seats, the tables were copiously covered with various cheer. Meanwhile the Parcæ, shaking their bodies with infirm gesture, began to utter soothsaying canticles. A white garment wrapping their tremulous bodies all round, *was* encircled with a purple hem *where it reached* their heels; snowy fillets sat on their ambrosial heads,[5] and their hands plied their eternal task, according to their custom. The left hand held the distaff covered with soft wool; the right hand, lightly drawing forth the threads, formed them with upturned fingers, then twisting them on the downward-pointed thumb, made the

[1] *Leaving Tempe to be,* &c.] The MSS. are very corrupt in this place, and nearly a score of various readings have been proposed. Nessonides: nymphs of Nessos, a lake near Tempe. Dorian choirs: the girls of the Dorian race danced naked on certain occasions.

[2] *Phaethon's flexible sister.*] Phaethon's sisters, inconsolable for the death of their brother, who perished in his mad attempt to drive the chariot of his father, the Sun, were changed into poplars.

[3] *Prometheus,* &c.] An eagle had preyed on his liver for thirty years.

[4] *Phœbus.*] Homer makes Apollo play the lyre at the nuptials of Peleus and Thetis. The reason why Catullus rejected this tradition, was probably that the prescient Apollo could not look with favour on a marriage which was to give birth to Achilles, the destroyer of his favourite Trojans, and whom the god himself was to slay.

[5] *Ambrosial heads.*] Ambrosio is manifestly preferable to the common reading *At roseo,* for roses are surely an incongruous ornament for the hoary heads of the awful Fates.

spindle revolve smoothly and swiftly; their nipping teeth always smoothed the work, and the woolly fibres which had stood out from the light thread, being bitten off, adhered to their dry lips. Wicker-baskets, before their feet, held fleeces of white wool. With shrill voices, as they drew out the threads, they poured forth these fates in divine song, in song which no after-time shall convict of falsehood: [1]

"O Peleus, of most illustrious birth,[2] safeguard of Thessaly, enhancing signal honour by great virtues, hear the truthtelling oracle which the sisters reveal to thee on this joyful day; and you, whereon fates depend, run, spindles, run, and draw out the threads.

"Hesperus will soon come, and bring thee what bridegrooms desire; with that auspicious star will come the spouse, who bathes thy mind in soul-softening love, and prepares to sink to sleep with thee in pleasing languor, putting her smooth arms under thy strong neck. Run, spindles, run, and draw out the threads.

"No house ever united such loves beneath one roof;[3] no love ever bound lovers together in such unanimity, so reciprocal is the concord between Thetis and Peleus. Run, spindles, run, and draw out the threads.

"To you shall be born Achilles void of fear, known to the foe, not by his back, but by his valiant breast; who many a time victor in the rapid race, shall outstrip the fiery steps of the swift stag. Run, spindles, run, and draw out the threads.

"No hero shall compare with him in war, when the Phrygian streams shall flow with Trojan blood, and the third heir of perjured Pelops,[4] waging long war against the Trojan city, shall lay it waste. Run, spindles, run, and draw out the threads.

[1] *Convict of falsehood.*] Whereas, says Muretus, this could not be said of the prophecy reported by others to have been delivered on the same occasion by Apollo.

[2] *Illustrious birth.*] Instead of *clarissime natu*, some read *clarissime nato*, "illustrious in thy son," a phrase which would not indeed be inappriate in the mouths of the Fates, though that son was not yet born; but which appears superfluous, since ample mention is subsequently made of the glories of Achilles.

[3] *United ... beneath one roof.*] So Achilles Statius interprets *con texit*.

[4] *Pelops.*] The first two successors of Pelops, were his sons Thyestes and Atreus; the third was Agamemnon, son of Atreus.

"Mothers shall often confess, in the death of their sons, his egregious valour and illustrious deeds, when they shall let fall their hair whitened with dust, and beat their livid breasts with their feeble hands. Run, spindles, run, and draw out the vital thread.

"For as the husbandman, prostrating the ears of corn, mows the crops that yellow under the hot sun, so shall he prostrate the bodies of the sons of Troy with hostile sword. Run, spindles, run, and draw out the threads.

"A witness of his great valour shall be the wave of Scamander, which is poured diffusely into the rapid Hellespont, and choking whose course with heaps of slain, he shall make the deep stream warm with mingled gore. Run, spindles, run, and draw out the threads.

"A witness too shall be the captive given to death, when the smooth pile heaped upon the lofty mound shall receive the snowy limbs of the slaughtered virgin.[1] Run, spindles, run, and draw out the threads.

"For as soon as fortune shall have enabled the Greeks to break through the Neptunian walls of the Dardanian city, the lofty sepulchre shall be wetted with Polyxena's blood; who, like a victim falling beneath a two-edged knife, kneeling to the stroke, shall fall a headless corpse. Run, spindles, run, and draw out the threads.

"Come then, consummate the amorous longings of your souls; let the bridegroom receive the goddess in happy wedlock; let the bride be delivered to the husband long eager for her. Run, spindles, run, and draw out the threads.

"Her nurse, when she visits her again at dawn of day, shall not be able to surround her neck with yesterday's thread.[2] Run, spindles, run, and draw out the threads.

---

[1] *The slaughtered virgin.*] Achilles was about to marry Polyxena, the daughter of Priam, when he was slain by Paris in the temple of Apollo. After the fall of Troy Pyrrhus, the son of Achilles, immolated her on his father's tomb.

[2] *Yesterday's thread.*] The swelling of the bride's neck, ascertained by measurement with a thread on the morning after the nuptials, was held to be sufficient proof of their happy consummation. The ancients, says Pezay, had faith in another equally absurd test of virginity. They measured the circumference of the neck with a thread. Then the girl under trial took the two ends of the magic thread in her teeth, and if it was found to be so long that its bight could be passed over her head, it

"Nor shall her mother grieve to see her daughter at discord with her mate, and sleeping apart; nor cease to hope
for grandchildren. Run, spindles, run, and draw out the
threads."

Thus prophesying in days of yore, the Fates sang the happy
destinies of Peleus with divine omen. For formerly, ere virtue
was yet despised, the inhabitants of heaven were wont to visit
in person the guiltless abodes of heroes, and to show themselves in mortal assemblies. Often did the father of the gods,
revisiting[1] his splendid temple, when the annual solemnities
arrived with the festal days, behold a hundred chariots running along the ground. Often did roving Bacchus drive his
screaming Thyads with dishevelled hair from the highest
peak of Parnassus,[2] when the Delphians, eagerly rushing out
from the whole city, joyfully welcomed the god with smoking
altars. Often, in the deadly strife of war, Mars, or the mistress
of the rapid Triton,[3] or the Rhamnusian virgin,[4] in person
exhorted armed troops of men. But after the earth was
stained with nefarious crime, and all men drove out justice
from their covetous souls; after brothers drenched their hands
in brothers' blood; the son ceased to mourn his dead parents;
the father desired the death of his firstborn son, that he might
be free to enjoy the beauty of an unwedded step-dame;[5] after

was clear she was not a maid. By this rule all the thin girls might pass
for vestals, and all the plump ones for the reverse.

[1] *Revisiting*, &c.] *Templo in fulgente revisens:* an archaic form of
expression, says Scaliger, like *reviso domi, reviso ad eum.*

[2] *Parnassus.*] One summit of the biforked hill was sacred to Bacchus,
(Pezay says, "in favour of the fine lines which wine inspires,") and his
worship was cultivated at Delphi, as well as that of Apollo. This we
learn from Lucian, book v.

> Between the ruddy west and eastern skies,
> In the mid-earth, Parnassus' tops arise :
> To Phœbus, and the cheerful god of wine,
> Sacred in common stands the hill divine.
> Still as the short revolving year comes round,
> The Mænades, with leafy chaplets crown'd,
> The double deity in solemn songs resound. Rowe.

[3] *Triton.*] A torrent in Bœotia; also a river and marsh in Africa;
both sacred to Pallas.

[4] *Rhamnusian virgin.*] Nemesis, so called from Rhamnus, a town in
Attica.

[5] *An unwedded step-dame.*] Unwedded, but whom he wished to wed.
Sallust states that Catiline murdered his son, because the young man
was an obstacle to his marriage with Aurelia Orestilla,

the impious mother, submitting herself to the embrace of her unconscious son,[1] feared not to contaminate her household gods with sacrilege; all right and wrong confounded together by the madness of guilt, averted from us the righteous minds of the gods. Wherefore they neither deign to visit assemblages so composed, nor suffer themselves to be encountered in the light of day.[2]

## LXV. TO HORTALUS.

THOUGH care, and incessant, consuming sorrow, alienate me, Hortalus, from the learned virgins, nor is my mind capable of drawing forth the sweet younglings of the Muses, with such afflictions is it agitated; for the wave that flows from the Lethæan gulf hath lately washed the pallid foot of my

---

[1] *The impious mother*, &c.] Semiramis is said to have done thus by her son Ninus.

[2] *Day.*] The Marriage of Peleus and Thetis fully justifies Scaliger's opinion that "it approached nearer to the divinity of the Iliad than any other poem." He might however have added, that some part of that divinity was even borrowed from it. The parting of Egeus and Theseus is the prototype of that of Evander and Pallas; the despair of Dido is worked up with sentiment and passion probably suggested by that of Ariadne; and even the beautiful commemoration of Marcellus is an improvement upon the prophecy of the career of Achilles.—*Lambe.* Ovid has treated the subject of Ariadne not less than four times, and has borrowed largely from Catullus. In the Epistle of Ariadne to Theseus he has painted, like his predecessor, her disordered person, her sense of desertion, and remembrance of the benefits she had conferred on Theseus. But the epistle is a cold production, chiefly because her grief is not immediately presented before us; and she merely tells that she had wept, and sighed, and raved. The minute detail, too, into which she enters, is inconsistent with her vehement passion. She recollects too well each heap of sand which retarded her steps, and the thorns on the summit of the mountain. Returning from her wanderings, she addresses her couch, of which she asks advice, till she becomes overpowered by apprehension for the wild beasts and marine monsters, of which she presents her false lover with a faithful catalogue. The simple ideas of Catullus are frequently converted into conceits, and his natural bursts of passion into quibbles and artificial points. In the eighth book of the *Metamorphoses*, the melancholy part of Ariadne's story is only recalled in order to introduce the transformation of her crown into a star. In the third book of the *Fasti*, she deplores the double desertion of Theseus and Bacchus. It is in the first book of the *Art of Love* that Ovid approaches nearest to Catullus, particularly in the sudden contrast between the solitude and melancholy of Ariadne, and the revelry of the Bacchanalians.—*Dunlop*

brother, whom, snatched from my eyes, the Trojan earth covers beneath the Rhœtean shore.[1] * * * * Ah brother dearer than life, shall I never henceforth behold thee? But surely I will always love thee; the songs I sing shall always be saddened by thy death, like those which the bird of Daulia[2] warbles beneath the shade of thick boughs, bewailing the fate of the lost Itys. Yet in the midst of such grief I send thee, Hortalus, these strains imitated from Battiades,[3] that you may not perchance suppose that your words have escaped from my mind, to be given idly to the passing winds, but as the apple,[4] the clandestine gift of the wooer, rolls out from the virgin's chaste bosom;[5] for she forgets, poor thing, that it is placed beneath her soft robe, and as she starts up at her mother's coming, it is shaken out; down it falls at once to the ground, whilst a conscious blush suffuses the face of the distressed damsel.[6]

[1] A line is wanting here.

[2] *The bird of Daulia.*] Daulia in Thrace was the scene of the tragedy of Itys. Tereus, king of Thrace, ravished Philomela and cut out her tongue. Her sister Procne, the wife of Tereus, revenged the deed by killing her son Itys, and cooking him for his father's supper. All four were transformed into birds. Philomela became a nightingale.

[3] *Battiades.*] The Greek poet Callimachus, who was descended from Battus the founder of Cyrene. It would seem that Hortalus had requested Catullus to translate from Callimachus the next poem after this, " Berenice's Hair."

[4] *The apple.*] The gift of an apple had a very tender meaning; according to Vossius it was *quasi pignus concubitus*, that is to say, it was the climax

> To " all those token flowers that tell
> What words can never speak so well."

The emperor Theodosius caused Paulinus to be murdered for receiving an apple from his empress. In one of the love epistles of Aristænetus, Phalaris complains to her friend Petala, how her younger sister, who had accompanied her to dine with Pamphilus, her lover, attempted to seduce him, and among other wanton tricks did as follows: " Pamphilus, biting off a piece of an apple, chucked it dexterously into her bosom; she took it, kissed it, and thrusting it under her sash, hid it between her breasts."

[5] *Bosom.*] The Romans had an ungallant proverb, *nec mulieri, nec gremio credi oportere*, nothing should be intrusted to a woman or a bosom, because, says Festus, the former are light and variable, and whatever is put in the latter is forgotten when one stands up.

[6] *The distressed damsel.*] The intrinsic beauty of this comparison is universally admitted, but many of its warmest admirers confess that they have little to say in defence of its appositeness. But, says Doering, this is because they have not rightly apprehended it. If, for instance, we ac-

## LXVI. BERENICE'S HAIR.[1]

### (THE HAIR SPEAKS.)

CONON, who hath investigated all the lights in the great firmament; who hath ascertained the rising and the setting of the stars, *and knows* how the splendour of the rapid sun is obscured, how the stars depart at certain times, and how sweet love detaining Diana among the crags of Latmos, withdraws her from her airy circuit; that same Conon saw, shining brilliantly with celestial light, me, the hair of Berenice's head, which she, outstretching her smooth arms, had promised to many gods, at the time when the king, recently blest in marriage, and bearing marks of the nocturnal struggle in which he had been engaged for the virgin's spoils, had gone to lay waste the Assyrian territory. Is Venus odious to the newly wedded? Why do brides frustrate their parents' joys by the feigned tears they pour out profusely within the nuptial chamber? Their grief is not real, so help me the gods!

cept the interpretation given by Muretus, " Do not think that your words have lapsed from my mind like an apple from a girl's bosom," then indeed the comparison is quite frigid. But this was not what Catullus intended; his meaning was, " It is true I forgot for a while what I had promised you, but forgot it just as it sometimes happens to a maiden to forget a thing she prizes most dearly, and to be overcome with shame and confusion when she is suddenly reminded of her inattention."

[1] *Berenice's Hair.*] According to Hyginus, whom all the commentators have implicitly followed, Berenice, the daughter of Ptolemy Philadelphus and Arsinoe, married her brother Ptolemy Euergetes, in accordance with the Egyptian custom. But we know from Justin, lib. xxvi. c. 3, that Berenice was not really Ptolemy's sister, but his cousin-german, a relationship to which ancient usage gave the name of sisterhood. Her husband having soon afterwards marched with his army into Syria, Berenice devoted her beautiful locks to Venus on condition of her husband's victorious return. Her prayers were heard, and she suspended her locks with her own hand in the temple of the goddess, whence they disappeared before the next morning, to the great vexation of both the royal consorts. Conon, a famous astronomer of Samos, and a no less adroit courtier, averred that a divine hand had withdrawn them, and placed them among the stars. On this hint Callimachus composed a poem, which Catullus has here imitated. But though the poem of Callimachus may have been seriously written, and gravely read by the court of Ptolemy, the lines of Catullus often approach to something like pleasantry or *persiflage*. The original is lost, which is the more unfortunate, as no work of Catullus has been more disfigured by transcribers than this.

This truth my queen taught me by her many lamentations, when her newly-wedded spouse set out for grim battles. It was not, however, for the loneliness of thy deserted bed that thou didst grieve, but for the sad departure of thy dear brother, when sorrow so consumed thy very marrow, and thy whole bosom was so racked, that sense and reason departed! But surely I have known thee magnanimous since thou wast but a little maiden. Hast thou forgotten that good deed,[1] by which thou didst win a royal marriage, a deed than which none ever dared to do a bolder?[2] But what words thou didst utter at thy sad parting from thy husband! O Jupiter! how often thou didst wipe thine eyes with thy hand! What

---

[1] *That good deed.*] Hyginus gives a romantic and incredible explanation of these verses, in which he is followed by modern commentators. Berenice is represented as a heroine, who broke horses, drove chariots, and practised all military exercises. The exploit here alluded to was, they say, her rescue of her father in battle, when surrounded by enemies; in reward for which her brother married her. But the poet certainly alludes to a memorable passage in history, related by Plutarch in his Life of Demetrius. Magas, the uterine brother of Ptolemy Philadelphus, was by the influence of his mother promoted to the government of Cyrene and Libya. (Pausanias in Attic.) He governed those provinces many years with ability, and having fortified his own power by the affection of the natives and by his marriage with Apame, daughter of Antiochus Soter, king of Syria, he determined to secure to his own family the dominion of the countries which he had long ruled as a viceroy. His revolt was successful; but the supposed contingency which had at first inspired him with disaffection to his brother, failed to happen. He had reached the extremity of old age, and his queen Apame had brought him no male children, and only one daughter, Berenice. Under this disappointment Magas expressed a desire to compose all differences with his brother Ptolemy Philadelphus, by marrying his only daughter with Ptolemy's eldest son, and giving as her dower the restored allegiance of Cyrene and Libya. The treaty was accepted, but Magas died before the conditions of it were executed. The ambitious Apame, unwilling that her husband's independent kingdom should sink into a tributary province, invited to Cyrene Demetrius, the brother of Antigonus Gonatas, king of Macedon, promising him her daughter in marriage. But the figure and accomplishments of this young prince changed her resolutions and captivated her affections. Demetrius, instead of marrying the daughter, became the paramour of the mother. But the slighted Berenice determined to avenge her wrongs. A conspiracy was formed in the palace. Demetrius was slain in the embraces of Apame; the daughter conducting the assassins to the chamber and bed of her mother. Apame was sent into Syria, and Berenice repaired to Alexandria, and consummated her marriage with young Ptolemy, afterwards called Euergetes.—*Tytler.*

[2] *A deed than which, &c.*] Quo non fortius ausit alis. Alis for alius.

mighty god thus changed thee? Was this because lovers are loth to be long absent from the beloved one? And there thou didst promise me, together with blood of bulls, to all the gods for thy dear spouse, if he returned in no long time, and added vanquished Asia to the bounds of Egypt. For these reasons, I, now numbered among the celestial assembly, discharge thy pristine vow by a new gift.

Unwillingly, O queen, did I quit thy crown;[1] unwillingly, I swear by thee and thy head; and fit chastisement befall whoever takes that oath lightly! But who can hope to withstand steel? That mountain too was cut down with steel, over which, the largest on the coasts, the illustrious race of Thia[2] was borne, when the Medes swept through a new sea, and the Barbarian youth navigated through the midst of Athos. What can hairs do when such things yield to steel? Perish, O Jupiter, the whole race of the Chalybes,[3] and whoever in the beginning instituted the practice of seeking out veins under ground and forging hard iron! My sister hairs, just before separated from me, were bewailing my fate, when Æthiopian Memnon's brother, the winged steed of Chloris, beating the air with quivering wings, presented himself in Arsinoe's temple, and catching me up flew through the dusky ether and laid me in the chaste bosom of Venus.[4] Zephyritis

[1] *Unwillingly*, &c.] Macrobius remarks that Virgil, who was well acquainted with the works of his predecessors, has borrowed this line from Catullus (Æn. iv. 460):

Invitus, Regina, tuo de littore cessi.

[2] *Thia.*] Macedon, who gave his name to Macedonia, the original country of the Ptolemies, was the son of Jupiter and Thia, the daughter of Deucalion. The Macedonians were among the auxiliaries of Xerxes when he invaded Greece, cutting a channel through Mount Athos on his way.

[3] *The Chalybes.*] A people of Asia Minor, descended from Chalybs, a son of Mars, who first taught the use of iron. Pope has imitated this passage in the third canto of the Rape of the Lock:

What time would spare, from steel receives its date,
And monuments, like men, submit to fate.
Steel could the labours of the gods destroy,
And strike to dust the imperial towers of Troy;
Steel could the works of mortal pride confound,
And hew triumphal arches to the ground;
What wonder then, fair nymph, thy hairs should feel
The conquering force of unresisted steel?

*The chaste bosom of Venus.*] The Venus here meant is the more

herself had sent her servant to the pleasant regions on the
Canopian shores, to the end that not only the golden crown
from Ariadne's temples should be fixed in the varied extent
of heaven, but that we, the consecrated spoils of *Berenice's*
yellow head, might shine there too.　As moist with tears I
entered the temple of the gods, divine *Venus* placed me as a
new constellation among the ancient ones.　For contiguous
to the stars of the Virgin and of the fierce Lion, adjoining
Calisto the daughter of Lycaon, I turn to the west, preceding the slow Bootes, who sinks late and reluctantly into the
deep ocean.　But though the footsteps of the gods press me
by night,[1] yet by day I am restored to the bosom of white-
haired Tethys.　Let me be allowed to say these things with
thy permission, Rhamnusian virgin, for I will not conceal the
truth from any fear; no, though the stars assail me with invectives, I will unfold the secret feelings of my sincere mind:
I am not so rejoiced by these events, as not to be tortured by
the thought that I am for ever parted from the head of my
mistress, with whom I imbibed many thousand fragrant ointments, though whilst she was yet a virgin I never had any.[2]

Now you, on whose union the marriage torch has shone
with its precious light, give not your persons to your fond
mates, nor throw off your robes and bare your bosoms, before
your onyx box presents me with pleasing libations ; *let* your
onyx box *do this*, all you who seek the rights of wedlock in
a chaste bed.　But whoso gives herself up to impure adultery,
let the light dust unwillingly imbibe her loathed gifts ; for I

reputable of the two goddesses of that name, the one who presides over
lawful wedlock.　Multitudinous blunders in the MSS. combine with
mythological intricacies to make this whole passage one of the most obscure in the works of Catullus.　Briefly, its meaning appears to be this :
Zephyrus, son of Aurora, brother of Memnon, and husband of Chloris,
carried off the hair by order of Venus, who is also called Arsinoe, from
her temple in the town of that name founded by Ptolemy Philadelphus
in honour of his sister-spouse ; and Zephyritis, from the Egyptian promontory of Zephyrium where she was worshipped.　Some commentators
make Zephyritis identical with Chloris.

　[1] *The footsteps of the gods press me.*]　The *Coma Berenices* is situated
in the Milky Way, the road by which the gods passed over the sky to
and from Olympus.

　[2] *Never had any.*]　Maidens used simple oil alone, and no perfumes
for their hair, or only such as were extracted from single plants, but not
those composite essences which were always implied by the words *un-
guentum* and μυρρα.　They wore no garlands of flowers, only plain fillets.

desire no offerings from the unworthy. Rather, O brides, may concord and constant love always abide in your dwellings.

But thou, O queen, when gazing on the stars thou shalt propitiate Venus with festive torches, let not me, thine own, be left without my share of sacrifice, but rather present me with copious offerings.

Why do the stars hold me? Would I might again become the hair of my royal mistress! Orion might then shine next to Aquarius [1] *for aught I cared*.

### LXVII. ON A WANTON'S DOOR. [2]

#### CATULLUS.

HAIL, door, dear to the amiable husband and dear to his father, and may Jove bless thee with his good aid, O door, who they say didst formerly serve Balbus with good will, when the old man lived here; and who they say again didst serve an evil intent after the old man was stretched out and *the mistress* was *again* made a bride. Come, tell me why thou art reported to be so changed and to have thus renounced thy old fidelity to thy master.

#### DOOR.

As I hope to please Cæcilius, to whom I now belong, it is not my fault, although it is said to be so; nor can any one say that any offence has been committed by me; but if you believe the people, everything is the door's doing: for whenever anything is known to have been done amiss, they all cry out at me, "It is your fault, door."

#### CATULLUS.

It is not enough to assert this by word only; but you must make it so plain that any one may understand and see it.

#### DOOR.

How can I? No one asks, or cares to know.

[1] *Orion .... Aquarius.*] These two constellations are very far asunder: the mention of them implies, Could I but get back to my old place, the whole order of the heavens might be upset for aught I cared.

[2] *On a wanton's door.*] The persons and the circumstances alluded to in this satire being totally unknown, our interest in it is greatly impaired. Several commentators have endeavoured to explain its personal allusions, but their conjectures are quite arbitrary and therefore worthless.

## CATULLUS.

I do: do not hesitate to tell me.

#### DOOR.

In the first place then it is false that she was delivered to
us a virgin: not that her impotent husband had first been intimate with her; but her own father is said to have violated
his son's bed, and to have dishonoured his unfortunate house;
whether it was that his incestuous soul burned with blind
passion, or that his enervated son was incapable of marital
functions, and that abler means to loose the virgin's zone had
to be sought elsewhere.

#### CATULLUS.

You make known to me a rare instance of admirable parental conscientiousness;—to cuckold his own son!

#### DOOR.

But this is not the only thing which Brixia professes to know,
Brixia, situated below the Cycnæan peak, beloved mother of
my Verona,[1] which the yellow Mela traverses with its gentle
stream. But it tells of the amours of Posthumius and of Cornelius, with whom she committed shameful adultery. Now
some one may say: "How do you know these things, door,
you who are never free to quit your master's threshold, nor
to hear the talk of the people, but, fastened to this post, are
wont only to shut or open the house?" I have often heard
her in private talking of these wicked deeds of hers, with her
handmaids, in a stealthy voice, and mentioning by name those
I have mentioned; for she did not of course expect that I had
tongue or ear. Moreover, she spake of a certain person whom
I do not wish to mention by name, lest he bristle up his red
eyebrows. He is a long, lanky fellow, who formerly got involved in great litigation about a simulated pregnancy and
false parturition.

[1] *Beloved mother,* &c.] Maffei (*Verona Illustrata*) maintains that the
two lines which predicate this relationship of Brescia and Verona contradict
history, and that they are spurious.

## LXVIII. TO MANLIUS.[1]

THAT, bowed down by misfortune and sore calamity, you
send me this epistle blotted with your tears, *praying me* to
raise you up as a shipwrecked man flung ashore by the foaming billows, and to rescue you from the gates of death; *and
telling me* that neither sacred Venus suffers you to enjoy soft
slumber in your lonely, deserted bed, nor do the Muses delight
you with the sweet strains of old poets, whilst your sorrowing mind knows no rest; this is gratifying to me, for as much
as you esteem me your friend, and therefore ask of me the
gifts of the Muses and of Venus. But that my sorrows may
not be unknown to you, Manlius, and that you may not suppose I shrink from the duties incumbent on your guest,[2] hear
now in what billows of misfortune I myself am plunged, and
ask no more for the gifts of the happy from a wretch like
me.

When first the white robe[3] was conferred upon me, when
my flowery years were in their jocund spring, I disported
variously enough;[4] I have not been unknown to the goddess

[1] *To Manlius.*] Most commentators conclude from the fifth and sixth lines
of this poem that it was addressed to Manlius on the occasion of the death
of his wife Julia, celebrated in the first epithalamium. But this seems
incongruous with the wish expressed at the end of the piece, that Manlius and the lady, whoever she was, who is emphatically termed " his
life," may long live happily together. Doering supposes that the fond
pair had quarrelled; but that hypothesis fails also if tried by the same
test; besides, the poet offers no hint or inducement towards reconciliation,
as he would naturally have done in such a case. It is to be regretted that
we are left in the dark as to the occasion on which this poem was composed, for we are thus deprived of the means of clearing up many of its
obscurities, and of becoming reconciled to many things in it which now
appear as blemishes upon a work which presents many extraordinary
beauties.

[2] *Your guest.*] The Romans regarded hospitality as a permanent
mutual relation, and assigned to it a high place among the duties of life.
Aulus Gellius thus classifies social duties in the order in which they are
to be preferred when they happen to clash with each other—First, the
duty towards parents and guardians; next, that towards clients and
adopted dependants; thirdly, the duties of those who accepted or inter-
changed hospitality; and lastly, duties towards kindred and relations.
The duties of hospitality, he says, are sometimes placed second.

[3] *The white robe.*] The *toga virilis*, assumed at the age of puberty, and
which was of but one colour; the boy's robe was bordered with purple.

[4] *I disported variously enough.*] Some interpret this to mean, I toved

G

who mingles sweet bitterness[1] with our cares. But my brother's death has absorbed all such tastes in grief. O my brother, whose loss hath left me wretched! Thou hast broken all my enjoyments by thy death, brother; our whole house is buried along with thee; with thee have perished all my delights, which thy dear love fostered in thy lifetime. Since thy departure I have wholly abandoned all my fondness for poetry, and all my favourite pursuits. Therefore as for what you write, that "It is a shame for Catullus to be at Verona, for there a man of mark must warm his cold limbs in his solitary bed;"[2] this is not shameful, Manlius; say rather it is pitiable. You will pardon me then if I do not send you those gifts of which sorrow has bereft me, since I am unable. For that I have no great stock of writings by me is a result of my living at Rome; that is my home, my domicile; there my life is passed. Only one case of books[3] out of many has accompanied me to this place. This being so, I would not have you conclude that it is from ill will, or illiberality of mind on my part, that both your requests are not fulfilled. I would

with the Muses; others, I dallied with love; we rather think that Catullus meant both.

[1] *Sweet bitterness.*] This was a familiar idea with the ancients, and Byron's imitation of Lucretius has naturalized it in England:

> Medio de fonte leporum
> Surgit amari aliquid quod in ipsis floribus angat.

> Full from the fount of joy's delicious springs
> Some bitter o'er the flowers its bubbling venom flings.

Anacreon, Ode 45, describes the manufacture of Cupid's arrow-heads: Vulcan forges them, Venus then dips them in honey, and Cupid afterwards in gall. Claudian gives a somewhat different account of the matter:

> Labuntur gemini fontes, hic dulcis, amarus
> Alter, et infusis corrumpit melle venenis,
> Unde Cupidineas armavit fama sagittas.

> In Cypris' isle two rippling fountains fall,
> And one with honey flows and one with gall;
> In these, if we may take the tale from fame,
> The son of Venus dips his darts of flame. MOORE.

[2] *It is a shame*, &c.] Lamb, and many others before him, have strangely mistaken the meaning of this passage, as though it signified that while Catullus buried himself in a provincial town, others were taking the place he left vacant by Lesbia's side at home.

*Case of books.*] *Capsula*, a portable case in which the ancients kept their books, whence the slaves who carried the books of patrician boys when they went to school were called *Capsarii*.

gladly send you *both books and verses*, if I had any supply of
them.

I cannot forbear, O goddesses, to tell in what things
Manlius has aided me, and how great has been his kindness,
lest fleeting, oblivious time veil in obscurity this friendship of
his for me. But I will tell you *all:* do you tell it again to
many thousands, and make this paper talk of it when it shall
have become an ancient writing. * * * * * * [Let him become
more and more famous when dead,[1]] and let not the pendent
spider, weaving her fine web, ply her work over the neglected
name of Manlius.

For you know, *Muses*, what anxiety wily Venus[2] caused
me, and in what manner she fired my bosom; when it boiled
like the bowels of Ætna, or the Malian fountain in Œtæan
Thermopylæ;[3] when my eyes were bedimmed with incessant
tears, and my cheeks were wet with sad showers. As the
limpid stream bursts from the mossy stone on the airy mountain's crest, and having rolled down the sloping valley, makes
its way through the midst of a dense population, presenting a
sweet refreshment to the weary traveller, when the oppressive
heat makes the parched fields crack and gape: and as a soft
and favouring wind comes to mariners whom a black tempest
has tossed, and who invoke the aid of Castor and Pollux; such,
and so helpful has Manlius been to me. He widely extended
the limits of my narrow domain; he gave me the house I dwell
in and its mistress, whom we might love in common.[4] Thither

[1] *Let him become*, &c.] Handius suspects this line to be an interpolation.
[2] *Wily Venus*.] We agree with Muretus in thinking that the epithet
*duplex* has the same meaning as that in which Horace applies it to
Ulysses. Scaliger understands by it Venus Urania and the common
Venus. Vossius and Vulpius think it alludes to the Venus with two
faces, one of them bearded, who was worshipped by the people of
Amathus.
[3] *The Malian fountain*, &c.] Thermopylæ is etymologically The Pass
of the Hot Wells: θερμὸς, warm, πύλη, gate.
[4] *Love in common*.] Vulpius quotes instances from Plautus and
other writers, to prove that this excess of friendship was not unusual
in Rome. An epigram in the Greek Anthology condemns the practice,
and thereby proves its existence; and Donatus states that Virgil refused
an invitation from Varius to establish such an intimacy. It seems to be
generally taken for granted that the mistress here in question was Lesbia;
but this is merely a conjecture, and a very improbable one, as it appears to us.

my fair divinity turned her light steps,[1] and halted on the
threshold, pressing it with her shining foot and creaking sandals.[2]   So came of yore Laodamia,[3] burning with love, to the
home of Protesilaus, *a home* she entered with hopes doomed to
be frustrated, since no victim had yet propitiated the lords of
heaven with consecrated blood.   May nothing, O Nemesis,
ever engage my affections so strongly, as that I should rashly
enter upon its enjoyment without the sanction of the gods.
Laodamia learned by the loss of her husband how hungrily
the altar craves for sacrificial blood ; *for she was* compelled to
quit the neck of her lately wedded spouse, before a second
return of the long winter nights had so satisfied her eager love,
that she could survive the dissolution of her marriage, which
the Fates knew would not be far remote in time, if her husband went in arms to the walls of Ilium.   For Troy had then
begun to provoke the leaders of the Greeks against it by the
rape of Helen : accursed Troy !  the common sepulchre of
Europe and Asia ; Troy, the cruel grave of brave men and
noble qualities ; to which I also owe the lamentable death of
my brother.   O brother, lost to my sorrow !  O light of gladness, lost to thy wretched brother !  Our whole house is buried
with thee.   With thee have perished all my delights, which
thy sweet love fostered in thy lifetime.   Now, an alien land
holds thee so far from me, in its remote soil, laid not among
familiar tombs, not near kindred ashes, but buried in infamous,
unhappy Troy.

Thither hastened from all quarters the whole manhood of
Greece, forsaking their domestic hearths, that Paris might not
enjoy his stolen adulteress in the ease and freedom of a peace-

---

[1] *Light steps.*]  *Molli pedi :* Noel, the French translator of Catullus,
understands by this, " The grace of a voluptuous gait ; a feminine at-
traction which was so highly prized, that we find it commemorated in
ancient inscriptions : *Sermone lepido, tum autem incessu commodo.*  Propertius has specified it in a pretty line :

*Et canit, ut solent molliter ire pedes.*"

[2] *Creaking sandals.*]  *Arguta solea* is susceptible of a different meaning, viz. " small and pretty : " we prefer that which we have given, for
reasons which no lover will be at a loss to assign.

[3] *Laodamia.*]  Too fondly impatient to consummate her marriage with
Protesilaus, Laodamia neglected previously to propitiate the gods with
sacrifices.  In revenge they caused her husband to be the first hero slain
before Troy.  She desired to see his shade, and died embracing it.

ful bed. Thus it happened that thou, O fairest Laodamia, wast bereft of a spouse dearer to thee than life and soul. A very whirlpool of love had sucked thee in, and plunged thee down a gulf as deep as the rich soil which the Greeks tell us was dried by the drainage of the marsh near Cyllenean Pheneus, and which the falsely supposed son of Amphitryon is said to have dug, when he cut through the hearts of mountains, at the time when he smote the Stymphalian monsters with his sure arrows, by command of a less valiant lord;[1] that the gateway of heaven might be trodden by a divinity the more, and that Hebe[2] might not be long a virgin. But thy deep love was deeper than that gulf which taught the god to bear tamely the yoke of a master.[3] For no only daughter rears a late-born child so dear to his aged grandsire, *a child* who, when hope was almost gone, appears at last as heir to his ancestral wealth, has had his name inserted in the attested will, and thus extinguishing the unkindly joy of the baffled next of kin, drives away the vulture that hovered over the grandsire's hoary head;[4] nor did any dove ever delight so much in its snowy mate, (though that bird is said to surpass all others in the indefatigable ardour of its billing kisses,) *as thou didst, Laodamia*, though woman is pre-eminently inconstant. But thou alone didst surpass every great love ever known, when once thou wast united with thy yellow-haired husband.[5]

[1] *The drainage of the marsh*, &c.] Hercules, son of Jupiter, by Alcmena, the wife of Amphitryon, was by an artifice of Juno's made subject to his less heroic uterine brother Eurystheus. The two labours of Hercules, here mentioned, are the destruction of the monstrous birds of prey that infested the neighbourhood of Stymphalus in Arcadia, and the draining of a marsh formed by the waters of the Pheneus, which he effected by opening a passage through a mountain.

[2] *Hebe.*] Whom Hercules married after his reception into heaven, and his reconciliation to her mother, Juno.

[3] *That taught the god*, &c.] The various readings of this passage are innumerable; Muretus, one of the most judicious of commentators, frankly confesses that he cannot make sense of it. It must be confessed that the whole of this allusion to Hercules has very much the air of an illustration, dragged in by the head and shoulders.

[4] *The vulture*, &c.] That is, the heir at law, who watched like a carrion bird of prey for the old man's death.

[5] *But thou alone*, &c.] Noel inclines to the opinion that the death of Julia was the real theme of this poem, notwithstanding the mention of the lady, who would seem to have anticipated Catullus in consoling the

Worthy to yield to her in no respect, or but little, the light of my life came to my bosom; while often fluttering round her here and there, fair Cupid shone in saffron tunic. And though indeed she is not content with Catullus alone, I will bear with the few infidelities of my discreet mistress, that I may not make myself intolerable as fools do. [Often, even Juno, the greatest of the celestial goddesses, raged at the daily faults of her consort, knowing the many amours of most volatile Jove. But it is not meet that men should be compared with gods.] Let me be rid *however* of the annoying burthen of her fidgetty father. *Why should he interfere?* For[1] she was not delivered to me by a father's hand, when she came to my house scented with Assyrian perfume; but quitting the very bosom of her husband, she bestowed furtive favours on me in that delicious night. Enough then, if she gives to me alone that day which she marks with a white stone.

I send you, Manlius, this gift of verse, the best I could compose, in return for many acts of friendship, that this day, or that, or another, may not touch your name with the unseemly rust *of oblivion.* May the gods add, moreover, all kinds of gifts which Themis was wont to bestow on the virtuous of yore. May you both be happy, yourself and she who is your life; and happy be the house in which we have dallied, and its mistress, and he who first made me known to you, and from whom all my good fortune was primarily derived; and happy beyond all others be that light of my days, who is dearer to me than myself, and who while she lives makes life sweet to me.

widower; for he says that the ancients were not so squeamish in such matters as the moderns. In confirmation of this conjecture, he asks: "Would it be unreasonable to suppose that this digression about Laodamia, which seems so foreign to the subject, is an allusion to the love of Julia for Manlius,—Julia carried off like her in the bloom of youth?"

[1] *Let me be rid,* &c.] We have given this line the only interpretation by which it seems possible to connect it with the received context; but the latter bears obvious marks of some clumsy interpolater's handiwork. If we reject with Handius the preceding passage enclosed between brackets, the meaning will come out clearly thus: "Let me not be unreasonably fretful *about such slight grievances,* after the manner of fools; away with the onerous and ungracious task *of watching and chiding, like* a fidgetty parent *rather than a lover.*"

## LXIX. TO RUFUS.

WONDER not, Rufus, why no woman will submit to your embrace, nor why you can tempt none by the gift of a choice robe, or an exquisite transparent gem. Your reputation suffers from a certain ugly story that is current, to the effect that a horrid buck goat is lodged in your armpits. They are all afraid of him, and no wonder, for he is a very dreadful beast, and one which no fair damsel could sleep along-side of. Wherefore either slay that dire foe to their noses, or cease to wonder why the women shun you.

## LXX. ON THE INCONSTANCY OF WOMAN'S LOVE.

MY mistress says there is none she would rather wed than me; not though Jove himself should woo her. She says so:[1]

[1] *She says so.*] *Dicit.* Noel traces a strong resemblance between this epigram and one by Callimachus, especially in the graceful repetition, which serves so well to introduce the closing thought. The Greek epigram is to this effect:

"Calignotus has sworn to Ionis that he will never love any one better than her. He has sworn it: but it is a true saying that lovers' oaths do not reach the ears of the immortals."

Some very pretty lines of similar tenor by Montemayor, a Spanish poet, have frequently been imitated in English:

"One eve of beauty, when the sun
    Was on the waves of Guadalquiver,
To gold converting one by one
    The ripples of the mighty river;
Beside me on the bank was seated
A Seville girl, with auburn hair,
And eyes that might the world have cheated,
A wild, bright, wicked diamond pair."

"She stoop'd and wrote upon the sand,
    Just as the loving sun was going,
With such a soft, small, shining hand,
    You would have sworn 'twas silver flowing.
Three words she wrote and not one more;
    What could Diana's motto be?
The syren wrote upon the shore:
    " Death, not inconstancy."

"And then her two large languid eyes
    So turn'd on mine, that, devil take me,
I set the air on fire with sighs,
    And was the fool she chose to make me.

but what a woman says to an eager lover, should be written
on the wind and the running water.

### LXXI.  TO VERRO.

IF ever, Verro, any worthy was infested with a cursed buck-
goatish effluvia from his armpits; or if hobbling gout ever
deservedly racked any one, that rival of yours, who supplants
you in your love, has with marvellous fitness acquired both
maladies; for as often as he enjoys his conquest, he avenges
you on the pair; her he stifles with his rank smell, and he
himself is half killed by the gout.

### LXXII.  TO LESBIA.

YOU used once to say, Lesbia, that you knew none but *your
own* Catullus, and that you would not prefer even Jove to me.
I loved you then not merely as men commonly love a mistress,
but as a father loves his sons and his sons-in-law.  Now I
know you.  Wherefore though I burn for you more vehe-
mently than ever, yet are you much more despicable and
worthless in my eyes.  How can this be?  you ask.  Because
such wrongs *as mine* compel a lover to love more, but to like
less.

### LXXIII.  ON AN INGRATE.

CEASE to wish to deserve well of any one, or to think that
any one can be made faithfully observant of his obligations.
The whole world is ungrateful: kind acts are of no avail;
nay, they even weary, they weary and offend rather.  [So it is
in my own case; for no one pursues me with more acrimonious
hostility than he who but lately had in me his one only friend.[1]]

### LXXIV.  ON GELLIUS.[2]  [*See Metrical Version.*]

---

Saint Francis would have been deceived
By such an eye, and such a hand:
But one week more, and I believed
As much the woman as the sand."

[1] *So it is*, &c.]  The passage enclosed between brackets is palpably
spurious.
[2] *On Gellius.*]  Les oncles sont grondeurs; Gellius n' ignorait pas que
le sien déclamait en rigoriste outré contre les propos gais et les galantes

## LXXV. TO LESBIA.

No woman can say truly she has been loved so well as thou, my Lesbia, hast been loved by me. Never was so much faith observed in any compact as hath been manifested on my part in my love for thee.[1] Now is my mind brought to this pass by thy perfidy, my Lesbia, and has so lost itself in its devotion to thee, that I can neither like thee, shouldst thou become faultless, nor cease to love thee, do what thou wilt.

## LXXVI. TO HIMSELF.

If there be any pleasure to a man in the remembrance of former good deeds, when he considers that his conduct is upright,[2] and that he has not broken sacred faith, or abused the sanction of the gods, in any compact, to the deception of men; many delights remain in store for thee, Catullus, for long years to come, out of that ill-requited love of thine. For all the kindness that men can show to any one by word or deed, has been evinced in thy words and deeds; but all has been lavished in vain on a thankless mind. Why then torture thyself more? Why not summon up resolution enough to withdraw utterly from that *illusion*, and cease to be wretched in defiance of the gods?[3] It is hard to put off sud-

---

fredaines. L' habile neveu a commencé par interesser sa tante en sa faveur, et a fini par faire de son oncle un Harpocrate. C' était le moyen de réussir ; car, pour faire taire la censure, il n' y a rien de mieux que de fermer la bouche au censeur. *Noel.*

There were two persons of the name of Gellius at Rome in the time of Catullus—an uncle and nephew. The first was a notorious profligate, who had wasted his patrimony, and afterwards headed mobs in the forum for hire (Cicero, *pro Sextio*, c. 51). The nephew was equally dissolute. After the death of Cæsar he conspired to assassinate Cassius in the midst of his army, and having been pardoned, deserted to Antony. One of the various crimes of which he was suspected identifies him as the Gellius branded by our poet, and whose vices were so enormous that all the water of the sea could not wash him clean. (lxxxvii.)

[1] *For thee.*] The first part of this poem, as far as the words "for thee," appears in some editions as a separate poem or fragment, numbered lxxxvii.

[2] *Upright.*] *Pium;* a term which implies a conscientious regard for all social as well as religious duties.

[3] *In defiance of the gods.*] Viz. Venus and Cupid.

denly a long-cherished love : it is hard, but do it how thou
mayest.   This is thine only safety ; this must be achieved by
thee ; this thou shalt do, be it possible or impossible.   O ye
gods, if it is your attribute to have pity, or if ever you
granted aid to mortals in the very crisis of mortal agony, look
upon my misery ; and if I have led a pure life, pluck from me
this plague and destruction, which, creeping like a lethargy
through every fibre of my frame, has expelled all gladness
from my breast.    I do not now ask that she may love me in
return, or, what is impossible, that she should be chaste ; I
desire myself to be healed, and to cast off this dire disease.
Grant me this, O gods, in reward of my piety.

### LXXVII.  TO RUFUS.

RUFUS, whom fruitlessly and in vain I treated as a friend ;
fruitlessly ? nay, to my great loss and damage ; hast thou thus
cajoled me, and consuming my vitals, ravished from me all
my joys ? Thou hast ravished them from me.   O cruel poison
of my life !  O plague of my friendship !   And now I grieve
that thou hast beslavered my girl's sweet lips with thy filthy
kisses.    But thou shalt not escape with impunity ; for all
ages shall know thee, and long-lived fame shall tell what
thou art.

### LXXVIII.  ON GALLUS.

GALLUS has brothers, one of whom has a very charming
wife ; the other a charming son.    Gallus is a nice man ; for
he panders sweetly, and puts the handsome aunt and the
handsome nephew to bed together.    Gallus is a fool ; for he
does not stop to consider that he is a husband and an uncle,
before he demonstrates how an uncle may be made a cuckold.

### LXXIX.  ON GELLIUS.

GELLIUS is handsome : who can doubt it ? since Lesbia
prefers him to you, Catullus, and your whole race.   Nevertheless this handsome youth is at liberty to sell Catullus and his
race, if he find three men of condition to salute him.

### LXXX.  TO GELLIUS.[1]   [See Metrical Version.]

---

[1] To Gellius.]   Nous diras tu, G llius, pourquoi tes lèvres de rose ont

### LXXXI. TO JUVENTIUS.

Was there no one in so great a multitude, Juventius, no nice fellow, to whom you might take it into your head to become attached, besides that host of yours from deadly malarious Pisaurum,[1] wanner then a gilded statue ; who is now dear to you, whom you dare to prefer to me ? Ah ! you know not what you do.

### LXXXII. TO QUINTIUS.

If you would have Catullus owe his eyes to you, Quintius, or aught else dearer to him than his eyes, if such thing there be, do not ravish from him what is much dearer to him than his eyes, or than anything still dearer.

### LXXXIII. ON LESBIA'S HUSBAND.

Lesbia says all sorts of abusive things of me, when her husband is by, and this is a great delight to that numskull. Ass! do you not see that if she forgot me and said nothing, she would be all right ? Whereas now she snarls and rails, she not only remembers, but what is worse, she is angry: that is to say, she is on fire and she speaks.

### LXXXIV. ON ARRIUS.

Whenever Arrius had occasion to say the word *commodious* he would say *chommodious*, and *hinsidious* when he meant *insidious*, and he hoped that he had spoken marvellously well when he had aspirated *hinsidious* as much as he could. I believe his mother, his uncle Liber, and his maternal grandfather and grandmother spoke thus. When he was sent into Syria, our ears had all a respite, for they heard the same words

pris la blancheur de la neige, lorsque dans les longs jours d' été, la huitième heure t' arrache à la mollesse d' un repos voluptueux ? En croirons nous les bruits qui t' accusent de prêter ta bouche à d' infâmes complaissances ? Il le faut bien ; l' épulsement de ton ami Victor, et les traces honteuses que conservent tes lèvres décolorées, ne déposent que trop contre vous deux. *Noel.*

[1] *Pisaurum.*] A town of Umbria noted for its insalubrity, now called Pesaro. Vossius says that in his time it had the same character, and there were few old inhabitants there.

pronounced smoothly and lightly.    Thenceforth they had no
dread of them, when suddenly the horrible news arrives, that
the Ionian waves, after Arrius had gone thither, were no
longer *Ionian* but *Hionian.*

### LXXXV.  ON HIS LOVE.

I HATE and love.   You ask perhaps how can that be.   I
know not; but I feel that it is so, and I am tortured.[1]

### LXXXVI.  ON QUINTIA AND LESBIA.

QUINTIA is handsome in the opinion of many; in mine she
is fair, tall, straight; this I acknowledge; I admit these
several details, but that aggregate " handsome" I deny; for
there is no loveliness, not a grain of piquancy, in her whole
person, large as it is.   Lesbia is handsome; for, beautiful all
over as she is, she combines in her single self all the graces
stolen from her whole sex.

### LXXXVII.  [*See note on LXXV.*]

### LXXXVIII.  AGAINST GELLIUS.

WHAT does he do, Gellius, who indulges his prurience with
his mother and his sister, and is naked and busy all night ?
What does he do, who suffers not his uncle to be a husband ?
Have you any idea, what a load of guilt he takes upon him ?
He takes upon him, Gellius, so much as not Tethys to her farthest bounds, not Oceanus the farthest of the Nymphs, can
wash away.[2]   For there is no possible kind or form of guilt
which can exceed this : Non si demisso se ipse voret capite.

### LXXXIX.  ON GELLIUS.

GELLIUS is thin ; and why not ? when he has such a kind

---

[1] *I hate and love*, &c.]   The reader may perhaps like to hear the opinion
of the pure and saintly Fenelon concerning our obscene pagan author.
" Catullus," he says, " whom we cannot name without shuddering at his
obscenities, is perfection itself in impassioned simplicity.   Odi et amo,
&c. Compare him here with Ovid and Martial; how far inferior are their
ingenious and artificial points to these unadorned words, in which the
suffering heart talks with itself alone in an access of despair."

[2] *Wash away.*]   The ancients believed the sea had the virtue to
purge moral impurity, and that not typically or metaphorically, but in
reality.

mother, such a buxom and comely sister, such a good easy
uncle, and such lots of female cousins,[1] how should he cease
to be lean ? Though he never touches anything but what it is
nefarious to touch, you will find cause enough why he should
be as lean as you please.

## XC. ON GELLIUS.

LET there be born from the nefarious commerce of
Gellius and his mother a Magus, who shall learn the Persian
system of augury. For a Magus must be born of a mother
and her son, if the impious religion of the Persians is true,
that their offspring may worship the gods with acceptable hymns,
melting the fat omentum[2] in the flame of the altar.

## XCI. ON GELLIUS.

IT was not because I know you well, Gellius, and thought
you constant, or capable of refraining from infamous villany,
that I hoped you would be faithful to me in this matter of my
wretched, my desperate love ; but because I saw that this girl,
for whom I was consumed with passion, was neither your
mother nor your sister ; and though I had the experience of
much personal intercourse to guide my judgment, I did not
believe that there was enough in such a case to tempt you.
You thought there was ; so great is your delight in every offence in which there is some mixture of enormous guilt.

## XCII. ON LESBIA.

LESBIA always abuses me, and never ceases to talk about
me. May I die but Lesbia loves me. How does that appear ?
As if I am not perpetually reviling her just as much ; yet may
I die but I love her.[3]

[1] *Lots of female cousins.*] *Omnia plena puellis cognatis.* This very
idiomatic expression is frequently used by Latin authors. *Omnia mise-
riarum plenissima.* Cic. Epist. 24, L. ii., ad Attic. *Lacrymis omnia
plena,* Tibul. Eleg. 9, L. i.
[2] *Omentum.*] The fat of the victim, wrapped in the omentum, a mem-
brane that covers the intestines, was thrown into the fire on the altar, and
auguries were drawn from the appearance of the flame.
[3] *Lesbia, &c.*] Bussy de Rabutin has pretty well imitated this epigram :

## XCIII. ON CÆSAR.

I DO not greatly care to court your good will, Cæsar, nor to
know whether you are white or black.

## XCIV. AGAINST MENTULA.

THE flesh sins: certainly the flesh sins.   That is as much
as to say, The pot gathers garden stuff for the pot.[1]

## XCV. ON THE "SMYRNA" OF THE POET CINNA.[2]

AT last my friend Cinna's Smyrna is published, after the
lapse of nine years since it was begun; whereas Hortensius
has in the mean while *thrown off* his fifty thousand verses in
one  *   *   *   *   The Smyrna shall reach as far as the
deep waves of Atrax;[3] distant ages shall peruse the Smyrna;
but the Annals of Volusius  *   *   *   and shall often furnish
loose wrappers for mackarel.   The brief works of my friend
*Cinna* are precious to me  *   *;  but let the mob delight in
the turgid Antimachus.[4]

> Phillis dit le diable de moi;
> De son amour et de sa foi
> C'est une preuve assez nouvelle:
> Ce qui me fait croire pourtant
> Qu' elle m' aime effectisement,
> C'est que je dis le diable d'elle,
> Et que je l'aime éperdument.

[1] *The flesh*, &c.] There is a double meaning in the original, and the
translator can give but half of it.   *Mentula*, synonymous with *penis*, is a
nickname applied by Catullus to Mamurra, of whom he says (cxv.) that
he is not a man, but a great thundering *mentula*.   Mahérault has happily rendered the meaning of the epigram in French, in which language
there is an equivalent for Mentula, that is to say, a man's name which is
also a popular synonyme for what characterizes the god Priapus.   "Jean
Chouard fornique; eh! sans doute, c'est bien Jean Chouard.   C'est
ainsi qu'on peut dire que c'est la marmite qui cueille les choux."

[2] *The Smyrna.*] The author of this lost poem was the unlucky Cinna,
who was torn "for his bad verses" by Antony's mob after the assassina-
tion of Cæsar.   The text of this poem is defective in three places.

[3] *Atrax.*] A town and river of Thessaly, introduced here merely to
express distance.   Volusius' Annals have been before celebrated.

[4] *Turgid Antimachus.*] A Greek poet who wrote an Epic poem on the
Theban war; and having composed twenty-four books without mentioning Thebes, unfortunately died, and never got to his subject in this
world.   His name is used here for any prolix and tiresome poet.

## XCVI. TO CALVUS ON QUINTILIA.

IF anything pleasing and acceptable can accrue to the mute grave from our sorrow, Calvus, and from the yearning with which we revive the memory of old loves, and weep over long-lost friendships;[1] surely Quintilia mourns less her premature death, than she is gladdened by your love.

## XCVII. ON ÆMILIUS.[2]  [*See Metrical Version.*]

## XCVIII. TO VETTIUS.[3]

To you, stinking Vettius, if to any one, may be applied what is said to babblers and fools. With that tongue of yours

[1] *The yearning*, &c.]  "The two lines of the original," says Lamb, "beginning Quo desideris, flow with a sweet melancholy that defies imitation. Shakspeare has a sonnet much resembling it in idea and expression:

> When to the sessions of sweet silent thought
> I summon up remembrance of things past,
> I sigh the lack of many a thing I sought,
> And with old woes new wail my time's dear waste.
> Then can I drown an eye (unused to flow)
> For precious friends hid in death's dateless night,
> And weep afresh love's long since cancell'd woe,
> And moan th' expense of many a ravish'd sight.

[2] *On Æmilius.*]  There is in the Greek Anthology a similar epigram by Nicarchus, which has been thus translated by Grotius:

> Non culo, Theodore, minus tibi fœtida bucca est
>   Noscere discrimen sit sapientis opus.
> Scribere debueras hîc podex est meus, hic os :
>   Nunc tu cum pedas atque loquare simul,
> Discere non valeo, quid venerit inde vel inde ;
>   Vipera namque infra sibilat atque supra.

[3] *To Vettius.*]  Justus Lipsius has written a dissertation with regard to Vettius, whom he supposes to be the person mentioned in Cicero's Letters to Atticus, and by Suetonius, as having been suborned by Cæsar to allow himself to be seized with a weapon on his person, and to confess that he had been employed by the chiefs of the senate to assassinate Pompey—a device contrived by Cæsar in order to set Pompey and the senate at variance. Vettius was strangled in prison, and Cicero charged Vatinius with the murder. He had previously served Cicero as a spy in the affair of Catiline's conspiracy, and had accused Cæsar of being implicated in it. He was a dirty fellow (see Poem liv.) and ready for any dirty work.

you may wipe cowkeepers' shoes and nastier things yet, if you
have occasion.   If you wish utterly to destroy us all, Vettius,
open your mouth ; you will effect your purpose to a certainty

### XCIX.  TO ———

I SNATCHED from you, while you played, honeyed one, a kiss
sweeter than sweet ambrosia ; but not with impunity ; for
I remember that I hung for more than an hour on the cross, all
the while endeavouring to excuse myself, but unable to abate
your cruelty in the least.  For as soon as the act was committed,
you rinsed your lips again and again, and rubbed them with
every joint of your fingers ; that no particle from my mouth
should remain on them, as though it were the filthy slaver of
a common trull.   Moreover you have never ceased to subject
my miserable being to the despites of love, and to torture me
in every way : so that now that kiss is changed for me from
ambrosia to be bitterer than bitter hellebore.   Since such is
the penalty you impose on unfortunate love, never more will
I steal kisses.

### C. ON CŒLIUS AND QUINCTIUS.[1]   [See Metrical Version.]

### CI.  FUNERAL CEREMONIES AT HIS BROTHER'S TOMB.

THROUGH many nations, over many seas I am come, brother, to these sad funeral rites, to bestow upon thee the last
gifts to the dead, and vainly to address thy mute ashes, since
fortune has bereft me of thyself, ah ! poor brother, cruelly
taken from me !  Now then accept those gifts, profusely
watered with a brother's tears, which the ancient usage, derived from our ancestors, prescribes for the sad rites of the
grave ; and now for ever hail, brother, and farewell !

[1] On Cœlius and Quinctius.]   Cœlius et Quinctius, la fleur de la jeu-
nesse de Vérone, brûlent tous deux, l' un pour Aufilénus, l' autre pour
Aufiléna.   Voilà ce qu' on peut appeler une charmante confraternité.
Pour qui seront mes vœux ?   Pour l' ami du frère, on pour l' amant de
la sœur ?   O Cœlius !  j' ai trop reconnu la sincerité de ton amitié, lors
que les feux d' amour qui m' embrasaient me rendaient son indulgence
nécessaire.   Puisse donc l' amour couronner tes ardeurs !  Puisses tu
te montrer digne des faveurs de l' amour !

## CII. TO CORNELIUS.

IF ever anything was committed by a confiding friend to the secret keeping of another whose fidelity was thoroughly known, you will find me too, Cornelius, religiously bound to secrecy ; so think that I am become Harpocrates.

## CIII. TO SILO.

EITHER be good enough to return me ten thousand sesterces, and then be as surly and savage as you please ; or if you like the money *too well*, cease, I beg, to be a pimp, and *at the same time* surly and savage.

## CIV. TO A CERTAIN PERSON, CONCERNING LESBIA.

Do you believe that I could revile my life, who is dearer to me than both my eyes ? I neither could do so, nor if I could, should I love her so desperately. But you invent all sorts of monstrous things with *your friend* the tavern-keeper.

## CV. ON MENTULA.

MENTULA strives to climb the Pimplæan mountain : the Muses pitch him down headlong with forks.

## CVI. ON A BOY AND A PUBLIC CRIER.[1] [*See Metrical Version.*]

## CVII. TO LESBIA.

IF ever any one who desires and longs for anything, but has no hope of it, obtains *the object of his wishes,* then is it peculiarly welcome to his soul : therefore it is welcome to me, and more precious than gold, that you, Lesbia, restore yourself to my longing breast. You restore yourself, and of your own accord give yourself back to me unexpectedly. O day of whiter mark ! Who can say what happier man lives than I, or what there is more to be desired in life than this ?

[1] *On a Boy,* &c.] Un crieur paraître en public à côté d' un jeune et beau garcon ! C' est donc pour afficher qu' il est à vendre et qu' il cherche chaland ?

### CVIII. ON COMINIUS.

IF your hoary age, Cominius, defiled by foul habits, were to perish by the sentence of the people, I make no doubt but that your tongue, so hostile to the good, would be cut out and thrown to a vulture; the crow would pick out your eyes and swallow them down its black throat; dogs would devour your intestines, and wolves the rest of your carcase.

### CIX. TO LESBIA.

MY life, my Lesbia, you profess that this love of ours shall be mutually fond and perpetual. Great gods! grant that she may be able to promise truly, and that she say this sincerely and from her soul; that we may be permitted to maintain throughout our lives this hallowed bond of affection.

### CX. TO AUFILENA.

GOOD friendly wenches are always praised, Aufilena; they take the price of what they mean to perform. But you are the reverse of good and friendly, because you have made me promises and not kept them; and forasmuch as you never give, and often take, you are criminal. It became you, Aufilena, either as a frank, honest girl to keep your word, or as a modest girl not to promise. But to clutch what is given you, and bilk the giver, exceeds the infamy of the greediest harlot, that prostitutes herself with her whole body.

### CXI. TO AUFILENA.

TO live content with one husband, Aufilena, is the first among the choicest glories of married women; but it is allowable to yield to any lover, rather than to be the mother of one's own cousins german.[1]

### CXII. ON NASO.[2] [See Metrical Version.]

---

[1] *Cousins german.*] *Fratres ex patruo.* Uncles' sons were called *fratres* or *fratres patrueles.* Thus in Ovid, Ajax claims as a brother's right the arms of his dead cousin Achilles: *Frater erat, fraterna peto. Metam.* 13.

[2] *On Naso.*] A tes yeux, Nason, tu es un grand personnage. Mais comment concilier cette haute opinion de toi même avec l' étrange humiliation à la quelle tu te soumets?

### CXIII. TO CINNA.

WHEN Pompey was consul the first time, there were two known adulterers in Rome ; when he was again made consul, the number was still two ; but several thousands have been superadded to each one of the pair. Adultery is prolific.

### CXIV. ON MENTULA.

YOUR Formian estate, Mentula, is not untruly reputed rich, for how many fine things does it comprise ! Feathered game of all kinds, fish, beasts, pasture and arable lands. All in vain ; for your expenditure exceeds the income. I grant then *your estate* is rich, but you are destitute ; let us praise the wealth of your estate, but you are a beggar.

### CXV. AGAINST MENTULA.

MENTULA has something like thirty acres of meadow and forty of arable land : the rest is *as wide as* the sea. Why can he not surpass Crœsus in wealth, who possesses so many fine things in one domain ; meadows, arable land, vast woods and forests, and marshes, stretching away to the world's end and to the ocean ? All these are great ; but greatest of all by far is himself, no man, but truly a great threatening MENTULA.

### CXVI. TO GELLIUS.

THOUGH often inquiring how I might send you the poems of Battiades to be carefully investigated, that so I might soften you towards me, and that you might not attempt to prick my head with your gnat's sting ; I now see that I took all this trouble in vain, Gellius, and that my prayers to that effect were of no avail.[1] So then I will ward off your weapons with my cloak alone, but you shall suffer condign punishment, pierced by mine.

[1] *Though often inquiring*, &c.] On this epigram Lamb remarks : " From the former poems on Gellius, it would not be expected to find Catullus at last trying to conciliate him by the compliment of asking for his criticisms. This poem however shows that it was so, and that the attempt had failed." We notice this remark as an instance of the false inferences often drawn from the order in which the poems of Catullus are arranged, as if that was chronological. For aught we know to the contrary, this epigram is just as likely to have been the first as the last addressed to Gellius.

# THE VIGIL OF VENUS.[1]

To-morrow let those love, who have never loved; let those who have loved, love to-morrow.

The new spring is come, the warbling spring, the season in which the world was born. In spring the loves impel to union; in spring the birds mate together, and the woods, quickened by prolific showers, shake loose their locks of verdure. To-morrow she who knits the bonds of love will visit the shady groves, and twine the myrtle sprays into green bowers: to-morrow, seated on her lofty throne, Dione publishes her edicts.

To-morrow, &c.

It was in spring that, from its foamy womb, impregnated by celestial blood, the mighty deep produced Dione,[2] floating

---

[1] *The Vigil of Venus.*] This pretty poem has been by turns ascribed to a great number of authors, among the rest, to Catullus; but all the learned are now agreed that it is certainly the work of an anonymous writer, and probably of the second century, if not of later date. The language of the piece is evidently that of an age of degenerate Latinity, and in its florid luxuriance, as well as in certain peculiarities of expression, it exhibits the closest affinity to that African school, of which Apuleius is the most remarkable example. When the poem was first rescued from oblivion by Pierre Pithou and Claude Saumaise, the text was corrupt in every line, sometimes in every word of a line; and although much labour has since been bestowed on its correction, its condition in many places is still far from satisfactory. The subject of the poem is the Festival of Venus, which was celebrated on the first three days of April, beginning at nightfall on the last day of March. For, says Macrobius, *Saturnal.* i. 21, "When the sun ascends above the lower parts of the earth, and passes the bounds of the vernal equinox, lengthening the days, then is Venus *glad*, the fair fields are green with corn, the meadows with grass, the trees with leaves. For this reason our forefathers dedicated the month of April to Venus."

[2] *Produced Dione.*] The "celestial blood" of which Dione or Venus was engendered, was that which fell from the god Cœlus, when he was mutilated by his son Saturn, the father of Jove.

over the waves, amidst the azure throngs *of Tritons and Nereids*, and the biped horses.[1]

To-morrow, &c.

She paints the year with flowers that purple it as with gems; she urges the buds, swelling with the breath of Zephyr, into the warm bridal bed of air;[2] she scatters the bright dewy moisture left by the humid air of night; how its tears glitter and tremble as if they would fall; but each pendent drop remains self-balanced by its little orb. That moisture which the stars shed in the calm night loosens the virgin buds in the morning from their humid robe, and displays the crimson blushes of the flower. She has commanded that to-morrow all the virgins shall wear roses. The rose tinged with the blood of Venus,[3] perfumed by the kisses of Love, and glowing with the lustre of gems, of flames, of the sun's orient splendours, to-morrow will not be ashamed to loose as a bride her last knot, and display the crimson concealed beneath her robe of fire.

To-morrow, &c.

The goddess hath bidden the Nymphs assemble in the myrtle grove. Her boy accompanies them; but Love cannot be trusted as a harmless associate in the festival if he carries his arrows. Go, Nymphs; Love has laid aside his arms, he is harmless. He is ordered to go unarmed and naked, that he may do no mischief with his bow, or his arrows, or his torch. Yet, Nymphs, beware, for Cupid is beautiful. Love is all armed even when he is naked.

To-morrow, &c.

[1] *Biped horses.*] The horses of Neptune were, like seals, furnished only with fore feet, and these were webbed.

[2] *The warm bridal bed of air.*] We read with Lipsius *in toros tepentis*.

[3] *The blood of Venus.*] The following epigram tells how this happened:

> Illa quidem studiosa suum defendere Adonim,
>   Gradivus stricto quem petit ense ferox,
> Affixit duris vestigia cœca rosetis,
>   Albaque divino picta cruore rosa est.

> While the enamour'd queen of joy
> Flies to protect her lovely boy,
>   On whom the jealous war-god rushes;
> She treads upon a thorned rose,
> And while the wound with crimson flows,
>   The snowy flowret feels her blood, and blushes! MOORE.

Virgin of Delos, Venus sends thee virgins modest as thyself. There is one thing we beg of thee. Leave this grove to her awhile unsullied by the slaughters of the chase. She would fain invite thee if thy maiden modesty would yield to her prayer. She would gladly see thee at her festival if the scene were not repugnant to thy virgin mind. For three nights thou wouldst see the festive choirs, crowned with flowers, wandering through the groves, or disporting in its myrtle bowers. Ceres and Bacchus[1] will be there, and the god of the poets; the whole wakeful night will resound with song. Dione shall reign in the woods; give place to her, Delia.

To-morrow, &c.

The goddess hath commanded a tribunal to be reared of flowers of Hybla. She will preside there; the Graces will be her assessors. Hybla, pour out every flower that the year produces; Hybla, cast forth a tapestry of flowers, vast as that which adorns the plain of Enna. Hither will come the Nymphs of the fields and the mountains, and those that dwell in forests, groves, and streams. The mother of the winged boy has bidden them all to attend, and has enjoined them not to trust Love though he be naked.

To-morrow let those love, who have never loved; let those who have loved, love to-morrow, and weave a verdant shade with new-opened flowers. The day returns to-morrow on

---

[1] *Ceres and Bacchus.*] Every one knows the aphorism in Terence's Eunuch, "Sine Cerere et Baccho friget Venus," "Without Ceres and Bacchus Venus freezes;" or, as Le Noble oddly paraphrases it,

> Point de beau feu sans la marmite ;
> Mille accidens m'ont convaincu
> Que l'Amour n'est qu'un froid-au-cu,
> Si Cérès et Bacchus ne marchent à sa suite.

After the line of the original beginning *Nec Ceres, nec Bacchus*, Lipsius places the four following, which he believes to be by the author of the Vigil :

> Hic Apollo, deinde Liber hic videtur ignifer ;
> Ambo flammis sunt creati, prosatique ex ignibus ;
> Ambo de comis calorem, vite, radio conserunt :
> Noctis hic rumpit tenebras, hic tenebras pectoris.

" Here are seen Apollo and fire-giving Bacchus ; both were born of flames and begotten of fire ; both shed warmth from what crowns their brows, the vine, and the rays : the one bursts the gloom of night, the other the gloom of the breast."

which the primal æther consummated its nuptials;[1] that he, the father of the dew, might beget the year with his innumerable clouds. The bridegroom-shower flowed into the bosom of his genial spouse, and spread throughout her vast body to nurture all its germs of life. The great procreant goddess herself breathing through all the veins and the mind, governs them with occult powers; suffuses her penetrating influence by every channel of generation through heaven and earth, and the sea's depths; and bids the world know the ways of reproduction.

To-morrow, &c.

She transported the Trojan Penates to the shores of Latium; she gave the Laurentian maid as a spouse to her son Æneas; she gave a chaste vestal to the arms of Mars; she effected the marriage of the Romans with the Sabines, whence sprang the Ramnes and the Quirites, and for the weal of Romulus's remote descendants—the Cæsars, father and nephew.

To-morrow, &c.

The goddess of Pleasure fructifies the fields; they feel the presence of Venus; Love himself, Dione's son, is said to have been born among them.[2] It was when they were in their season of parturition that his mother first folded him to her bosom, and she reared his infancy on the perfumed juice of flowers.

To-morrow, &c.

[1] *Consummated its nuptials.*] Of all marriages the most ancient is that of the air with the earth, and it is renewed every year in spring. This idea, and the very forms in which it is here expressed, are taken from Virgil, Georg. ii. 325. Stanley cites a kindred passage from Euripides, which he thus renders:

> How far Cythera's power extends
> No speech, no fancy comprehends.
> Me, thee, and all she doth sustain.
> The barren earth affects the rain:
> Heaven big with showers, this Queen of Loves
> To fall into Earth's bosom moves:
> These two, commixed with mutual heat,
> All things that serve mankind, beget.

[2] *Love himself,* &c.] Tibullus gives the same account of the birth of Love. Book ii. El. 1.

The bonds of marriage bind all creatures. See the bulls spread their broad flanks over the brooms; the bleating ewes flock to the shade with the rams; the lakes resound with the hoarse voice of the swan; and the goddess has forbidden the tuneful birds to be silent. The nightingale sings in the shade of the poplar, that you would suppose she was uttering in music the emotions of love, not that she was complaining to her sister of the barbarity of Tereus. She sings: we are silent! When shall my spring come? When shall I be like Chelidon, and silent never more? I have lost the Muse's favour by keeping silence, and Phœbus no longer regards me. So was Amyclæ undone by silence.[1]

To-morrow, &c.[2]

[1] *Amyclæ undone by silence.*] Amyclæ was a town of Italy between Cuieta and Terracina. Its people having been frequently terrified by false alarms of the approach of besiegers, passed a law forbidding that any one should make report of danger on any grounds whatever. The besiegers came at last, and the place was taken by surprise.

[2] It was with reference to this poem that Dousa (Van des Deos) planned a hoax upon his learned contemporaries, like that which Muretus practised on Scaliger. He gave out that one of his friends had seen another *Vigil* in a library in France, and had retained these four lines of it in his memory—

Nemo tentis mentulis det, nemo nervis otium.
Ecce passeres salaces, ecce rauci turtures,
Hac super virenti myrto nos amoris admonent.
Nemo tentis, etc.

The trick succeeded; the learned unanimously recognised the genuine air of antiquity in this fragment; and when they were undeceived, they consoled them as Scaliger had done, by virulently abusing the clever mystifier.

# ELEGIES OF TIBULLUS.

## BOOK I.

### ELEGY I.[1]

LET another heap up wealthy store of yellow gold,[2] and hold many thousand acres[3] of cultivated land; so shall he be troubled with incessant dread of the approaching enemy, and his sleep be scared by the trumpet's blast.  As for me, let my poverty consign me to a life without excitement, whilst the

---

[1] *Elegy I.*]  An invitation from Messala to accompany him to the wars, with a view to repairing the poet's fortunes, appears to have been the occasion of this Elegy, in which Tibullus declares his determination to abandon the pursuit of wealth and power, and to retire to the country, there to lead a life of calm and simple enjoyment with the girl of his heart.  We may confidently fix the date of the poem about the beginning of B. C. 31, the year in which Messala won the battle of Actium for Octavius.  According to Scaliger and Bronkhusius, whose arrangement of the text we generally follow, this Elegy consists of 92 lines: Heyne and the Vulgate give it 78.  Tibullus has suffered a twofold injury at the hands of ignorant copyists, who, not content with mutilating and changing his words, have in many instances broken the order of his lines, and shuffled them about in pairs and in scores in the most random manner.

[2] *Gold*, &c.]  The poet here specifies wealth in money and wealth in land, both however with reference to the " præmia militiæ."  The soldier acquired gold by direct plunder from his foes, and at this period it was the practice to make an assignment of land to each veteran when discharged from service.

[3] *Many acres.*]  *Jugera.*  The Roman *jugerum* contained two *actus*, the *actus* being a square whose side was one hundred and twenty Roman feet.  The Roman foot was equal to 11·64 English inches.  From these data it is easily calculated that the *jugerum* was not quite two-thirds of an English acre.

fire on my hearth is always bright;[1] nor let hope disappoint me, but always yield me heaps of fruit, and a vat full of rich must. Myself a rustic, I will plant my tender vines and large apples with ready hand in due season. Nor yet will I shame to handle the fork at times, or to hasten the slow oxen with the goad. I will not be loth to carry home the lamb in my bosom, or the kid deserted by its mother. Here it is my yearly custom to fumigate my shepherd, and to sprinkle the altar of the placid Pales[2] with milk ; for I revere *every divinity*, whether a forlorn bole in the fields, or an old stone in a forking of the roads bear flowery garlands ; and whatever apples the new year rears for me, their firstlings are placed before the goddess of the fields.

Yellow Ceres, let there be a crown woven from the corn-ears of our crop, to hang before the door of thy temple ; and let Priapus, ruddy[3] guardian, stand in my orchard to frighten the birds with his menacing sickle. And you too receive your offerings, my Lares,[4] guardians of a once rich, now poor,

[1] *The fire—always bright.*] *Assiduo luceat igne focus :* or, if we read *exiguo*, for which there is equal MS. authority, " whilst my hearth shines with a small fire." The chief objection to *assiduo* is the occurrence of the same word three lines before. On the other hand *exiguo* would per-haps imply sordid poverty, as Ramsay remarks. The " blazing hearth" was the emblem of domestic comfort among the Romans as well as among ourselves. There is a sepulchral inscription preserved in Fabretti, c. iv. 283, apparently engraved by a husband as a memorial to his wife and friend, which concludes with these words,—TVNC. MEVS. ASSIDVE. SEMPER. BENE LVXIT. AMICE. FOCVS.

[2] *Pales.*] The goddess of shepherds. See II. v.

[3] *Ruddy.*] *Ruber.* Painted with vermilion. See Virg. E. x. 26. Pliny has a curious passage (N. H. xxxiii. 7) on the custom practised by the early Romans of adorning the faces of their gods, and even the bodies of their triumphant generals, *triumphantumque corpora*, with red paint. Camillus, he says, followed that fashion when he triumphed.

[4] *Lares.*] The word *Lar* is of Tuscan origin, and in that language was a title of honour, equivalent, apparently, to chief or prince. Thus we read of Lar Porsenna, king of Clusium, Lar Tolumnius, king of the Veientes. The testimony of those among the Romans who were best quali-fied to form an opinion upon such a subject is so precise that we can enter-tain no doubt that, according to the popular belief, the deities denominated Lares were certain spirits of dead men, who were supposed to watch over and protect the living. They were very numerous, and were ranked in classes according to the departments over which they presided, the first grand division being into private and public Lares. The former were tutelary spirits who received the homage of all the individuals residing under the same roof. The spot peculiarly sacred to them was the *focus*

domain. In those days a slaughtered calf was the propitiatory sacrifice for vast herds; now a lamb is a sumptuous victim to come from my small estate. A lamb shall fall before you, and round it the rustic youth shall cry: "Io! give us a plenteous harvest and a good vintage." Favour us with your presence, gods; scorn not the gifts of a poor table, nor libations from clean pottery. Such vessels the husbandman of yore made for himself and formed them of ductile clay.

And you, ye thieves and wolves, spare my few heads of cattle, and take your prey from large herds. I do not regret the wealth of my fathers, and the plenty which their stored harvests afforded of yore. For me a small crop is enough; it is enough to rest under my own roof, if I may, and to stretch my limbs on my wonted couch. How delightful it is to hear the pitiless winds as we lie in bed, and fold the mistress we love to our bosom; or when the wintry south wind pours down its sleety waters, to sleep on securely, lulled by the plashing rain! Let this be my lot. Let him grow rich, as is but fair, who can bear the rage of the sea and the dismal rain. Now I, who am content to live on a little, cannot do this, nor can I be alway resigned to long wayfaring;[1] but my choice is

---

or hearth, situated in the principal apartment (*atrium*), and considered the central point of the mansion. Here stood the altar for domestic sacrifice, and near to this there was usually a niche, containing little images of these gods, and denominated *lararium ædicula*, which in the sumptuous palaces of later times was not unfrequently enlarged into a chapel with magnificent decorations. The public Lares were of several kinds: e. g. *Lares Rurales*, guardians of flocks, herds, and fruits of the earth: the poet addresses these in the lines before us: *Lares Compitales*, worshipped at the spot where two or more roads crossed; *Lares Præstites*, protectors of the city, &c. &c. The Lares bear a striking resemblance to the saints of modern Italy. Moreover the holy books of the Etruscans described certain sacred rites, by means of which the souls of men might be changed into gods, a process somewhat analogous to canonization. The *Penates* were the deities worshipped in the *penus*, or innermost part of the house. Penates is a generic term, and includes the *Lares* and certain other gods who were worshipped at the hearth, especially Vesta, who was herself the Goddess of the Hearth.—*Ramsay*.

[1] *Now I, who am content,* &c.]

> Jam modo non possum contentus vivere parvo,
> Nec semper longæ deditus esse viæ.

The first of these lines has greatly perplexed all the editors; for, separated from its true context, and punctuated as above, it seems to express the very reverse of its author's undoubted meaning. The difficulty arises

to shun the heat when the sultry dogstar is in the ascendant,
reposing under the shade of foliage, beside the running stream.[1]
Oh perish all the gold and gems[2] in the world rather than any
girl should weep for my wayfaring !

It is for thee, Messala, to war by land and sea, that thy
house may display the spoils of the foe.   Me the bonds of a
fair girl hold captive, and I sit like a gate-keeper[3] before her
obdurate door.   I care not to be praised, my Delia ; only let
me be with thee, and I am content to be called slow and

entirely from the dislocation we have spoken of in a preceding note ; for
in most editions the foregoing twenty-five lines, from "Adsitis divi,"
"Favour us with your presence, gods," down to "ferre potest pluvias,"
"can bear, &c. the dismal rain," are printed out of their proper place.
After their restoration to it, nothing more is wanted to make the sense
quite clear, except a comma after *possum*.

   [1] *Under the shade of foliage,* &c.]   In Dunlop's notice of Catullus (Hist.
Rom. Lit.) we find a passage which commends itself especially to the reader
of Tibullus : "The Romans, and particularly the Roman poets, as if the
rustic spirit of their Italian ancestry was not altogether banished by the
buildings of Rome, appear to have had a genuine and exquisite relish for
the delights of the country ; not as we are apt to enjoy it, for the sake of
exercise or field sports, but for its amenity and repose, and the mental
tranquillity which it diffused.   With them it seems to have been truly—

> 'The relish for the calm delight
>     Of verdant fields and fountains bright ;
> Trees that nod on sloping hills,
>     And caves that echo tinkling rills.'

Love of the country among the Romans thus became conjoined with the
idea of a life of pastoral tranquillity and retirement, a life of friendship,
liberty, and repose, free from labour and from care, and from all turbu-
lent passions.   Scenes of this kind delight and interest us supremely,
whether they be painted as what is hoped or what is enjoyed.   We feel
how natural it is for a mind with a certain disposition to relaxation and
indolence, when fatigued with the bustle of life, to long for serenity and
quiet, and for those sequestered scenes in which they can be most exquisitely enjoyed.   There is much less of this in the writings of the Greeks,
who were originally a seafaring and piratical, not, like the Italians, a pastoral, people.   It is thus that even in their highest stage of refinement
the manners and feelings of nations bear some affinity to their original
rudeness, though that rudeness itself has been imperceptibly converted
into a source of elegance and ornament."

   [2] *Gems.*]   *Smaragdi.*   It appears extremely probable that the ancients
gave this name not merely to the precious gem which we call an emerald,
but also to fluor spar, green vitrified lava, (green Iceland agate,) green
jasper, and green glass.

   [3] *I sit,* &c.]   A remark of Heyne's happily disposes of the apparent
incongruity between the two images of wearing chains and sitting as a
door-keeper.   Porters in Rome were chained to the doors.

spiritless. Let me be free to yoke my oxen , so I be but with thee, my Delia, and to feed my flock on the lone mountain ; and, if I may but hold thee in my fond arms, soft be my sleep on the rude ground ! What boots it to lie down on a Tyrian couch without favouring love, when the sleepless night must be passed in tears ? Vain then are down, and richly dyed tapestry, and even the gentle murmuring of water, to induce slumber. The man were iron who, when he could have thee, should stupidly prefer to follow arms and rapine. He may drive before him vanquished troops of Cilicians, and pitch his martial camp on the conquered soil ; caparisoned all over with gold and silver, he may bestride his swift steed in all the pomp of his glory. Let me behold thee when my last hour is come, thee let me hold with my dying hand.[1] Thou wilt weep, Delia, when I am laid on the funeral pile, and thou wilt give me kisses mingled with sad tears ; thy bosom is not cased in hard iron, nor hast thou flint in thy tender heart. No youth, no virgin will be able to return from that funeral with dry eyes. But pain not my Manes ; spare thy dishevelled hair, Delia, and spare thy tender cheeks.

Meanwhile, as long as the fates permit, let us indulge our mutual love. Soon death will come with its head wrapt in gloom ; soon sluggish age will creep upon us ; nor will it be seemly to love or to talk amorously with hoary heads. Now is our time to ply light Venus, whilst we may without blushing break doors, and commit riotous frolics. In this warfare I am a captain and a good soldier. Banners and trumpets, begone ! Bestow wounds and rich booty on heroes who long for them ; as for me, secure in the store I possess, I will despise both opulence and penury.

[1] *Let me behold thee.*] No other poet so often introduces the dismal images of death. Tibullus does not, like Anacreon or Catullus, present them for a moment, or on the back-ground of his pictures of joy, but exhibits them at full length and on the front of the canvass. When he thinks of death he thinks so profoundly, and so long contemplates its image, that the ideas it suggests must have occupied a large space in his soul. Even to the most joyous thoughts of Tibullus some mournful or plaintive sentiment is generally united, and his most gay and smiling figures wear chaplets of cypress on their brows. While deeming himself happy in comparison with the great Messala, because he will pass his life unknown in the arms of Delia, he thus concludes his address to this beloved mistress: "Let me behold thee," &c. *Dunlop.*

## ELEGY II.[1]

MORE wine! Lull my new pains with wine, till sleep hold
my weary eyes in subjection. Let no one wake me as I lie
with my brain drenched by Bacchus, and have a respite from
the wretchedness of love. *Let me drink;* for a stern watch
is set upon my girl, and the obdurate door is firmly barred
upon her for the night. Surly door, may the rain beat upon
thee, may the lightning smite thee by Jove's command.
Open, door, for me only, subdued by my plaintive entreaties,
and make no noise as thou turnest stealthily on thy hinges.
And if my crazy passion has given thee any bad words, pardon me; let them be upon my own head, I pray. Remember
all the thousand things I said to thee in suppliant tone, when
I hung thy frame with garlands of flowers.[2] And thou too,
Delia, be not afraid to elude thy guards. Be venturous;
Venus herself aids the bold. She favours *enterprise* whether
some youth assays new thresholds or a girl opens the barred
doors. She teaches how to creep stealthily out of the soft
bed; how to step with noiseless foot; how to converse in
speaking signs in presence of a husband, and to convey hidden
phrases of soft import in preconcerted tokens.

Nor does she teach this to all, but only to those who are
neither laggards, nor forbidden by fear to rise in the dark night.
As for me, when I wander anxiously over the whole city in
darkness, Venus makes me fearless in the darkness, nor does
she let any one meet me to wound my body with steel, or to

---

[1] *Elegy II.*] Delia having married during her lover's absence from
Rome, he tries to drown his grief in wine. Then he alternately abuses
and coaxes her obdurate door, and begs her to summon courage enough
to admit him, assuring her that he has procured magic means to hinder
all discovery.

[2] *Garlands.*] We have already seen that this kind of gallantry was
much practised by the Romans: thus Lucretius:

> At lacrimans exclusus amator limina sæpe
> Floribus, et sertis operit, postesque superbos
> Ungit amaracyno.

> Meantime excluded, and exposed to cold,
> The whining lover stands before the gates,
> And there with humble adoration waits;
> Crowning with flowers the threshold and the **floor,**
> And printing kisses on the obdurate door. DRYDEN.

make booty of my garments.[1]  Whoever is possessed by love,
may go where he will, safe and sacred; it is not for him to
fear any lurking dangers.  I am not hurt by the numbing
cold of the winter nights ; nor when the rain falls in torrents ;
all this does not harm me, if only Delia unclose the door,
and mutely summon me to the beck of her finger.  Man or
woman who come in my way, hold off with lights !  Venus
chooses that her thefts should be concealed.  Alarm me not
with the sound of your feet ; ask not my name, nor bring the
light of a blazing torch near me.  If any indiscreet person see
me, let him forget who I am, and swear by all the gods he
does not know me.  For should any one chatter, he shall be
made to feel that Venus is born of blood and of the swiftly-
roused sea.

Your husband however will not believe this *impertinent
meddler,* as a truth-telling sorceress hath assured me by means
of her magic art.  I have seen her draw down the stars from
heaven; she turns the course of the swift lightning by her
incantations ; she cleaves the earth, brings out the Manes from
the sepulchres, and calls down the bones from the still
smouldering pile.  Now she makes the infernal hosts swarm
round her with her magic screamings, and now she bids them
be gone, sprinkling them with milk.  When she pleases, she
sweeps away the clouds from the sombre sky ; when she
pleases, she calls down the snow in summer by a word from
her mouth.  She is said to possess alone all the evil herbs
known to Medea, alone to have brought the fierce dogs of He-
cate under subjection.  This witch has composed for me chants
by which you may deceive *all eyes.*  Chant thrice, spit thrice[2]
after reciting the charm ; your husband will be unable to be-

---

[1] *To wound my body,* &c.]  During the civil wars, and for a long time
after them, Rome was full of thieves and cut-throats.

[2] *Spit thrice.*]  The poor Irishwoman who spits for luck on the first
coin she takes in the day, has classical authority for the practice.  The
reader who wishes to be informed of the many uses made of spittle in
medicine, in magic, in expiations, in averting witchcraft, and in concili-
ating love, may consult Pliny the Elder, and those commentators whom
Brockhusius has quoted.  The Romans had great faith in it as a preservative against fascination.  Accordingly on the day when an infant
was named (the eighth after birth for girls, the ninth for boys) the grandmother or aunt, walking round it in a ring, rubbed, with her middle finger,
the child's forehead with spittle, which was hence called *lustralis saliva.*
The occult potency of odd numbers is well known.

lieve any one's tale about us, or even himself though he see us with his own eyes on the soft bed. Abstain however from others ; for he will discern all else ; of me alone he will know nothing.

What shall I think of it ? This same witch actually told me that she could dissolve my love by incantations or herbs. She fumigated me with torches, and a black victim was sacrificed in the dead of night to the magic gods. I prayed not that my love should wholly depart, but that it should be reciprocated ; nor can I wish to be able to live without you.[1]

## ELEGY III.[2]

You will traverse the Ægean waves without me, Messala! may the gods grant that you and your followers remember me. Phæacia[3] detains me, a sick man in her unknown land : keep off thy hands, violent death ; keep them off, black death, I implore. My mother is not here to gather my burned bones to her sad bosom ; nor my sister to pour Assyrian odours on my ashes, and weep with dishevelled hair before my sepulchre. There is no Delia here, who, when she was about to let me go from the city, is said to have first consulted all the gods. Thrice she drew the boy's sacred lots ;[4] the boy brought

---

[1] *To live without you.*] Though this is evidently the conclusion of the Elegy, yet some editors have strangely tacked to it " Ferreus ille fuit," and the thirteen following lines, which belong to the first Elegy. And not content with this, they have forced " Num Veneris magnæ," and the seven succeeding verses, from their natural place in the fifth Elegy of this book, and have added them to the other transposition.

[2] *Elegy III.*] Soon after his successful campaign in Aquitania, Messala was despatched by Augustus on a mission to the East. Tibullus formed one of his retinue, but was taken ill and compelled to remain behind at Corcyra, where this Elegy was composed, B. C. 29.

[3] *Phæacia.*] The island of Corcyra, now Corfu.

[4] *The lots.*] *Sortes.* These were of various kinds. The first words spoken by the virgin in the temple of Juno were the *sortes* in cases of marriage ; as the first spoken by a boy in the high-way, gave the omen commonly depended upon before a journey was undertaken. An example will better explain this obscure piece of superstition. A lady who was betrothed went with a young companion to the temple of the goddess of marriage to watch the first words spoken by a woman. Anxiously attentive, she seated herself while her companion stood. Two hours having passed without a word being uttered, or anybody entering the temple, the younger at last said, " My dear, I am tired ; will you permit me to

her news of sure omens from the streets. Everything prog-
nosticated my return, yet nothing could hinder her from weeping and turning to look after me as I went. I myself, to
console her, when I had already given orders for my departure,
still anxiously sought for pretexts to delay; and alleged
either an unpromising appearance of the birds, or dire omens,
or that Saturn's unlucky day[1] detained me. Oh how often
at the outset of my journey did I say that a stumble at the
threshold[2] had given me sinister warning! Let no one dare
to set out on a journey in spite of love, or *if he does*, let him
know that his course is begun under the prohibition of the
god.

What does your Isis for me now, Delia? What avail me
those brazen sistra of hers so often shaken by your hand?[3]
Or what am I the better for remembering that, while you
were pursuing her rites, you bathed purely and lay alone in

sit in your chair a little?" These were the first words. The sequel ac-
corded with them. The betrothed lady died soon after, and the other was
married to the bridegroom in her stead. Another way of taking the lots
was by means of slips of parchment or pieces of wood, upon which certain
words or sentences were inscribed. They were shuffled together in a box
or urn; one was drawn or shaken out at random, and a conclusion drawn
from the import of its inscription. Fortune-tellers drove a brisk trade in
Rome, and frequented the Forum, the Circus Maximus, and other places
of public resort. In the case before us, Delia sent a boy to a place where
three ways met, that he might watch for an omen; or if we read *trinis*
instead of *triviis*, she employed him to draw the lots from the urn three
times—the mystical number.

[1] *Saturn's unlucky day.*] It was doubtless from observing the conduct
of the Jews on their sabbath, which corresponded with Saturn's day,
(Saturday,) that the superstitious Romans thought that an unlucky day
to begin a journey. Thus Ovid, A. A. i. 415,

Quaque dies redeunt rebus minus apta gerendis
Culta Palæstino septima sacra Syro.

"The passage before us," says Ramsay, "is remarkable as being the first
in which we find mention of a day of the week named after a planet,
and it is by no means certain that the planetary names for the other six
were at this time known to the Romans."

[2] *Stumble at the threshold.*] The worst of all omens to a person setting out upon a journey, or about to begin any important undertaking.

[3] *Sistrum.*] A bronze instrument which the worshippers of Isis held
in their hands, and shook whilst performing their devotions. It re-
sembled the frame of a racket or battledore in miniature, with trans-
verse rods loosely fitted in, by means of which a jingling sound was
produced.

a pure bed. Now, now, goddess, succour me; for that man may be healed by thee, is proved by many a picture in thy temples. Let my Delia, dressed in linen,[1] sit before thy sacred doors, performing vigils vowed for me; and twice a day, with hair unbound, conspicuous among the Pharian crowd, let her recite thy due praises; but be it my lot to celebrate my native Penates, and to offer monthly incense to my ancient Lar.

How happily men lived when Saturn reigned, before the earth was laid open by long roads! Not yet had the pine contemned the azure waves, and shaken out its bellying sails to the winds, nor had the roving mariner, seeking gain in unknown lands, loaded his ship with foreign merchandise. In those days the strong bull did not bear the yoke; the horse did not champ the bit in his subject mouth; no house had doors; there was no stone fixed on the fields, to mark the precise boundaries of each man's crop; the very oaks yielded honey, and the sheep spontaneously offered their milky udders, and gave no trouble to those who wanted them. There were no armies, no enmity, no wars; nor had the cruel smith forged the sword with ruthless art.

Now under the rule of Jove, slaughter and swords are incessant; now sea and land offer a thousand ways of sudden death. Spare me, Father; I have not a conscience frightened by any perjuries, or impious words uttered against the holy gods. But if I have now completed my destined years, let a stone stand over my bones, with this inscription:—Here lies Tibullus, consumed by pitiless death, while following Messala by land and sea.

But because I am always obsequious to tender Love, Venus herself will conduct me to the Elysian fields. There dance and song are perpetual, and birds flitting in all directions warble sweetly with their small throats. The uncultivated vegetation bears cinnamon, and the benignant ground blooms all over with fragrant roses. Groups of youth sport with

---

[1] *Linen.*] The priests of Egypt were compelled to pay the most scrupulous regard to personal cleanliness. To insure this, they shaved their heads, and wore no garments but such as were made of linen, and perhaps cotton. It appears from this passage that the worshippers of Isis, when they appeared at his shrine, wore habits of this description, which would be very remarkable at Rome, where the clothing of all ranks was chiefly woollen. The fullest account of the worship of Isis is given by Apuleius in the eleventh book of his Metamorphoses

tender damsels, and love incessantly mingles them in pleasing
strife.   There is the place of every one whom rapacious death
interrupts in the midst of his love, and he bears myrtle wreaths
on his distinguished head.

But the abode of guilt lies buried in deep night, and black
floods roar around it.   There rages Tisiphone with fierce
tangled snakes for hair, and the crowd of the wicked flies
hither and thither *before her.*   Black Cerberus hisses with
his serpents[1] at the entrance, and watches before the brazen
gates.   There the guilty limbs of Ixion, who dared to attempt
Juno, are whirled round on the rapid wheel, and Tityos, extended over nine acres of ground, feeds the ever-ravening
birds with his dark entrails.   Tantalus is there, with a lake
around him ; but the water baffles his hot thirst just as he is
about to drink : and the children of Danaus, who committed
sacrilege against Venus, carry the water of Lethe into pierced
casks.   There let him be, whosoever troubled my love, and
wished for me the tedious anxieties of warfare.

But, Delia, remain faithful, I implore, and let an old woman
always sit by your side, a sedulous guardian of your sacred
modesty.   Let her tell you stories, and fill long spindles with
the threads she draws from the distaff by lamp-light ; and let
the girl near her, intent on her busy task, yield gradually to
sleep and leave off her work.   Then I will come suddenly ;
no one shall announce me, but I shall seem to you as if I had
dropped from the sky.   Then run to me, Delia, just as you
are, with bare feet and your long hair in disorder.   This is my
prayer ; may fair Aurora bring us that bright day with her
rosy horses.

## ELEGY IV.[2]

So may you always have a shady canopy, Priapus, to defend your head from sun and snow; *but tell me* by what

---

[1] *Cerberus hisses*, &c.]   The three-headed dog Cerberus had a crest
and mane of hissing serpents, and the tail of a dragon.

[2] *Elegy IV.*]   Unsuccessful in an amour, Tibullus consults Priapus,
who delivers so animated a lecture on the art of conducting such matters,
that his pupil at once proclaims himself advanced to the ranks of a professor ; but ends by confessing that he has still much to learn.   Bach
thinks it probable the date of the poem is not earlier than B. c. 24.   The
translator has been compelled to be unfaithful to the original with regard

cunning art of yours do you captivate the fair? Truly your
beard is not glossy, your hair is not neat; naked you endure
the winter's frost, and naked you endure the parching season
of the dog-star.

So said I, and thus answered the rustic son of Bacchus
armed with his curved sickle. "Be not disheartened, if haply
a girl refuse you at first; by degrees she will give her neck to
the yoke. Time has taught lions to obey man; with time soft
water cuts its way through stone. A year ripens the grapes
on the sunny hills; a year brings round the changes of the
constellations in sure order. Be not afraid to swear; the
oaths broken in the sight of Venus the winds scatter over
land and sea. For this, great thanks to Jove: the great father
himself has forbidden to have any force, whatever oaths
thoughtless love may have eagerly sworn; and Diana allows
you to pledge yourself with impunity by her arrows, and
Minerva by her hair. But if you are not prompt you will
miss all. Time passes away! The day does not stand still,
or return. How soon the earth loses its brilliant hues! How
soon the tall poplar its comely tresses! How helpless lies,
when the fates of old age are come upon him, the courser that
was first to bound forth from the Elæan starting-place. I have
seen one who was but now a youth, lamenting, when graver
years pressed upon him, the days that had passed foolishly
away. Cruel gods! the serpent casts his skin and comes forth
anew every year: but the Fates have granted no delay to
beauty. Eternal youth belongs to Phœbus and Bacchus alone,
for unshorn locks adorn both gods.

"Whatever your fair one has a mind to do, let her have
her own way. Love achieves many victories by compliance.
Do not refuse to accompany her, though a long journey
is intended, and the fiery dog-star parches the fields; though
the watery bow, marking the sky with its parti-coloured
dyes, portend the coming rain. Or if she desires to roam
over the azure waves, ply the oar yourself and speed the light
bark over the waters. Grudge not to undergo hard labour,
and to chafe your hands unused to such work. And if she
wishes to enclose deep valleys with the hunter's toils, let not

to gender. This change has occasioned some awkwardness in a few
places; but without it the poem, which is one of the most elegant of the
author's works, could not have been presented in English.

your shoulders refuse to carry the nets, if so you may please her. If she will practise arms, you will try to fence with a light hand, and often expose your unguarded side that she may make a hit. Then she will be indulgent; then you will be allowed to snatch sweet kisses; she will struggle, but give them after all. First she will give what you steal; afterwards she will offer them for you to take, and at last she will freely clasp your neck.

"Alas, how vilely these times treat unfortunate art. The tender girl is now grown used to desire presents. Now may the stone press wretchedly on thy bones, whoever thou art, that first taught Venus to sell her favours. O love the Muses, young beauties, and love learned poets; let not golden gifts out-do the Muses. Through song is the hair of Nisus [1] purple; if song were not, ivory would not have shone from the shoulder of Pelops. Whom the Muses extol, shall live whilst the earth has trees, the sky has stars, the river rolls waters. But whoso hears not the Muses, whoso [buys or] sells love, be it theirs to follow the chariot of Idan Ops, let them fill three hundred cities with their wanderings, and mutilate their vile bodies in Phrygian fashion. Venus desires that there be room for the winning ways of courtship; she favours plaintive supplications and piteous tears."

These precepts the god delivered to me that I might sing them to Titia, but Titia's spouse bids her not mind them. "O beware of trusting the amorous crowd of youths," he says, "for they never want a plausible pretext for love. This one finds favour because he reins the steed with address; that one, because he cleaves the calm waters with snowy breast; another captivates, because he is strong and daring; and a fourth, because maiden modesty sits upon his soft cheeks."

Let her obey her monitor; but as for you, whom the wily boy maltreats, extol me as your guide and master. To each belongs her own glory; to me let all lovers who are scorned come for consultation: my door is open to them all. The time will come when a studious crowd of youths will attend the aged Tibullus as he expounds the doctrines of Venus.

Alas, alas, with what slow tortures Titia racks me. Vain

---

[1] *The hair of Nisus.*] Nisus, king of Megara, had among his white locks a single purple one, on the preservation of which his life depended. Ovid. Met. viii. 8.

are all my arts, vain all my wiles.    Spare me, **Titia,** I implore,
let me not become the laughing-stock of my acolytes, when
they see how idle is the science I profess.

## ELEGY V.[1]

I was cross, and said that I could bear a rupture well, but
now my brave boasting is far away; for I am whirled like the
top[2] which the nimble boy with practised skill lashes along
the smooth ground.    Burn, torture me for my insolence; cure
me of all desire to talk big in future; put down my blustering.    Yet spare me, I implore you, by our confederate bed-
thefts, by Venus, and by your own comely head.

I am he who is declared to have snatched you from the
grasp of death by my vows when you lay overcome by griev-
ous illness.    I myself performed fumigations round you with
pure sulphur, whilst the old woman was busied with magic
incantations.    I took care that you should not be troubled
with painful dreams, which I caused to be charmed away by
a thrice-consecrated cake.[3]    Veiled in linen, with robes unbound, I paid nine vows to Trivia in the silent night.    I did
all; another now enjoys your love, and is happy in the fruits
of my prayers; whilst, fool that I was, I pictured to myself
the happy life that should be mine, if you were saved; but the
gods opposed my hopes.

I will cultivate my fields; my **Delia** will be the keeper of
my garners, whilst the harvest is threshed under the hot sun;
or she will keep my grapes in full baskets, and my rich must
pressed with nimble feet.    She will grow used to number

---

[1] *Elegy V.*] Tibullus recants the boast he had made, that he could easily
reconcile himself to the loss of Delia, and pleads to her the care he had
bestowed when she was ill, and the hopes he had built on her recovery.
Bach concludes from internal evidence that the Elegy was written not
earlier than B. C. 29.

[2] *Like the top.*] No poet perhaps ever used fewer similes than Tibullus.
The principal object always employed him too much to think of resem-
blances.    Virgil has applied the simile of the top to Amata in the seventh
book of the Æneid; as Valerius Flaccus does to Medea in the eighth
book of his Argonautus.    Things of no dignity in themselves become important in the hands of a real poet.—*Grainger.*

[3] *Thrice-consecrated cake.*]    This cake, which was made three times a
year by the Vestal virgins, was a composition of flour and two kinds of
salt.

my flock; the prattling boy born in my house will grow used to play on the lap of my mistress; she will know how to offer to the god of the husbandman grapes for the vines, ears of corn for the crops, meat-offerings for the flock. Let her rule all my people; let her have charge of everything, and let it be a pleasure to me to be as nothing in my house and all that belongs to it. Hither will come my Messala; Delia will set before him sweet apples from choice trees; and reverencing so great a man, she will sedulously entertain him, obey his wishes, and herself serve the banquet and wait upon him. These things I pictured to myself, but now Eurus and Notus have swept the fond visions to the odorous shores of Armenia.

Have I outraged the divinity of great Venus by any words of mine, and do I now suffer the penalty due to my impious tongue? Am I charged with having assailed the abodes of the gods, and torn the garlands from their sacred shrines? Let me not hesitate, if I have incurred this guilt, to prostrate myself in their temples and kiss their sanctified thresholds; I will not refuse to crawl suppliantly on my knees, and beat my wretched head against the holy doors.[1] But you who ex-ultingly deride my woe, beware; your own turn will come by and by; one god will not always be wroth alone. I have seen an old man, because he had mocked the unfortunate loves of his juniors, himself afterwards forced to bend his neck to the bonds of Venus; and to shape his quavering voice to the utterance of soft things, and to try to arrange his white hairs with his hands. Nor was he ashamed to stand before the dear girl's doors, and to stop her servant in the middle of the forum. Boys and youths encompassed him in dense crowds, and each one spat upon his own soft bosom.[2]

But spare me, Venus: my mind has always been devoted to thy service; why dost thou rancorously consume thy own harvests?

[1] *Beat my head.*] According to Broekhusius, the beating of the head against the sacred threshold was an expiatory ceremony brought from Egypt along with the goddess Isis. This is the only passage of antiquity where this extraordinary rite is mentioned; whence that commentator concludes that it neither prevailed long, nor was generally received at Rome.

[2] *Spat upon his own soft bosom.*] As a preservative against the bad omen of such preposterous love.

## ELEGY VI.[1]

OFTEN have I tried to dispel my cares with wine; but grief turned all my wine to tears. I have often clasped another fair one in my arms; but just as I was at the point of enjoyment, Venus reminded me of my mistress and deserted me. Then the woman quitted me, saying I was bewitched,[2] and, oh shame! she goes about telling that she knows abominable things about me.

No witch does this by magic words; my girl it is that bewitches me with her face, her gentle arms, and her yellow hair; lovely as Thetis,[3] the daughter of Nereus, when she was wafted of yore by a bridled fish to Æmonian Peleus. This is what wrought my hurt. That she has a rich lover, is the work of a cunning bawd who interferes for my destruction. May she eat bloody food, and drink with gory mouth cups all bitter with gall. May souls complaining of their fate always hover round her, and the screech-owl hoot wildly on her roof. Goaded to madness by hunger, may she pluck grass from the sepulchres, and the bones left by ravening wolves. May she run naked and howling through the towns, and snarling packs of dogs hunt her from the cross-ways. It will come to pass; a god forebodes it; there is a divinity in a lover, and Venus unjustly forsaken takes dire vengeance.

But you, my girl, reject forthwith the counsels of this greedy witch. Is all love overcome by gifts? The poor lover

---

[1] *Elegy VI.*] Tibullus relates the failure of sundry remedies he has tried for his unfortunate passion; curses the go-between who has introduced a wealthier lover to Delia; and demonstrates the error committed by ladies who prefer a rich lover to a poor one—a general doctrine which he applies to his own advantage. Some editors have very injudiciously tacked this Elegy to the preceding one, with which it coincides in date.

[2] *Bewitched.*] *Devotum.* Devovere, says Broekhusius, properly signifies, frigore ferire eam partem qua viri sumus, ut quantumvis cupiamus, tamen minime possumus. The French call it *nouer l'aiguillette;* and the doctors of the canon law say that such persons are frigidi and malificiati.

[3] *Lovely as Thetis.*] The heathen poets, in comparing a person to any of their deities, had a sure method of giving the reader a picture of that person, as the statues of their gods were known to every one and their features ascertained; and this, says the ingenious author of the Polymetis, is one reason why similes of this kind are so frequent in ancient authors.

will be ever at your command; the poor lover will be the first to fly to you, and will cling inseparably to your side. The poor lover will be your faithful escort through the crowd, will fend off the pressure with his hands, and make way for you. The poor lover will furtively conduct you to the secret *carousals of* his friends, and will himself untie your shoes and take them off your snow-white feet. Alas, I sing in vain; the door will not open for words alone, but must be knocked at by a well-filled hand.

But you who now have the advantage, beware; light-wheeled fortune spins rapidly round.

### ELEGY VII.

LOVE, thou offerest me always a smiling countenance in order to allure me; but afterwards I find thee, to my sorrow, gloomy and severe. What quarrel hast thou with me, cruel boy? Is it a great glory for a god to have laid snares for a man? Toils are now spread for me; now crafty Delia furtively cherishes I know not whom [2] in the silent night. She indeed denies this over and over again; but it is hard to believe her, for she makes just as pertinacious denials about me to her husband. Unfortunate that I am, I taught her myself how to elude her guardians; alas, alas! I am now the victim of my own art. She has now learned how to invent pretences for lying alone, and how to make the doors turn on noiseless hinges. And then I gave her juices and herbs, for

[1] *Elegy VII.*] This must have been written before the preceding Elegy, (and probably in A. U. C. 724,) for here he only suspects what there he speaks of as a fact already beyond all doubt. The unfortunate lover complains that he is caught in his own trap, for he has taught Delia how to deceive. Then he appeals to her husband, makes a clean breast of it, and invites the poor man to make common cause with him. This is rather a bold step, it must be owned; it is asking too much, as Ovid says, Trist. ii. 457:

> Denique ab incauto nimium petit ille marito
> Se quoque uti servet, peccet ut illa minus.

Grainger and Dunlop are shocked at the impropriety of this proceeding, but without much reason. They forget the class to which Delia belonged, and the probability that her intimacy with Tibullus was no news to her husband. The address to that person is an exquisite piece of persiflage and nothing more.

[2] *I know not whom.*] *Nescio quem:* this is not to be understood literally, but as an expression of contempt.

removing the livid marks which mutual Venus makes by the impress of the teeth.

But you, incautious husband of the tricksome girl, keep me too, that she may be hindered from erring at all. Take care that she is not profuse in her compliments to young men, nor let her recline with her robe loose so as to expose her bosom; let her not betray you with secret looks and nods, nor dip her finger in liquid, and draw marks on the table. If she goes out very often, be on your guard; or if she says she intends to visit the rites of the Bona Dea to which males are not admitted. But if you will intrust her to me, I will follow her alone to the altar; and then far it be from me to doubt the vigilance of my own eyes. I remember that I often touched her hand under pretence of examining her jewels or her seal. Often I plied you with strong wine till you fell asleep, while I secured my victory by drinking sober draughts mingled with water. I did not wrong you intentionally; forgive me, as I confess my fault; Love commanded it should be so, and who can fight against the gods? I am the very man, nor will I now be ashamed to tell the truth, at whom your dog used to bark all night long. It is not for nothing that some one just now is always stopping before your threshold; that he looks about, retreats, pretends to pass the house, and presently comes back alone, and hawks and hems close by the door. Some furtive amour is preparing for you, I know not what; bestir yourself, I beg, while you may; as yet your boat swims in smooth water. What use is it to have a charming wife, if you cannot keep what you have got? It is in vain you have locks to your doors. While she embraces you, she sighs for other absent loves, and suddenly feigns a head-ache. But intrust her to my keeping; I do not refuse to endure stripes, I do not object to have my feet put in fetters, *if I let her escape*. Then keep off, all you who dress your hair with art, whose tunics hang loose upon your breasts. Any man that comes this way, to hinder all chance of his doing mischief, let him keep off, and not stop until he is far away in another street.

Thus the god himself commands it to be done; thus the great priestess has conveyed to me the injunctions of the divine oracle. Once she is agitated and distraught by the impulse of Bellona, she fears neither scorching flame, nor lashes; she lacerates her own arms with an axe, and unmurmuringly sprinkles the goddess with her blood; with a spike thrust through her side, and her bosom torn, she stands, and chants the events which the great goddess foretells. "Forbear from assailing a girl whom Love guards, lest you be afterwards taught a terrible lesson. Touch her, and your wealth shall pass away, like the blood from my wounds, like these ashes scattered by the winds." And on you, my Delia, she denounced I know not what penalties: but if you receive me, I will pray her to be light with you. I do not spare you for your own sake; but your mother moves me, and the excellent old woman subdues my resentment. She brings you to me in the dark, and mutely and in great fear joins our hands together. She waits for me by night, fixed to the door, and recognises the sound of my footstep a long way off. Long may you live for me, sweet old woman: fain would I compound my own years with yours, were it possible. I will always love you, and your daughter for your sake; whatever she does, she is, after all, your blood. Teach her only to be chaste, though no fillet binds her hair, no long robe impedes her feet.[1] And on me, too, let hard laws be imposed, nor let it be possible for me to praise any beauty, unless she is before my eyes. And if I am adjudged to have offended in any way, and am pulled by the hair undeservedly, and am dragged along the sloping street;[2] let me not think of striking of you; but if such madness seizes me, I should wish myself without hands. And be not chaste through fear alone, but let mutual love keep you faithful in mind to me when I am absent. The girl who was faithful to no lover, after age has overcome her, sinks into want, and draws out the twisted threads with her

---

[1] *Though no fillet*, &c.] The *vitta* and the *stola* were worn only by matrons and maidens of free descent (ingenuæ). Delia was therefore *libertinæ conditionis*, a foreigner, or the daughter or grand-daughter of one who had been a slave. The condition of such women in Rome was very like that of the free quadroon girls of New Orleans, who are all destined to become the mistresses of white men, never their wives. This is confirmed by Ovid, Ep. ex Pont. iii. 3 :

Scio tamen, ut liquido juratus dicere possis
Non me legitimos solicitasse toros.
Scripsimus hæc istis, quarum nec vitta pudicos
Contingit crines, nec stola longa pedes.

[2] *The sloping street.*] *Pronas vias*: most of the streets in Rome ran up and down hill.

tremulous hand, and interweaves the woof with the firm warp,
and picks off the rough fibres drawn from the snowy fleece.
The young men gather round her rejoicing to see her so employed, and remark that she deserves to bear all this in her
old age. Venus looks down disdainfully on her tears from
the summit of Olympus, and shows by such an example how
severe she is to the faithless.

May these curses befall others; may we, Delia, be examples
of love when we are both white-haired.

## ELEGY VIII.[1]

THE Fates, who weave the threads which no god can break,
sang of this day; they foretold that He would be, who should
overthrow the tribes of Aquitania,[2] and whom vanquished Atur
should tremble to see approaching in martial might. The
Roman youth has seen new triumphs, and kings with their
arms bound. And thou, Messala, crowned with laurel, wast
borne in an ivory chariot drawn by white horses. Thy honours were not won without me; Tarbella[3] of the Pyrenees is
witness, and the shores of the Santonic Sea;[4] witness the Arar
and the rapid Rhone, and the great Garonne, the yellow-haired
Carnuto, and the Loire's blue water. And thee, Cydnus, I
will sing, which flowest softly with noiseless water, and vast

[1] *Elegy VIII.*] On his return from the East, B. c. 27, Messala enjoyed
the honour of a magnificent triumph for his victories over the Aquitani.
His birthday, which occurred soon after in the same year, is celebrated
in this Elegy. The poet enumerates Messala's exploits in Gaul, Cilicia,
Syria, Egypt, dwelling especially on the wonders and fertility of the latter,
and singing the praises of Osiris the inventor of agriculture. He then
calls upon the genius of Messala to come and receive the honours which
were peculiarly his own upon such an occasion, and concludes with
prayers for his patron and his descendants.

[2] *Aquitania.*] The southern part of Gaul, extending from the Garumna,
the modern Garonne, to the Pyrenees. The river Atax is now the Ande.

[3] *Tarbella.*] The Tarbelli, one of the tribes of Aquitaine, have left their
name to the city of Tarbes. They occupied the valley of the Atur
(Adour).

[4] *Santonic Sea,* &c.] The Santones were another tribe of Aquitania,
who dwelt north of the Garumna (Garonne) in the province lately called
Saintonge. The Arar is the modern Saone; the "Rhodanus celer" is
"the arrowy Rhone:" the Liger is the Loire; the principal town of the
Carnuti was Autricum (Chartres).

frozen Taurus lifting its head among the clouds, the mountain
of the bearded Cilicians.

Why need I tell how the sacred white dove[1] flutters untouched about the numerous cities of Syrian Palestine? Or
how Tyre, which first learned how to give the bark to the
gale, looks out over the vast sea from its towers. And how
the fertile Nile abounds in summer floods when the dog-star
splits the parched ground? Father Nile, wherefore or in
what lands can I say that thou hast hidden thy head? Through
thee thy land has no need of rain, nor does the parched grass
supplicate pluvious Jove. The barbarian youth, taught to
bewail the bull of Memphis, sings thee, and admires its own
Osiris.[2] Osiris with skilful hand first fashioned the plough,
and fretted the soft soil with iron. He first committed seed
to the inexperienced earth, and gathered fruit from unknown
trees. He taught the practice of attaching the tender vine
to the stake, and lopping the green foliage with the pruning-
hook. To him first the ripe grape, pressed by the feet of
clowns,[3] yielded sweet juice. That liquor taught men to mo-
dulate their voices in song, and move their unpractised limbs to
certain measures. Bacchus gave the over-laboured husband-
men what cheers their heavy hearts; and Bacchus brings rest
to oppressed mortals, though their legs sound to the knock-
ings of their hard fetters. No sad cares or wailings are

[1] *Sacred dove.*] The dove was not used as food by the Syrians, being
sacred to their goddess Astarte, whom the Greeks identified with Aphro-
dite (Venus).

[2] *Osiris.*] The chief god of the Egyptians. The inventor of agriculture and vine husbandry. The Greeks and Latins confounded him with
Bacchus; and this is probably the reason why the latter was represented
with horns; for the bull was an incarnation of Osiris: *Memphitem . . .
bovem.* The sacred animal was called *Apis*, and was kept at Memphis
in Lower Egypt in a magnificent temple and park. He was said to live
for twenty-five years, at the end of which period he was supposed to
drown himself by leaping into the Nile. He was then buried with great
pomp, and the priests wandered about for some days shrieking, beating
their breasts (*plangere bovem*), and exhibiting every outward sign of grief
until a new Apis was found, when the discovery was celebrated by a joyful festival.

[3] *By the feet of clowns.*] *Incultis—pedibus* does not mean " with slovenly,
dirty feet," as most commentators suppose: a disgusting mistake! Dissen
alone has pointed out that the phrase is an example of a very common
poetical figure, and equivalent to *incultorum pedibus*, " by the feet of men
as yet rude and uncivilized."

thine, Osiris, but dance, and song, and light, ready love ; various flowers, and a forehead wreathed with ivy ; yellow robes flowing down to thy soft feet ; and Tyrian garments, and the sweet flute, and the light ark with its hidden mysteries.——
——Come hither and celebrate a hundred games, and delight the Genius[1] with dances, and steep the brain in wine.  Let perfumed ointments drop from his smooth hair, and let him wear soft garlands on his head and neck.  Come thus to-day, that I may honour thee with incense, and offer thee cates sweetened with Arcadian honey.

But may a progeny spring from thee, *Messala*, which shall add to their father's deeds, and stand in honour round the old man.  Nor silent be the road-monuments[2] which the Tusculan

---

[1] *Genius.*]  The Genius was a spiritual being who presided over the birth of man, watched over him during life, and perished at his death.  Each individual had a separate Genius who regulated his lot, and was represented as black or white according to his fortunes.  The Genius of women was called a Juno.  It was natural that the birthday should be particularly set apart for the worship of the Genius, and that the marriage bed should be under his special protection, and hence called *genialis torus*.  Genialis is used generally as an epithet for anything which conduces to festivity, mirth, or pleasure.  To practise abstinence is "to defraud one's Genius ;" on the other hand, " to indulge one's Genius " is to eat, drink, and be merry.

[2] *The monuments,* &c.]  The passage refers to some repairs executed upon the Via Latina by Messala at the command of Augustus.  This road began at the Porta Capena, ran through the Albana Vallis, and joined the Via Appia at Beneventum.  Messala's road must have been esteemed a strong and durable work, since Martial, to represent that perpetuity of fame, to which he thought himself entitled as a poet, alludes to it in these words, (B. viii. E. 3,) Et cum rupta situ Messalæ saxa jacebunt.  "The public ways ranked among the most important works of Roman magnificence.  Amazing labour, with vast expense, were devoted and combined in extending them from the capital to the utmost limits of the known world ; and in many instances they seem to have been calculated by their construction to outlast the empire, of which they have not inaptly been termed the arteries.  Nor was their construction alone the object of solicitude, the care of looking to their repair was not thought unworthy the greatest men of the republic.  None but those of the highest rank were eligible to the office of superintending that service ; and we find Augustus himself taking the charge of a district.  The Appian Way, the most ancient as well as the most noble, being distinguished by the epithet *regina viarum*, as originally made by Appius Claudius the censor, extended from Rome to Capua.  It was composed of three strata ; the lower of rough stones or flint cemented together, formed a foundation or statumen ; the middle stratum or *rudera* was of gravel ; the upper of well-jointed stones of irregular forms.  It remains in many places perfect to the present day."—*Sir William Gell's "Pompeii."*

land holds, and fair Alba in its ancient abode.  For by thy command here the hard pebbles are compacted together, there the blocks of stone are aptly fitted to each other.  The husbandman sings thy praise when he comes home late from the great city, and finds his feet uninjured.

And thou, Messala's natal day, return and be celebrated through many years, ever fairer and fairer.

## ELEGY IX.[1]

IT cannot be concealed from me what import there is in a lover's language of signs, and his softly-whispered words. I have not the gift of sortilege, or of reading the secrets of the gods in entrails; nor does the song of birds forewarn me of things to come; but Venus, binding my arms behind me with a magic knot, hath thoroughly instructed me, not without many stripes.

Cease to dissemble.  The god of love burns more mercilessly those whom he sees to have succumbed to him unwillingly.  You, Marathon, have done this.  What does it avail you now to have bestowed such pains on your soft locks, and to have so often changed their arrangement? to have adorned your cheeks with shining dye? to have had your nails trimmed by the artist's skilful hand?  In vain are your garments frequently changed, and your feet compressed in tight shoes. She charms though she comes with a face which she has taken no pains to beautify, and though she has not spent much time and art in dressing her shining head.  Has an old woman bewitched you with incantations and potent herbs in the silent time of night?  Incantations steal away the crops from the fields; incantations stop the course of the enraged serpent; incantations attempt to drag down the moon from her chariot, and would do it, were it not for the sound of the clashing brasses.  But why do I accuse incantations of having worked you woe?  Why do I talk of herbs?  Beauty has no need of

---

[1] *Elegy IX.*]  Tibullus pleads the cause of his favourite Marathus, who was ill-used by the coquette, Pholoë, and lectures the former on his foppishness, and the latter on her arrogance and avarice.  The date of the poem is not determined, but it is later than that of El. iv.  Certain allusions to a theme more extensively treated in the latter, have again rendered necessary some infidelity in the translation.

magic auxiliaries. The charm that is really noxious, is to have touched the fair body, to have given long kisses, to have been mutually entwined.

Remember this, *Pholoë*, and be not unkind to the youth; Venus punishes such misdeeds. Ask not for presents; let the white-headed lover give presents, that you may warm his frigid frame in your bosom. More precious than gold is a youth with smooth shining face, and no rough beard to scrape the bosom he embraces. Put your white arms beneath his shoulder, and despise the treasures of kings. Venus will find you opportunities to yield furtively to the ardent boy, when he presses your tender bosom, and to give him moist kisses with tilting tongue as he pants for breath, and to mark his neck with your teeth.

No joy can precious stones and jewels yield to her who sleeps alone in the cold, and who is an object of desire to no man. Alas, too late is love, too late is youth recalled, when age has shed its whiteness on the head. Then is the toilette a serious business; then are the locks tinctured and changed with the green husk of the walnut, to disguise the effect of years; then what pains are taken to root out white hairs, and to make the face cast its skin and be new again.

But you whose life is in its blooming prime, use it while you may; it is gliding away with no slow foot. And torture not Marathus: what glory is there in smiting a boy? Be obdurate to the old; but spare the tender youth, I beseech you. It is not bodily ailment, but excessive love, that tinges his complexion with yellow. Poor lad! How often, when you are far away, he pours out piteous complaints and sheds no end of tears!

"Why does she scorn me?" he says. "The vigilance of those who watch her might be defeated. The god of love himself has given lovers the power of eluding restraint. I know the arts of furtive Venus, how to breathe softly, and how to snatch kisses without letting them be heard. I can creep in noiselessly even in the dead of night, and open the doors without the least sound. But what avail these arts, if she spurns her wretched lover, and flies, cruel girl, from the very bed in which I would embrace her? Even when she promises, with sudden perfidy she breaks her word, and I must watch the livelong night in countless torments. While

I delude myself with the thought that she will come, I think every movement I hear is the sound of her steps. Ah, perish all vain arts and observances of wooing! I will clothe my squalid body in shaggy garments. If my girl's door is shut, if I have few opportunities of seeing her, alas, what good does it do an unfortunate wretch like me to wear a flowing toga?"

Cease your tears, poor youth; her hard heart is unmoved, and your wearied eyes are swollen with weeping. The gods hate disdain, I warn you, Pholoë, and those who are guilty of it offer incense in vain at their holy altars. This Marathus used formerly to mock unhappy lovers, not aware that an avenging god was behind him. He is said even to have often laughed at the tears of an anguished lover, and purposely to have thrown obstacles in his way. Now he hates all arrogant disdain; now he loathes every door that is shut fast at night. Your punishment too will come unless you cease to be haughty. With what yearning you will then desire to recall this day!

### ELEGY X.[1]

WHY, if you were to wrong my wretched love, why did you give me pledges in the name of the gods, which were to be secretly broken? Ah! cruel one, though perjuries be at first concealed, yet chastisement comes at last with noiseless steps. Spare her, gods; it is just that the lovely should be free once to break with impunity oaths sworn by your sacred names. In hope of gain the husbandman yokes his bulls to the plough, and plies the hard work of agriculture. In hope of gain unstable ships are led by sure stars over seas that obey the winds. My girl has been seduced by gifts: but may an avenging god turn them into ashes and water. I shall soon see her punished; dust shall disfigure her beauty; her hair shall be roughened by the winds; her face and her locks shall be sun-burnt, and her delicate feet shall be way-worn.

How often have I admonished you thus! "Sully not your loveliness for gold, countless ills often lurk beneath it. If any one, beguiled by wealth, does violence to Love, Venus visits her with rigorous severity. Rather give my head to the

---

[1] Elegy X.] Happily this is the last occasion on which the translator will have had to ask the reader's indulgence for a necessary, but not always successful, remodelling of the original.

K

flames, smite my body with steel, and gore my back with lashes. Nor hope when you are about to sin that you can conceal it: there is a god who will not let perfidy be hidden. That god makes the taciturn confederate speak out freely when he has drunk largely. That god compels dreamers to articulate, and unwillingly to declare things they would hide." Thus did I say; and now I blush to think that I spoke in tears, and prostrated myself before your fair feet. Then you swore to me that you would not barter your faith for heaps of gold or gems; no, not if all Campania, not if the Falernian soil so dear to Bacchus, were offered to you. With such words as these you might have brought me to deny that the stars shine in heaven, or that there was purity in the water of the stream. You wept too; and I, unpractised in deceit, and credulous, wiped your moist cheeks assiduously. How would you treat me, were you not yourself in love? [1] I pray that the object of your passion may follow the example you give of fickleness. * * * * [2] Wretch that I was, I believed that I was loved; believed it foolishly, for I might have been more wary against your snares. Smitten with your charms, I sang your praises; but now I am ashamed of myself and my Muses. May Vulcan consume those songs with swift flame; may they be washed out by the waters of the stream. Out upon you, whose only care is how to sell your beauty, and to fill your hand with a large payment.

But you, who have dared to corrupt my girl with presents, may your wife make you with impunity the dupe of her incessant wiles; and when she shall have tired out her favoured youth in furtive concourse, may she keep you aloof in bed. May strangers always press your bed, and may your house always lie open and at the command of wooers. Let not even your lascivious sister be said to have drained more cups, or used up more men, than your wife; and that sister, they

---

[1] *Were you not yourself in love.*] And therefore partly softened by the thought that you are liable to the same unkindness as that which I complain of.

[2]    O quoties, verbis ne quisquam conscius esset
         Ipse comes multa lumina nocte tuli !
       Sæpe insperanti venit tibi munere nostro,
         Et latuit clausas post adoperta fores.

As these lines are incapable of being modified in the same way as the rest. we have not translated them.

say, often prolongs her Bacchic revels until the risen orb of
Lucifer portends the day; nor is any one abler than she to
consume the night, and to fill it with variety of occupation.
But your wife has learned these accomplishments; and you,
dolt, do not perceive this when she practises with you the
lesson she has learned from another.[1] Do you imagine it is
for you she arranges her hair, and parts it with a close-
toothed comb? Is it that face of yours that induces her to
wear golden bracelets, and to fold her bosom in a purple robe?
It is not in your eyes she wishes to seem beautiful, but in
those of a certain youth, for whom she would let your house
and fortune go to ruin. Nor is it with evil intent she does
this; but like a girl of cultured taste she shuns your gouty
deformed body, and your senile embraces.

And this man my girl has taken to her bed: after this I
can believe her capable of fondling a wild beast. Have you
dared to sell to others the endearments that were mine? to
give my kisses, infatuated girl, to others? But your turn
will come to weep when another shall claim me as her conquest, and shall imperiously rule the bosom that was yours.
Then will I rejoice in your punishment, and a golden shield
suspended in the temple of my kind protectress, Venus, shall
make known my case in these words: "Freed from the toils
of a perfidious mistress, Tibullus dedicates this to thee, goddess, and prays thee to regard him with favour."

## ELEGY XI.[3]

WHO was it that first produced horrid swords? How
savage, how utterly iron-hearted he was! From that day
began battles and carnage, and a shorter way was opened to
dire death. But the unhappy inventor apprehended nothing
like this; we turn to our own destruction the weapons he gave
us against wild beasts. This is the fault of gold; there were

---

[1] *When she practises*, &c.] *Quum tibi non solita corpus ab arte movet.*

[3] *Elegy XI.*] The poet, being about to quit Rome on military service,
expresses his abhorrence of war, and of avarice, the cause of war; and
praises the blissful security of those simple ages when strife was yet unknown. He prays to his Lares to preserve him that he may end his days
in the quiet of his rural home; and concludes with an enumeration of
the joys of peace. This Elegy appears to have been written on the eve of
Messala's expedition to Aquitaine, A. U. 724.

no wars when the beechen platter held the feast; there were no citadels or ramparts, and the shepherd slept secure amidst his particoloured flock.[1]  Would I had lived then, and had not known the horrors of arms, nor heard with quivering heart the blast of the trumpet.  Now I am forced away to war, and now perhaps some enemy carries the weapon that is to be buried in my body.  Preserve me, paternal Lares; you who nurtured me when I ran about in childhood before your feet.  Be it no shame that you are fashioned out of an old trunk, for even so you inhabited the abode of my old grandfather.  The men of those days kept better faith, when a wooden idol stood in a small shrine, and received poor offerings.  The deity was propitiated, if one gave it a libation from the new vintage, or set a crown of corn-ears on its sacred head.  Whoever had had his wishes fulfilled, carried offerings to the god with his own hand, followed by a little girl bearing fine honeycomb.

Turn away keen-pointed shafts from us, O Lares; your victim shall be a pig from the full rustic stye.  I will follow it dressed in white, with a myrtle wreath on my head, and carrying baskets twined with myrtle.  So may I please you: let any one else be mighty in arms, and prostrate hostile captains by favour of Mars; enough for me that the soldier narrate his deeds to me as I drink, and sketch his camp on the table with his finger dipped in wine.  What madness to seek dark death in war!  It is always at hand, and approaches unseen with silent step.  There are no corn-crops below, no cultivated vineyards; but fierce Cerberus and the Stygian ferry-boat.  There a pale crowd, with fleshless chaps and burnt hair, wander by the gloomy marsh.

How much more to be praised is the lot of him who, with his progeny round him, passes his old age in his little cabin.  He follows his sheep, his son attends to the lambs; and his wife prepares warm water to refresh him when he returns home weary.  So may I live; may my head grow white, and may I relate as an old man the deeds done in my early days.

[1] *Parti-coloured flock.*]  *Varias.*  This epithet, says Ramsay, points to the primitive simplicity of those ancient times.  The sheep in the flock were *variæ*—that is, *spotted*, no anxiety having been as yet displayed with regard to the fineness and purity of the fleece.  Bach thinks that *varias* means, *roaming at pleasure as they fed*—an image of security more apposite than any question of colour.  Brukhusius, not satisfied with any explanation of *varias*, reads *saturas*, "full pastured."

Meanwhile may peace bless our fields. Fair peace first brought the steers under the curved yoke of the plough. Peace reared the vines, and stored the juice of the grape, that the cask filled by the father might yield cheering draughts to the son. In peace the mattock and plough are in full play, but cobwebs gather in dark lumber-holes over the weapons of the stern soldier. The rustic, not very sober, carries home his wife and his children in his cart from the grove.[1] But then the wars of Venus grow hot; a woman complains of locks cut off her head, and of her doors broken open; she weeps and shows the bruises on her tender cheeks; and then the victor himself weeps to think that his mad hands were so strong. Meanwhile wanton Love suggests spiteful words to swell the quarrel, and seats himself at his ease between the angry pair. Ah, he must be stone or iron, who beats his own girl; he brings down the swift vengeance of the gods from heaven. Be it enough to cut off the fine hem of her robe; to undo the arrangement of her tresses; to make her shed tears; thrice happy he whose anger has the power to make a gentle girl weep. But whoever shall be guilty of ill usage with his hands, let him carry shield and pike, and keep far aloof from gentle Venus.

Come to us, bounteous peace, holding ears of corn in thy hand, whilst thy lap overflows with fruit.

---

# BOOK II.

### ELEGY I.[2]

FAVOUR us, each and all who are present; we perform the lustration of our crops and fields, as the rite has been handed

[1] *The grove.*] The consecrated grove, where he had been paying homage to the gods, and feasting with his wife and children.

[2] *Elegy I.*] Written apparently in the spring of B. C. 26. The subject is the *ambarvalia* celebrated in spring for the purification of the fields and all belonging to them. The name was derived from the ceremony of leading the victims in procession round the limits of the farm or district on behalf of which they were to be offered. Ceres and Bacchus are invoked to

down from times of yore. Come, Bacchus, and let the sweet
grape hang from thy horns ; and Ceres, bind thy brows with
ears of corn. Let the earth rest on this sacred day ; let the
ploughman rest, and suspend the hard labour of the furrow.
Unfasten the yokes ; the oxen must now stand at the full man-
gers with garlanded heads. Let all things be devoted to the god :
let no woman dare to put her hand to the spindle. You too I
command to stand aloof, approach not the altars, you who last
night enjoyed the pleasures of Venus. Chaste things are
pleasing to the gods ; come in clean garments, and cleanse
your hands in spring water.

See where the consecrated lamb advances to the glowing
altar ; a crowd follows it crowned with fair olive branches.
Gods of our native land, we purify our fields, we purify our
hinds ; repel, ye gods, all evils from our boundaries. Let not
our crops cheat the labours of the harvest with deceitful
blades,[1] nor the slow-footed lamb fear the swift wolves. Then
the sleek rustic, cheered by the plenteousness of his fields, will
heap large logs on the blazing hearth ; and a crowd of born-
thralls,[2] good signs of a thriving farmer, will sport, and erect
bowers of twigs before the altar.[3]

My prayers for the future will be fulfilled. See you how
the presaging entrails give happy tokens that the gods are
placid. Now bring me smoky Falernian of an old consulship, and unbind the Chian cask. Let wine celebrate the day ;

bless the farm, and the omens appearing favourable, all present are encouraged to spend the day in jollity. Then follows a hymn in honour of
the rural deities, and of Love, their foster-brother. The phrase "favour
us" is sacerdotal ; favour us with your tongues, is implied, that is to say,
either with words proper to the occasion, or with silence. See the beginning of the next Elegy.

[1] *Deceitful blades.*] *Fallacibus herbis :* with corn that looks well in the
blade but carries light ears, and yields less grain in proportion than straw.

[2] *Born-thralls.*] *Turba vernarum.* The *vernæ* were slaves born in
their owner's house or on his estate.

[3] *Bowers of twigs.*] Many of the best commentators understand these
words to refer to the erection of little temporary bowers by the slaves,
under the shelter of which they might drink and amuse themselves.
Others suppose that the *vernæ* in question are the slave children (the
"picaninnies") of the family, who are represented as building baby-houses,
one of the amusements enumerated in the catalogue of Horace, Sat. II.
iii. 247,

> Ædificare casas, plostello adjungere mures,
> Ludere par impar, equitare in arundine longa.

it is no shame to be tipsy on a holiday and to reel and stagger. But, Health to Messala! say every one as he takes his cup, and in every phrase that is uttered let the name of the absent hero be heard.

Messala, renowned for thy triumphs over the Aquitanian nation, victor who reflectest glory on thy rough-haired ancestors,[1] come hither, inspire me while I raise my song of thanks to the rural gods. I sing the country and the gods of the country: under their instruction, mankind ceased to relieve their hunger with acorns. They first taught how to cover the little log-hut with green thatch. They too are said to have first taught bulls to serve under the yoke, and to have put wheels to the cart. Then wild food was dressed; then apples were grafted; then the fertile garden drank irrigating waters; then the golden grape yielded its pressed juices to the feet; and sober water was mingled with the care-dispelling liquor of the vine. The country yields harvests, when the earth annually sheds its locks in the season of the hot star. In the vernal country the light-winged bee gathers the spoil of flowers in its hive, and busily fills its combs with sweet honey. The husbandman, wearied with the continual labours of the plough, first sang rustic words in determinate measure; and first modulated, after his repasts, on the dry oaten pipe, the airs he prepared to sing before the adorned images of the gods. The husbandman, with cheeks reddened with ochre, first led thy unfashioned chorus, O Bacchus; a he-goat, the leader of the flock, was given to him from the full fold—a notable reward.[2] In the country the youth first wove crowns of flowers, and placed them on the heads of his ancient Lares. In the country too the bright-fleeced sheep bears on its back the wool that is to be the care of the tender damsels. Hence is derived the labour of the females in the household, the distaff clothed with wool, and the spindle that revolves under

---

[1] *Rough-haired ancestors.*] Barbers were unknown in Rome until four hundred and fifty-four years after the foundation of the city, when they were imported from Sicily. In earlier times the Romans universally wore flowing hair and long beards; Scipio Africanus is said to have first set the example of shaving.

[2] *A he-goat, &c.*] Tragedy was at first nothing but an annual hymn, sung by peasants in honour of Bacchus; and he who acquitted himself best upon this topic was rewarded with a goat. Hence the Greek name τραγῳδια.

the touch of the thumb ; and hence the task of the weaver, who sings as she busily plies the work of Minerva, and the web sounds to the stroke of the lay.

Cupid himself too is said to have been born in the fields among the herds and the unbroken mares. There he made his first inexpert efforts with the bow: ah me! what expert hands he has now ! Nor does he take cattle for his mark, as he did then; his delight is to transfix girls and to bring down proud-spirited men. He strips the young man of his wealth ; and constrains the old man to utter words that disgrace him at the angry fair one's door. Led by him, the girl steps furtively over the bodies of the sleeping watch, and meets the youth alone in the dark. Timorously she treads the ground on tiptoe, and gropes her blind way. Alas, unhappy they whom the god severely persecutes; and happy he on whom kind Love breathes gently.

Come, sacred boy, to our festive banquet; but lay aside thy arrows, and hide far, far hence, thy glowing torch. Celebrate the god, all of you, in song, and summon him with your voices to the flock ; let each summon openly to the flock, and secretly to himself; or even openly each to himself, for the jocund rout is boisterous, and the curved pipe dins in Phrygian tone. Be merry : Night is now yoking her horses, and the yellow Stars are following the chariot of their mother in wanton dance ; after them comes silent Sleep with sombre wings outspread, and black Dreams with dubious gait.

### ELEGY II.[1]

LET us speak good words at the altars; the natal day is come. All who are present, man and woman, favour us with your tongues. Let pious incense be burnt on the hearths, and odours which the luxurious Arab sends us from his rich land. Let the Genius himself be present to behold his own honours, with his sacred locks adorned with soft garlands. Let his temples drop with pure spikenard, and let him have his fill of libations of pure wine. May he grant you, Cerinthus, whatever you shall demand. Come, why do you delay? He will grant; make your request. I augur that

---

[1] *Elegy II.*] This Elegy properly belongs to the fourth book, for it celebrates the birth-day of Cerinthus, the lover of Sulpicia.

you will wish for the faithful love of a wife. I suspect the gods themselves are already aware of this,[1] and that you would be less pleased to have all the fields in the whole world which the stout rustic ploughs with the strong ox, or all the gems produced by the earth in wealthy India, where shines the ruddy wave of the eastern sea. Your vows are ratified.[2] See you how Love flies hither with quivering wings, and bears the yellow bonds of marriage? Bonds which will endure for ever, until decrepit age brings wrinkles and hoary hair. Come with this winged omen, O natal day, and supply a progeny; and may a young group sport before thy feet.

### ELEGY III.[3]

THE country and her villa detain my girl, Cornutus; oh, one must be made of iron to remain in the city. Venus herself has now migrated to the glad fields. And Love is learning the ploughman's rustic words. Oh, if I might behold my mistress the while, how bravely would I there turn up the ground with the stout prong! I would follow the curved plough, like a husbandman, when the bullocks prepare the ground for sowing; nor would I complain that the sun scorched my delicate limbs, and the burst blisters made my soft hands sore.

Even beauteous Apollo fed the oxen of Admetus; neither his harp nor his unshorn locks availed him, nor could he cure his amorous distresses with wholesome herbs; love had conquered all the powers of his medical art. The god himself

[1] *I suspect the gods*, &c.] That is, I suspect that this is the burthen of all your prayers to them.

[2] *Your vows are ratified.*] *Vota cadunt.* Most editors take this to mean just the reverse, "your vows are made in vain;" the same words are used in this sense in Propertius, i. 17. But we have the authority of Bach and others for the sense which we have adopted, and which is alone consistent with what follows.

[3] *Elegy III.*] Nemesis, to whom the remaining Elegies of this book are addressed, had gone from Rome to her country house, and Tibullus declares his intention of becoming a peasant, and working in her fields, after the example of Apollo, who in similar circumstances became the herdsman of Admetus. So exasperated is he by the departure of his mistress, that he curses his favourite pursuit of agriculture for having caused it, and wishes for a return of the happy times when men fed on acorns.

was wont to drive the cows from the stalls, and take them after feeding time to the streams to drink. Then the light rush basket was woven by his hand, and fine openings were left between the meshes for the passage of the whey. Oh how often is his sister said to have blushed when she met him carrying a calf across the fields! Oh how often when he sang in some deep valley did the cattle dare to interrupt his exquisite strains with their lowing! Often did princes seek oracles in their anxiety, *but found them not,* and the crowd returned home, frustrated, from the temple. Often did Latona grieve to see the rough disorder of those sacred locks, which a step-dame herself had before admired. Whoever had seen that undressed head and that unbound hair, would have asked where were the locks of Phœbus? Where is thy Delos now, Phœbus? Where is the Delphic Pythoness? Love commands thee to dwell in a little cabin.

Happy the days of yore, when, as story tells, the immortals were not ashamed to serve Venus. That *love-smitten* god is now a common jest; but one to whom his mistress is dear, would rather be a common jest than a god without love.

But oh, cruel Ceres, who wilest away Nemesis from the city, may the earth never faithfully return thee the seed committed to it. And thou, youthful Bacchus, planter of the pleasant vine, do thou abandon the accursed vats. Thou canst not bury lovely woman in the dreary fields with impunity; thy vintage is not worth such a price, father. O farewell to the fruits of the earth; rather than our girls should be banished to the country, let us eat acorns and drink water in primitive fashion. What were the men of those times the worse for not having sown furrows? When love inspired them, kind Venus gave them joys in the shady valley. There were no guards then, no doors that shut out those who would come in; charming customs, return, if it be possible!

Lead on: I will till the land in obedience to my mistress. I do not shrink from chains and blows.

## ELEGY IV.[1]

I SEE my slavery, and a mistress ready: farewell now, freedom of my fathers. A hard servitude is imposed upon me; I am held in chains; and Love will never relax my bonds. And whether I have done well or ill, he burns me. I am burned; oh remove the torch, cruel girl! Oh, that I might not feel such pangs, how much rather would I be a stone on the frosty mountain; or stand like a rock breasting the mad winds, and beaten by the wrecking rage of the vast sea! Now bitter is the day, and more bitter the shades of night: all seasons are now filled with gall and wretchedness. Elegies help me not, nor Apollo, the author of song: her craving hand is always stretched out for pay. Avaunt, Muses, if you are of no help to a lover. I do not worship you in order to sing of wars; I describe not the journeyings of the Sun, nor how the Moon, when she has completed her orbit, turns her horses back again. I seek easy access to my mistress by my songs: avaunt, Muses, if they are of no avail.

But means of largess must be won by me by slaughter and crime, that I may not lie weeping before her closed doors. Or I will carry off the tokens suspended in the holy fanes; and Venus above all others shall be the object of my violence. She tempts me to wickedness by giving me a rapacious mistress: let her feel my sacrilegious hands.

O perish, whoever gathers green emeralds, and dyes the snowy fleece with the Tyrian shell! He gives girls motives for avarice, and so does the Coan robe, and the clear pearl from

---

[1] *Elegy IV.*] Hopelessly devoted to a thankless mistress, Tibullus execrates her venality, but is ready to indulge it at all hazards. "The whole poem," says Grainger, "is a tempest of amorous and contrary affections. By these our author is particularly distinguished from Ovid and Propertius. These poets generally begin and end their elegies with the same passion; whereas the reader will often find in one of Tibullus's all those contrarieties and transitions which peculiarly characterize the passion of love, and are so beautiful in poetry. This justifies the elegant encomium which Joannes Baptista Pius bestows on our author: Princeps elegorum poetarum est dubio procul Al. Tibullus, quia vere amantem agit. Modo superbit, modo supplicat; annuit, renuit; minatur, inter-cedit; dedignatur, devovet, orat; inconstans est, quod voluit non vult, quod optavit, refugit; secum dissidens, ut in vera Cupidinis rota circumagi credas.

the Red Sea.[1] These things have made them ill-natured;
hence the door has come to know the key, and the dog has
begun to guard the threshold. But if you offer a large present, the guard is overcome, the locks do not oppose your
entrance, and the dog is dumb.[2] Alas, whosoever of the gods
gave beauty to an avaricious woman, what a good thing he
buried under many bad ones! Hence tears and quarrels;
this in fine is what has made Love an ill-famed god. But you
who bar the door against lovers scorned for lucre, may wind
and fire rob you of your ill-got gain. Let young men look
with joy on the conflagration of your property, and not one of
them trouble himself to throw water on the flames. Or death
will overtake you; and there will be none to mourn, or sadly
to minister to your obsequies. But the girl who was good-
natured and not avaricious, though she live a hundred years,
shall be wept for before the blazing pyre; and some aged
man, revering the memory of his old love, shall yearly deck
her reared tomb with flowers, and say as he quits it, "Rest
well and placidly, and light be the earth above thy quiet
bones!"

My warnings are true; but what does truth avail me?
I must love her upon her own conditions. Even if she bid
me sell my ancestral domain, go, my Lares, pass into the prætor's hands and into the schedule.[3] All the poisons of Circe
and of Medea, all the deadly herbs produced by the soil of
Thessaly, and the virulent hippomanes[4] which drops from the

---

[1] *O perish*, &c.] Stanley has rendered this passage in the notes on
his translation of Anacreon, first published in 1655:

> Oh may the man who digg'd green emeralds first,
> And dipt white wool in Tyrian dye, be curs'd!
> Garments from Cos, and orient pearls he brought
> From the Red Sea, and women avarice taught.

[2] *The dog is dumb.*] We know not who is the author of the following
sarcastic epitaph on a dog which belonged to a married lady:

> Latratu fures excepi, mutus amantes:
> Sic placui domino, sic placui dominæ.

> I barked at thieves, was mute when lovers came;
> And thus I pleased my master, pleased my dame.

[3] *Pass into the prætor's hands*, &c.] *Ite sub imperium, sub titulumque
Lares:* Be placed at the disposal of the prætor to be sold by auction, and
be inscribed in the public lists of property for sale.

[4] *Hippomanes.*] Both authors and critics vary greatly in their opinions

lustful mare, when Venus inspires the unbroken herd,—if only Nemesis looks upon me complacently—let her mix these and a thousand other dreadful ingredients, and I will drink them.

## ELEGY V.[1]

THY favour, Phœbus! A new priest enters thy temple : hither, come hither with harp and song; I entreat thee now

respecting this mysterious ingredient of witchcraft. Aristotle and Theocritus mention a plant of that name, the smell of which made mares turn mad for the stallion. Pliny says the *hippomanes* was a fig-like excrescence on the forehead of the new-born foal, which the dam immediately bit off and swallowed; and if she was prevented, she would not let the foal suck. Virgil, Georg. iii., agrees with Tibullus in making it a liquid exudation.

[1] *Elegy V.*] The subject of this Elegy is the appointment of Messalinus, Messala's eldest son, as one of the Quindecemviri, the fifteen priests of Apollo, who had charge of the Sibylline books. "The Romans," says Grainger, "were proud of being thought the posterity of the Trojans; and their poets embraced every opportunity of making their court to the people by adopting that notion. Nor was this prejudice confined to the meaner sort of Romans; Julius Cæsar, and his successor, either believed, or affected from political motives to believe, that they were descendants of Æneas. Nay, so far was this folly carried, that Augustus entertained a design of transferring the seat of empire from Rome to Troy. This the Romans dreaded not a little; and to such a height did their apprehensions increase, A. U. C. 734, when Augustus was in Syria, that Horace, all courtier as he was, is supposed to have written that noble ode, *Justum et tenacem*, lib. iii. od. 5, obliquely to dissuade the emperor from that measure. As this, however, was a very delicate subject, and none knew better how to flatter his patron than Horace, he abruptly breaks off, —non hæc jocosæ conveniunt lyræ: these things are unsuited to the sportive lyre. Tibullus, however, not lying under the same obligations to Augustus as the lyric poet, and neither courting the smiles nor dreading the frowns of the court, he, like a true patriot in all the enthusiasm of poetry, introduces the Sibyl pushing on Æneas to the new settlement destined by heaven for him and his followers in Italy. As Augustus professed a great veneration for the Sibylline books, and was anxious to be thought the son of Apollo, who, he said, fought for him at the battle of Actium; the people (whose prejudices to the removing of their seat of empire must have been augmented by our poet's well-timed prophecy) would have regarded Augustus's breach of the Sibyl's orders as the most impious of violations. Besides, so flagrant a disrespect, and in one too of such eminence, might have produced the most fatal consequences to his government, by weakening the reverence which his subjects entertained for the Sibylline writings. This, Augustus was too sensible not to perceive, and too politic not to avoid."

to strike the vocal chords with thy thumb, and shape the strains to words of praise. With thy temples bound with triumphal laurel, come to thy own rites, while they heap the altar; but come neat and fair; put on now thy choicest garment;[1] comb well thy long locks, and appear as they say thou didst, when after the rout of King Saturn thou sangest praises to victorious Jove. Thou seest coming events long beforehand; the augur, vowed to thee, knows well what the prescient bird sings. Thou governest lots; through thee the aruspex forecasts the future, when a god has set marks on the slippery entrails. Guided by thee, the Sibyl who sings in hexameters the hidden things of fate, has never misled the Romans. Phœbus, suffer Messalinus to touch the books of the prophetess, and expound to him thyself, I beseech thee, what she sings.

She made known his destiny to Æneas, after, as the legend tells, he bore off his father and his rescued Lares, nor thought that Rome would be, when he looked back in sorrow from the deep on Ilion and its burning gods. Romulus had not yet formed the walls of the eternal city, in which his associate Remus was not destined to dwell; but cows fed there on the grassy Palatine, and humble cabins stood on the site of Jove's citadel. Milk-swilling Pan lodged there under the shade of the holm-oak, and wooden Pales carved with a rustic bill-hook. The garrulous pipe, sacred to the woodland god, hung on a tree, as the homage of the roving shepherd: the pipe, in which the range of reeds decreases continually, for a smaller tube is joined with wax to the first, and so on to the end. But where the open region of the Velabrum[2] extends, a little boat used to ply over the water. In it the girl who was to charm the rich master of the flock, was often ferried over to the youth on festal days. Gifts of the fruitful country returned with her, a cheese, and the white lamb of a snowy ewe.

[1] *Thy choicest garment.*] *Sepositum.* The poet in plain terms requests the god to wash his face, comb his hair, and put on his best suit, the one which is *laid by* for high days and holidays.

[2] *The Velabrum.*] The low ground lying between the Capitoline and the Aventine hills, and stretching from the forum to the river. It was anciently a swamp, until drained by the Cloaca Maxima and its branches, after which it was covered with streets and became one of the most populous districts of the city.

"Intrepid Æneas," *sang the Sibyl*, "brother of winged Love, who carriest the sacred things of Troy in thy ships as thou fliest, Jupiter now assigns to thee the Laurentian fields; that hospitable land now invites thy wandering Lares. Troy will then indeed marvel at itself, and own that thou hast done wisely in traversing so long a way. There thou wilt be sanctified when the honoured water of Numicus[1] shall have sent thee to heaven as one of the Dii Indigetes. Lo, victory hovers over thy wave-worn ships. At last the haughty goddess joins the Trojans. Lo, the flames gleam before me in the camp of the Rutuli; now I foretell death to thee, barbarian Turnus. Before my eyes is the Laurentian camp and the wall of Lavinium, and Alba Longa founded by Prince Ascanius. Thee, too, I see, priestess, who wilt charm Mars; Ilia, thou hast deserted the altars of Vesta; I see your stealthy embraces, and the fillets cast on the ground, and the arms of the ardent god left on the shore. Pluck, bulls, the grass from the seven mountains while now you may; this will be the site of a great city. Rome, thy name is destined by fate to rule the earth, wherever Ceres looks down from heaven on her fields, from where the rising of the sun is seen, to where his panting steeds bathe in the restless waves. I sing true things: so may I ever feed unharmed on the sacred laurel,[2] and my virginity be eternal."

Thus the prophetess sang, and called thee, Phœbus, to her, and tossed her head and her dishevelled hair. *Expound also to Messalinus* whatever Amalthea, whatever Mermessia told; what Herophile, beloved of Phœbus, announced; and the sacred oracles which Aniena of Tibur carried dry in her bosom through the floods.[3] These foretold that there would be a

---

[1] *Numicus.*] Æneas lost his life either in the river Numicus or in a battle fought near it. See Livy, i. 2. Modern topographers fix on a small stream called the Rio Torto as the ancient Numicus; it passes within a short distance of Pontica, which is generally recognised as the ancient Lavinium.

[2] *Feed on the sacred laurel.*] The Pythia before she ascended the tripod bathed in the water of Castalia, crowned herself with laurel, and chewed its leaves to increase the inspiration.

[3] *Amalthea, Mermessia, &c.*] According to the most learned of the Romans there were ten Sibyls: the Persian, Libyan, Delphic, Cumæan, Erythræan, Samian, Cuman, Hellespontic, Phrygian, and Tiburtine. But the list may be greatly curtailed, for in some cases two or more of these local titles were given to the same person. It seems certain that the

comet, evil sign of war, and that many stones would rain down upon the earth; and they say that trumpets and clashing arms were heard in the sky, and that the sacred groves predicted flight. The cloudy year, too, saw the rayless sun yoke his pale horses; and the images of the gods shedding warm tears; and heard oxen foretelling the fates with human voices.

These things were of old; but now, mild Apollo, sink such portents beneath the tameless ocean; and may the lighted laurel crackle well in the sacred fire, giving omen of a happy and sacred year. Ho, the laurel hath given good tokens; farmers, rejoice! Ceres will distend the full granaries with corn, and the rustic, tipsy with must, will tread the grapes till cisterns and vats shall fail to hold the abundant liquor. The shepherd bedewed by Bacchus shall celebrate his festival of Pales; then keep aloof from the stalls, ye wolves. Filled with drink he will set fire solemnly to heaps of straw, and leap through the sacred flames. And the matron will bear children, and the son will catch hold of his father by the ears and kiss him; nor will the grandfather weary of watching over his little grandson, and prattling broken words with the child. Then the lads who have done service to the gods will stretch themselves on the grass where falls the light shade of an ancient tree. Or they will spread out their garments for screens and tie them with flowery sprays; and a crowned goblet shall stand before them. Each spreads a banquet for himself, and erects a table and a couch of turf. There the youth will fling spiteful words at his girl in his drink, which he will soon wish unsaid; for savage as he is just now, he will weep when he is sober, and swear that he was not in his right senses.

So please thee, Phœbus, perish bows, perish arrows, only let Love roam the earth unarmed. Good is the art of archery, but since Cupid took up arms, alas, alas, to how many has that art been woeful! And to myself especially, for I have lain wounded for this year past; and I encourage the festering sore, so pleased am I with the pain! Scarcely have I

Cumæan, Cuman, Erythræan, and Hellespontic were one and the same. The names of these prophetesses, Amalthea, Herophile, &c., are involved in almost hopeless confusion. Tibullus appears to have taken at random names commonly current without investigating very closely their origin or their relations to each other.

power left to sing my Nemesis, without whom I cannot find words or measure for a line.

But thee, girl, I warn (for poets are under the safeguard of the gods) spare the sacred poet; that I may celebrate Messalinus, when vanquished towns[1] shall be borne as honours of war before the chariot in which he sits crowned with laurel; whilst the soldier also, bound with the laurel of the fields, shall sing aloud, Io, triumphe! Then let his father, my Messala, present a hallowed spectacle to the crowd,[2] as he applauds the son who passes before him in the chariot of victory. Grant this, Phœbus: so may thy locks be unshorn; so may thy sister be ever pure.

## ELEGY VI.[3]

MACER is bound for the camp: what will become of tender Love? Shall he go with him, and bravely bear arms on his neck? And whether Macer toils on the long march by land, or crosses the uncertain sea, will Love be ready to go by his side equipped with weapons? Burn him, boy, I beseech thee, for thus savagely forsaking the leisure of thy service, and bring back the deserter beneath thy banners. If thou sparest soldiers, here too is one who will be a soldier, *ay, and even* fetch his own thin potation of water in his helmet.

[1] *Vanquished towns.*] Plans of towns taken in war formed part of the pageantry of triumphs. They were at first of wood; but in Cæsar's last triumph they were of silver.

[2] *Then let his father*, &c.] *Tum Messala meus det pia spectacula turbæ, Et plaudat curru prætereunte pater.* Grainger, following the false lead of most commentators, translates these lines thus:

His father hails him as he rides along,
And entertains with pompous shows the throng.

The interpretation we have given above is that of Heyne; the father applauding his son's triumph were a spectacle of paternal pride and affection that would claim the sympathy of the beholders: such is the force of the word *pia.*

[3] *Elegy VI.*] Impatient of the cruelty of Nemesis, Tibullus proposes to follow the example of his brother poet, Macer, and go to the wars, but quickly recollects how often he had made similar resolutions, but wanted firmness to persevere in them. The poem must have been written about B. C. 24, when Augustus was preparing to send Ælius Gallus into Arabia Felix. The latter part of this Elegy, beginning with, "But come, whoever thou art," is, in the common text, inserted into the third Elegy of the second book, where, as the best editors admit, it is quite out of place.

I am for the camp: farewell Venus, farewell the girls! I, too, am valiant, and the trumpet was made for me. I talk big; but when I have talked magnificently big, the barred door upsets all my brave words. How often have I sworn that I would never return to her threshold! And when I have sworn stoutly, my foot goes back there of its own accord. Cruel Love, may I see thy arrows broken, and thy torch extinguished, if it be possible! Wretch that I am, thou torturest me, and forcest me to curse myself, and to utter mad blasphemies.

But come, whoever thou art, to whom Cupid is a grim-visaged commander, come to my tent and let us share the toils of war together. This iron age prizes not Venus, but booty; yet booty is won with many hardships. Booty hath girded fierce ranks with hostile arms; hence comes bloodshed, and slaughter, and expedited death. Booty impelled men to double their dangers on the restless sea, when it put warlike prows to insecure ships. He who fights for booty longs to possess immense fields, that he may have countless flocks feeding over multitudes of acres. He is anxious to procure foreign stone; a column is carried to his mansion, amidst the confusion of the city, by a thousand strong pairs of oxen; and a mole locks in the tameless sea, that the fish at ease within it may disregard the wintry billows. But let Samian pottery, and plastic clay fashioned on the Cuman wheel, bear glad cheer for you. Alas, alas, I see that our girls delight in wealthy lovers. Come then spoil and plunder, if Venus craves for opulence; that my Nemesis may swim in luxury, and be made conspicuous by my presents as she walks through the city. Let her wear thin robes spun by the Coan women and inwoven with gold; let her be attended by dark-skinned servants scorched in India, and blackened by the fire from the near chariot of the sun; let Africa and Tyre vie in supplying her with their choicest colours, their purples of violet and crimson tinge.

I speak things notorious to all lovers: that fellow is now royally installed, who was often forced to show his chalked feet[1] on the barbarian platform.

[1] *Chalked feet.*] Slaves imported from abroad, when they were exposed for sale, had their feet whitened with chalk or gypsum (plaster of Paris). The poet's successful rival was some wealthy freedman.

## ELEGY VII.[1]

I WOULD ere this have put an end to my woes by death; but credulous hope cherishes life, and always says that to-morrow will be better. Hope cheers the husbandman; hope commits the seed to the ploughed furrow, to be repaid by the field with large interest. She catches birds with the snare, and fishes with the rod, when the bait has previously concealed the fine hooks. Hope consoles even the slave who is fastened in strong fetters: the irons rattle on his legs, yet he sings at his work. Hope assures me that Nemesis will be kind; but she refuses. Oh, stubborn girl, be not stronger than a goddess! Spare me, I implore you by the bones and premature death of your sister; so may the little one rest well beneath the gentle earth. She is sacred to me; I will offer gifts upon her tomb, and garlands wet with my tears. I will fly to her tomb, and sit there a suppliant, and complain of my fate to her mute dust. She will not suffer me, her client, always to weep for your sake. I deprecate her words, that you be kind to me, lest her neglected manes send you bad dreams, and your sad sister stand before your bed as you sleep, such in appearance as when, falling head-long from a high window, she went all bloody to the shades.

I drop the subject, lest the bitter grief of my mistress be renewed. I am not worth that she should weep once *through me;* nor does she deserve that her speaking eyes should be spoiled with tears. It is a bawd that injures me; my girl herself is good-natured. Phryne, the bawd, denies me admittance, and goes backwards and forwards carrying notes concealed in her bosom. Often when I hear sweet tones from my mistress's hard threshold, that old wretch says she is not at home. Often when a night has been promised me she brings me word that my girl is ill, or that she is frightened by some threatening events or other. Then I am mortally

---

[1] *Elegy VII.*] The poet would long ago have ended his woes by death, had he not been sustained by the catholic cordial of hope. He implores Nemesis to have pity on him, adjuring her by the manes of her sister, to whose tomb he will repair as a suppliant; and he inveighs against the go-between who thwarts his passion. In many editions this poem is joined to the preceding one.

tormented; then my mind is lost in conjecturing who it is
that enjoys my girl, and in how many ways. Then, bawd, I
curse you; you will have a sore life enough, if the gods fulfil
the least part of my prayers.

---

# BOOK III.

## ELEGY I.[1]

THE festive calends of Roman Mars are come. This was
the beginning of the year for our ancestors; and now, according to established custom, gifts fly about in all directions
through the streets of the city, and the houses. Say, Muses,
with what gift shall I do homage to her who, mine or not
mine, is always dear Neæra?

### THE MUSES.

" The lovely are won with song, the avaricious with gold.
Let her rejoice, as she is worthy to do, in your verses. But
let a yellow wrapper enclose the snow-white book, and let the
pumice first of all smooth its white leaves. On the surface
of the thin paper let there be a finely-executed inscription,
declaring your name, and between the two fronts let there be
stained ornamental tips; for thus should the work be adorned
to be fit to send to her."

### TIBULLUS.

I entreat you by yourselves, who have dictated my strains,
and by the Castalian shade and the Pierian waters, go to her
house, and give her the handsome book as it was; let it lose
none of its gloss. She will send me back word, whether she

---

[1] *Elegy I.*] This is a dedication, in the form of a dialogue between
the poet and the Muses. Romulus, who divided the year into ten months,
dedicated the first to his father Mars. Numa Pompilius added the months
of January and February to the calendar of Romulus; but the custom
of presenting New-year's gifts continued, nevertheless, to be observed on
the first of March.

regards me with mutual affection, or with less, or whether I have lost all place in her bosom. But first wish her long health as she deserves, and say thus to her in submissive tone: " Your husband that will be, your brother that now is, chaste Neæra, sends you this little gift and begs you to accept it. And he swears that you are dearer to him than his vitals, whether you are to be his wife or his sister; but his wife rather: nothing but Pluto's pallid water shall take from him the hope of that name."

## ELEGY II.[1]

HE was made of iron who first tore the beloved maid from the youth, and the beloved youth from the maid. Hard too was he who could bear such grief, and survive the loss of his mistress. I have not such fortitude; such power of endurance is not in my nature. Sorrow breaks even stout hearts. Nor am I ashamed to speak the truth, and to confess my disgust for a life that has suffered so many woes. So when I shall have been changed into a thin shade, and the black dust shall cover my white bones, may Neæra with long dishevelled hair come and weep before my funeral pile. But let her come accompanied by her dear sorrowing mother; and let the one mourn a son-in-law, the other a husband. Then having addressed my manes, invoked my soul, and washed their pious hands in water, let them with their black robes unbound collect all that will remain of my body, my whitened bones. And when they have collected them, let them first sprinkle them with old wine, then wash them with white milk; afterwards soak the moisture from them with linen cloths, and lay them dry in their marble home. Then be there poured upon them the materials supplied by rich Panchaia, the Eastern Arabians, and fruitful Assyria, and with them tears to my memory. Thus I desire to be disposed of when I am turned to bones. And let an inscription declare the sad cause of my death, and display these words on the conspicuous front of the tomb: Here lies Lygdamus; grief and pining love for his lost bride Neæra were the cause of his death.

[1] *Elegy II.*] Written on the occasion of Neæra's departure from Rome with her mother.

### ELEGY III.[1]

WHAT avails it, Neæra, to have wearied the gods with
vows, and to have offered them pleasing incense with many
prayers? I have not done this that I might issue forth from
a marble mansion, as the distinguished scion of an illustrious
house; or that my oxen might till many acres of land, and
the kindly earth yield me large crops; but that I might share
with you the joys of a long life, and that my age might sink
to rest on your bosom, when I should have completed my
allotted span of life, and should be compelled to be ferried
naked in the Lethæan boat. For what were I the better for
a vast weight of gold? Or though a thousand oxen tilled my
fertile land? What to me were a mansion supported on
Phrygian columns, or on those from your quarries, Tænarus
or Caristus?[2] Or to have in my house plantations resembling
sacred groves, and gilded beams, and a marble floor? What
delight have I in cloths dyed with the shell collected on the
Red Sea's shore, or with the murex of Sidon, or in all the
things besides which the vulgar admire? These things excite
envy. The things which the vulgar love are mostly worthless.
A man's mind is not lightened or his cares removed by wealth,
for Fortune rules time and its events by her own law. To
me let poverty be welcome with thee, Neæra, but without
thee I care for no gifts of kings. O brightly fair day, that
shall restore thee to me! O day for me thrice and four times
blessed! But if my god hears with no averted ears whatever
vows are offered for that sweet return, I care not for kingdoms,

---

[1] *Elegy III.*] Tibullus complains of the inflexible cruelty of Neæra,
and of the failure of all his vows and offerings to the gods—vows and
offerings the object of which was not wealth, but that he might enjoy the
society of his beloved one until the close of life. He values not wealth
without love, and would gladly embrace poverty with Neæra. Without
her, he would gladly die.

[2] *Phrygian columns,* &c.] The Phrygian marble, so highly prized by
the Romans, was obtained from the quarries of Dorimia, a village near
Synnada, one of the chief towns of Phrygia Magna. It was white with
purple spots. Black marble, now known as *Nero Antico*, was obtained
from the promontory of Tænarus in Laconia (Cape Matapan). Carystus
in the island of Eubœa produced a white and green marble, resembling
in hue the lower part of the stalk and outer coat of an onion or leek;
and hence it has received the name of *Cipollino marble*.

nor for the golden stream of Lydia,[1] nor for all the riches
which the whole earth contains. Let others covet them; to
me be it granted to enjoy my dear spouse, content in humble
competence.

Come, daughter of Saturn, and favour my timid vows; come,
Cyprian goddess, wafted on thy shell, and favour them. But
if the return I pray for is denied by fate and by the sad
sisters who spin the threads and sing the things that are to
be, may lurid Orcus in his dull water call me to the vast
rivers and the black marsh of the realms below.

### ELEGY IV.[2]

MAY the gods grant me better things; nor let those dreams
be true which hateful sleep presented to me last night. Avaunt,
dreams; turn away your false, delusive faces, and expect no
longer to be believed. The gods give true warnings of coming destiny; the entrails examined by the Tuscan seers give
true warnings; but idle dreams beguile us in the deceitful
night, and fill our timorous minds with false fears; yet mankind, born for trouble, deprecate the omens of night with consecrated meal and crackling salt. Be this as it may, whether
they will believe the true soothsayer or a lying dream, *I will
pray* that Lucina make my nightly fears to be vain, and grant
that my anticipations be not fulfilled; if my mind is conscious
of no base deed, nor has my tongue impiously blasphemed
the great gods.

Night having traversed the firmament in her black chariot,
had washed her wheels in the azure flood, nor had I been
lulled by the god that is wholesome to the sick mind. Sleep
fails before the house of care. At length when Phœbus looked
forth from the verge of the orient, tardy sleep closed my weary
eyes. Then a youth, with temples wreathed in chaste laurel,
was seen to set foot within my dwelling. His unshorn locks
flowed down his long neck, and breathed Syrian perfumes.
His fairness was like that which shines from the face of
Latona's daughter, and a rosy hue mingled with his snowy

---

[1] *The golden stream of Lydia.*] The Pactolus. The name is now
corrupted by the Turks into Bagouly.

[2] *Elegy IV*]. Tibullus describes a dream in which Apollo appeared to
him, and warned him of Neæra's inconstancy.

whiteness; like the blush that suffuses the soft cheeks of the maid when first she is delivered to her young husband; like as when maidens twine white lilies with amaranths; like as when autumn ruddies the white apples. A palla[1] played upon his ankles, for that was the garb in which his fair body was clothed. On his left side hung the speaking lyre, a work of rare art, shining with tortoise-shell and gold. Striking its chords with an ivory plectrum as soon as he entered, he gave forth auspicious sounds, accompanying them with his lips. And when his fingers and his voice had mingled in harmony, he uttered these words in sweet, sad measure:

"Hail, favourite of gods; for Phœbus, and Bacchus, and the Muses constantly favour the chaste poet. But Bacchus, son of Semele, and the learned Sisters, are unable to declare what the future will bring, but to me my father has given to be able to see the laws of fate, and the events of coming time. Hear therefore what I, unfailing prophet, what I, the Cynthian god, will utter with true lips. She who is dear to thee as no daughter is to her mother, as no fair girl is to the eager bridegroom; she for whom thou dost weary the gods with vows, who suffers not thy days to pass in peace, and who mocks thee with nightly visions when sleep has wrapped thee in her sombre mantle; she who is celebrated in thy songs, the beautiful Neæra, prefers to be the bride of another. The unkind girl has her own amorous cares which are not for thee; Neæra rejoices not in the thought of entering a pure house as a bride. Ah, cruel sex! woman, faithless name! Ah perish whosoever she be that has learned to betray a lover's hopes! But she may be bent; their minds are changeable; only stretch out thy arms to her with abundant prayers. Harsh Love hath taught his votaries to perform stubborn tasks; harsh Love hath taught them to bear stripes. That I once pastured the white herds of Admetus, is not a tale invented for idle pastime. At that time I could neither take pleasure in my tuneful lute, nor accompany its chords with my voice; but I practised airs on a shining oaten pipe, I, the great son of Latona and Jove. Thou knowest not what love is, young man, if thou refusest to bear with a cruel and intractable mistress. Hesitate not therefore to employ the per-

---

[1] *A palla.*] This was a loose robe reaching from the head to the feet. It was the appropriate garb of harpers, and of their patron Apollo.

suasive accents of sorrow; hard hearts are overcome by soft prayer. If there be truth in the oracles chanted in the sacred temples, report these words to her in my name: The Delian god himself promises thee this marriage, this happy marriage! Cease to wish for another husband."

He said, and dull sleep departed from me. Ah may I escape the sight of such ills! I cannot believe that thy wishes are contrary to mine, nor that there is such guilt in thy heart. For thou wast not born of the waters of the vast deep, nor of the fierce, fire-vomiting Chimæra; nor of the dog with three tongues and three heads, whose back is covered with a serpent brood; nor of Scylla, whose virgin form is cinctured with dogs; nor did a savage lioness conceive and bring thee forth, nor the barbarous land of Scythia, nor dread Syrtis; but thou wast born in a civilized dwelling, not inhabited by cruel beings, and of a mother exceeding all others in gentleness, and of the most amiable of fathers.

May the god turn these cruel dreams to a better result, and bid the soft south winds sweep them away as frustrated presages.

## ELEGY V.[1]

YOU are staying at the waters that flow from the Tuscan fountains, waters not to be visited in the dog-days, but now excelling even the sacred wells of Baiæ,[2] whilst the earth is renewing itself in the purple spring. To me Persephone announces the fatal hour; spare, goddess, an innocent youth! I have not attempted audaciously to reveal the inviolable rites of the goddess worthy of all praise. My hand has not tainted the cup with deadly juices, nor given sure poisons to any one; I have not sacrilegiously set fire to temples; no impious deeds rack my heart with remorse; nor have I opened my mouth to utter mad blasphemies against the gods. My black hair is

[1] *Elegy V.*] The poet, suffering under a protracted fever, addresses some friends who were visiting the hot springs of Etruria. He laments his prospect of untimely death, and entreats his friends to offer sacrifices for his recovery.

[2] *But now excelling,* &c.] The common reading of the original is unanimously given up as unintelligible. We have adopted Bach's conjectural emendation, which appears to us one of the happiest efforts of the kind with which we are acquainted: *Nunc autem ante sacras Baiarum maxima lymphas.*

not yet touched with grey, nor has age, bent and slow-footed, come upon me. [My parents first saw my birth-day when both consuls fell by the same fate.][1] Why rob the vine of its growing grapes; and pluck with marring hand the just-formed apples? Spare me, all ye gods who possess the pale waters, you to whose lot has fallen the third dread realm! Let me become acquainted hereafter with the Elysian fields, and the bark of Lethe, and the Cimmerian lakes,[2] when my face is pale with wrinkled age, and I, an old man, relate the events of early days to youths.[3]  May the fear which this fever causes

---

[1] *Both consuls fell.*]  Meaning Hirtius and Pansa, who were mortally wounded at Mutina, in the battle against Antony, B. C. 43.  The passage enclosed between brackets is certainly an interpolation; not only has it no necessary dependence on the context, but the latter would be improved if it were taken away.  The original consists of two lines, the second of which is found *verbatim* in Ovid, Trist. iv. 10, 6;

> Here was I born: then rose my natal day,
> When by one fate both consuls slaughter'd lay.

If Tibullus was born in the same year with Ovid, it is singular that the latter, who was so minutely communicative, should have omitted so remarkable a fact, the mention of which would seem naturally prompted by his esteem for Tibullus.  But on the contrary he leaves us to suppose, from a successive enumeration of poets, that Tibullus was considerably his senior; and he regrets that fate had not allowed him to cultivate his friendship.  Moreover the chronology which these lines would establish, can by no means be reconciled with various known events of our poet's life.  For instance, it would show him to have been only thirteen or fourteen years of age when he bore a distinguished part in his patron Messala's victorious campaign in Gaul.  Tibullus fell sick at Corcyra on his voyage with Messala to Syria, which was undertaken at the latest in 726 (B. C. 28); and it appears from the Elegy which he wrote on that occasion that he must have been for some time the favoured lover of Delia.  That Elegy is one of his most successful compositions, and his precocity is unexampled, if before reaching the age of sixteen, he had earned all these triumphs in war, and love, and poetry.  Lastly, Horace must have been forty when he wrote the Epistle in which he compliments Tibullus as the candid critic of his satirical and epistolary " discourses:" a very unlikely sort of deference to one who was more than twenty years his junior.

[2] *Cimmerian lakes.*]  In Homer and his imitators the Cimmerians are a people who dwell in the mysterious regions of the far west, in a sunless land, shrouded in mists and clouds on the borders of the Ocean Stream, near the entrance to the realms of Hades.

[3] *My black hair . . . to youths.*]  These lines have been happily imitated by Hammond :—

> No stealth of time has thinned my flowing hair,
> Nor age yet bent me with her iron hand;

me prove groundless! I have now lain ill these fifteen days, whilst you are celebrating the divine powers of the Tuscan waters, and the yielding wave is parted by your straining arms. Live happy, and remember me, whether I remain on earth, or the Fates will that I shall be no more. Meanwhile, promise black victims to Pluto, and libations of white milk mingled with wine.

## ELEGY VI.[1]

COME, fair Bacchus: so may the mystic vine be thine perpetually; so may thy brows be ever bound with ivy. Take away my pangs, thou who hast thyself had need of the same medication: often has Love succumbed beneath the power of thy attribute. Dear boy, let the goblets mantle with generous Bacchus; go pour out Falernian for me with prone hand. Be gone far hence, cares and troubles, a tormenting race! Here let the Delian god show his radiant presence with white birds *of good omen.* And you, sweet friends, second my purpose, and let no one decline to follow my example. Or if any one refuses the friendly strife of wine, may the girl he loves deceive him by some impenetrable artifice.

That god makes the soul wealthy; he tames the haughty spirit, and makes it obedient to the will of a mistress; he conquers Armenian tigers and tawny lions, and gives soft hearts to savage beasts. These things, and greater yet, Love can do. But call for the gifts of Bacchus! Which of you likes an empty cup? Bacchus is equitable; he does not look grimly on those who honour him, and with him merry wine; but to the sober he shows his wrath more and more: whoso fears the might of an angry god, let him drink! How dread-

> Ah why so soon the tender blossom tear,
>  Ere autumn yet the ripened fruit demand?
> Ye gods who dwell in gloomy shades below,
>  Now slowly tread your melancholy round;
> Now wandering view the baleful rivers flow,
>  And musing hearken to their solemn sound ·
> O let me still enjoy the cheerful day,
>  Till, many years unheeded o'er me rolled,
> Pleased in my age I trifle life away,
>  And tell how much I loved ere I grew old.

[1] *Elegy VI.*] Neæra has married a man of her own rank in life, and Tibullus seeks solace in wine for his disappointed affections.

ful he is to such, and with what chastisement he visits them,
the gory victim of the Cadmean matron teaches us.[1]  But far
from us be this fear; let her feel, wherever she be, what is
the force of an offended deity's anger!

What prayer do I utter, insensate that I am!  Let my rash
wishes be scattered to the winds and the clouds.  Though
thou no longer carest for me, Neæra, be happy, and fair be
thy destiny.  For us, let us give our careless moments to the
table; one serene day is come after many bad ones.—Ah me,
it is hard to affect false joys; it is hard to feign merriment
when the mind is sad; the forced smile sits ill on lips that
belie the heart, and the words of drunken revelry ill befit the
anxious.—Why do I grieve and whine?  Base cares, begone!
Father Lenæus hates sad talk.

Thus didst thou weep of yore the perjury of Theseus, O
Gnosian maid, deserted on the unknown shore.  Thus,
daughter of Minos, did skilled Catullus sing for thee, and tell
of the abominable acts of the ungrateful man.  And I now
warn you, *my comrades:* Happy will you be if you learn from
another's suffering to avoid your own.  Be not insnared by
arms that hang round your neck, nor beguiled by the coaxing
prayers of a crafty tongue.  Though the false one swear by
her own eyes, and by her Juno and her Venus, there will be
no faith in her oaths: Jupiter smiles at lovers' perjuries, and
bids the winds scatter them.  Why then do I complain so
often of the words of a deceiving girl?  Away from me, all
serious words.—How gladly would I rest with thee the live-
long night, and wake with thee the live-long day!  False to
me without cause; not kind to me though with cause to be
so; false, but though false, yet dear!

Bacchus loves the Naiads; why do you loiter, slow attendant?  Dilute this old wine with water.  If my fickle mistress shuns my table, preferring the bed of a low rival, I
will not spend the whole night in sighing.  Go, boy, bring
stronger wine.  I ought long ago to have perfumed my head
with Syrian nard, and have twined flowers in my hair.

---

[1] *The gory victim,* &c.]  Pentheus, king of Thebes, having denied the
divinity of Bacchus, and given orders that he should be treated as a criminal, the god inspired all the women of the land with raving madness, and
the king's own mother, Agave, the daughter of Cadmus, headed the
Bacchanals who tore him to pieces.

# BOOK IV.

## POEM I.[1]

### A PANEGYRIC. TO MESSALA.

I WILL sing of thee, Messala. Though thy known worth makes me fear that my feeble powers may be unequal to the task, yet I will begin. But if my song fails to express the praise due to thee, though I be a humble recorder of such great deeds as thine, and no one by thyself can so commit thy exploits to writing but that still greater things shall remain to tell, it is enough for me to have had the will. Nor do thou scorn my humble offering. Even the Cretan[2] offered acceptable gifts to Phœbus; and Icarus[3] was the most pleasing of all hosts to Bacchus, as the constellations of Erigone and the Dog testify in the clear sky, beyond denial by any future age. Moreover Alcides, who was to ascend Olympus as a god, set his glad feet within the house of Molorchus.[4] Often have the celestials been propitiated with a little salt, nor are bulls with gilded horns always sacrificed to them. Let this little work too be accepted by thee, that I may have courage thence to compose many another copy of verses in thy praise. Be it another's task to tell of the wondrous work of the great universe; how the earth hath taken its place beneath the im-

[1] *Poem I.*] A laboured, clumsy, dull production, such as could not have been written by Tibullus. Some editors apologize for it upon the assumption that it was a juvenile effort; but that cannot be admitted, since it is certain that it cannot be referred to an earlier date than that of the first Elegy of the first book, which is perhaps the most beautiful in the whole collection.

[2] *The Cretan.*] The legend to which this refers is not known.

[3] *Icarus.*] A king of Laconia. Bacchus taught him the art of making wine, a favour for which he paid dearly; for some peasants whom he treated with the strange liquor thought they were poisoned, and murdered him. His daughter Erigone hanged herself for grief. Bacchus changed the father and daughter and their bitch Mera into constellations.

[4] *Molorchus.*] A shepherd of Cleonia, who gave hospitality to Hercules. The hero rewarded him by killing the Nemæan lion, the ravager of the shepherd's flock.

mense atmosphere; how the ocean hath gathered itself into
a globular form; how the unstable air where it strives to
rise from the earth, is everywhere mingled with the fiery
ether, and how the whole is enclosed above by the pendent
sky.   But whatever my Muses may avail to do, whether they
can match thy glory, or, surpass it, which I have no hope of,
or fall short, and they will certainly fall short of it, I will dedicate all this song to thee, that my poem may not want the
dignity of thy great name.

Though thou hast inherited the abundant renown of thy
ancient race, thy glory was not content with ancestral fame;
nor dost thou inquire only what the inscription states beneath
each bust, but thou strivest to surpass the old honour of thy
line, and to shed more lustre on thy ancestors than they on
thee.   But not the inscription alone beneath thy image, shall
contain thy deeds, but great volumes shall be filled for thee
with immortal verse; and writers will spring up on all sides to
celebrate thee in verse and prose.   There will be a contest
among them, who best praises thee.   May I be victor among
them, that I may inscribe my name upon such great acts.

For who does greater things than thou dost, in camps and in
the forum?   Thy merit is neither greater nor less in the one
or the other; as when a just balance is pressed down by
equal weights in both scales, and neither falls nor rises;
whereas if the weights in either scale be unequal; it fluctu-
ates alternately up and down.   If the inconstant, discordant
populace is in commotion, no other can appease them like
thee; or if the anger of the judge is to be assuaged, no orator
can soften him more.   Pylos or Ithaca had not such a man
in Nestor, or Ulysses, that great glory of a small state, though
the former lived until Titan in his orbit had completed three
centuries with prosperous hours; and the latter had daringly
roamed through unknown cities where the earth is enclosed
by the farthest waters of the sea. For he defeated the Cicones
in arms, nor could the lotus stop him from his course.   The
Neptunian dweller among the crags of Ætna was vanquished
by him, and, drunk with Thracian wine, was deprived of sight.
He carried the winds of Æolus with him over the smooth sea,
and visited the savage Lestrigonians, and Antiphates, through
whose territory flows the cold stream of the noble Artacia.
Him alone the magic beverage of the learned Circe did not

transform, although she was the child of the Sun, and skilled in changing old forms by herbs or incantations. He arrived too at the cities of the Cimmerians on which day never rose, whether Phœbus was on that part of his course above the earth or on that below it. He saw how the great progeny of gods, made subjects of Pluto's realm below, went about among the light shades. He passed swiftly the shores of the Syrens in his ship. Swimming between two confines of death, he was not affrighted by the ravening mouths of Scylla, when the monster writhed with her dogs amidst the mad waves; nor did violent Charybdis swallow him as was her wont, whether she rose aloft from the depths of the waves, or with yawning gulf laid bare the bottom of the sea. Nor let the slaughtered herds of the journeying Sun be passed in silence, nor the love of Calypso the daughter of Atlas, and her fruitful fields, nor the Phæacian lands, the end of his weary wanderings. But whether these things are facts known to our earth, or whether fable has given them a new world, his may have been the greater toil, but thine is the greater eloquence.

No one is more expert than thyself in the arts of war; how to encircle the camp with a safe ditch; how to plant palisades against the approach of the enemy; what spot is most fit to enclose with intrenchments; how the earth throws out springs of fresh water; how the approach may be made easy for thy own men, and difficult for the enemy, and how the soldier may be kept in vigour by continual rivalry for praise; who best casts the heavy javelin or the light arrow, or bursts through impediments with the stiff pike; who can restrain the swift steed with a tight rein, or throw the reins loose to the slow one, and urge the animal straight forward, or compel it to wheel round in a narrow circle; who excels with the shield, in guarding right or left, whether the shock of the spear come this way or that; or in hitting the mark with the sling. When comes the strife of bold Mars, and the adverse lines prepare to meet, then thy promptitude is seen in forming the order of battle, whether it is requisite that the forces should be drawn up in a square with a long and even front, or in two wings, so that the right should attack the enemy's left, the left his right, and that the two should achieve a double victory. Nor does my song praise at random; for I state things proved in war: witness for me the brave soldier

of the vanquished Iapydia; witness the crafty Pannonian,
everywhere driven back into the cold Alps; and witness that
poor Arupinian, a soldier born, to see whom, so unbroken by
age, might make one wonder less at Pylian Nestor's reputed
three centuries.   For though the old man may have seen
Titan bring back a hundred fruitful years, yet he will spring
boldly on a swift courser's back, and govern him with the
reins.  Under thy command the horse-taming nation, that
never turned their backs before, bent their free necks to the
Roman chain.

Nor shalt thou be content with these things ; for greater
are at hand, as I have ascertained by veracious auguries such
as Melampus son of Amythaon[1] could not surpass.  Thou
hadst just put on a garment shining with Tyrian woof at the
dawn of the day that led in the fertile years; when the Sun
rose brighter out of the waves, and the discordant winds held
their rude breath, nor did the sinuous streams run their ac-
customed course; even the stormy sea was calm, no bird
swept through the air, no rough quadruped depastured the
dense woods, when deep silence was afforded for the hearing
of thy wishes.  Jupiter himself came in his light chariot
through the empty air, left the heaven-touching top of Olympus, lent an attentive ear to thy prayers, and assented to
them all with his infallible nod.   The fire applied to the altar
shone out joyously above the heaped brands.  Begin then
with divine encouragement to do great deeds ; be thy triumphs
unlike those of others.   Neighbouring Gaul will not be able
to withstand thee in war, nor the bold warriors of broad Spain;
nor the wild land possessed by the Tyrian colonists, nor those
through which flows the Nile, or the royal water of Choaspes,[2]
or when the rapid Gyndes wears away the Arectæan plains
with its many mouths, monuments of the infatuation of Cyrus,[3]
nor the realms to which Tomyris gave the Araxes for bound-

---

[1] *Melampus.*]  A great soothsayer, extolled in the Odyssey.
[2] *Choaspes.*]  A river of Media, a confluent of the Tigris.  The Persian kings drank no other water, and were provided with a supply of it
wherever they went.
[3] *The infatuation of Cyrus.*]  When about to attack Babylon, Cyrus
drew off the waters of the river Gyndes through three hundred and sixty
new-made channels, and spent so much time on the work, that the Baby-
lonians were enabled to collect large forces against him.

ary;[1] nor the remotest land where the Padæans, nearest of men to the rising sun, hold their inhuman banquets;[2] nor the Getæ, whose country is watered by the Hebrus, the Tanaïs, and the Mosynos. Why dwell on details? Far as Oceanus bounds the habitable globe with his waters, there is no region which will stand against thee in arms. The Briton, yet unconquered by Roman warfare, awaits thee, and the other part of the world beyond the course of the sun. For the earth is seated in the midst of the ambient air, and its whole orb is divided into five parts; and two of these are always made waste by icy cold. There the ground is always covered with thick mist, and the flowing wave is arrested in its course by frost, and stiffens into dense ice and snow; for Titan has never carried his beams above those regions. But the middle region is always exposed to the heat of Phœbus, whether he approaches nearer the earth in his summer orbit, or hurries swiftly through the short days of winter. There therefore the earth is not thrown up by the ploughshare, nor does it yield corn-crops or fodder. Neither Bacchus nor Ceres blesses the fields, nor do animals inhabit the scorched region. Between it and the cold regions are placed the two fertile zones, our own and that which is opposite to it. Both these are tempered alike by the climate that adjoins them on either hand, in such wise that the one climate counteracts the other. Hence the year revolves for us through mild seasons; hence the bull has learned to submit his neck to the yoke, and the flexible vine to ascend the lofty branches of the elm; the annual crop yields mature harvests, the earth is cleft with steel, the sea with the keel, and towns arise with walls of masonry. So when thy deeds shall have marched through new triumphs, thou alone wilt be declared the greatest in the two worlds.

I am not adequate to the heralding of such glory, not though Phœbus himself should dictate to me the strains I should sing. Thou hast Valgius, who may gird himself up for this great effort; no one comes nearer than he to immortal Homer. I too will not be idle, but will devote my labour to

---

[1] *The Araxes for boundary.*] Tomyris, queen of the Scythians, defeated Cyrus on the Araxes.

[2] *Inhuman banquets.*] Herodotus (Thalia) mentions the Padæi as a cannibal people of India, who ate their sick relations.

thy praises, though Fortune, adverse to me, impairs my powers, as is her wont.  For whereas of old my house shone with great wealth, I had yellow crops to enrich granaries that were too small for my exuberant harvests, and vast flocks and herds feeding on the hills, plenty for their master, and too much for thieves and wolves; now regret remains; for my grief is renewed as often as sad memory recalls the years that are past. But though worse befall, and I am despoiled of what is left, my Muses will not fail to celebrate thee.  Nor shall Pierian honours alone be paid to thee; for thee I would dare to go through the wild waves, though the wintry billows swell beneath the winds; for thee I would stand alone in the thick of battle, or cast my small body into the flames of Ætna.  All I am is thine; if then thou hast a little regard for me; be it as much or as little as thou wilt, if it be but at all; the Lydian realm or the fame of Gylippus[1] were not more precious to me, nor would I choose in preference the ability to write books like Homer's.  But if this poem of mine, the whole or a part of it, be either well approved or slightly skimmed by thee, no Fates shall put an end to my poetic laudations of thee.  Even when the tomb shall have covered my bones; whether my death is near at hand, or a long life remains for me; should I be transformed, and range the solid plains as a horse, or become a bull, the glory of the slow herd, or as a bird be wafted with wings through the liquid air, whatever human form I may assume again after a long lapse of time, I will add new poems in thy praise to those I have begun.

## POEM II.

### IN PRAISE OF SULPICIA.

SULPICIA is adorned on thy calends, great Mars; come thyself from heaven to behold her if thou art wise.  Venus will pardon this; but thou, truculent god, beware, lest, struck with admiration, thou let thy arms fall ignobly.  When Love wants to fire gods, he lights two torches at her eyes.  Whatever she does, wherever she goes, Grace attends her unseen, and arranges her attire.  If she unbinds her hair, loose locks be-

---

[1] *Gylippus.*]  Commander of the Lacedæmonians, who defeated the Athenians in the Syracusan war.

come her; if she braids it, she is adorable in braided hair. She inflames all hearts if she walks abroad in a purple robe; she inflames them if she is clad in pure white. So they say blessed Vertumnus wears a thousand dresses in eternal Olympus, and wears a thousand becomingly. She alone among girls is worthy of robes twice dipped in the precious dye of Tyre, and to possess all the odorous produce gathered by the wealthy Arab husbandman in his fragrant fields, and all the gems which the black Indian, nearest neighbour of the Eastern waves, collects on the red shore. Sound her praise, ye Muses, on the festive calends, and thou, proud Phœbus, on the vocal shell. May she enjoy this solemn rite for many years. No girl is worthier of your choir.

## POEM III.

### SULPICIA TO CERINTHUS.

Spare my dear youth, boar that rangest the good pastures of the plain, or the intricacies of the shady mountain; be it of no avail for thee to have whetted thy hard teeth for fight, but may Love preserve him safe for me. But Diana and the chase drive all thoughts of me from his mind. Oh perish the forests and the hounds! What infatuation to wish to hurt your soft hands in enclosing thick, wooded hills with toils! What pleasure is it to creep stealthily into the lairs of wild beasts, and scar your white legs with hooked brambles? Yet that I might roam with you, Cerinthus, I myself would carry the twisted nets through the mountains. I myself would track the steps of the swift stag, and loose the iron chains from the hound. Then, then would the forests please me, though I be convicted of lying down with you, light of my eyes, before the very toils. Then let the boar come to them; he shall escape unhurt, rather than he shall disturb the joys of eager Venus. Now let there be no Venus without me; but, obedient to Diana's law, spread the nets, chaste youth, with chaste hands. And whosoever shall surreptitiously trespass upon my delight, may she fall into the grasp of wild beasts and be torn to pieces. But you, Cerinthus, leave the chase to your father, and come back quickly to my bosom.

## POEM IV.

### TO PHŒBUS.

Come hither and dispel the sickness of my tender mistress, come hither, superb Phœbus of the unshorn locks! Hasten, Phœbus, and believe me thou wilt not be sorry to have applied thy healing hands to the beautiful girl. Suffer not pale emaciation to settle upon her limbs, nor a sickly hue to blemish her fair body; and let the running waters of the river sweep all her malady and all our sad fears into the sea. Come, god, and bring with thee all the medicinal juices and all the chants that relieve bodily suffering. Torture not a youth, who fears the death of his mistress, and makes innumerable vows for her recovery. At times he vows, at times he utters angry words against the immortal gods, because she lies ill. Lay aside your fears, Cerinthus; no god does hurt to lovers. Only love always, and your girl's safety is insured to you. There is no need to weep; it will be a fitter time to use tears if ever she becomes a little unkind to you. But now she is wholly yours; the fair girl thinks of you alone, and the credulous crowd of suitors beset her doors in vain. Be favourable, Phœbus; it will be a great renown for thee, in saving one to have restored two. Thou wilt be celebrated, thou wilt be joyful, when both shall joyfully vie in paying their vows on thy holy altar. Then the blessed assembly of the gods will pronounce thee happy, and each will covet the possession of thy arts.

### POEM V.

#### SULPICIA TO CERINTHUS.

This day which gave you birth, Cerinthus, is sacred for me, and always to be reckoned among festal days. At your birth the Fates foretold new servitude for girls, and bestowed proud sovereignty on you. I beyond all others am inflamed; and pleased am I, Cerinthus, to be inflamed, if you burn with a mutual flame for me. Be it so, I entreat you, by our sweet secret blisses, by your eyes, and by your Genius! Divine Genius, take graciously the gifts I offer, and favour my vows, if only he glows when he thinks of me. But if haply he now

sighs for other loves, then, I beseech thee, quit his faithless
hearth. Nor be thou unjust, Venus; either let both serve thee,
bound alike, or take off my bonds. But rather let us both be
held in a strong chain, which no day to come shall be able to
break. The youth wishes the same things as I, but wishes
them more covertly; for he is ashamed to speak these words
openly. But thou, O natal god, since thou· knowest all, assent; what matters it whether he ask in secret or openly?

## POEM VI.
### TO JUNO.

TAKE, Natal Juno, the sacred tribute of incense which an
accomplished girl presents with her tender hand. To-day is
wholly thine; to-day she has with a heart full of gladness
adorned herself, that she might stand before thy altar worthy
to be seen. She ascribes indeed the cause of her adornment
to the goddess, yet there is one whom in secret she wishes to
please. But grant thy favour, divine Juno, and let nothing
part the lovers; but prepare mutual bonds, I implore thee,
for the youth. Thus wilt thou well unite them. He cannot more worthily serve any girl, nor she any man. Let
not the watchful guard be able to detect the longing pair, but
let Love supply a thousand ways of eluding them. Give
thy assent; come resplendent in thy purple robe; thrice,
chaste goddess, libation is made to thee of wine. The careful mother prescribes her own wishes to the daughter, but she
in her secret heart prays for another thing. She burns like
the swift flames on the altar, nor would she, though she could,
be cured. Let her be dear to the youth, and when the next
year is come, let this love, then mutual and old, assist at her
vows.

## POEM VII.
### SULPICIA TO VENUS.

THE love is come at last, which I glory less in modestly
concealing, than in openly confessing. Moved by the supplications of my Muse, Cytherea has brought it, and laid it in
my bosom. Venus fulfils her promises; let any one tattle of
my joys who is known not to have had the favours of his own

mistress. I will not commit anything to a sealed letter, that none may read me before my own lover; but I rejoice to have sinned; I loathe to shape my face in deference to public opinion; let it be told of me that I have been with one who was worthy of me, and I of him.

## POEM VIII.
### SULPICIA TO MESSALA.

THE unwelcome natal day is come, which must be sadly spent in the odious country and without Cerinthus. What is sweeter than the city? Is a villa a fit place for a girl? And the cold Arnus in the Aretine district? Now stay here, Messala, who indeed are too importunately anxious about me, and too often ready to take me on an unseasonable journey. Carried hence, I leave my soul and my senses behind me, since you will not let me exercise my own will..

## POEM IX.
### SULPICIA TO CERINTHUS.

Do you know that your girl has put all thoughts of the unwelcome journey out of her mind? We may now remain in Rome on her birthday. Let that day be passed by us all as a birthday, which now comes to you perhaps unexpectedly.

## X. EPISTLE.
### SULPICIA TO CERINTHUS.

I AM glad that you very securely promise yourself that I will not in foolish infatuation suddenly fall. If you like the harlot with her toga and her basket better than Sulpicia the daughter of Servius; others care for me and regard her with anger; nor will I, who am an object of the greatest interest to many, patiently bear to have a low wench preferred to me.

## XI. EPISTLE.
### SULPICIA TO CERINTHUS.

Do you feel an affectionate concern, Cerinthus, for your girl, whose weary frame is now racked by fever? Ah, I can-

not wish to overcome this painful illness, unless I think that
you wish it too. For what were I the better for recovering
from illness, if you can bear my sufferings with easy mind?

### XII. EPISTLE.

#### SULPICIA TO CERINTHUS.

LIGHT of my eyes, let me no longer be so fervently loved
by you as I think I was some days ago, if ever I committed
a fault in all my foolish youth of which I confess myself more
penitent, than that I left you alone last night, wishing to dissemble the ardour of my passion.

### XIII. ELEGY.

#### TIBULLUS TO HIS MISTRESS.

No woman shall steal me from your bed; our compact of
love was made from the first on this condition. You alone
charm me, and no girl but you in the whole city is lovely in
my eyes. And I would that you might seem lovely to me
alone. Be without charms for others! so shall I be safe. I
want not to be envied; away with vulgar notoriety; let him
who is wise rejoice in his own silent heart. So may I be
able to live happily in the sequestered woods, where there is
no path trodden by human foot. You are rest to my cares;
you are my light even in the black night; you are for me a
numerous company in lonely places. Were a mistress sent
down this moment from heaven to Tibullus, she would be
sent in vain, and would move no desire.[1] This I swear to

[1] *Were a mistress,* &c.] Thus smartly imitated by Croxall:

Were I invited to a nectar feast
In heaven, and Venus named me for her guest;
Though Mercury the messenger should prove,
Or her own son, the mighty god of love;
At the same instant let but honest Tom
From Sylvia's dear terrestrial lodging come,
With look important say, " Desires—at three,
Alone—your company—to drink some tea;"
Though Tom were mortal, Mercury divine,
Though Sylvia gave me water, Venus wine,
Though heaven was here, and Bow Street lay as far
As the vast distance of the utmost star;
To Sylvia's arms with all my strength I'd fly:
Let who would meet the Beauty of the sky.

you by the divinity of your Juno, whom alone I revere before the other gods. Fool that I am! what have I done? I have given up my securities. How stupid I was to swear! that fear on your part made me safe. Now you will be bold, now you will torture me more daringly. This is the unfortunate result of letting my tongue run on too fast. I will now do whatever you please; I will remain yours for ever, nor seek to escape from the service of my acknowledged mistress; but I will sit down in bonds before the altar of blessed Venus; she lashes the unjust, and favours suppliants.

## XIV. EPIGRAM.

RUMOUR says that my girl often wrongs me; now would I that my ears were deaf. These charges are not made without pain to me. Why dost thou torture me, importunate Rumour? Be silent.

## XV. EPIGRAM BY DOMITIUS MARSUS,
### ON THE DEATH OF TIBULLUS.

THEE too, Tibullus, an untimely death has sent young to the Elysian fields, as a companion to Virgil, that there should be none to breathe the tenderness of love in plaintive elegies, or to sing of royal wars in heroic measure.

# THE POEMS

OF

# VALERIUS CATULLUS.

---

## I. DEDICATION OF HIS POEMS,

### TO CORNELIUS NEPOS.

My little volume is complete,
With all the care and polish neat
   That makes it fair to see:
To whom shall I then, to whose praise,
Inscribe my lively, graceful lays?
   Cornelius, friend, to thee.

Thou only of th' Italian race
Hast dared in three small books to trace
   All time's remotest flight:
O Jove, how labour'd, learn'd, and wise!
Yet still thou ne'er wouldst quite despise
   The trifles that I write.

Then take the book I now address,
Though small its size, its merit less,
   'Tis all thy friend can give;
And let me, guardian Muse, implore
That when at least one age is o'er,
   This volume yet may live.    LAMB.

## II. TO LESBIA'S SPARROW.

SPARROW! my nymph's delicious pleasure!
Who with thee, her pretty treasure,
Fanciful in frolic, plays
Thousand, thousand wanton ways;
And, fluttering, lays to panting rest
On the soft orbings of her breast;
Thy beak with finger-tip incites,
And dallies with thy becks and bites;
When my beauty, my desire,
Feels her darling whim inspire,
With nameless triflings, such as these,
To snatch, I trow, a tiny ease
For some keen fever of the breast,
While passion toys itself to rest;
I would that happy lady be,
And so in pastime sport with thee,
And lighten love's soft agony.
The sweet resource were bliss untold,
Dear as that apple of ripe gold,
Which, by the nimble virgin found,
Unloos'd the zone that had so fast been bound.

ELTON

### THE SAME.

DEAR sparrow, long my fair's delight,
    Which in her breast to lay,
To give her finger to whose bite,
Whose puny anger to excite,
    She oft is wont in play.

For thus, when we are forced to part,
    Her thoughts she from me steals;
Thus solaces by sportive art
The soft regret, the fretful smart,
    I fondly hope she feels.

Then may not I in absence play,
    As she has play'd with thee;
Nor thou, who couldst her grief allay,
Assuage my pangs when she's away,
    And bring relief to me.

Thou wilt be welcome, as 't is known
　　Was to the nimble maid
The golden fruit that loosed the zone,
Her virgin guard, and bade her own
　　A lover's warmth repaid. 　　　LAMB.


### III. ON THE DEATH OF LESBIA'S SPARROW.

MOURN, all ye loves and graces; mourn,
　　Ye wits, ye gallant, and ye gay;
Death from my fair her bird has torn,
　　Her much-loved sparrow's snatch'd away.

Her very eyes she prized not so,
　　For he was fond, and knew my fair
Well as young girls their mothers know,
　　Flew to her breast and nestled there.

When fluttering round from place to place,
　　He gaily chirp'd to her alone;
He now that gloomy path must trace,
　　Whence Fate permits return to none.

Accursed shades o'er hell that lower,
　　Oh be my curses on you heard!
Ye, that all pretty things devour,
　　Have torn from me my pretty bird.

Oh evil deed! oh sparrow dead!
　　Oh what a wretch, if thou canst see
My fair one's eyes with weeping red,
　　And know how much she grieves for thee!! 　LAMB.


### THE SAME.

EACH Love, each Venus, mourn with me!
Mourn, every son of gallantry!
The sparrow, my own nymph's delight,
The joy and apple of her sight;
The honey-bird, the darling, dies,
To Lesbia dearer than her eyes.
As the fair one knew her mother,
So he knew her from another.

¹ The preposterous phrase, "Oh what a wretch," is most unlike the original, "O miselle passer!"

With his gentle lady wrestling,
In her snowy bosom nestling;
With a flutter, and a bound,
Quiv'ring round her and around;
Chirping, twitt'ring, ever near,
Notes meant only for her ear.
Now he skims the shadowy way,
Whence none return to cheerful day.
Beshrew the shades! that thus devour
All that's pretty in an hour.
The pretty sparrow thus is dead;
The tiny fugitive is fled.
Deed of spite! poor bird!—ah! see,
For thy dear sake, alas! for me!—
My nymph with brimful eyes appears
Red from the flushing of her tears.        ELTON

## IV. DEDICATION OF A PINNACE,

### TO CASTOR AND POLLUX.

THAT pinnace, friends, can boast that erst
    'Twas swiftest of its kind;
Nor swam the bark whose fleetest burst
    It could not leave behind;
Whether the toiling rower's force,
Or swelling sail, impell'd its course.

This boast, it dares the shores that bound
    The Adrian's stormy space,
The Cyclad islands sea-girt round,
    Bright Rhodes or rugged Thrace,
The wide Propontis to gainsay,
Or still tempestuous Pontic bay.

There, ere it swam 'mid fleetest prows,
    A grove of spreading trees
On high Cytorus' hill, its boughs
    Oft whisper'd in the breeze.
Amastris, pride of Pontic floods,
Cytorus, green with boxen woods,

Ye knew it then, and all its race,
  And know the pinnace too,
Which, from its earliest rise, to grace
  Thy lofty summit grew;
And in the waves that wash thy shores
Which moisten'd first its sturdy oars.

Thence many vainly-raging seas
  It bore its master through;
Whether from right or left the breeze
  Upon the canvass blew;
Or prosperous to its course the gale
Spread full and square the straining sail.

No vows to Ocean's gods it gave,
  For then no storm could shake;
When erst from that remotest wave
  It sought this limpid lake:
But, ah! those days are fled at length,
And fled with them are speed and strength.

Now old, worn out, and lost to fame,
  In rest that's justly due,
It dedicates this shatter'd frame,
  Ye glorious Twins, to you—
To you, whose often cheering ray
Beam'd light and safety on its way.   LAMB.

## V. TO LESBIA.

LOVE, my Lesbia, while we live;
  Value all the cross advice
That the surly greybeards give
  At a single farthing's price.

Suns that set again may rise;
  We, when once our fleeting light,
Once our day in darkness dies,
  Sleep in one eternal night.

Give me kisses thousand-fold,
  Add to them a hundred more;
Other thousands still be told
  Other hundreds o'er and o'er.

But, with thousands when we burn,
    Mix, confuse the sums at last,
That we may not blushing learn
    All that have between us past.

None shall know to what amount
    Envy's due for so much bliss;
None—for none shall ever count
    All the kisses we will kiss.   LAMB.


THE SAME.

LET us, my Lesbia! live and love;
Though the old should disapprove:
Let us rate their saws severe
At the worth of a denier.
    Suns can set beneath the main,
And lift their faded orbs again:
But we, when sets our scanted light,
Must slumber in perpetual night.
    Give me, then, a thousand kisses
Add a hundred billing blisses:
Give me a thousand kisses more;
Then repeat the hundred o'er:
Give me other thousand kisses
Give me other hundred blisses;
And when thousands now are done,
Let us confuse them every one:
That we the number cannot know;
And none that saw us kissing so,
Might glut his envious busy spleen,
By counting o'er the kisses that had been.   ELTON


VI.  TO FLAVIUS.

AH, Flavius, you would gladly tell
Catullus, whom you love so well,
    What girl your favourite reigns:
Nor could your restless tongue forbear
To speak her name; unless you wear
    Some jade's disgraceful chains.

And now you love, I fain must guess,
Some shameless wanton's coarse caress,
   Whom you would blush to own:
For, vainly mute, your couch that smells
Of flowers and Syrian essence, tells
   You never lie alone.

Your fragrant room, disorder'd bed,
And, ah! 'bove all, your drooping head,
   Your thin and languid frame,
The fruits of love-sick loose excess,
Speak what your silence would suppress,
   And all the truth proclaim.

Oh! boldly then your flame declare,
Or false or true, or plain or fair,
   The damsel that you prize:
My sprightly verse will lend a grace
To deck your worst amours, and place
   With honour in the skies.    LAMB.

## VII. TO LESBIA.

THY kisses dost thou bid me count,
And tell thee, Lesbia, what amount
My rage for love and thee could tire,
And satisfy and cloy desire?

Many as grains of Libyan sand
Upon Cyrene's spicy land
From prescient Ammon's sultry dome
To sacred Battus' ancient tomb:
Many as stars that silent ken
At night the stolen loves of men.
Yes, when the kisses thou shalt kiss
Have reach'd a number vast as this,
Then may desire at length be stay'd,
And e'en my madness be allay'd:
Then when infinity defies
The calculations of the wise;
Nor evil voice's deadly charm
Can work the unknown number harm.    LAMB.

PART OF THE SAME.

As many stellar eyes of light,
As through the silent waste of night,
Gazing upon the world of shade,
Witness some secret youth and maid,
Who fair as thou and fond as I,
In stolen joys enamour'd lie!
So many kisses, ere I slumber,
Upon those dew-bright lips I'll number;
So many vermil, honied kisses,
Envy can never count our blisses:
No tongue shall tell the sum, but mine;
No lips shall fascinate but thine!        MOORE

VIII.  TO HIMSELF,

ON LESBIA'S INCONSTANCY.

CEASE from this idle fooling trade—
    Cease, wretch Catullus, all is o'er;
And what thou seest has long decay'd,
    E'en think it lost for evermore.

Of old thy suns were bright and clear,
    When thou, where'er her path has lain,
Wouldst chase the damsel, loved so dear
    As none will e'er be loved again.

Then were the sports of amorous jest
    Still urged by thee with new delight;
While she scarce chid and not repress'd—
    Oh then thy suns were truly bright!

She now rejects thee—cast her off,
    Nor weakly chase a flying fair;
Nor grieving live to be her scoff,
    But coldly steel thy mind to bear.

Damsel, farewell! Catullus stern
    Thy scorn disdains, thy love will shun;
And soon thy pride to grief shall turn,
    When left by him, and woo'd by none.

Think, wanton, what remains for thee:
  Who will pursue thy lonely way?
Who in thy form will beauty see?
  Whose fervent love shalt thou repay?

Whose fondling care shalt thou avow?
  Whose kisses now shalt thou return?
Whose lip in rapture bite?—But thou—
  Hold! hold! Catullus, cold and stern.   LAMB.

## THE SAME.

CEASE the sighing fool to play;
Cease to trifle life away;
Nor vainly think those joys thine own,
Which all, alas, have falsely flown.
What hours, Catullus, once were thine,
How fairly seem'd thy day to shine,
When lightly thou didst fly to meet
The girl whose smile was then so sweet—
The girl thou lov'dst with fonder pain
Than e'er thy heart can feel again.
  Ye met—your souls seem'd all in one,
Like tapers that commingling shone;
Thy heart was warm enough for both,
And hers in truth was nothing loth.
  Such were the hours that once were thine;
But, ah! those hours no longer shine.
For now the nymph delights no more
In what she loved so much before;
And all Catullus now can do,
Is to be proud and frigid too;
Nor follow where the wanton flies,
Nor sue the bliss that she denies.
False maid! he bids farewell to thee,
To love, and all love's misery;
The hey-day of his heart is o'er,
Nor will he court one favour more.
  Fly, perjured girl!—but whither fly?
Who now will praise thy cheek and eye?

N

Who now will drink the syren tone,
Which tells him thou art all his own?
Oh, none:—and he who loved before
Can never, never love thee more.     MOORE.


### THE SAME.

CATULLUS! give thy follies o'er:
Ah! wretch! what's lost expect no more:
Thy suns shone bright, when to and fro
Thou, at her beck, didst come and go:
The nymph who once thy passion proved
As never nymph shall e'er be loved.
What frolic joys would then enchant,
When thou wouldst ask and she would grant!
Then clear and bright thy suns would shine:
And doth she now thy love decline?
Then be alike refusal thine.
Follow not her, who flies from thee;
Nor wretched in despondence be.
But scorn the weakness that can feel,
And bear thy grief with breast of steel.
Farewell, O girl! whom I adore!
Catullus now laments no more:
Firm he persists: he will not woo,
Nor for unwilling favours sue.
Yet wilt thou grieve, when ask'd by none,
Think, cruel! how thy days will run!
Who to thy side shall now repair?
In whose fond eyes shalt thou be fair?
Whom wilt thou for thy lover choose?
Whose shall they call thee? false one! whose?
Who shall thy darted kisses sip,
While thy keen love-bites scar his lip?
But thou, Catullus! scorn to feel:
Persist—and let thy heart be steel.     ELTON.

## IX. TO VERANNIUS,

### ON HIS RETURN FROM SPAIN.

OF all the many loved by me,
　Of all my friends most dear,
　　Verannius, is thy travel o'er,
　　And art thou home return'd once more
To light thy brother's smile of glee,
　Thy mother's age to cheer?

Thou'rt come.　Oh blissful, blessed news!—
　Thou'rt come, and I again
　　Shall see and hear thee, in the way
　　I loved in former time, portray
The splendid towns, the mountain views,
　The tribes, and deeds of Spain.

I warm shall press thee to my breast,
　Where fervent welcomes burn.
　　What mortal, though he dare to think
　　Of pleasure he may largely drink,
Is half so joyful, or so blest,
　As I in his return?　　　LAMB.

X　THE INTERVIEW WITH VARUS AND HIS MISTRESS.

As I was idling time away
Just by the Forum t'other day,
　My Varus took me thence
To see the wanton, his delight;
And, faith! she struck me at first sight
　To want nor charms nor sense.

We then fell into conversation.
About Bithynia's situation,
　The value of the land,
And what my profit there had been:
I mention'd truly all I'd seen,
　And how things really stand.

N 2

" That not the Pretor nor his train
Could there afford from any gain
    More sumptuous dress or fare ;
And sure not we, that Pretor's slaves,
The worst of profligates and knaves,
    Who prized us not a hair."

" Of course," she said, " as they relate
'Tis usual, you some slaves for state
    To bear your litter bought."
I felt a little pride arise ;
And was not willing in her eyes
    To be a pauper thought.

So cried, " Oh, yes.   Though luck was bad,
It was not on the whole so sad,
    That I eight slaves should lack."
In truth, I never here nor there
Possess'd a single slave to bear
    My litter on his back.

Said she, a harlot thorough-bred !
" Catullus, lend me, pray, that bed,
    I wish but to be taken
To where Serapis holds his fane "——
" Stay ! stay !" said I, " let's think again—
    I 've none—I was mistaken.

" 'Tis Cinna's bed, scarce his alone,
I use it just as 'twere my own :
    Who's owner nought care I.
Thou 'rt an uncivil, troublous jade,
Whose artful, mercenary trade
    Won't let one tell a lie."          LAMB.


XI.  THE PARTING MESSAGE TO LESBIA.
ADDRESSED TO FURIUS AND AURELIUS.

COMPANIONS, who would gladly go
With me through every toil below
    To man's remotest seats :
Whether Catullus should explore
Far India, on whose echoing shore
    The eastern billow beats :

Whether he seek Hyrcania wild,
The Tartar hordes, or Arabs mild,
  Or Parthia's archer train:
Or tread that intersected isle,
Whence pouring forth the sev'n-fold Nile
  Discolours all the main.

Whether across the Alps he toil,
To view the war-ennobled soil
  Where Cæsar's trophies stand ;
The Rhine that saw its Gaul's disgrace,
Or dare the painted Briton race
  In their extremest land.

Companions dear, prepared to wend
Where'er the gods may place your friend,
  And every lot to share ;
A few unwelcome words receive,
And to that once-loved fair I leave
  My latest message bear.

Still let her live and still be blest,
By profligates in hundreds prest,
  Still sport in ease and wealth ;
Still of those hundreds love not one,
Still cast off each by turns undone
  In fortune and in health.

But let her deem my passion o'er :
Her guilt has crush'd, to bloom no more,
  The love her beauty raised ;
As droops the flower, the meadow's pride,
Which springing by the furrow's side
  The passing share has grazed.        LAMB.


PART OF THE SAME.

COMRADES and friends, with whom where'er
  The Fates have will'd through life I've roved,
Now speed ye home, and with you bear
  These bitter words to her I've loved.

Tell her from fool to fool to run,
   Where'er her vain caprice may call;
Of all her dupes, not loving one,
   But ruining and maddening all.

Bid her forget—what now is past—
   Our once dear love, whose ruin lies
Like a fair flower, the meadow's last,
   That feels the ploughshare's edge, and dies.
MOORE.

### XII. TO ASINIUS,

#### ON HIS PRACTICAL JOKES.

ASINIUS, Marrucinian vile,
   Think you, when wine gives life to jest,
'Tis wit to filch with left-hand wile
   The napkin of the careless guest?

Poor idiot, can you not perceive
   How rude, how low the deed you do?
But should you not my words believe,
   Your brother, Pollio, says so too.

Pollio with hoards of gold would part
   No more to see you thus disgraced;
For that's a youth of generous heart,
   Of lively wit, and purest taste.

Expect a satire coarse and keen,
   Or back to me your plunder send;
'Tis not its value moves my spleen,
   But it's the keepsake of a friend.

A dearest friend from Spanish skies
   Sent me the gift you stole so sly;
And when the giver's love I prize,
   I prize his smallest gift as high.   LAMB.

### XIII. INVITATION TO FABULLUS.

FABULLUS, thou shalt be my guest
At supper soon, if Heaven's behest
   No otherwise decree:

The feast too must be rich and rare,
And since thou lov'st luxurious fare,
  Bring such a feast with thee.

And bring the girl with breast of snow,
And wine and wit of ready flow,
  And laughter's joyous peal;
Bid but all these my board attend,
And then no doubt, my gallant friend.
  We 'll have a glorious meal.

For in my coffers spiders weave
Their webs in peace: so thou receive
  For all thy kind expense
My lays, of love alone that sing,
Or aught, if aught thy friend can bring,
  To please some finer sense.

And I can give thee essence rare
That Loves and Graces gave my fair:
  So sweet its odour flows;
Thou 'lt pray the gods " may touch and taste
Be quite in smell alone effaced,
  And I become all nose."    LAMB.

### XIV. TO CALVUS, AN ADVOCATE,

IN RETURN FOR A PRESENT OF POEMS.

DID I not dearer than my eyes
Your friendship, lively Calvus, prize,
With fiercer hate I should regard you,
Than e'en Vatinius feels toward you.

For what can I have ever done,
Or ever said in spite or fun,
That you my leisure hours should curse
With such a heap of wretched verse?
Gods, on that client curses send,
Who gave these poems to my friend!
Yet, if the gift so choice and pleasant
Was that poor pedant Sulla's present,
I'm glad, your legal toil to aid,
So vile a wretch is thus repaid.

Great gods!—I cannot calmly look
Upon the dreadful cursed book,
Which cruel Calvus yet could send
Catullus, whom he calls his friend.
I bore from morn till day was flying,
The torments of protracted dying;
E'en while the Saturnalia gay
Rejoiced the year's most festive day.

But, wag, you shall not 'scape me so;
With earliest sunrise will I go
Round every library and stall,
Collect Suffenus' works, and all
That e'er that crew of viler note,
The Cesii and Aquinii wrote;
All foolish odes, and poisonous trash,
And dull bombast and balderdash;
And send them, to repay to thee
The torments thou hast heap'd on me.

For you, ye scribblers, hence! I spurn you
Again to that same place return ye
Whence ye began your cursed journey.
Avaunt, our age's worst disasters!
Avaunt, ye wretched poetasters!        LAMB

## XV.  TO AURELIUS.

MYSELF and my best loves to thee,
'Tis a small boon of modesty,
 Aurelius, I commend;
Then spare, although thy pamper'd taste
May long for what is fresh and chaste,
 The favourite of thy friend.

I mean not from the harmless throng,
Who busy walk the streets along,
 Intent on sordid pelf,
But from thy passion's rampant rage,
That dares both old and young engage,
 From thy lascivious self.

Let this one single instance be
Of thy surprising chastity ;—
    When gone, indulge thy flame ;
But should thy lustful heat now dare
To wound me where I least can bear,
    And clothe my head with shame ;

Soon may the punishment, prepared
For such offence, be thy reward ;
    Exposed to public view,
Oh may thy legs be fitly tied,
Radish and mullets then applied
    Inflict the torture due !          NOTT.

## XVI.   DEFENCE OF HIS AMATORY POEMS

### TO AURELIUS AND FURIUS.

AND dare ye, profligates, arraign
The ardour of my sprightly strain,
    And e'en myself asperse ?
And, if his lines are gay and free,
Deem ye the poet's self must be
    As wanton as his verse ?

The sacred bard, to Muses dear,
Himself should pass a chaste career,
    And pure his blood should roll :
But let his numbers warmly flow,
And paint in all their native glow
    The passions of the soul.

His verse should be of power to move
Not only fervent boys with love,
    And feed the blazing flame ;
But torpid age should feel the strain
Raise every youthful heat again,
    And nerve the feeblest frame.

No more, ye rakes, peruse my line :
By minds debauch'd and base as thine
    It scarce is understood.

It sings of wine, of woman's charms,
Of love, of all that cheers and warms
   The generous and the good.

But ye, on whom no fair one smiles,
Whose hours no social board beguiles,
   I scorn your blame or praise.
Whom love and favouring woman bless,
Who taste the raptures they express,
   Will never blame my lays.     Lamb.


### XVII.  ON A STUPID HUSBAND.

ADDRESSED TO THE TOWN WHERE HE RESIDED.

Thou lively town, that wouldst with gladness see
On thy long bridge the sports of rustic glee,
   And nimble dancers bounding to the strain,
Didst thou not fear the rotten props would throw
Thy tottering bridge into the marsh below,
   Ne'er from its muddy bed to rise again ;

One boon, one sight, to raise my laughter, grant ;
And may a bridge so strong supply thy want,
   That the wild Salii's dance can nothing hurt.
I ask that one, a townsman of thine own,
May only from thy bridge be headlong thrown,
   And neck and shoulders plump into the dirt.

It should be there, where lies the deepest mud,
And greenest mire of all the stagnant flood.
   The man's a senseless dolt, whom nought can warm
His wit or sense no rivalry can hold
With any boy, who is but two years old,
   And rock'd to sleep upon his father's arm.

His wife's a girl in blooming beauty's dawn,
More soft and tender than the youngling fawn ;
   Like ripest grapes demanding gentlest care.
He lets her rove uncheck'd her giddy way,
Where'er, with whom she lists, to jest and play,
   Nor values all her charms a single hair.

Life, for his only care himself, he keeps,
Dull as the axe-fell'd alder tree, that sleeps
  In some remote Ligurian ditch confined:
He scarcely seems to know he has a wife;
And dozes on his lethargy of life
  Deaf to her accents, to her beauty blind.

E'en while he breathes, while strong his life-blood flows,
Whether he lives or not he scarcely knows.
  Oh, let him from thy bridge be headlong cast,
Plunged deep with all his stupor in the flood;
And his dull soul in the congenial mud,
  Like the mule's iron shoe, leave sticking fast! LAMB.

## XVIII. TO THE GARDEN GOD.

To thee I dedicate this green retreat;
  Priapus, sacred be the shade to thee:
Whether some grove, or Lampsacus thy seat,
  Detains thy steps, O sylvan deity!
Thou who in towns that deck the shelly coast
Of much-famed Hellespont art worshipp'd most. NOTT.

## XIX. THE GARDEN GOD'S ADDRESS.

THIS farm, young passengers, these marshy meads,
This cottage thatch'd with sedge and matted reeds,
Hewn from the season'd oak by rustic skill,
I long have nursed, and am their guardian still.

Years still succeeding by my influence bear
Some wealth, some added blessing to my care.
For sire and sons, who live and prosper here,
Worship my name, and as their god revere.
The grateful siro is careful to erase
Moss and rough brambles round my altar's base.
The gifts are small that childish hands impart,
But gain their value from the giver's heart;
A crown of flowers, the earliest of the year,
And the green corn's yet moist and tender ear.
Round me the purple violets are pour'd;
The poppy's crimson flower, the pallid gourd,

The fragrant apple, are as offerings paid,
And grapes that ripen in the vineyard's shade.
Oft bearded goats (but tell it not again)
And their hoof'd ewes with blood my altar stain.

For all these honours, fix'd upon this spot,
I guard my master's vines and humble cot.
Then, boys, refrain from theft, nor pilfer here;
Rich is our neighbour, and his garden's near:
There a small loss Priapus little heeds;
There's plenteous spoil. This pathway thither leads.

LAMB

## XX.  THE GARDEN GOD'S THREAT.

FORM'D from the season'd poplar's heart
By the unskilful rustic's art,
From every foe and danger free,
I guard the little spot you see;
And save from theft and rapine's hand
My humble master's cot and land.

To me the flowery chaplet, Spring;
The deep brown ear doth Summer bring;
Autumn the luscious grape bestows;
The pale-green olive, Winter snows.
The she-goat bears from my rich down
Dugs swoll'n with milk to yonder town.
The lamb that's fatten'd in my fold
Sends back its owner chinking gold.
The tender heifer hence that goes,
While here the frantic mother lows,
Oft pours its gushing blood to stain
The threshold of the richest fane.

Then, trav'ller, view this god with fear,
And check all thirst for plunder here.
'Twere well thou didst; for I can be
Quick means of punishment to thee.
Say'st thou, " Come on," and scorn'st advice?
Behold the cotter in a trice;
And, if he please thy sides to drub,
Myself will serve him for a club.     LAMB.

## XXI. TO AURELIUS.

Aurelius, father of the treat,
Where hunger finds not aught to eat ;
Such fasting treats were ne'er of yore,
Nor are, nor ever will be more ;
Thy lustful thoughts too freely rove,
Fain wouldst thou tempt my pretty love,
Nor mak'st a secret of the thing,
But to my charmer's side dost cling ;
Dost boldly, impudently toy,
And every wanton art employ ;
Yet vain shall prove thy base intent,
For e'en my guilt should thine prevent :
Wert thou high fed, all this I 'd bear ;
But that the one I hold most dear
Should learn to hunger and to thirst,
So moves my choler that 'twill burst.
Then hold, while thou canst honest be ;
If not, I 'll do a deed for thee.       Nott.


## XXII. ON SUFFENUS.

### ADDRESSED TO VARRUS.

Varrus, you well Suffenus know,
The wit, the scholar, and the beau.
Alas ! he also makes at times
A fearful quantity of rhymes.
I think a thousand lines, ay ten,
Or more, have issued from his pen.
Not written upon foolscap base,
To blot, and alter, and erase ;
On royal paper smooth and fine
He pens at once the perfect line ;
With edges gilt, and binding new,
And silver clasp, and silken clew,
Its shape by rule exactly right,
And all with highest polish bright.

But, if his verses are but read,
The wit's, the scholar's fame is fled.

The veriest oaf, the dullest proser,
Must seem more bright than the composer:
Such different lights to those will show him
Who see himself, or read his poem.

What title can this creature fit,
Who now appears a very wit,
Or aught, if ever aught arises,
Society more seeks and prizes;
But, when to verse he turns his mind,
Is duller than the dullest hind;
Yet, ah! for ever spends his time
In toil to build the lofty rhyme?
He's ne'er so truly blest, as when
He uses his poetic pen;
So high he rates his wit, and ever
Wonders to find himself so clever.

Yet we are all, I doubt, in truth
Deceived like this complacent youth;
All, I am much afraid, demean us
In some one thing just like Suffenus.
For still to every man that lives
His share of errors nature gives;
But they, as 'tis in fable sung,
Are in a bag behind us hung;
And our formation kindly lacks
The power to see behind our backs.          LAMB.

### THE SAME.

VARRUS, that wretch Suffenus, whom you know
Is handsome, talkative, and is a beau;
What's more, the coxcomb makes pretence to wit,
And verses has incontinently writ.
So great his stock of rhymes, so large his store,
He has at least ten thousand lines or more,
All written out so curious and so clean,
That common writing paper's thought too mean.
His paper's royal, and his books are new,
With silver bosses tempting to the view,
Tied up with ribbons of the deepest red,          [lead.
Each page with pumice smooth'd, and ruled with crimson

But read him, and this fop so neat and nice
Is changed into a sloven in a trice.
Suffenus—Oh! the foolish scribbling dotard
In's writings seems a ditcher or a goatherd;
So much he's altered from the man he was.
How can this be? and what can be the cause?
Yet he that but just now in others' sense
Was destitute of every excellence,
Was made the common jest of all the town,
And thought much more unlearned than a clown,
Is wise, and to perfection, in his own.
When he puts pen to paper and indites,
No man so blest as he in what he writes.
He joys so much, and wonders at his skill,
As if the Muses had inspired his quill.
No wonder; all are subject to mistakes;
None but in something a Suffenus makes.
Our neighbour's bunch upon his back is known,
But we forget what rises from our own.        ANON.

### XXIII. CONGRATULATIONS ON POVERTY.

#### TO FURIUS.

FURIUS, thy life no servants tease,
  No chests of gold with watchings tire;
No downy bed to harbour fleas,
  No blazing hearth thy house to fire.

Thou feed'st thy father and his wife,
  Whose sharp-set teeth on flints could browse.
How blest must be your careless life
  With him, and his old wooden spouse!

Oh truly blest!—ye keep your health,
  Digest your food with ease; nor dread
Nor fire, nor ruin's curse, nor stealth,
  Plunder, nor poison in your bread.

Ye all the ills and dangers scorn,
  The fear of which makes many sigh;
Your bodies drier are than horn,
  Or aught, if there is aught more dry.

Still warm'd by Summer's burning rays,
  Or cool'd in Winter's snowy vest,
Physick'd by famine, can your days
  Be otherwise than truly blest?

All fears of plethora ye may spurn,
  And gout's and fever's anguish keen.
When others swell, and throb, and burn,
  Ye still continue cool and clean.

Furius, no more these gifts disdain,
  Nor rate them small, nor e'er infest
The gods with prayers for wealth again;
  For really thou art very blest.    LAMB

### THE SAME.

NOR menial slave, nor coffer strong,
Nor blazing hearth to thee belong;
Nor e'en a spider, nor a louse,
Can live within thy famish'd house:
Yet does my Furius to his cost
A father and a step-dame boast;
So hungry, so extremely thin,
Their teeth a very flint would skin;
And such thy sire, so lean his wife,
You needs must lead a pleasant life:
What wonder? when, beyond a question,
You all are blest with good digestion;
Have nought to fear, nor fire, nor losses,
Nor impious deeds, nor poisonous doses;
Nor all the dangers which await
The wretchedness of human state.
  Your harden'd bodies drier are
Than horn, or aught that's drier far;
And nursed by hunger, cold, and heat,
How can your bliss but be complete?
From you no sweat, no spittle flows;
No rheum, no snivel from your nose:
Besides, one cleanliness superior
To all you boast, that your posterior
Is so exceeding trim and sweet,
A salt-cellar's not half so neat:

Scarce ten times in a year you vent
Your indurated excrement;
So indurated ne'er was known
Or shrivell'd bean, or hardest stone;
Which, rubb'd, and crumbled o'er and o'er,
Would leave the finger as before.
Then hold not cheap, nor yet despise
Blessings, my Furius, you should prize;
Nor, as you're wont, ask more of heaven,
To thee enough's already given! NOTT.

## XXIV. TO JUVENTIUS.

### ON HIS CHOICE OF A FRIEND.

DEAR boy, of thy race thou'rt the blossom and pride;
 Not only of all who these days may adorn,
But all who through ages long distant have died,
 And of all who shall ever hereafter be born.

With a wretch, who commands neither servant nor purse,
 Wilt *thou* then thus warmly in friendship combine?
Oh! rather than thee his affection should curse,
 I would almost have made him a crony of mine.

"He's a gallant," thou say'st. May be so; still 'tis plain
 This gallant nor slave has, nor cash at command;
And, whate'er thou may'st deem him, the world will disdain,
 Till a slave's at his heels, or a purse in his hand.
          LAMB.

### THE SAME.

O LOVELIEST of Juventian bloom!
 Thou bud with early beauty graced!
Unequall'd by the age to come,
 Or by the present or the past!

Oh hadst thou given but paltry pelf
 To him who wants both slave and chest,
I had not grieved!—But that thyself
 By yon lewd wretch should be possest!

o

You 'll cry, " He 's handsome !"—so he **may ;**
 Still that he 's poor you needs must grant :
Reject, extenuate all I say ;
 Both slave and chest he 's doom'd to want !   Noтт


### XXV.   TO THALLUS.

Voluptuous Thallus ! soft, I own,
 As rabbit's fur, as cygnet's down ;
 Soft as the tip of softest ear ;
As flimsy age, or spider's silken snare !

Yet more rapacious than the sea,
 Which vext with storms sweeps all away ;
 Whilst boding birds, with dismal cry,
O'er the tempestuous, wintry billows fly.

My cloak thou shalt return, I vow,
 My fine Setabian napkin too ;
 My tablets from the Thynian coast ;
All which as lineal wealth, vain fool, you boast !

Unglue thy hands, my things restore !
 Lest thy soft breech and sides made sore
 With unaccustom'd stripes, you rave,
Lash'd like some skiff that dares wild ocean's wave.
                                        Noтт.


### XXVI.   TO FURIUS, ON HIS VILLA.

Thy villa, Furius, is not placed
 The southern gales to bear ;
Nor north, nor east, nor west is faced,
 But screen'd from every air.

But, oh ! 'tis out at mortgage placed,
 'Gainst sums thou can'tst repay ;
And that 's of all the likeliest blast
 To sweep it quite away.        Lamb.


### XXVII.   TO HIS CUP-BEARER.

Boy, who in my festive home
Mak'st the rich Falernian foam.

Broach my oldest wine, and pour
Till the goblet mantles o'er.
Gay Postumia thus ordains,
When she at my banquet reigns.
Not the juice that swells its shape
Is so native to the grape,
As the draught that fills the bowl
Is congenial to her soul.

Hence, ye waters ! hence abstain,
Generous liquor's chilly bane !
Hence, where'er it please you, flow !
Hence, to surly wisdom go !
Pure this draught as from the vine
Bacchus' self had press'd the wine.    LAMB.


### XXVIII. TO VERANNIUS AND FABULLUS,

#### ON THEIR RETURN FROM SPAIN.

WELL, friends, who big with hopes of gain,
Have follow'd Piso into Spain,
Your luggage is compact and tight,
And as it went of carriage light.
Verannius, friend, Fabullus, say,
What wealth ye gather'd in your way ?

Did ye in that curmudgeon's suite
Enough of cold and hunger meet ;
And do now your accounts contain
Expenses in the place of gain,
Like me, who from my Pretor's tour
Came, 'stead of richer, much more poor ?

Ah, Memmius ! ill your train you treated,
And all the time abused and cheated :
And now, for all that I can view,
It's just the same with both of you.
Ye, by your scoundrel trick'd, repine ;
Your scoundrel is as great as mine.

Now speed, thou fool, whoe'er intends
To thrive by courting noble friends ;

And every evil man can know
May gods and goddesses bestow
On you, ye Pretors, who disgrace
The Roman name and Roman race.    LAMB.


### XXIX. UPON MAMURRA.

#### ADDRESSED TO CÆSAR.

WHO can behold, or who endure;
    Save rakes devoid of truth and shame,
    Or gambling cheats, or gluttons tame;
That base Mamurra should procure
And squander free the spoil and products all
Of farthest Britain's isle, and rich Transalpine Gaul?

Miscreant Romulus, canst thou see,
    And suffer this?—Then thine the shame,
    The rake's, the cheat's, the glutton's name.
Soon proud and all-abounding he
Through all our marriage beds shall wanton rove,
Gay as Adonis young, or Venus' snowy dove.

Canst thou still see and bear this thing,
    Miscreant Romulus?—Thine the shame,
    The rake's, the cheat's, the glutton's name.
And for this name, unrivall'd king,
Proud didst thou bear afar thy conquering crest,
E'en to the farthest isle that gems the distant West,

That he, thy lustful friend, should prey
    On all the spoil, thy valour's prize?
    "What matters it?" thy bounty cries,
"A little wealth he throws away."
And has he then but little wealth devour'd?
First he his father's hoards on low companions shower'd

Then by the spoil of Pontus fed,
    And then by all Iberia gave,
    And Tagus from its golden wave.
Him justly Gaul and Britain dread.
Justly his grasping sway may cause alarms
More than his emperor's name and all-victorious arms.

Oh! why so base a favourite choose,
　Who has nor wit, nor use, nor power,
　　Save all thy riches to devour?
Didst thou, O son-in-law! then lose,
Didst thou, O conquering father! then obtain
The empire of the world to be this minion's gain? LAMB.

## XXX. TO ALPHENUS, ON HIS PERFIDY.

FORGETFUL, false to those who love thee best,
Alphenus, can no kindness from thy breast
　E'en I, thy loved companion, know?
No pitying pause, no doubts relenting stay
Thy reckless course, still eager to betray
　With equal falsehood friend or foe.

Yet faithless deeds the lords of heaven offend;
Though thou regardless canst behold thy friend
　By anguish and despair opprest.
All trust is past, let man of man beware.
Thou, who by show of faith and friendliest care
　Hadst made me open all my breast,

Changed from thyself, now bid'st the roving air
Thine oaths, thy pledges, far from memory bear,
　And scatter in the tempest's course.
The gods, though thou forgett'st, remember all,
And outraged faith will to thy breast recall
　Thy perjury, and its due remorse. LAMB.

## XXXI. TO THE PENINSULA OF SIRMIO.

### UPON HIS RETURN TO HIS COUNTRY HOUSE THERE.

SIRMIO, of all the shores the gem,
　The isles where circling Neptune strays;
　　Whether the vast and boisterous main
Or lake's more limpid waves they stem,
　How gladly on thy lands I gaze!
　　How blest to visit thee again!

I scarce believe, while rapt I stand,
　That I have left the Thynian fields,
　　And all Bithynia far behind,

And safely view my favourite land.
  Oh bliss, when care dispersing yields
    To full repose the placid mind!

Then when the mind its load lays down;
  When we regain, all hazards past,
    And with long ceaseless travel tired,
Our household god again our own;
  And press in tranquil sleep at last
    The well-known bed so oft desired—

This can alone atonement make
  For every toil.   Hail, Sirmio sweet!
    Be gay, thy lord hath ceased to roam!
Ye laughing waves of Lydia's lake,
  Smile all around!  Thy master greet
    With all thy smiles, my pleasant home!  Lamb

#### THE SAME.

Sirmio! the lovely eye of every isle
And green peninsula, where'er they smile;
Whether the fresh or briny wave surround,
The floating lake, or ocean's blue profound;
With what a joyous willingness of mind
I thee revisit, leaving far behind,
Still half incredulous, Bithynia's plain,
And gaze in safety on thy scenes again!
Oh! what more blissful than to loose the breast
From cares, and bid the unburden'd spirit rest?
Sit by our home fire-side; forget the toil
Of weary wanderings on a foreign soil;
And on the long'd-for bed sink down at last
In full-felt ease; o'erpaid for hardships past!
Hail, pleasant Sirmio! for thy master's sake
Rejoice! ye waters of the Lydian lake,
Brighten in joy! and each remember'd thing,
That laughs of home, shall smile my welcoming!
                                Elton.

#### THE SAME.

Sweet Sirmio! thou the very eye
  Of all peninsulas and isles,

That in our lakes of silver lie,
   Or sleep, enwreath'd by Neptune's smiles—

How gladly back to thee I fly!
   Still doubting, asking—*can* it be
That I have left Bithynia's sky,
   And gaze in safety upon thee?

Oh! what is happier than to find
   Our hearts at ease, our perils past;
When, anxious long, the lighten'd mind
   Lays down its load of care at last.

When tired with toil o'er land and deep,
   Again we tread the welcome floor
Of our own home, and sink to sleep
   On the long-wish'd-for bed once more.

This, this it is, that pays alone
   The ills of all life's former track.—
Shine out, my beautiful, my own
   Sweet Sirmio, greet thy master back.

And thou, fair Lake, whose water quaffs
   The light of heaven like Lydia's sea,
Rejoice, rejoice—let all that laughs
   Abroad, at home, laugh out for me! MOORE.

### THE SAME.

O BEST of all the scatter'd spots that lie
In sea or lake,—apple of landscape's eye,—
How gladly do I drop within thy nest,
With what a sigh of full, contented rest,
Scarce able to believe my journey's o'er,
And that these eyes behold thee safe once more!
Oh where's the luxury like the smile at heart,
When the mind breathing, lays its load apart,—
When we come home again, tired out, and spread
The loosen'd limbs o'er all the wish'd-for bed!
This, this alone is worth an age of toil.
Hail, lovely Sirmio! Hail, paternal soil!
Joy, my bright waters, joy: your master's come!
Laugh every dimple on the cheek of home!
                   LEIGH HUNT.

## XXXII. THE RENDEZVOUS.

### TO HYPSITHILLA.

KIND of heart, of beauty bright,
Pleasure's soul, and love's delight,
None by nature graced above thee,
Hypsithilla, let me love thee.

Tell me then, that I shall be
Welcome when I come to thee;
And at noon's inspiring tide
Close thy gate to all beside.
Let no idle wish to roam
Steal thy thought from joys at home;
But prepare thy charms to aid
Every frolic love e'er play'd.
Speed thy message. Day goes fast.
Now's the hour; the banquet's past:
Mid-day suns and goblets flowing
Set my frame with passion glowing.

Speed thee, wanton, fair and free!
Tell me I must haste to thee. LAMB

### THE SAME.

MY Hypsithilla, charming fair,
My life, my soul, ah! hear my prayer:
Thy grateful summons quickly send,
And bless at noon, with joy, thy friend.
And if my fair one will comply,
And not her sighing swain deny,
Take care the door be then unbarr'd,
And let no spy be on the guard.
And thou, the aim of my desire,
Attend at home my amorous fire.
Prepare thy bosom to receive
All that so much love can give:
Prepare to meet repeated joy,
Continued bliss without alloy,
Dissolving still in thy dear arms,
Still raised by thy reviving charms,

To onsets fresh of sprightly pleasure,
Tumultuous joy beyond all measure.
But dally not with my desire,
Nor quash with thy delays my fire.
Bursting with love upon my couch I lie,
Forestalling with desire the distant joy.    ANON.

### XXXIII. ON THE VIBENNII.

OLD Vibennius of all the bath thieves thou first thief!
Of all monsters in lust, young Vibennius thou chief!
This is gifted with hands which are ever rapacious,
That is gifted with parts which are full as voracious;
Then, oh why don't ye both into banishment go,
And deservedly wander in deserts of woe?
Not a soul but the father's mean rapines must tell;
And thou, son, canst no more thy stale infamy sell.    NOTT.

### XXXIV. ODE TO DIANA.

VIRGINS fair, and boys yet chaste,
    We Diana's service bear;
Raise her votive chorus, haste,
    Spotless youths and virgins fair!

Mighty child of mightiest Jove,
    Thee, Latona, we adore;
In the Delian olive grove
    Thee thy beauteous mother bore.

Born to be the sacred queen
    Of the mountain and the wood,
Of the valley's placid scene,
    Of the river's echoing flood.

Soothing woman's labouring throe,
    Goddess, thou Lucina hight;
Thee, we powerful Trivia know,
    Luna, thee, with borrow'd light.

By thy monthly rise and wane
    Still th' apportion'd year is sped;
Still thy power with fruits and grain
    Stores the peasant's homely shed.

Be thou, by whatever name
  Please thee, sacred ; and embrace
Still with guardian care the same
  Ancient Rome's heroic race.    LAMB.


### XXXV.  INVITATION TO CECILIUS.

Go, paper, to Cecilius say,
To him I love, the bard whose lay
  The sweetest thoughts attend ;
Say, he must quit his loved retreat,
Comum and Larius' lake, to greet
  Verona and his friend.

Here let him some advice receive,
A friend of his and mine will give.
  If wise, he 'll speed his way ;
Although the fair his haste may check
A thousand times, and on his neck
  May hang, and beg his stay.

For, when of old she read his strains
To her on Dindymus who reigns,
  Did raging passion seize
On all her heart ; and since that day
She idly wears his youth away
  In love and slothful ease.

Yet thee, fair girl, I not abuse,
More learned than the Sapphic Muse,
  And warm with all her fire ;
For, ah ! so soft, so sweetly flow'd
His melting strains, his tender ode,
  They well might love inspire.    LAMB.


### XXXVI.  TO "THE ANNALS."

#### A POEM, BY VOLUSIUS.

VOLUSIUS' Annals—worthless lay !
  E'en than thy writer's self more stupid ;
'Tis thou, my damsel's vow must pay
  To sacred Venus, and to Cupid.

She vow'd, that, should my soften'd heart
   Be reconciled to her again;
And at her I should cease to dart
   My cross and keen Iambic strain;

That she would give to him, the lame
   Grim god, whom yet Jove's anger curses,
To be consumed by evil flame,
   The chosen worst of all bad verses.

No fruitful tree must form the pyre,
   Which heaven protects and man loves well;
Ill-omen'd wood shall feed the fire,
   Dear only to the gods of hell.

Thou art the poem, all declare,
   Fore-destined by her frolic oath;
Then, oh, thou goddess bright and fair,
   Form'd of the azure ocean's froth;

Goddess of Syria's open meads,
   Of sacred woods, Idalia's boast,
Cnidus, where grow the poet's reeds,
   Amathus, and Ancona's coast,

Of Golgos, and Dyrrachium's port,
   The market of the Adrian main;
Accept the vow, nor deem our sport
   That taste should shun, or wit disdain.

Then come, ye pointless, rugged lays,
   Into the fire; 'tis there you're due.
Then, whether Venus blame or praise,
   We shall at least get rid of you.    Lamb.


### XXXVII. THE COMPLAINT.

#### TO CORNIFICIUS.

O Cornificius! all goes ill,
   With wasting cares I bend;
And more each day and hour they still
   Oppress thy wretched friend.

The tender lay which thou couldst frame
   Might somewhat grief remove;
And oft thy reckless heart I blame,
   That thus neglects my love.

Some plaintive strain my grief might please,
   How sad soe'er it be:
The sighs of old Simonides
   Are not too sad for me.        LAMB.

### THE SAME.

Sick, Cornificius, is thy friend,
Sick to the heart; and sees no end
Of wretched thoughts, that gathering fast
Threaten to wear him out at last.
And yet you never come and bring—
Though 't were the least and easiest thing—
A comfort in that talk of thine:—
You vex me:—this, to love like mine?
Prithee, a little talk for ease, for ease,
Full as the tears of poor Simonides.  LEIGH HUNT.

### XXXVIII.  TO THE FREQUENTERS OF A CERTAIN TAVERN

O THOU brothel most lewd, and you dissolute host,
From the cup-honour'd brothers who hold the ninth post!
Do you think that you only have passions and power,
Thus to mingle with wantons and spend the soft hour?
That no girl, be she dwarfish, tall, snowy, or brown,
—Each soul else a rank goat—but must kiss you alone?
What; because a good hundred at least, if not two,
You for ever sit down at the door of your stew;
Do you fancy, you fools, as resentment may call,
I'll not venture one stroke, and let fly at you all?
Oh, in faith, but I will!—and 'twere serving you right,
With my stick, duly burnt, o'er your brothel to write:
Since my girl, whom these arms could no longer detain;
So beloved that none e'er shall be so loved again;
For whose sake in a thousand mad riots I've bled;
Hath with you ta'en her place both to board and to bed:

And you love her forsooth ; you sweet, delicate souls !
Oh 'tis shameful, you wretches, fit only for trulls !
But of all the lewd, infamous posse, I vow,
The most lewd, the most worthless, Egnatius, art thou.
Celtiberia's soft son, for long tresses renown'd ;
Celtiberia, the country where rabbits abound ;
Of thy bushy, black beard, who canst only be vain,
And thy teeth nicely polish'd with urine of Spain.    NOTT.

### XXXIX. ON EGNATIUS.

BECAUSE Egnatius' teeth are nicely white,
To grin and show them is his sole delight.
If haply at some trial he appear,
Where eloquence commands the gushing tear,
He grins.—If, at the pile, the duteous son,
The childless mother weeps, for ever gone,
He grins.—In short, whate'er the time or place,
Do as he may, the grin still marks his face :
'Tis his disease ; and, speaking as I feel,
We cannot call it decent or genteel.
Then, good Egnatius, list to what I sing :
Didst thou from Roman or from Sabine spring,
From Tiburine, or Umbrian highly fed ;
Or with Etrurians greasy wert thou bred ;
Wert thou descended of Lanuvian race,
Remark'd alike for teeth, and swarthy face ;
Or—that my native land may mention claim—
Wert thou like me of Transpadanian name ;
Wert thou a son of any region, where
Teeth are kept clean with water that is fair ?
E'en then that ceaseless, ill-timed grin forego :
A silly laugh 's the silliest thing I know :
But, Celtiberian ! in that country born,
Where what you make at night you every morn
Rub on your teeth and scarlet gums ; for you
To smirk and smile but proves this scandal true :
The more your teeth are polish'd white and fine,
The more you 've only swill'd of filthy brine.    NOTT.

### XL.  TO RAVIDUS.

WRETCH Ravidus, what impulse ill
 Has hurried thee away
A base, unenvied place to fill
 In my Iambic lay?
What deity thus ill-invoked
This senseless squabble hath provoked?

Wouldst thou be known and mention'd wide
 The theme of trite report?
Well, have thy wish.—Since thou hast tried
 My fair one's love to court;
My verses shall preserve thy name
In everlasting scorn and shame.  LAMB.


### XLI.  ON MAMURRA'S MISTRESS.

CAN that hackney'd jade be sane?
 She, whom dirt and vice surrounds,
Spendthrift Formian's mistress plain
 Asks me for two hundred pounds.

Neighbours, quick, physicians have in,
 All her friends and kinsmen summon.
Doubt not she is mad; she's raving,
 Thinks herself a pretty woman.  LAMB


### XLII.  ON A COURTESAN,

#### WHO KEPT HIS TABLETS FROM HIM.

COME, verses, come at my request;
 Nor, Satire, now thy coarseness lack;
Yon filthy wench makes me her jest,
 And will not give your tablets back.

If ye can bear the task, with me
 Come claim them, worry, tease, and bait.
Ask ye of whom?—Of her ye see
 Who struts with yon affected gait;

Who gapes with stunning laughter wide
   As is the Gallic beagle's grin.
Come, Satire, come, demand, and chide,
   And persecute with ceaseless din.

Restore them, wench of vilest trade!
   Restore the tablets, wretch accurst!
Dost thou not heed?   Oh filth! oh jade!
   Oh all that's lowest, basest, worst!

And will not this abuse prevail?
   At least, however rare, let's place
One blush, if in all else we fail,
   Upon the strumpet's iron face.

Shout then, in terms more loud and keen,
   "Drab, harlot! give them back again!
Give back the tablets, filthy quean!"
   Yet she's not moved, and all is vain.

Ah! we must breathe a softer tale.
   Then, "Chaste and modest maid, restore
Our tablets, pray!"—That must prevail,
   For that she never heard before.   LAMB.


### XLIII. TO MAMURRA'S MISTRESS.

THOUGH splaw thy feet, and snub thy nose,
Thy fingers short, and unlike sloes
   Thine eyes in hue may be ;
Thy lip with driv'lling moisture dew'd,
Thy language vulgar, manners rude,
   Yet, wanton, hail to thee !

And does the province praise thy grace ;
And e'en presume thy form and face
   With Lesbia to compare?
Then why should I thy charms dispraise?
Mid vulgar fools, in tasteless days,
   'Tis useless to be fair.   LAMB.

### XLIV.  TO HIS OWN FARM,

#### WHILE RESIDING THERE.

WHETHER, my farm, the Sabine bounds,
Or Tibur hold thy peaceful grounds;
  (For those who love me like a friend
Call thee of Tibur; those who come
To vex my pride, with any sum
  That thou art Sabine will contend.)

But whether that, or truly class'd
'Mong Tibur's lands, well pleased I've pass'd
  Some days in thy sequester'd seat.
Thou from my loaded breast hast driven
A cough my stomach's sins had given,
  Deserved by many a costly treat.

And when I plainly hoped to feed
As Sextius' guest, my host would read
  His speech 'gainst Attius, made of old.
'Twas full of poison and disease;
It made me shiver, made me sneeze,
  And gave me a bad cough and cold.

At length I fled into thy breast;
And there with med'cine and with rest
  Have cured myself in little time:
So now, in health and spirits gay,
My warmest thanks to thee I pay,
  Who thus hast done away my crime.

And, when I e'er again shall go
To hear his works, may they bestow
  Their cough and cold, not on my head,
But upon Sextius' self, who ne'er
Asks me to sup, but when the fare
  Is hearing his own nonsense read!    LAMB

### XLV.  ACME AND SEPTIMIUS

SEPTIMIUS said, and fondly prest
The doting Acme to his breast :—

" My Acme, if I prize not thee
With love as warm as love can be,
With passion spurning any fears
Of growing faint in length of years,
Alone may I defenceless stand
To meet, on Libya's desert sand,
Or under India's torrid sky,
The tawny lion's glaring eye !"

Love, before who utter'd still
On the left-hand omens ill,
As he ceased his faith to plight
Laugh'd propitious on the right.

Then Acme gently bent her head,
Kiss'd with those lips of cherry red
The eyes of the delighted boy,
That swam with glistening floods of joy;
And whisper'd as she closely prest—

" Septimius, soul of Acme's breast,
Let all our lives and feelings own
One lord, one sovereign, Love alone !
I yield to love, and yield to thee,
For thou and love art one to me.
Though fond thy fervent heart may beat,
My feelings glow with greater heat,
And madder flames my bosom melt
Than all that thou hast ever felt."

Love, before who utter'd still
On the left-hand omens ill,
As she ceased her faith to plight
Laugh'd propitious on the right.

Since favouring omens thus approved,
They mutual love and are beloved ;
Septimius prizes Acme more
Than Syria's realm and Britain's shore ;
And from Septimius only flows
The bliss that faithful Acme knows.

Then search the world, and search in vain
For fonder maid or happier swain.

P

Ask men below, and gods above,
Ask Venus kind, and potent Love,
If e'er they with propitious care
Heap'd equal bliss on any pair.          LAMB.


### THE SAME.

On Septimius' lap entwining,
While his Acme sank reclining;
" If I love thee not," he cried,
" Oh my Acme! oh my bride!
Even to perdition love thee,
And shall feel thy beauties move me,
As the rapid years roll by,
Like men who love distractedly,
Then, where Afric's sands are spread,
Or India's sun flames overhead,
May a lion cross me there
With his green-eyed, angry glare."
  Love stood listening in delight,
  And sneezed his auspice on the right.

Acme, as her lover said,
Lightly bending back her head,
And with lips of ruby skimming
His tipsy eyes, in pleasure swimming;
" Septimillus! darling mine!
So may we thus ever twine,
Victims vow'd at Cupid's shrine,
As with still more keen requitals
Thou art felt within my vitals!"
  Love stood listening in delight,
  And sneezed his auspice on the right.

In the heavenly omen blest
They love, caressing and carest;
The poor youth would lightlier prize
Syria's groves than Acme's eyes;
Acme centres in the boy
All her longings, all her joy.
Who more bless'd has mortals seen?
When has a kinder passion been?   ELTON

### THE SAME.

" O Acme, love ! " Septimius cried,
As on his lap he held his bride,—
" If all my heart is not for thee,
And dotes not on thee desperately,
And if it dote not more and more,
As desperate heart ne'er did before,
May I be doom'd on desert ground
To meet the lion in his round ! "
    He said ; and Love on tiptoe near him,
    Kind at last and come to cheer him,
    Clapp'd his little hands to hear him.

But Acme to the bending youth
Just dropping back that rosy mouth,
Kiss'd his reeling, hovering eyes,
And, " O my life, my love ! " replies,
" So may our constant service be
To this one only deity,
As with a transport doubly true
He thrills your Acme's being through ! "
    She said ; and Love on tiptoe near her,
    Kind at last, and come to cheer her,
    Clapp'd his little hands to hear her.

Favour'd thus by heaven above,
Their lives are one return of love ;
For he, poor fellow, so possess'd,
Is richer than with east and west,—
And she, in her enamour'd boy,
Finds all that she can frame of joy.
    Now who has seen, in Love's subjection,
    Two more blest in their connexion,
    Or a more entire affection ?   LEIGH HUNT.


### XLVI.  TO HIMSELF.

#### ON THE APPROACH OF SPRING.

SPRING returns, and blended meet
Winter's cold and Summer's heat.
Zephyr's soothing airs assuage
Heaven's equinoctial rage.

Leave, Catullus, Phrygia's plains,
Leave Nicæa's rich domains;
And to Asia take thy flight
Where her splendid towns invite.

All my mind's for travel fired;
Hope hath all my limbs inspired:
Loved society, farewell,
Friends with whom I've joy'd to dwell;
From our happy jovial home
Now we all together roam;
Very soon how far and wide
Various paths shall all divide.          LAMB.

### THE SAME.

Now Spring renews her gentle charms,
And lull'd in Zephyr's balmy arms,
  Soft grows the angry sky;
Haste then, and leaving Phrygia's plains,
Leaving Nicæa's rich domains,
  To Asia's cities fly.

My soul all trembling pants to stray,
My bounding feet the call obey;
  Friends of my youth, farewell!
Loved friends with whom I left my home,
Now doom'd through various ways to roam,
  In different lands to dwell.          PETER

### XLVII. TO PORCIUS AND SOCRATION.

OH Porcius and Socration! minions base,
  Panders to Piso's avarice, lust, and lies,
You, 'bove my friends, does that vile Pretor grace,
  Above Verannius and Fabullus prize?

While ye at splendid banquets daily meet,
  Revel from morn till day its light has hidden;
My loved companions wandering in the street
  Might vainly beg a place, where ye are bidden.

Still are they my companions, still most dear,
  Though vice abhor and poverty pursue:

Their honest lot is mine, and mine their cheer,
  More blest to starve with them than feast with you!
                                          LAMB.

## XLVIII. TO HIS LOVE.

If, all-complying, thou wouldst grant
  Thy lovely eyes to kiss, my fair,
Long as I pleased; oh! I would plant
  Three hundred thousand kisses there.

Nor could I even then refrain,
  Nor satiate leave that fount of blisses;
Though thicker than autumnal grain
  Should be our growing crop of kisses.   LAMB.

## XLIX. TO M. T. CICERO,

### WHO HAD PLEADED SUCCESSFULLY FOR CATULLUS.

Tully, most eloquent, most sage
  Of all the Roman race,
That deck the past or present age,
  Or future days may grace.

Oh! may Catullus thus declare
  An overflowing heart;
And, though the worst of poets, dare
  A grateful lay impart!

'T will teach thee how thou hast surpast
  All others in thy line;
For, far as he in his is last,
  Art thou the first in thine.   LAMB.

## L. TO LICINIUS.

'T was yesterday our careless sport,
Licinius, made the day seem short;
As suited men of taste and wit,
We sported just as fancy hit;
And in my tablets all day long
Wrote various kinds of verse and song;
While mutual jokes and flowing bowls
United all our jovial souls.

When home I went, my fancy run
So wholly on your wit and fun,
I loathed my lonely, cheerless meal,
Nor sleep would o'er my senses steal:
All night I toss'd from side to side,
Each corner of my bed I tried,
Still vainly wishing night would end,
And dawn bring pleasure and my friend.

Now listless, weary, almost dead,
I lie unrested on my bed;
And 't is from thence this verse I write,
To let you know my cheerless plight.

Now be not stern, but have a care;
Nor dare neglect my sportive prayer.
My earnest wishes cannot brook
One scoffing word or sneering look.
Neglect me!—I shall straight avow
Hatred as warm as friendship now;
And Nemesis herself shall be
Invoked for vengeance upon thee.
She is a goddess little tender:
Beware, beware, how you offend her!   LAMB.


LI.  SAPPHO'S ODE.

BLEST as th' immortal gods is he,
The youth, who fondly sits by thee,
And hears and sees thee all the while
Softly speak, and sweetly smile.

'T was that deprived my soul of rest,
And raised such tumults in my breast;
For while I gazed, in transport toss'd,
My breath was gone, my voice was lost.

My bosom glow'd; the subtle flame
Ran quick through all my vital frame;
On my dim eyes a darkness hung;
My ears with hollow murmurs rung;

With dewy damp my limbs were chill'd;
My blood with gentle horrors thrill'd;

My feeble pulse forgot to play ;
I fainted, sank, and died away.

AMBROSE PHILLIPS.


### THE SAME.

THAT man is like a god to me
Who, sitting face to face with thee,
Shall hear thee sweetly speak, and see
   Thy laughter's gentle blandishing.

'Tis this astounds my trembling heart:
I see thee, lovely as thou art:
My fluttering words in murmurs start,
   My broken tongue is faltering.

My flushing skin the fire betrays
That through my blood electric strays :
My eyes seem darkening as I gaze,
   My ringing ears re-echoing.

Cold from my forehead glides the dew :
A shuddering tremour thrills me through :
My cheek a green and yellow hue :
   All gasping, dying, languishing.   ELTON.


### LII.  TO HIMSELF, ON THE TIMES.

How now, wretch Catullus ? say,
   Why you still your death delay ?
For Struma Nonius fills the Curule chair ;
Perjured Vatinius holds the Consul's care :
   How now, wretch Catullus? say,
   Why you still your death delay ?  LAMB.


### LIII.  CALVUS' ORATORY.

WHEN Calvus short denounced aloud
   Vatinius' venal rule ;
And, to be level with the crowd,
   Had jump'd upon a stool :

" O learned stool !" cried some one near,
   " How high thy fame should shine !

Since, but for thee, the words we cheer,
Nor he could speak, nor we could hear;
   The eloquence is thine!"          LAMB.


LIV.  TO CÆSAR, ON HIS COMPANIONS.

O THOU to taste, to feeling dead!
If neither Otho's dwarfish head,
   Nor Libo's filthy gibe,
Nor Vettius' unwash'd feet; if these
Thee nor Fuffecius can displease,
   Thine old and hackney'd scribe.

Then, mighty emperor, once again
I'll pour forth my Iambic strain
   Uncourtly, bold, and free:
Again shalt thou my truth condemn;
And he, who will be friend to them,
   Shall still be foe to me.          LAMB.


THE SAME.

MAYST thou, though fond of all the vicious tribe,
May old Fuffitius too, thy hackney'd scribe,
At least detest vile Otho's shallow brain,
That vulgar upstart of the rabble train!
May stinking Libo your displeasure share,
Whose unbathed feet the filthy brute declare!
Fume on, proud monarch, as thou read'st this strain;
It breathes but truth; then fume, and read again.
                             NOTT


LV.  INQUIRIES AFTER CAMERIUS.

OH! tell me, dear friend, if it can be reveal'd,
In what dark abode you are lying conceal'd;
   For I vainly have traversed of late
The campus, the libraries all, and above
The circus, the temple of thundering Jove,
   And the gardens of Pompey the Great.

I question'd the damsels that roam'd through the place,
Whenever I met any fair one, whose face
   Was bedeck'd in contentment and smiles:

" Restore me Camerius !" I confident cried.
" Restore me Camerius ! nor venture to hide
   Any more by your profligate wiles."

Then one of them laughing and wantonly said,
Who drew down her vest and her bosom display'd—
   " Hidden here in these roses he lies:
But, ah ! 't were a labour Herculean to tear
Your friend from that seat; for while revelling there,
   He all friendship will proudly despise."

Then say where you are, whither going, I pray,
And boldly declare it in face of the day;
   If some snow-bosom'd fair one employs
Your moments in bliss, you by secrecy blight
The fruits of your love; for to love 't is delight.
   To converse and to boast of its joys.

Or secret be still, if your pleasure it be:
But yet, oh ! preserve, I entreat it, for me
   As of old, in your friendship a place;
For if I were Talus, the guardian of Crete,
Or rode I the winds upon Pegasus fleet,
   Or were Ladas, the first in the race,

Or could I the sandals of Perseus obtain,
The speed with which Rhesus rush'd over the plain
   When he urged on his horses of snow;
The force and the lightness of all living things
That gods ever gifted with swiftness or wings
   Of the winds when the fiercest they blow:

All these might be join'd in my body alone;
Yet wearied and faint in each sinew and bone,
   Every nerve, every limb I should be;
And failing, and sinking, exhausted and lame,
Would languor eat up all the strength of my frame,
   O Camerius! in searching for thee.    LAMB.

## LVI. TO CATO.

'Tis ridiculous, Cato, 'tis really droll;
When you hear it, I 'm sure you will laugh from your soul:
Cato, laugh! if to thee thy Catullus is dear;
For 'tis droll and ridiculous past all compare:

The fact is, this moment I caught my young blade
Just attempting to rifle an innocent maid:
Then, sweet Venus, if thou wilt not take it amiss,
I will find out the shaft that shall punish for this!

NOTT.

### LVII.  ON MAMURRA AND CÆSAR.

No debauchees were better pair'd
Than vile Mamurra and his lord;
   Nor can we think it strange;
The Roman's and the Formian's name,
With equal infamy and shame
   Deep stampt, no time can change.

Vicious alike one couch they press;
A little learning both possess;
   Both rank adulterers are:
No debauchees were better pair'd
Than vile Mamurra and his lord,
   Twin rivals of the fair.    NOTT.

### LVIII.  LESBIA'S DISGRACE.

#### ADDRESSED TO CELIUS.

O Celius! think, our Lesbia, once thy pride;
   Lesbia, that Lesbia whom Catullus prized
More than himself, and all the world beside,
   Now gives for hire to profligates despised
In the dark alley, or the common lane,
The charms he loved, the love he sigh'd to gain!  LAMB

### LIX.  ON RUFA.

Can that wretch of Bononia, can Rufa, mean soul!
Can that vile wife of Menius, Rufulus cajole?
She who haunted each burying-place, merely to steal
From the pile that was burning her infamous meal;
Who from funeral flames as collecting her meat,
By the low-lived, half-shaved body-burners was beat.

NOTT.

## LX. FRAGMENT.

WHENCE sprang that savage, that unfeeling mind?
Art thou some offspring of the lion kind,
On scorching Libya's thirsty mountains born;
Or from the womb of barking Scylla torn?
That thus thou'rt deaf to all my urgent woes;
O heart too harden'd that no pity knows!　　NOTT.

## LXI. EPITHALAMIUM

### ON THE MARRIAGE OF MANLIUS AND JULIA.

O THOU, Urania's heaven-born son,
Whose loved abode is Helicon;
Whose power bestows the virgin's charms
To bless the youthful bridegroom's arms;
O Hymen! friend to faithful pairs;
O Hymen! hear our fervent prayers!

Around thy brow the chaplet bind,
Of fragrant marjoram entwined;
And bring the veil with crimson dyed,
The refuge of the blushing bride.
Come, joyous, while thy feet of snow
With yellow sandals brightly glow!

Arouse thee on this happy day;
Carol the hymeneal lay;
Raise in the strain thy silver voice,
And in the festal dance rejoice;
And brandish high the blissful sign,
The guiding torch of flaming pine.

When Venus claim'd the golden prize,
And bless'd the Phrygian shepherd's eyes;
No brighter charms his judgment sway'd
Than those that grace this mortal maid;
And every sigh and omen fair
The nuptials hail, and greet the pair.

The myrtle's sweet on Asia's ground,
Its branches fair with blossoms crown'd
Which oft the Hamadryad crew
In frolic nourish with the dew :
But not less fair, but not less sweet,
Her Manlius now does Julia meet.

Then hither speed thy course to take :
Awhile the Thespian hill forsake ;
Nor waste awhile the lingering hours
Reclining in Aonian bowers,
Where Aganippe's springing fount
Refreshes all the sacred mount.

Propitiate here the maiden's vows,
And lead her fondly to her spouse ;
And firm as ivy clinging holds
The tree it grasps in mazy folds,
Let virtuous love as firmly bind
The tender passions of her mind.

Ye virgins, whom a day like this
Awaits to greet with equal bliss,
Oh ! join the song, your voices raise
To hail the god ye love to praise.
O Hymen ! god of faithful pairs ;
O Hymen ! hear our earnest prayers !

The god, who loves the pure, will hear
A virgin's prayer with willing ear,
Will swiftly to his office haste
To bless the fond, reward the chaste ;
The god, who ever feels delight
When virtuous hearts in love unite.

O ye ! who warmly, truly love ;
Invoke no other god above :
To none beside address your sighs
Of all enthroned amid the skies.
O Hymen ! god of faithful pairs ;
O Hymen ! hear our earnest prayers !

Invoked by sires, with anxious fear,
Their children's days with bliss to cheer;
By maidens, who to thee alone
Unloose the chaste, the virgin zone;
By fervid bridegrooms, whose delight
Is staid till thou hast blest the rite.

Thy influence tears, thy fond behest,
The damsel from her mother's breast;
And yields her blooming, blushing charms
To fiery man's resistless arms.
O Hymen! god of faithful pairs;
O Hymen! hear our earnest prayers!

Though wanton Venus feed the flame;
Nor grateful praise, nor virtuous fame
Can wait on those, who loose and free
Indulge a love unblest by thee.
What other god can mortals dare
With genial Hymen to compare?

No house can boast a lengthen'd race;
No heir can parents' honours grace;
They serve to deck their tombs alone,
If parents' lives thy sway disown.
What other god can mortals dare
With genial Hymen to compare?

In vain the son, if scorn'd thy band,
Seeks power or greatness in the land;
If blest by thee his natal day,
The proudest realm may own his sway.
What other god can mortals dare
With genial Hymen to compare?

Unbar the door, the gates unfold!
The bashful virgin comes.—Behold,
How red the nuptial torches glare;
How bright they shake their splendid hair!
Come, gentle bride!—The waning day
Rebukes thy lingering, cold delay.

We will not blame thy bashful fears,
Reluctant step, and gushing tears,
That chide the swift approach of night
To give thy bridegroom all his right.
Yet come, sweet bride!—The waning day
Rebukes thy lingering, cold delay.

Daughter of Cotta, cease to weep,
For love shall watch, and falsehood sleep.
The sun, at dawn that lifts his blaze
From ocean, and the world surveys,
Shall never look, shall never shine
On beauties that shall rival thine.

Thus blooms, amid the gay parterre,
Some wealthy owner's pride and care,
The hyacinth with colours proud,
The loveliest of the varied crowd.
Come, gentle bride!—The waning day
Rebukes thy lingering, cold delay.

Then come, sweet bride, and bless thy spouse
And sanction love by nuptial vows.
At length our friendly numbers hear:
The torches high their brilliance rear,
And richly shake with glowing pride
Their golden hair.—Then come, sweet bride!

No profligate, no faithless swain,
No follower of the wanton train,
No rake, who joys in wild excess,
Now woos thee to his warm caress.
He ne'er will taste of welcome rest,
But pillow'd on thy tender breast.

As round the husband elm entwine
The tendrils of the clinging vine,
Thus will he woo thee still to place
Round him a fondling close embrace.
Come, gentle bride!—The waning day
Rebukes thy lingering, cold delay.

O festal couch! with garlands sweet,
What joys thy happy lord will greet!
What joys in many a sleepless night!
What joys in day's inspiring light!
Come, gentle bride!—The waning day
Rebukes thy lingering, cold delay.

Raise, boys, the beaming torches high!
She comes—but veil'd from every eye;
The deeper dyes her blushes hide:
With songs, with pæans greet the bride!
Hail, Hymen! god of faithful pairs!
Hail, Hymen! who hast heard our prayers!

Now pour the warm Fescennine lays,
And all the bridegroom's passion raise:
Now let his pure, his plighted hand
Throw nuts to all the youthful band,
Base emblems of the looser joys
He henceforth leaves to wanton boys.

Throw, bridegroom, throw thy nuts away!
Enough in joy's voluptuous day
Hast thou beguiled thy youthful time;
But now thy manhood's riper prime
Let pure, let bless'd Thalassus sway:
Then throw thy mystic nuts away.

'Tis whisper'd, that the wanton's charms
Will yet allure thee to her arms:
Oh! let no shameless rival's pride
Degrade and pain thy gentle bride.
Hail, Hymen! god of faithful pairs!
Hail, Hymen! who hast heard our prayers!

Unloved, unwedded youths and boys
May freely sport in wanton joys:
Let him, that's blest by wedlock's rite,
In wedlock seek his sole delight.
Hail, Hymen! god of faithful pairs!
Hail, Hymen! who hast heard our prayers!

And let no coldness damp his fire,
Fair bride, nor coyness check desire.
Oh ! make his heart less sweet confess
All lawless love, than thy caress.
Hail, Hymen ! god of faithful pairs !
Hail, Hymen ! who hast heard our prayers !

Riches, and power, and rank, and state,
With Manlius' love thy days await:
These all thy youth shall proudly cheer,
And these shall nurse thy latest year.
Hail, Hymen ! god of faithful pairs !
Hail, Hymen ! who hast heard our prayers !

Till dotage, with enfeebling sway,
Shall tremble in thy temples grey ;
And shake the brow, as if it meant
To nod perpetual assent.
Hail, Hymen ! god of faithful pairs !
Hail, Hymen ! who hast heard our prayers !

Let not the threshold, omen blest !
Be with thy golden slipper prest ;
But swiftly spring with lightness o'er,
And swiftly pass the polish'd door.
Hail, Hymen ! god of faithful pairs !
Hail, Hymen ! who hast heard our prayers !

See, on the Tyrian couch reclining,
The bridegroom for thy summons pining :
By thee are all his senses fired ;
By thee is all his frame inspired.
Hail, Hymen ! god of faithful pairs !
Hail, Hymen ! who hast heard our prayers !

As warm as thine, his passion's heat,
As strong his rapturous pulses beat ;
Nay, fiercer flames must still pervade
The bridegroom than the timid maid.
Hail, Hymen ! god of faithful pairs !
Hail, Hymen ! who hast heard our prayers !

Purple-robed boy, whose pleasing care
Has been to lead the lingering fair,
Release her arm:—By others led
She now ascends the bridal bed.
Hail, Hymen! god of faithful pairs!
Hail, Hymen! who hast heard our prayers!

Ye chaster matrons, who have known
One honour'd husband's love alone,
Of truth in years long virtuous tried,
'Tis yours to place the lovely bride.
Hail, Hymen! god of faithful pairs!
Hail, Hymen! who hast heard our prayers!

Now haste, young bridegroom, swiftly haste;
The bride is in the chamber placed:
Inspiring blushes warmly streak
The fairness of her snowy cheek.
So mix'd with poppies' crimson glow
The white parthenium's flow'rets blow.

Nor is thy form, by heaven above!
Unworthy such a fair one's love.
Venus in rival charms array'd
The manly youth and tender maid.
Haste, bridegroom, haste!—One western ray,
Still faintly lingering, chides delay.

Needs not to chide; thou swift hast sped.
Propitious Venus bless thy bed!
For sanction'd passion, solemn rites,
On thee bestow thy wish'd delights:
Not lust perverted, shame supprest,
The pure desires that warm thy breast.

Whoe'er the number would define
Of sports and joys that shall be thine,
He first must count the grains of sand
That spread the Erythræan strand,
And every star and twinkling light
That stud the glistening arch of night.

o

Oh! boundless be your love's excess,
And soon our hopes let children bless!
Let not this ancient honour'd name
Want heirs to guard its future fame;
Nor any length of years assign
A limit to the glorious line.

Soon may we see a baby rest
Upon its lovely mother's breast;
Which, feebly playful, stretching out
Its little arms to those about,
With lips apart a tiny space,
Is laughing in its father's face.

Let young Torquatus' look avow
All Manlius' features in his brow;
That those, who know him not, may trace
The knowledge of his noble race;
And by his lineal brow declare
His lovely mother chaste as fair.

Then shall maternal virtue claim
As splendid praise, as pure a name
To deck her child, as erst was known
To young Telemachus alone,
Whom, then of all most fair and chaste,
Penelope with honour graced.

Now close the doors, ye maiden friends;
Our sports, our rite, our service ends.
With you let virtue still reside,
O bridegroom brave, and gentle bride!
And youth its lusty hours employ
In constant love and ardent joy.      LAMB


### LXII.  THE BRIDAL SONG.

#### YOUTHS.

'TIS Hesper beams!—Behold his rising light
Brings on, at length, the long-expected night
Then, youths, arise; the festal banquet leave
Obey the summons of the star of eve!

The virgin comes, led by his genial ray;
'Tis yours to greet her with the nuptial lay.
O Hymen, hear! O sacred Hymen, haste;
Come, god and guardian of the fond and chaste!

### MAIDENS.

Behold, the youths are ris'n!—Rise, maidens, rise;
Hesper o'er Eta's height illumes the skies.
Blithe are the youths; with tuneful art they frame
A tender song, that to surpass were fame.
O Hymen, hear! O sacred Hymen, haste;
Come, god and guardian of the fond and chaste!

### YOUTHS.

Not to an easy conquest we aspire;
Mark with what studious zeal the lovely quire
Polish their lay; nor will the care be vain,
Fame long shall cherish their harmonious strain.
Our minds, while verse should be their only care,
Still muse enraptured on th' attendant fair;
Heedless how wild the measure flows along,
Our ears still dwell on their entrancing song.
We shall be justly conquer'd.   Victory wise
On zeal and labour still bestows her prize.
At least, then, rally all our mental powers,
And let the palm of poetry be ours.
They sing—let us then pour responsive lays,
Repel their chiding or return their praise.
O Hymen, hear! O sacred Hymen, haste;
Come, god and guardian of the fond and chaste!

### MAIDENS.

Hesper, whose fatal splendour flames on high,
Most cruel star of all that stud the sky!
Who still art prompt, while no remorse can check,
To tear the daughter from her mother's neck,
E'en while that daughter clinging begs delay;
And give to man her chastity a prey.
What blacker deed do brutal victors act
In cities doom'd by vengeance to be sack'd?
Yet, Hymen, hear! O sacred Hymen, haste;
Come, god and guardian of the fond and chaste!

### YOUTHS.

Hesper, most blissful star of all above,
Thy torch still ratifies the bond of love.
Long since their sires the sacred compact made,
Long since their youthful hearts the call obey'd.
Yet still their ardent breasts apart have sigh'd,
Till thy kind light would bless the knot they tied.
What god can give, what proud celestial power,
A richer boon than thy connubial hour?
O Hymen, hear! O sacred Hymen, haste;
Come, god and guardian of the fond and chaste!

### MAIDENS.

Hesper, sweet maids, hath from us dared to rend
A childish playmate and a youthful friend.
Guards, star of ill! at thy appearing light,
Watch for the various plunderers of the night:
Then prowl, when bright thy favouring beams above,
Seduction, ravishment, and lawless love;
Till changed thy task, thy renovated ray,
As morning's star forewarns them of the day.

### YOUTHS.

Hear not the maids who these reproaches feign,
Their secret breasts adore thine amorous reign.
Shine still serene! then, Hesper, proudly shine.
Nor heed their words, whose hearts are wholly thine.
O Hymen hear! O sacred Hymen, haste;
Come, god and guardian of the fond and chaste!

### MAIDENS.

When in the garden's fenced and cultured ground,
Where browse no flocks, where ploughshares never wound
By sunbeams strengthen'd, nourish'd by the shower,
And sooth'd by zephyr, blooms the lovely flower:
Maids long to place it in their modest zone,
And youths enraptured wish it for their own.
But, from the stem once pluck'd, in dust it lies,
Nor youth nor maid will then desire or prize.
The virgin thus her blushing beauty rears,
Loved by her kindred and her young compeers;

But, if her simple charm, her maiden grace,
Is sullied by one spoiler's rude embrace,
Adoring youths no more her steps attend,
Nor loving maidens greet the maiden friend.
O Hymen, hear! O sacred Hymen, haste;
Come, god and guardian of the fond and chaste!

### YOUTHS.

As in the naked field the vine's weak shoot
Nor lifts its languid stem, nor glows with fruit;
But by itself weigh'd down it lowly strays,
And on its root its highest tendril lays:
The herdsmen then, the passing hinds, neglect
The lonely vine, nor cherish, nor protect.
If by some happy chance its feeble boughs
Twined round the trunk shall make the elm a spouse;
No herdsmen then, nor passing hinds, neglect
The wedded vine, but cherish and protect.
So scorn'd the maid, who flies the fond embrace,
And withering adds no honours to her race.
So is the fair beloved, who binds her fate
In wedlock chaste to some accordant mate:
She gives the joys that warm her husband's breast,
And doting parents by her bliss are blest.

### YOUTHS AND MAIDENS.

Then, gentle maiden, shun no more the spouse
To whom thy father pledged thy bridal vows.
If thou hast loved as daughters should, obey
The latest dictate of parental sway.
Thou must thy timid wish to his resign;
Nor is thy chastity entirely thine;
Thy parents gave it thee with life and light;
Part is thy father's, part thy mother's right.
They to thy bridegroom yielded with his bride
Her filial duty and her maiden pride.
Then yield, nor damp by chill reluctant shame
Thy parents' wishes and thy lover's flame.
O Hymen, hear! O sacred Hymen, haste;
Come, god and guardian of the fond and chaste.    LAMB.

### THE SAME.

#### A YOUTH.

VESPER ascends: ye youths! together rise:
Eve's long-expected star has gilt the skies.
Rise, leave the feast; the bride will soon appear;
The bridal song be sung: O Hymen, Hymen, hear!

#### A VIRGIN.

Mark ye the youths? to face them, maidens, rise;
Night-shedding Hesper lights the spangled skies:
Look up; 'tis so; and saw ye how their throng
Sprang forth? nor idly: soon to raise the song:
Let us in rival strain surpass the lay:
O Hymen, Hymen, bless the wedding day!

#### A YOUTH.

Arduous the palm of strife: oh, friends! be strong:
For see yon maidens muse some mutter'd song:
Nor idly muse: some memorable lay;
While we our ears and thoughts have turn'd away:
We merit shame, since victory favours care:
Yet now your parts with emulation bear:
'Tis theirs to speak: let us responses frame!
O Hymen, Hymen, bless the marriage flame!

#### VIRGINS.

Hesper! knows heaven a star like thee severe,
That tear'st the maiden from her mother dear?
The ling'ring maiden from her mother's arms,
And yield'st some fervid youth her spotless charms;
What wrongs more fierce can cities storm'd display!
Come, Hymen, hither! Hymen, grace the day!

#### YOUTHS.

Hesper! what star more joyous shines above?
Thy flames confirm the plighted troth of love:
By covenants of men, of parents seal'd,
Thy dawn alone the wish'd embrace can yield:
What hour can gods bestow more wish'd than this?
Come, Hymen, hither! crown the hour of bliss!

## VIRGINS.

Alas, companions!   Hesper's dawning ray
Has stolen a playmate of our sports away.
Oh, dreaded star! how many sentries wait
At thy pale glance to watch the guarded gate!
Through nightly shades the stealthy robbers rove,
The soft, th' insidious ravishers of love:
And oft, as Lucifer, from morning skies
Does thy pale gleam their hairbreadth 'scapes surprise.

## YOUTHS.

This, Hesper! is th' unwedded fair one's joy:
To rail on thee who dost her thoughts employ.
What if their railing be a trick of art,
And him they flout, they worship in their heart?
They long for him whom prudishly they chide,
O Hymen, Hymen, at this hour preside!

## VIRGINS.

As in fenced gardens blows some floweret rare,
Safe from the nibbling flock, or griding share:
Which gales refresh, sun strengthens, rain-drops rear,
To many a youth and many a maiden dear:
Clipt by the nail, it bends the stem and fades:
No more by youths admired, or wish'd by maids;
So loved the unpolluted virgin blooms;
But when the blighting touch her flower consumes,
No more she charms the youth, or charms the maid.
Come, Hymen, Hymen, give the nuptials aid!

## YOUTHS.

As on the naked field the lonely vine
Yields no sweet grape, nor lifts its tendril twine:
Droops with its weight, and winds its tendril shoots
With earthward bend around their twisted roots,
Nor herd nor peasant, in the noon-day heat,
Beneath its chequer'd, bow'ry shade retreat:
But if it clasp some elm with married leaves,
Its shade the peasant and the herd receives:
Such is the virgin who untouch'd remains,
While still unwoo'd her useless beauty wanes.

But wedded in her bloom, those charms delight
Her husband's eyes, nor shame her parents' sight.

### YOUTHS AND VIRGINS.

Resist not fiercely, virgin !—but obey
Thy mother, father: thy betrothers they:
Not thine thy virgin flower: a part is theirs:
Thy sire a third ; a third thy mother shares ;
A third thy own: then struggle not, coy maid !
For in thy bridegroom both are disobeyed:
They with thy dower have yielded every right.
Come, Hymen, Hymen, bless the marriage night !  ELTON


### LXIII. ATYS.

BORNE swiftly o'er the seas to Phrygia's woody strand,
Atys with rapid haste infuriate leap'd to land ;
Where high-inwoven groves in solemn darkness meet,
Rush'd to the mighty deity's remote and awful seat,
And wilder'd in his brain, fierce inspiration's prey,
There with a broken flint he struck his sex away.

Soon as he then beheld his comely form unmann'd,
While yet the purple blood flow'd reeking on the land ;
Seized in his snowy grasp the drum, the timbrel light,
That still is heard, dread Cybele, at thine initiate rite,
And struck the quivering skin, whence hollow echoes flew,
And raised this panting song to his infuriate crew.

" Ye priests of Cybele, or rather let me say,
For ye are men no longer, ye priestesses, away !
Together pierce the forest, great Cybele's domains,
Ye vagrant flocks of her on Dindymus who reigns.
Ye, like devoted exiles, who, seeking foreign lands,
Have follow'd me your leader, have bow'd to my commands ;
Have cross'd the salt-sea wave, have dared the raging storms
And, loathing woman's love, unmann'd your lusty forms ;
The sense of error past let laughing frenzy blind ;
Let doubt, let thought itself be driven from the mind.
Haste, haste, together haste to Cybele divine !
Seek we her Phrygian grove and dark sequester'd shrine,

Where cymbals clash, where drums resound their deepening
    tone,
Where Phrygia's crooked pipe breathes out its solemn drone,
Where votaresses toss their ivy-circled brows,
And urge with piercing yells their consecrated vows,
Where the delirious train disport as chance may lead:
Thither our vows command in mystic dance to speed."

Thus Atys, female now, to female comrades sung.
The frantic chorus rose from many a panting tongue;
Re-echoes the deep timbrel, the hollow cymbals ring,
And all to verdant Ida run madly as they sing.
Though breathless, still impetuous with inspiration's force,
Raving and bewilder'd, scarce conscious of her course,
As the unbroken heifer will fly the threaten'd yoke,
Atys through gloomy woods, where never sun-beam broke,
Loud-striking the light timbrel, rush'd on with bounding stride,
And all the frantic priestesses pursue their rapid guide.
The fearful fane at length their panting ardour stops,
Each, faint and unrefresh'd, in leaden slumber drops.
In languor most profound their eyelids are deprest,
And all ecstatic rage is lull'd in torpid rest.

But when again the sun returning to the skies
Put forth his golden brow, when now his radiant eyes
Throughout white heaven, and earth, and ocean pour'd their
    light,
And with thunder-pacing steeds he chased the shades of night,
Sleep then leaving Atys, who started from her rest,
To fair Pasithea fled, and sunk upon her breast.
When slumber's reign serene had frenzy's flame subdued;
When Atys her fell deed in clearer reason view'd,
Beheld in what abode her future lot was placed,
And, ah! how low she stood in nature's rank disgraced;
Then, hurried to despair by passion's rising tide,
Again she wildly sought the country's sea-girt side;
There, casting her full eyes o'er boundless ocean's flow,
Address'd her native land in plaintive words of woe.

" My country, oh my mother! creatress, parent earth!
My country, oh my nurse that fed me from my birth!
From whom, as churlish slaves their kindly lord have fled,
To Ida's gloomy wood an exile I have sped,

With beasts their frozen dens for my abode to share,
And madly roaming rouse the fierce one from his lair.
Ah! where, in what far point of this surrounding sky,
Shall I now deem, my native land, thy loved shores lie?
My longing eyeballs strain to cast their sight to thee,
While yet awhile my mind is from its frenzy free.
Must I for dreary woods forsake my native shore,
And see my friends, my home, my parents never more?
No more the Forum seek, the gay Palestra's court,
The Stadium, urge no more each famed gymnastic sport?
O wretched, wretched man! while years shall slowly roll
For ever o'er and o'er again, grieve, grieve, my soul!

" What grace, what beauty is there, that I did not enjoy?
I, when in manhood's prime, a youth, or yet a boy,
The flower of all who trod the firm gymnastic soil,
The victor 'mid the crowd who wore the wrestler's oil.
My gates were ever throng'd, and full my threshold swarm'd
With blooming garlands hung, that lovesick maidens form'd
My mansion gaily glitter'd each morning as I sped
At earliest blush of sunrise with lightness from my bed.

" And must I ever now a maniac votaress rave,
Heaven's devoted handmaid, to Cybele a slave,
Her frantic orgies ply, disgraced in nature's plan,
A part of what I was, a maim'd, a barren man;
And dwell in Ida's caves which snow for ever chills;
And pass my savage life on Phrygia's rugged hills,
Placed with the sylvan stag, the forest-ranging boar?
Oh! now how soon I rue the deed, how bitterly deplore!"

As from her rosy lips these wandering murmurs broke,
They rose to heaven and bore th' unwonted words she spoke
Indignantly unyoking her lions on the plain,
And rousing the grim beast that bore the left-hand rein,
Great Cybele, enraged, her dread injunction told;
And thus to fury waked the tyrant of the fold.

" Haste, fierce one, haste away! rush on with glaring ire;
With inspiration's rage, with frenzy's goad of fire,
Drive the too-daring youth, who would my service fly,
Again to seek the gloom of yonder forest high.

Haste: lash thyself to rage till all thy flank be sore:
Let all around re-echo to thine appalling roar:
Toss with thy sinewy neck on high thy glossy mane."
So spake terrific Cybele, and loosed her lion's rein.
Gladly the beast awakes his ruthlessness of mind,
Bounds, rages, reckless leaves the thicket crush'd behind,
Then swiftly gain'd the beach, wash'd by the foamy flood,
Where Atys in despair amid the breakers stood,
And springing fiercely forth—the wretch, no longer brave,
Into the forest plunged, and in a living grave
There pass'd her long devoted life, a priestess and a slave.

O great, O fearful goddess! O Cybele divine!
O goddess, who hast placed on Dindymus thy shrine!
Far be from my abode thy sacred frenzy's fire,
Madden more willing votaries, more daring minds inspire!
LAMB.

### THE SAME.

ATYS o'er the distant waters, driving in his rapid bark,
Soon with foot of wild impatience touch'd the Phrygian forest
    dark,
Where amid the awful shades possess'd by mighty Cybele,
       In his zealous frenzy blind,
       And wand'ring in his hapless mind,
With flinty knife he gave to earth the weights that stamp
    virility.
Then as the widow'd being saw its wretched limbs bereft of
    man,
And the unaccustom'd blood that on the ground polluting ran,
With snowy hand it snatch'd in haste the timbrel's airy
    round on high,
That opens with the trumpet's blast, thy rites, Maternal
    Mystery;
And upon its whirling fingers, while the hollow parchment
    rung,
Thus in outcry tremulous to its wild companions sung:—

      "Now come along, come along with me,
      Worshippers of Cybele,
      To the lofty groves of the deity!

Ye vagabond herds that bear the name
  Of the Dindymenian dame !
Who seeking strange lands, like the banish'd of home,
With Atys, with Atys distractedly roam ;
Who your limbs have unmann'd in a desperate hour,
With a frantic disdain of the Cyprian power ;
Who have carried my sect through the dreadful salt sea,
Rouse, rouse your wild spirits careeringly !
    No delay, no delay,
    But together away,
And follow me up to the Dame all-compelling,
To her high Phrygian groves, and her dark Phrygian
    dwelling,
Where the cymbals they clash, and the drums they resound,
And the Phrygian's curved pipe pours its moanings around ;
Where the ivy-crown'd priestesses toss with their brows,
And send the shrill howl through their deity's house ;
Where they shriek, and they scour, and they madden about,—
'Tis there we go bounding in mystical rout."


    No sooner had spoken
    This voice half-broken,
When suddenly from quivering tongues arose the universal cry.
The timbrels with a boom resound, the cymbals with a clash
    reply,
And up the verdant Ida with a quicken'd step the chorus flew,
While Atys with the timbrels' smite the terrible procession
    drew ;
Raging, panting, wild, and witless, through the sullen shades
    it broke,
Like the fierce, unconquer'd heifer bursting from her galling
    yoke ;
And on pursue the sacred crew, till at the door of Cybele,
Faint and fasting, down they sink, in pale immovability :
The heavy sleep—the heavy sleep—grows o'er their failing
    eyes,
And lock'd in dead repose the rabid frenzy lies.
But when the Sun look'd out with eyes of light
Found the firm earth, wild seas, and skies of morning white,
    Scaring the lingering shades
    With echo-footed steeds.

Sleep took his flight from Atys, hurrying
To his Pasithea's arms on tremulous wing;
And the poor dreamer woke, oppress'd with sadness,
To memory woke and to collected madness.—
Struck with its loss, with what it was, and where,
Back trod the wretched being in despair
To the sea-shore, and stretching forth its eye
O'er the wide waste of waters and of sky,
Thus to its country cried with tears of misery:—

"My country, oh my country, parent state,
Whom like a very slave and runagate,
Wretch that I am, I left for wilds like these,
This wilderness of snows and matted trees,
To house with shivering beasts and learn their wants,
A fierce intruder on their sullen haunts,—
Where shall I fancy thee? Where cheat mine eye
With tricking out thy quarter in the sky?
Fain, while my wits a little space are free,
Would my poor eye-balls strain their points on thee!
Am I then torn from home and far away!
Doom'd through these woods to trample day by day,
Far from my kindred friends and native soil,
The mall, the race, and wrestlers bright with oil?
Ah wretch, bewail, bewail; and think for this
On all thy past variety of bliss.
I was the charm of life, the social spring,
First in the race, and brightest in the ring:
Warm with the stir of welcome was my home;
And when I rose betimes, my friends would come
Smiling and pressing in officious scores,
Thick as the flowers that hang at lovers' doors:—
And shall I then a minist'ring madman be
To angry gods? A howling devotee?—
A slave to bear what never senses can,—
Half of myself, sexless,—a sterile man?
And must I feel, with never-varied woes,
The o'erhanging winter of these mountain snows,
Skulking through ghastly woods for evermore,
Like the lean stag, or the brute vagrant boar?

Ah me ! ah me ! Already I repent ;
E'en now, e'en now I feel my shame and punishment !"

As thus with rosy lips the wretch grew loud,
Startling the ears of heaven's imperial crowd,
The Mighty Mistress o'er her lion yoke
Bow'd in her wrath,—and loosening as she spoke
The left-hand savage, scatterer of herds,
Roused his fell nature with impetuous words.
" Fly, ruffian, fly, indignant and amain,
And scare this being, who resists my reign,
Back to the horror-breathing woods again.
Lash thee, and fly and shake with sinewy might
Thine ireful hair, and as at dead of night
Fill the wild echoes with rebellowing fright."
Threatening she spoke, and loosed the vengeance dire,
Who gathering all his rage and glaring fire,
Starts with a roar, and scours beneath her eyes,
Scattering the splinter'd bushes as he flies :
Down by the sea he spies the wretch at last,
And springs precipitous :—the wretch as fast,
Flies raving back into his living grave,
And there for ever dwells, a savage and a slave

O goddess ! Mistress.  Cybele ! dread name !
O mighty power !  O Dindymenian dame !
Far from my home thy visitations be :
Drive others mad, not me :
Drive others into impulse wild, and fierce insanity.
                                        LEIGH HUNT

## LXIV.  THE NUPTIALS OF PELEUS AND THETIS.

WHEN erst the pines, hewn from the towering wood
On Pelion's summit, swam o'er Neptune's flood
Far as the streams of Phasis, and the land
Aetes ruled : what time the daring band,
The chosen strength of all the youth of Greece,
Resolved to plunder Colchos of its fleece,
In their swift vessel braved the salt domain,
And swept with oars of fir its azure plain ;

(For them the goddess, whose proud empire frowns
From lofty citadels o'er vassal towns,
Form'd the light chariot that from every blast
Collects its vigour till it flies as fast ;
Fix'd to the crooked keel the knitted trees,
And bade them first profane the virgin seas.)
Soon as its beak the turbid billows clove,
And with the wreathing foam the steerage strove ;
Strange forms arose amid the tossing spray,
Sea-Nereids wondering at the monster's way.
For two succeeding suns the gallant crew,
(A sight before unknown to human view,)
With breasts exposed above the liquid plain,
Beheld the naked daughters of the main.
Then Peleus first with love for Thetis burn'd,
Nor Thetis then a mortal bridegroom spurn'd ;
Then Jove himself, to whom all nature bows,
Deem'd Peleus worthy a celestial spouse.

Oh ! born in that proud day, that age of earth
Most blest, hail, heroes ! hail, of heavenly birth !
Hail, mighty bark, that like a mother bore
The living host enwomb'd from shore to shore !
Ye I 'll invoke ; ye shall my verse address ;
And Peleus, thee, whom glorious spousals bless,
Thessalia's shield, to whom all-powerful Jove
Yielded the fair himself had sought with love :
Thetis, of all the offspring of the sea
The loveliest nymph, bestows her love on thee ;
Ocean, who earth encircles with his tide,
And Tethys, give their grandchild as thy bride.

At length the weary interval was spent
'Twixt love's avowal and its full content.
Thessalia's crowds with gifts the palace seek,
And looks of greater joy than words can speak.
The throng from Tempe's vale, from Scyros roams,
From Cranon's turrets and Larissa's homes,
And seek from every side the rich Pharsalian domes.
The earth 's untill'd, the bullock's callous throat,
Free from the yoke, regains its softer coat :

The lowly vineyard knows no weeding rakes,
Nor ox with sloping share the furrow breaks:
No pruner lops the trees' encumbering boughs,
And rust grows thick on the neglected ploughs.
But through the halls of Peleus' vast abode
Pale silver shone, or gold more warmly glow'd ;
Thrones white with ivory, tables rich with plate ;
The dome all gladden'd with its regal state.
'Twas in the central chamber had been spread
For her, the bride divine, the nuptial bed ;
Of Indian ivory form'd, it shunn'd the eye,
Veil'd by its covering of the crimson dye.
On that were pictured men and times of old,
And wondrous art the deeds of heroes told.
There Ariadne, whose distracted soul
Felt every passion that defies control,
From Dia's coast, where foaming billows beat,
On Theseus gazed and his receding fleet.
She scarce believes, though sleep beguiles no more,
Though waking sense beholds the lonely shore,
That she, so lately to her Theseus dear,
Can be the wretched maid forsaken here.
But he, the treacherous youth, spreads all his sails,
And gives his vows of love to passing gales.
Him Minos' daughter, left to weep alone,
Like some wild Bacchant's form in sculptured stone
Looks on afar from ocean's barren side,
While anguish heaves her with its silent tide.
No more the fillet wreaths her locks of gold ;
Her snowy bosom no light garments fold,
Nor the thin laces of the girdle bind
Her swelling breast that scarce will be confined :
Before her feet the scatter'd vestments fall,
And restless surf is sporting with them all.
She nor her fillet heeds, nor floating vest :
Theseus, on thee alone her turbid breast,
Her tearful eyes, her thoughts are all engrost,
And every sense is in thy falsehood lost.

Ah ! how thy mind was madden'd, hapless fair !
By the keen woes that Venus planted there,

When cruel Theseus from th' Athenian road
Sail'd to proud Crete, thy tyrant sire's abode.
For Athens, forced by pestilence's reign
To dire atonement for Androgeus slain,
Took from her sons the glories of the race,
Cull'd from her virgin train the flower and grace,
And to the Minotaur desponding bore
Recurring banquets on her native gore.
When Theseus learnt his noble country's woes,
Peril and painful death he rather chose,
Than still to see from Athens sadly led
These woeful funerals of the living dead.
Swiftly with pleasant gales his vessel gain'd
The sea-girt realm where awful Minos reign'd;
There with enraptured eyes the royal maid,
There Ariadne first his form survey'd.
Her bed yet breathed its fragrance o'er her charms
To lull them chastely in a mother's arms,
Pure as the myrtle on Eurotas' side
That draws its limpid nurture from the tide,
Or as the flower, whose varied colours blow
Warm'd by the breath of spring with all their glow.
Now, ere she turn'd away her doting sight,
Her eyes were glistening with impassion'd light;
Her breast was heated with the fiercest flame,
And springing pulses throbb'd o'er all her frame.

O maddener of the mind! immortal boy,
Whose power still blends with woe our richest joy!
O beauty's goddess! O celestial queen
Of Golgos rugged and Idalia green!
With what wild storms ye toss'd that virgin's breast,
Who sigh'd whene'er she met the fair-hair'd guest
What chilling terror made her heart-blood cold;
How sicklier far her cheek than pallid gold,
When Theseus, burning the fell brute to tame,
Sought instant death or everlasting fame!
Rich gifts in secret to the gods she vow'd
To gain the wish she dared not breathe aloud:
Those pious offerings could another save,
But vainly sought the bliss of her who gave.

R

For as the whirlwind hurls from Taurus' brow
The oak, and twists like reeds each giant bough,
Or thick with cones the oozy pine will tear;
And whirl the massive trunk aloft in air:
Far from the broken roots it falls to ground,
And scatters crashing devastation round:
So Theseus down the ponderous monster cast,
Who vainly raging gored the passing blast.
Thence back the victor bent his cautious tread,
Led through the labyrinth by a slender thread,
Which mark'd those tortuous paths, that thought in vain
Had toil'd to trace, or memory to retain.
But why in long digression need I tell
The further fortune that the fair befell?
Who from a sister's arms, a father's eye,
And e'en a mother's dear embrace could fly,
(Ah! mother doom'd with flowing tears to moan!)
And gave up all for Theseus' love alone.
Nor need I tell, how the swift vessel bore
The pair to Dia's isle; how from that shore
The traitor fled, while sleep her eyelids prest,
And lull'd her senses in unkindly rest.
Then, as with burning pangs she madly grieved,
Oft piercing shrieks her bursting heart relieved:
Often she climb'd the craggy cliff to gain
A larger prospect o'er the boundless main;
Then rush'd, her ankles naked to the breeze,
Amid the breakers of repelling seas,
And there with half-drawn sighs, and moanings faint,
And streaming eyes, pour'd forth this wild complaint.

" And hast thou, Theseus, on this desert strand
Left her, who fled for thee my native land;
And has thy double perfidy beguiled
The trusting father to betray the child?
Darest thou, in scorn of heaven's attested host,
Bear fated perjury to thy native coast?
Could nothing check the deed thy soul design'd;
Did rising pity never touch thy mind;
Nor e'er thy bosom to itself pourtray
Those burning pangs that now make mine their prey?

Not these thy promises so fondly vow'd,
When all affections to thine accent bow'd :
Thou never bad'st me hope a fate like this,
But festive spousals and connubial bliss.
The oaths thy passion urged thee then to swear
Are now all scatter'd to the senseless air.
Then let no woman hence in man believe,
Or think a lover speaks but to deceive.
He, while ungratified desire is high,
Shrinks from no oath, no promise will deny ;
Soon as his lust is satiate with its prize,
He spurns his vows, and perjury's curse defies.
I snatch'd thee, lost, from death's ingulfing wave ;
I rather doom'd my brother to the grave,
Than fail in peril's desperate hour to aid
Thee, hard and false ; and I am thus repaid ;
Am giv'n to beasts a prey ; nor shall remorse
Heap e'en the rudest grave upon my corse.

" What lonely lioness thy childhood fed,
What raging sea disgorged, what quicksand bred,
What vast Charybdis, or what Scylla stern ;
Who mak'st for life preserved such fell return ?
Though by the will of thy harsh father tied
Thou couldst not wed, and hail me as thy bride ;
Thou might'st have borne me to thy native soil,
And I, thine handmaid, plied my pleasing toil ;
O'er thy fair feet the tepid stream have shed,
And smoothed the purple covering of thy bed.

" But, ah ! has grief subdued my tortured mind,
Or why complain I to the reckless wind ;
Which with no sense endow'd, no feeling warm,
Nor hears my utterance, nor can answer form ?
The midmost sea his barks already reach ;
No man, no creature treads the silent beach.
Harsh fate, insulting thus my latest pain,
Denies the last sad solace, to complain.
Oh ! would, all-powerful Jove, th' Athenian fleet
Had never touch'd upon the shore of Crete ;
Nor treacherous sailor to its port convey'd
The fatal tribute to the monster paid ;

Nor he, whose form too bright, whose look too kind,
Cloak'd well the savage purpose of his mind,
This heartless, cruel man, had never prest
My father's threshold, a perfidious guest!
Lost as I am, what path, what hopes remain?
Shall I my native mountains seek again?
Ah! the wide depth of ocean's pathless roar
Bars my approach; and dare I hope once more
My sire's affection, whom I left to wed
The reeking murderer of my brother dead?
Can love's sweet musings any solace give,
Or pictured truth, or promised rapture live;
When the dear youth, on whom this heart relied,
Forsakes my bed and flies o'er yonder tide?
No home, no busy cots around me smile,
And seas confine me to this hapless isle.
No means, no hope of flight, no living breath,
All round is desert, but all big with death.

" But yet, ere fate shall close my languid eye,
Ere from my woe-worn breast my senses fly;
I from the gods some ample curse will claim
On him who outraged their attested name;
Will still, betray'd, invoke their awful power,
And pray for vengeance in my latest hour.

" Ye, who avenge their crimes on all mankind,
Furies, whose hair with angry snakes entwined
Paint on the threatening brow the hell-born breast,
Haste, hither haste, and hear my fell request.
'Tis helpless frenzy, senseless, blind despair;
Teach me, 'tis all that's left, my frantic prayer;
Rend from my secret heart each cold restraint,
And pour forth all my soul in my complaint.
Since then it warmly flows from heartfelt pain,
Let me not speak my rage, my grief in vain;
But grant, that still the reckless, ruthless mind
Which made him fly, and leave a wretch behind,
May guide, may urge his life with headlong pace,
Till Theseus curse alike himself and all his race."

As from her burning breast this prayer she pour'd,
And vengeful penance on his crime implored,

The heavenly ruler, Jove, all-powerful god!
Nodded his stern assent ; and at that nod
Earth and wild ocean trembled, and on high
The glistening stars were shaken in the sky.
Then dark oblivion every thought supprest
Which Theseus yet had treasured in his breast:
Of the fond precepts he had long revered
He kept no memory, and no sign he rear'd,
No wish'd-for signal, that his sire might learn
His glorious triumph and his safe return.

For story tells, that Egeus, when the fleet
Unmoor'd to leave Minerva's favour'd seat,
Ere yet he launch'd him on the boisterous wave,
Embraced his son, and this injunction gave.

"My son, my only child, more dear than life,
Son I am forced to send 'mid deadly strife ;
Oh ! late restored to cheer my closing day,
While age yet lingers in its last decay !
Since my stern doom and thy too generous heart
Parts thee from me ; alas ! how loth to part !
While these weak eyes of fastly-dying flame
Yet long to gaze upon thy manly frame ;
I do not send thee forth with hope elate,
Nor shalt thou bear the garb of prosperous fate.
Let me with dust strew my grey temples o'er ;
Let all its sighs my swelling bosom pour :
Then will I hang to your loose yards on high
Funereal sails dark with Iberian dye ;
And let their hue proclaim to every wind
The black despair and misery of my mind.

"But should the goddess in Itone known,
Pallas, who still protects our race and throne,
Propitious grant thy conquering arm to stain
In gushing life-blood of the monster slain ;
Then heed, my son, that treasured in thy heart
This precept live, nor e'er with time depart.
Soon as these hills once more thine eyes shall hail,
Let every yard cast off its gloomy sail ;
And hoisted high in air let every rope
With snow-white canvass greet thy father's hope.

I still shall watch, and I the first be blest,
If happier days give thee return and rest."

Theseus had kept these words in memory bright
'Mid peril's turmoil, and through love's delight;
Now light as clouds, when tempests rudely sweep
The sky-hid summit of some frozen steep,
They fled his mind, nor bless'd the prosperous time,
Forgot in safety's hour and victory's prime.
Wearing with constant tears his eager sight,
His sire still watch'd upon the rampart's height,
Saw the dark sails the clear horizon stain,
Madden'd with thoughts of Theseus fiercely slain,
And from the lofty rock plunged headlong to the main

Thus, when his natal threshold Theseus prest,
A father's death reproach'd his reckless breast.
Scarce less his woe, scarce lighter was his care
Than he had heap'd on the deserted fair ;
Whose hopeless gaze there linger'd to descry
His sails just fading into viewless sky,
While, broken-hearted, in her thoughts she drew
All shapes of woe and miseries ever new.

On the rich covering from another part,
With love for thee high raging in his heart,
Thee seeking, Ariadne, Bacchus young
Hurries with flying steps the shores along.
Before his path the Satyrs madly prance,
The gay Sileni, Nysa's offspring, dance ;
Wild sporting round him range the frantic rout,
And toss their brows, and Evæ, Evæ! shout.
Some brandish high their ivy-cover'd spears ;
Some tear the quivering limbs from mangled steers.
Some round their waists enwrithing serpents tie ;
Some with their stores from ozier caskets ply
Those fearful orgies, that high mystic rite
That's ever hid from uninitiate sight ;
Some their lank arms on echoing timbrels dash ;
Some from the cymbals their thin tinklings clash ;
Some wake the trumpet's hoarser blast and strife,
Or the sharp note of the discordant fife.

Such were the portraitures profusely spread
O'er the rich covering of the nuptial bed.
Pall'd with the sight the throng now bending home
Left for celestial guests the festal dome.
As when young Zephyr flits across the plain,
Rippling with early breath the placid main ;
What time Aurora smiles on day begun
With all the freshest glory of the sun ;
Soft break the waves, and low their laughing sound,
But soon with blasts increasing swell around,
And loud and louder roar, and far away
Raging toss back the purple beams of day ;
So the close crowd, that left the palace, spread,
And wide dispersing urged their quickening tread.

Chiron the first, when all the dome was still,
His rural offering bore from Pelion's hill.
Whatever flowers the meads produce, whate'er
Thessalia's broad and fertile mountains bear,
Whatever blossom some poor streamlet near
The tepid breezes of Favonius rear,
He brought in chaplets of promiscuous bloom ;
And all the palace breathed their glad perfume.

Then Peneus came from Tempe's verdant glades,
Tempe, encircled by o'erhanging shades,
Where Nessos' lovely maids their carols pour.
Peneus the towering beech uprooted bore,
The plane, whose leaves in every zephyr play,
The lofty cypress, and the tapering bay,
And that tall tree whose form the sisters fair
Of blasted Phaeton were doom'd to bear.
These round the dome he placed, a blooming screen,
And veil'd the porch with interwoven green.

Next came Prometheus, rich in craftiest lore,
Who yet faint marks of ancient penance bore ;
When erst his limbs in flinty bondage stiff
Were hung extended on the dizzy cliff.

Then with his sacred queen and all his race
The sire of gods the palace deign'd to grace ;

All, save thee, Phœbus, and thy sister bright,
The sylvan huntress upon Ida's height ;
Alike ye Peleus both beheld with scorn,
Nor Thetis' nuptials would as guests adorn.
Soon as the glorious host were seated round,
A lavish feast the costly table crown'd ;
Then through their frames while aged tremors ran,
The ancient Fates their prescient song began.
Round their weak bodies a white robe was flung,
Whose crimson border o'er their ankles hung ;
Their purple locks with snowy bands were tied ;
And aye their hands the sacred labour plied.
The left the distaff grasp'd, the right hand drew
The wool from thence, and twisted in the clew,
On the bent thumb the winding spindle held,
And as the whirlwind moves its course impell'd.
Still as they spun they bit off every shred
That roughly hung about the new-made thread ;
And the coarse fibres rent in ragged strips
Clung white and dry upon their shrivell'd lips.
Rush-baskets held of wool a snowy choice :
Still as they toil'd they pour'd a piercing voice,
And hymn'd prophetic destiny's behest,
Whose truth all future ages shall attest.

"Peleus, Emathia's stay, and virtue's care,
Renown'd thyself and glorious in thine heir,
Hear on thy nuptial day the Sisters sing
The splendid destiny that time shall bring ;
And, spindles, speed, so life and fate are sped ;
Speed ye, who ceaseless draw the mortal thread !

"Hesper, who gives the bridegroom's sweetest right
Shall lead thy bride with his auspicious light :
Then she and Love, Love that all hearts obey,
Shall make thy soul in bliss dissolve away ;
Fix'd round thy neck her smooth embrace will keep,
And both in soothing languor sink to sleep.
O spindles, speed, thus love and life are sped ;
Speed ye, who ceaseless twine the vital thread !

"No festal palace e'er such loves possess'd,
No loves were ever by such nuptials blest,

As those that Peleus to his Thetis wed.
Ye spindles, speed, who draw the vital thread !

" Achilles' birth shall bless your fond career,
Of heart unstrung to know the touch of fear.
Ne'er his receding back, but well the foe
His breast exposed, and fierce attack, shall know :
He, in the devious race for ever first,
Shall leave behind the stag's most fiery burst.
Ye spindles, speed, so life and fate are sped ;
Speed ye, who ceaseless twine the vital thread !

" No other warrior equal fame shall gain,
When Trojan gore shall Phrygian rivers stain ;
And perjured Pelops' grandson shall destroy
With weary siege the towering walls of Troy.
Speed, spindles, speed, thus life and fate are sped ;
Speed ye, who ceaseless draw the mortal thread !

" His valour oft, his ever dauntless breast
Shall mothers' grief o'er children's biers attest ;
While each with dust her hoary forehead strows,
And beats her livid breast with trembling blows.
Ye spindles, speed, thus fate and death are sped ;
Speed ye, who ceaseless draw the fatal thread !

" As, when the corn by autumn's heat is brown'd,
The reaper strews the crowded stalks around ;
Thus shall his sword the falling Trojans spread.
Speed ye, who ceaseless draw the mortal thread !

" Scamander's waves, in hurrying eddies tost,
That roll to Hellespont, and there are lost,
Shall see his glorious deeds, his deadly force ;
When heaps of slain shall narrow all its course,
When its encumber'd stream the shore shall flood,
And all its depths shall glow with reeking blood.
Speed, spindles, speed, thus fate and death are sped ;
Speed ye, who ceaseless draw the fatal thread !

" At length the virgin too, by victory's doom,
Shall fall to grace his obsequies and tomb :
There shall her snowy limbs, an offering laid,
Attest his glory and appease his shade.

Speed, spindles, speed, so love and death are sped ;
Speed ye, who ceaseless twine the fatal thread !

"When to the war-worn Greeks by fraud shall fall
Neptune's proud work, the sacred Trojan wall ;
Then on his tomb Polyxena shall kneel,
A victim stooping to the two-edged steel ;
Shall there, a headless corpse, her life-blood pour,
And dye the sepulchre with maiden gore.
Speed, spindles, speed, thus love and life are sped ;
Speed ye, who ceaseless draw the fatal thread !

"Then haste, let wedlock's blissful knot be tied ;
Receive, great Peleus, thine immortal bride :
Now lead the fair one to the bridegroom's bed,
And, spindles, speed, and twine the vital thread !

"Her nurse the morrow's morn shall find too tight
The band that girds her slender neck to-night.
Speed, spindles, speed, thus love and life are sped ;
Speed ye, who ceaseless twine the vital thread !

"Ne'er shall the mother mourn, their passion o'er,
The separate homes and bride beloved no more ;
Nor see her hopes of playful grandsons fled.
Still, spindles, speed, thus life and fate are sped ;
Speed, ever ceaseless speed, and twine the mortal thread !

Such was the bliss to Peleus which of old
In lofty song the prescient Fates foretold.
For oft, while piety was yet revered
By pristine man, the gods on earth appear'd ;
And, entering oft some hero's pure abode,
To human crowds immortal beauty show'd.

Oft heaven's dread father, when the festal day
Would to his name its yearly rite display,
Himself would visit the resplendent fane,
And see his hundred chariots scour the plain.
Oft from Parnassus Bacchus drove his flocks
Of Thyads rev'lling with dishevell'd locks ;
When all the Delphians from their city pour'd,
And glad with smoking shrines the god adored.

Oft 'mid the deadly warfare, proudly seen,
Would horrid Mars, or rapid Triton's queen,
Or Nemesis, Rhamnusian maid, incite
Their armed throngs to brave the thickest fight.
But when this earth with impious crime was stain'd,
When virtue fled from man, and passion reign'd ;
When brothers dyed their hands in brothers' gore ;
When children wept a parent's death no more ;
When the harsh father sigh'd for early fate
To snatch the first-born of his buried mate ;
And leave him free from fonder ties, to press
Some blooming stepdame in his faint caress ;
When e'en the mother, warm'd by youthful charms,
Lured her unconscious offspring to her arms ;
Bade incest's curse her household gods condemn,
Impious alike to nature and to them ;
When rival honour crime and virtue knew ;
Their favour justly all the gods withdrew ;
No more to visit sinful earth would deign,
Nor let the eye of man their forms profane.   LAMB.

## ARIADNE.

### FROM THE NUPTIALS OF PELEUS AND THETIS.

No peasant tills the fields ; the steers are eased
Of the neck-galling yoke ; no bull upturns
With downward sloping share the mouldering glebe ;
Discolouring rust soils the deserted plough,
Nor the bent rake clears from the creeping vine
The crumbling earth ; nor he that prunes the bough
Lops with his lightening hook the leafy tree.
The palace, through its inner space discern'd
Of long receding halls, shone gorgeously
With gold and burnish'd silver ; couches gleam'd
Whitening with ivory ; tables glitter'd thick
With goblets ; all the splendid mansion laugh'd
With regal opulence.   The couch, prepared
In tho mid chamber for the goddess bride,
Rose high with plumy cushions.   It was carved
From teeth of Indic elephants, and spread
With the shell purple's crimson of the sea.

The tapestried covering, wrought with antique forms
Of men, display'd heroic lore, in threads
Of wondrous art.   For there upon the shore
Long echoing to the flowing sound of waves
Stood Ariadne, casting a far look
On Theseus as in rapid bark he pass'd
Away; and pangs of furious wild despair
Master'd her throbbing heart.   Nor yet believed
That she was Ariadne; while scarce waked
From her deceiving sleep, she saw herself
Left wretched on the solitary sands.
The youth, who could forget her, flying beat
The billows with his oars, and left his vows
Light scatter'd to the winds and to the storms.
Him when the princess from the weedy shore
Discern'd remote, she bent her straining eyes,
In posture like the statue of a nymph
Nodding in Bacchic orgies; troubled thoughts
Rush'd on her soul, like waves; nor suffer'd she
The slender mitre on her yellow hair;
Or the transparent scarf that o'er her breast
Spread light its covering; or the girdle's grasp
'Gainst which her bosom's struggling orbs rebell'd;
But all torn wildly off from all her form
Lay strewn on every side, and the salt seas,
White foaming at her feet, broke over them.
She nor her mitre, nor her floating zone
Regarded aught : on thee, O Theseus !—still
On thee she dwelt with heart and mind and soul
Distracted.   Ah ! unhappy one ! how grief
And senseless frenzy seized her ! and what thorns
Of anguish Venus planted in her breast !
In that heroic age did Theseus leave
Piræus' winding bay, and visited
The Cretan walls of that inhuman king.
For legends tell that Athens, erst constrain'd
By cruel pestilence, atoned the death
Of slain Androgeos ; and a tribute sent
Of chosen youths, and maids in beauty's flower,
To glut the monstrous Minotaur.   When thus
The noble city underneath its curse

Groan'd heavily, the gallant Theseus chose
To perish self-devoted, in behalf
Of his dear Athens, rather than these maids
Find graves in Crete, yet need a funeral rite.
So, in light bark, with gentle breeze he sail'd
To awful Minos, and his stately court.
When on the stranger fell the eager gaze
Of that same royal virgin, who reposed
Within her mother's arms, on pillow chaste
That breathed sweet perfumes, like the myrtle buds
On green Eurotas' river-banks, or breath
Of the spring gale, that draws the colours forth
From all the streaky flowers. No sooner then
The gazing maid withdrew her glowing eyes,
And bent them on the floor, than all her breast
Conceived a flame, and all her vitals burn'd.

Oh sacred boy ! that, merciless of heart,
Troublest, alas, how cruelly ! the soul
With passion's fury, yet with human griefs
Minglest delights ; and thou, O Venus ! queen
Of Golgos and Idalia's leafy lawns ;
With what a sea of troubles did ye toss
The maiden's heart ; with what a flame consume !
When for the stranger of the yellow locks
She drew full many a sigh. How languish'd she
In heart-struck terrors ! how her cheek grew pale
With yellowing tinge, like the wan shine of gold,
When Theseus, match'd against the monster, sought
Death or the palm of glory ! Nor to heaven
Vow'd she unpleasing offerings, though to her
Fruitless ; nor vainly on her silent lips
Whisper'd suspended hopes. For as the blast
Of irresistible whirlwind with a rush
Of sudden eddy shakes a branching oak
On the Mount Taurus ; or cone-rustling pine,
Dropping with gum ; and smites the knotted trunk ;
Wrench'd from the roots, the tree falls headlong down,
And crushes all beneath it : with such force
Did Theseus quell the savage prostrated
In dust, and beating with his horns the wind.

Then, in his glory, he secure retraced
His footsteps, governing with silken skein
His wandering feet; lest measuring forth his way
From winding of the labyrinth, he should err,
Foil'd by the cunning edifice, that spread
Its undiscoverable maze around.
But why, thus starting from my theme, recount
Superfluous tales ? how Ariadne left
Her father's aspect, and her sister's kiss,
And mother's folding arms ; who, wretched made,
Should with flush'd weeping mourn her daughter lost ?
But Theseus' love was dearer than them all.
Or how the ship was wafted to the shore
Of Naxos' foaming isle ; or how, when closed
Her heavy eyes in that disastrous sleep,
Ingrate he fled, and left her.—Oft, they say,
With burning indignation she pour'd forth
Shrill outcries from the bottom of her heart ;
Climb'd sad the steepy mountains, and threw out
A long glance o'er the vast and foamy deep ;
Or on the flat shore ran amidst the waves,
That swell'd their rippling surface opposite,
From her bared leg lifting the drapery light ;
Then, in extremity of anguish, spoke
These wild upbraidings, with her cheek all bathed
In tears, while shivering sobs confused her words:

"And is it thus, perfidious man ! led far
From my own country, thou forsak'st me now,
Perfidious Theseus ! on a desert shore ?
And dost thou then depart, of watchful gods
Heedless, and ah ! bear with thee to thy home
Those vows, accurs'd by me ?   Could nothing turn
Thy cruel purpose ? did no sudden thought
Of pity cross thee ? did thy hard heart feel
No soft, compunctious visitings for me ?
Not such thy utter'd promises ; not these
The hopes thy lips convey'd to me undone ;
But wedding joys and wishes all fulfill'd
Of marriage love : now to the winds of air
Blown and dispers'd ! Let never woman trust

The oath of man ; let never woman hope
Faith in his tender speeches ! He, while aught
Inflames his ardour to possess, will fear
No oath, will spare no promise.   But when once
His gust is sated, fears not what he spoke ;
Heeds not his perjured promise.   Yet 'twas I
That from death's whirlpool snatch'd thee, and resolved
To sacrifice my brother Minotaur,
That I might spend with thee life's latest hour,
Deceiver as thou art !—and 'tis for this
That forest beasts must tear me ; birds of prey
Dismember ; and no heap of friendly earth
Be scatter'd o'er my corpse !—What lioness
In wilderness of rocks first brought thee forth ?
What sea conceived thee in its roaring depths,
And from its foaming billows cast thee out ?
Syrt, Scylla, or Charybdis, which, or what
Art thou, that for the sweets of life bestow'd
Mak'st this return ?   But if thy heart repell'd
Union with me ; and if to thee seem stern
The laws of marriage which old Cecrops framed ;
Thou couldst at least have brought me to thy home,
That I with pleasant labour might have been
Thy handmaid ; tenderly thy snowy feet
Laving in limpid waters, or thy couch
Spreading with purple coverings.   Ah ! what boots
This frenzy of misfortune ?   Why complain
To the unconscious air, that neither hears
My utter'd speech, nor can in words reply ?
He now has nearly pass'd the middle seas ;
And not one solitary mortal meets
My gaze along the ocean's weedy shore ;
And Fate, insulting even my dying hour,
Envious denies the blessing of complaint
To listening ears.  Oh, mighty Jupiter !
Would that in time long past no ships had touch'd
From Athens on our coast ; no mariner
With dreadful tribute to the bull had loosed
His cable, and, perfidious, sail'd for Crete !
Nor e'er that stranger, masking in sweet form
His cruel purpose, rested in my home !

Whither shall I betake me? on what hope
Lean for support? Say, shall I seek again
The hills of Cretan Ide? ah me! the deep
Rolls broad its severing flood, and cruel forms
Of the wide seas a gulf impassable.
Or might I hope my father's succouring hand?
I, who could leave him, following this stern youth
While reeking with my brother's sprinkled blood?
Shall I console my sorrows with the love
Of that so faithful spouse, while now his oars
Bend pliant in the billows, as he flies?
Shall I pass inland, and forsake the shore?
No dwelling has this lone, unpeopled isle:
There is no egress hence; the sea-waves roll
A girdle round; no plan, no hope of flight;
All solitary, silent, desolate;
A prospect of inevitable death.
But let not yet my dying eyes grow dim,
Nor sense my faint limbs leave, ere, thus betray'd,
I ask the gods for vengeance, and attest
With my last breath the holy faith of heaven.
Ye, then, that with retributive revenge
Visit the deeds of men; whose forehead 'twined
With snaky hair, waves with th' avenging wrath
Of my expiring breast, arise and hear!
Come to my side: come listen the complaints,
Which, oh me miserable! I perforce
Now from my inmost vitals breathe, thus lost,
Burning, and blind with my delirious rage,
Since from the very bottom of my heart
I heave this plaintive voice, oh suffer not
My tears and groans to vanish on the winds!
But in the spirit that within him wrought,
When he forsook me on the desert shore,
In that same spirit, deadly to himself
And to his kindred, let him stain his house
With horror and pollution."

When she thus
Had given her sorrows utterance, and had call'd
In her distraction heavenly vengeance down
On Theseus' cruel deed, heaven's ruler bow'd

His head, and at his unresisted nod
Earth and sea trembled, and the firmament
Rock'd its bright orbs.   But Theseus, dark of mind,
Dismiss'd from memory all injunctions past,
Though long with heed retain'd : nor lifted up
The gladdening symbol, that he safe return'd
To his own country's harbours, in the eyes
Of his long sorrowing father.   Story tells
That when old Ægeus trusted to the winds
His son, who bent his galley's sails to leave
Minerva's towers, he clasp'd him in his arms,
And gave this mandate :—

                 " Oh, my only son !
More pleasant in mine eyes than length of life :
My son ! whom I, perforce, dismiss to cope
With doubtful perils ; son ! so lately lent
Again to these fond arms, in the last stage
Of feeble years : since now my mournful hap
And thy own fervid valour tear thee hence
From these unwilling eyes, whose languid orbs
Still gaze unsated on my son's dear face ;
Not glad I send thee hence ; nor shalt thou bear
Symbols of prosperous Fortune.   I will ease
My bosom of complaint, and soil in dust
My hoary locks ; and on thy flitting mast
Suspend discolour'd sails ; that this my grief
And soul-inflaming anguish may be read
In thy Iberian canvass, while its folds
Are tinged with dusky blue.   If she, who dwells
In blest Itonus, Pallas, who defends
Our race and city, grant that in the blood
Of that half human bull thy hand be red ;
Then bury these injunctions in thy heart ;
Let them take growth, and flourish, so that time
May never root them out.   Soon as thine eyes
Behold our hills again, then let thy crew
The dismal canvass on the yard-arm furl,
And hoist with ropes the sails of snowy white :
That, seeing, I may recognise the joy
Of that blest moment, when auspicious time
Returns thee present to mine eyes again."

s

These mandates, which before with constant mind
He cherish'd, now from Theseus' memory fled,
Like mists from airy ridge of snowy Alp
Swept by the whirlwind.   Still the father bent
From a high turret's top his straining eyes,
Anxious, and dim with weeping.   When he saw
The sable swelling sails, from the steep rocks
He cast himself down headlong ; deeming then
His Theseus lost by an inhuman death.
So Theseus, glorying in the monster slain,
Enter'd beneath his father's roof, now changed
With funeral horror ; and himself now felt
A portion of that anguish, which, ingrate
Of soul, he fix'd in Ariadne's breast :
When, wounded to the heart, a thousand griefs
Roll'd in her bosom, while she pensive bent
On the receding ship her lengthening gaze.

But in another part, Iacchus, flush'd
With bloom of youth, came flying from above,
With choirs of Satyrs, and Sileni, born
In Indian Nyse : seeking thee he came,
O Ariadne ! with thy love inflamed.
They, blithe, from every side came revelling on,
Distraught with jocund madness : with a burst
Of Bacchic outcries, and with tossing heads.
Some shook their ivy-shrouded spears ; and some
From hand to hand, in wild and fitful feast,
Snatch'd a torn heifer's limbs : some girt themselves
With twisted serpents : others bore along,
In hollow arks, the mysteries of the god :
Mysteries to uninitiated ear
In silence wrapt.   On timbrels others smote
With tapering hands, or from smooth orbs of brass
Clank'd shrill a tinkling sound ; and many blew
The horn's hoarse blare, and the barbaric pipe
Bray'd harsh upon the ear its dinning tune.

Thus gorgeously with colour'd figures wrought
The drapery spread its mantling folds, and veil'd
With arras coverlet the wedding couch.

When now the throng of Thessaly had gazed
Their eager fill, they rev'rently gave place
To step of gods approaching.  As the gale,
Ruffling the calm sea with its murm'ring breeze,
Stirs the sloped waves, at rising of the dawn,
Beneath the flitting lustre of the sun:
They, forward driven with gentle blast, roll on
Slowly, and as with sounds of laughter shrill
Dash their soft echo; till the growing wind
Freshens, and more and more in heaving swell
They float far glittering in the purple light:
So from the palace vestibule the throng
Flow'd gradual forth, and wander'd wide away.  ELTON.

## LXV.  TO HORTALUS.

### SENT TO HIM WITH THE POEM OF BERENICE'S HAIR.

THOUGH grief, my Hortalus, that wastes my heart,
    Forbids the culture of the learned Nine ;
Nor can the Muses with their sweetest art
    Inspire a bosom worn with grief like mine ;

For Lethe laves my brother's clay-cold foot,
    His spirit lingers o'er its lazy wave ;
The Trojan earth at high Rhetæum's root
    O'erwhelms his relics in a distant grave !

Shall I then never, in no future year,
    O brother, dearer far that vital breath !
See thee again ? yet will I hold thee dear,
    And in sad strains for ever mourn thy death.

Such as the Daulian bird so sadly pours ;
    As, in some gloomy grove, whose branches crost
Inweave their shade, she still at night deplores
    The hapless destinies of Itys lost.

Yet not forgetting thy request, my friend,
    My love awhile can anguish disregard ;
And, though opprest by heaviest woe, I send
    These lines, the chosen of Cyrene's bard.

Lest, vainly borne upon the zephyrs swift,
   Thou deem'st thy wishes fled my thought and care;
As the dear apple, love's clandestine gift,
   Falls from the bosom of the virgin fair;

Which she forgetting in her vest conceal'd,
   Springs her returning mother's kiss to claim,
It falls, and as it rolls to view reveal'd,
   Her blushes own, like me, neglect and shame.    LAMB

## LXVI.  THE HAIR OF BERENICE.

TRANSLATED BY CATULLUS FROM THE GREEK OF CALLIMACHUS.

(THE HAIR SPEAKS.)

CONON, who knew the lights of yonder skies,
Told how the constellations set and rise;
How the sun's glorious beam is clouded o'er;
How stars at certain times are seen no more;
How love calls Dian from her orbit's place
To steal in Latmos' cave the mute embrace;
He first mark'd me with heavenly light o'erspread,
The honours once of Berenice's head:
Which she, with arms outstretch'd in suppliant love,
Vow'd to devote to many gods above;
What time the king, scarce past the nuptial rite,
Warm from th' unequal contest of the night,
Flush'd with its spoil and proud of amorous wounds,
Had led his warriors to Assyria's bounds.

Do brides, O Venus! hate the bridal bed,
Or feign the tears they oft profusely shed,
The tears that parents gladly mark arise
At wedlock's summons in a daughter's eyes;
That to their doting hearts pay every debt
Of love, of gratitude, and fond regret?
Yes, by the gods, feign'd are the tears they shed
To grace the nuptial rite and bridal bed!
This truth my mistress taught, who wept each day
While war detain'd her youthful spouse away.
But, queen, thy sorrows did not mourn alone
A bridegroom's loss and nuptial rapture flown;

When from thy brother-husband forced to part,
A sister's purer love usurp'd thy heart:
That virtuous grief devour'd her pensive mind ;
Reason, by that subdued, all sway resign'd :
Then sunk that spirit, which had earn'd the praise
Of dauntless valour e'en in childish days.

Hadst thou forgotten the great deed, which won
A royal spouse, a deed yet dared by none ;
Jove ! that at parting thou couldst weakly plain,
While tears, still vainly dried, still gush'd again ?
What mighty god transform'd thee ? Could the woe
Which every lover must in absence know,
Make thee thus promise to the heavenly throne,
Nor wonted blood nor hecatombs alone,
But bid the lovesick offering e'en embrace
Thy temple's shade and forehead's wavy grace,
That heaven might speed thy lord's returning hour,
And Asia's nation bow to Egypt's power ?
He conquer'd and return'd.—The vow was paid,
And heaven received the sweet oblation made.
Reluctant, queen, by thee and by thy brow !
(Evil to him who heeds not such a vow !)
I swear, reluctant from that brow I fell.
But what can iron's mighty strength repel ?
For e'en that mountain, that the tallest height
In Greece o'ertopp'd by swift Hyperion's light,
E'en Athos yielded when the Median host
Form'd a new ocean on the wondering coast,
And through its hills their gorgeous navy bore
The youth barbaric to the Grecian shore.
Could feeble hair that potent metal brave
Which cleaves the mountain, and directs the wave ?

Accursed, O Jove, be all the Scythian race,
And they who, daring first her veins to trace,
Earth's hidden product from her entrails tore,
And shaped and harden'd the destructive ore !

The sister locks I left bewail'd my fate,
When Ethiop Memnon's brother, Flora's mate,

Fanning the yielding air with pennons fleet,
Young Zephyr sought Arsinoe's sacred seat.
Through gloomy night he hurried me away
To the pure regions of ethereal day ;
On Venus' bosom placed me then to rest,
And drink celestial nature from her breast.
Such, where Canopus crowns the fertile wave,
The mandate Flora to her Zephyr gave.

"Permit no more," she cried, "the crown, that shed
Its radiance erst round Ariadne's head,
Alone in heaven to lift its lovely flame,
Nor any star possess congenial fame :
Bid the rich spoil of Berenice's brow
Dart rival beams and share that glory now."

To heaven the goddess raised me, bathed in tears,
An added splendour to the starry spheres.
Betwixt the Lion and the Virgin chaste,
Close to Lycaon's child Callisto placed,
Turn'd from the east, I slow Boötes guide
In tardy progress to the western tide.
I stud that way, in that bright path I lie,
Oft pass'd by gods when journeying o'er the sky :
When night is still, and dark the solar blaze,
They tread my light, and trample on my rays ;
But dawn returning bids me Tethys greet,
And hide my splendour in her cool retreat.

But still—and let me, Nemesis, reveal
In peace the truth no terror shall conceal ;
Let every star reproachful curses dart,
I will unfold the secret of my heart !
Though high 'mid heaven's immortal splendour placed,
I still regret the fair whom erst I graced.
Upon her polish'd brows, while yet a maid,
Unbraided, unperfumed, my ringlets stray'd ;
And drank the breath in wedlock's costlier hours
Of rarest unguents and the balmiest flowers.

And, O ye fair ! allured by Hymen's light,
Ere yet the husband gains his dearest right,
Ere your smooth bosoms heave from cincture free,
Let sweets in rich libation flow to me.

Dear is the incense on my altar spread
By all who seek the chaste, the nuptial bed ;
But the foul offering of disgraceful lust
Shall sink forgotten in the barren dust :
Adulterers' gifts with loathing I reject,
Nor prize their worship, nor their love protect.
But bliss and passion ever young reside
With the fond bridegroom and the faithful bride.

But, queen, when thou shalt gaze upon the skies,
And bid thine orisons to Venus rise,
Though blood must never stain the Paphian shrine ;
Hope not by prayers alone to make me thine :
With purest offerings urge thy costly vows,
And speed my wish'd return to deck thy brows.
There will I wave, nor heed what ills betide,
Though dark Orion seek Aquarius' side,
And constant storms and elemental wars
Proclaim the wild disorder of the stars.          LAMB.

### THE SAME.

THE sage who view'd the shining heav'ns on high,
Explored the glories of th' expanded sky ;
Whence rise the radiant orbs, where still they bend
Their wand'ring course, and where at length descend ;
Why dim eclipse obscures the blazing sun ;
Why stars at certain times to darkness run ;
How Trivia nightly stole from realms above
To taste on Latmos' rocks the sweets of love.
Immortal Conon, blest with skill divine,
Amid the sacred skies beheld me shine,
Ev'n me, the beauteous hair, that lately shed
Refulgent beams from Berenice's head ;
The lock she fondly vow'd with lifted arms,
Imploring all the powers to save from harms
Her dearer lord, when from his bride he flew,
To wreak stern vengeance on th' Assyrian crew ;
While yet the monarch bore the pleasing scars
Of softer triumphs and nocturnal wars.

O sacred queen, do virgins still despise
The joys of Venus and the nuptial ties,

When oft in bridal rooms their sighs and tears
Distract the parent's heart with anxious fears?
The tears descend from friendly powers above;
The sighs, ye gods! are only sighs of love.
With tears like these fair Berenice mourn'd
When for her virgin spoils the monarch burn'd;
With sighs like these she gave him all her charms,
And bless'd the raptured bridegroom in her arms.

But on the widow'd bed you wept alone,
And mourn'd the brother in the husband gone.
What sorrow then my pensive queen opprest,
What pangs of absence tore her tender breast;
When, lost in woe, no trace remain'd behind
Of all her virgin mirth and strength of mind.
Hadst thou forgot the deed thy worth achieved,
For which thy brows the imperial crown received;
The wondrous deed that placed thee far beyond
Thy fair compeers and made a monarch fond?

But when for wars he left your tender arms,
What words you spoke, with what endearing charms
Still breathed your soft complaints in mournful sighs,
And wiped with lifted hands your streaming eyes.
Didst thou, fair nymph, lament by power divine,
Or for an absent lover only pine?
Then to the gods you vow'd with pious care
A sacred offering, your immortal hair,
With blood of slaughter'd bulls, would heaven restore
Your lord in triumph to his native shore;
Should he, returning soon, with high renown
Add vanquish'd Asia to the Egyptian crown:
And I, fair lock, from orbs of radiance now
Diffuse new light to pay thy former vow.
But hear, O queen, the sacred oath I swear,
By thy bright head, and yet remaining hair,
I join'd unwilling the ethereal sphere;
And well I know what woes the perjured feel:
But none can conquer unresisted steel.
Steel heaved the mightiest mountain to the ground
That Sol beholds in his diurnal round.

Through Athos' rocky sides a passage tore,
When first the Medes arrived at Phthia's shore.
Then winds and waves drove their swift ships along,
And through the new-made gulf impell'd the throng.
If these withstood not steel's all-conquering blow,
What could thy hairs against so dire a foe?
O mighty Jove! may still thy wrath divine
Pour fierce destruction on their impious line,
Who dug with hands accurst the hollow mine;
Who first from earth could shining ore produce,
First temper'd steel, and taught its various use.

As thy bright locks bewail'd their sister gone,
Arsinoe's horseman, Memnon's only son,
On flutt'ring wings descended from on high,
To bear the beauteous hairs above the sky;
Then upward bent his flight, and softly placed
Thy radiant lock in chaste Arsinoe's breast,
Whom we Zephyritis and Venus name,
And on Canopus' shores her altars flame;
When late the winged messenger came down
At her desire, lest Ariadne's crown
Should still unrivall'd glitter in the skies;
And that thy precious hair, a richer prize,
The spoils devoted to the powers divine,
Might from the fields of light as brightly shine.
Yet bathed in tears I wing'd my rapid flight,
Swift from her shrine to this ethereal height,
And, placed amidst the fair celestial signs,
Thy lock for ever with new glory shines,
Just by the Virgin in the starry sphere,
The savage Lion, and the Northern Bear.
Full to the west with sparkling beams I lead,
And bright Boötes in my course precede,
Who scarcely moves along the ethereal plain,
And late and slowly sinks beneath the main.

Though feet of gods surround my throne by night:
And in the seas I sleep with morning light,
Yet, O Rhamnusian maid, propitious hear
The words of sacred truth unawed by fear.

The words of truth I wish not to conceal,
But still the dictates of my breast reveal.
Though these resplendent orbs in wrath should **rise**
And hurl me headlong from the flaming skies,
Though placed on high, sad absence I deplore,
Condemn'd to join my lovely queen no more,
On whose fair head, while yet in virgin bloom,
I drank unmeasured sweets and rich perfume.

But now, ye maids, and every beauteous dame,
For whom on nuptial nights the torches flame,
Though fondly wedded to some lovely boy,
Your virgin choice, and partner of your joy,
Forbear to taste the pleasures of a bride,
Nor from your bosoms draw the veil aside,
Till oils in alabaster ye prepare,
And chastely pour on Berenice's hair.
But I th' impure adulteress will confound,
And dash the ungrateful offering on the ground.
From her no rich libation I demand ;
I scorn the gift of her unhallow'd hand :
But if the virtuous fair invoke my power,
Unbounded bliss shall crown the nuptial hour ;
To her shall concord from high heaven descend,
And constant love her soft retreats attend.

And when, bright queen, on solemn feasts your eyes
Shall hail Arsinoe radiant in the skies ;
When she demands, bright opening on your view,
The sacred rites to heavenly Venus due ;
If thy loved lock appear resplendent there,
Let me with her an equal offering share.
But why should these surrounding stars detain
Thy golden hairs in this ethereal plain ?
Oh could I join thy beauteous head once more,
The sacred head on which I grew before ;
Though I should ever lose my light divine,
And moist Arcturus next the Virgin shine.    TYTLER

## LXVII. ON A WANTON'S DOOR.

### PASSENGER.

HAIL, door, to husband and to father dear!
And may Jove make thee his peculiar care!
Thou who, when Balbus lived, if fame say true,
Wast wont a thousand sorry things to do;
And, when they carried forth the good old man,
For the new bride who didst them o'er again;
Say, how have people this strange notion got,
As if thy former faith thou hadst forgot?

### DOOR.

So may Cæcilius help me, whom I now
Must own my master, as I truly vow!—
Be the offences talk'd of great or small;
Still I am free, and ignorant of all:
I boldly dare the worst that can be said;
And yet, what charges to my fault are laid!
No deed so infamous, but straight they cry,
"Fie, wicked door! this is your doing, fie!"

### PASSENGER.

This downright, bold assertion ne'er will do;
You must speak plainer, and convince us too.

### DOOR.

I would;—but how, when no one wants to know?

### PASSENGER.

I want;—collect your facts, and tell them now.

### DOOR.

First, then, I will deny, for so 'tis thought,
That a young virgin to my charge was brought:
Not that her husband, with ungovern'd flame,
Had stolen, in hasty joy, that sacred name;
So vile his manhood, and so cold his blood,
Poor, languid tool! he could not, if he would:
But his own father, 'tis expressly said,
Had stain'd the honours of his nuptial bed;

Whether because, to virtue's image blind,
Thick clouds of lust had darken'd all his mind;
Or, conscious of his son's unfruitful seed,
He thought some abler man should do the deed.

### PASSENGER.

A pious deed, in truth; and nobly done—
A father makes a cuckold of his son!

### DOOR.

Nor was this all that conscious Brixia knew;
Sweet mother of the country where I grew
In earliest youth! who, from Chinæa's height,
Sees boundless landscapes burst upon the sight;
Brixia! whose sides the yellow Mela laves
With the calm current of its gentle waves:
She also knows what bliss Posthumius proved;
And how, in triumph, gay Cornelius loved;
With both of whom, so wanton was the fair,
She did not blush her choicest gifts to share.
" But how," you'll ask, "could you, a senseless door,
These secrets, and these mysteries explore;
Who never from your master's threshold stirr'd,
Nor what the people talk'd of ever heard;
Content upon your hinges to remain,
To ope, and shut, and then to ope again."—
Learn, that full oft I've heard the whispering fair,
Who ne'er suspected I had tongue or ear,
To her own slaves her shameful actions tell,
And speak the very names I now reveal.
One more she mention'd, whom I will not speak,
Lest warm displeasure flush his angry cheek:
Thus far I'll tell thee; he's an awkward brute,
Whose spurious birth once caused no small dispute.

NOTT

### LXVIII.  EPISTLE TO MANLIUS.

THE plaintive letter, Manlius, thou hast sent,
While low by fate and sudden misery bent,
That bids me raise thee from the whelming wave,
And rescue from the threshold of the grave;

Since mighty Venus lets not slumber shed
Its lulling influence o'er thy lonely bed ;
Nor all the verse, our tuneful sires' bequests,
Can soothe thy mind where anguish never rests ;
That hapless letter still my bosom cheers,
Those lines are dear, though written with thy tears :
For, ah ! they speak thy love, and bid me send
Verse from the bard, affection from the friend.
Think not I wish my duty to disown
To the first friend my life has ever known ;
But, Manlius, learn my own unhappy state ;
Learn in how rough a sea of troublous fate
I sink o'erwhelm'd ; nor ask from hopeless woe
For gifts the happy only can bestow.

When the white robe of man I first assumed,
When youth's light Spring with every pleasure bloom'd,
Free were my sports, nor did that goddess spare,
Who blends the bitter sweets of lovers' care.
But all these joys my brother's death has torn
From the lone wretch whom he hath left to mourn.
Brother, thy death has wrapt my days in gloom,
And all our house lies buried in thy tomb ;
Thy friendship still my life with pleasures fed,
And every pleasure now with thee is dead.
His early fate has from my bosom chased
All former joys, and all the mind can taste.
Then cry not, " Shame, Catullus should be known
To droop and linger in Verona's town,
While any noble's frigid form partakes
The warmth of that soft bed which he forsakes !"
No, Manlius, call it not disgrace or shame,
For keenest misery is the fitter name.
Forgive me then, if thou shalt ask in vain
The gifts that sorrow from myself has ta'en.
No hoard of writers here their fires infuse,
To guide my taste and cheer my drooping Muse :
Few favourite volumes serve to fill the void,
And chase the gloom of leisure unemploy'd.
Rome holds my home, my comfort, and my care,
And life is only life when I am there.

Then think not fretful envy prompts my part,
Or gratitude is irksome to my heart ;
Forced to refuse to each request of thine
Gifts I had sent unask'd, had they been mine.
Yet can I not, ye Nine, the tale repress,
How Manlius still has toil'd my life to bless ;
Nor let oblivious time its gloom extend
O'er the dear memory of so true a friend.
To you I speak his praise, do ye unfold
To countless crowds the praises I have told.
Let this time-honour'd verse for ever tell
To future days the name I loved so well ;
And when at length, alas ! his aged head
Shall rest inurn'd among the noble dead,
Wider and wider still his praise proclaim,
When all of him that lives will be his fame.
Thus, by its theme immortal, shall my page
Live still perused in every distant age ;
Nor spider ever venture to profane
With lazy web my laudatory strain.

Ye know how Venus false my life oppress'd,
With what destroying flame she scorch'd my breast
Hot as the fires that Etna's crater fill,
Or Malia's springs that boil near Eta's hill.
With wasting tears my eyes were dim and weak,
And sorrow's drops for ever bathed my cheek.
As, springing on some mountain's airy throne,
The crystal streamlet from the mossy stone
Through the slope valley hurrying headlong down,
Crosses the busy road to some rich town ;
A blest refreshment to the trav'ller's toil,
When arid heat has crack'd the fever'd soil.
As, when through storms the sailor long has pray'd
To Pollux now, and now for Castor's aid,
Soft breathes the favouring air and calms the sea ;
Such Manlius was, such help and bliss to me.
When narrow bounds confined my poor domain,
He made me master of a spacious plain ;
He bounteous placed me in a rich abode,
And the fond girl, whose love we shared, bestow'd

That home my goddess blest: that mansion bore
Her graceful foot upon its tell-tale floor ;
There oft her creaking sandal, sweet to hear,
Foretold the fair one to her lover's ear.

Thus erst, while love warm'd every blissful thought,
Her husband's home Laodamia sought.
Too eager bride !  No victim led to die
Had yet propitiated the gods on high.
(Thy power, dread Nemesis, hath still suppress'd
All hopes unsanction'd by the heavens' behest :
Hapless, who grasp, unless the gods approve,
The proffer'd gift of glory, wealth, or love !)
Soon did she learn how keen the thirsty fane
Desires the sacred blood of victims slain,
Forced from her parting husband's neck to tear
The close embrace that long'd to linger there ;
Ere yet two winters in their length of nights
Had glutted passion with its own delights ;
Or taught the bride, a strength how hard to give !
To lose the mate she loved, and yet to live.
The Fates well knew this doom not distant far
If the bold chieftain sought the Trojan war.
For then had Troy by stealth of Helen's charms
Roused 'gainst herself the kings of Greece to arms.
Troy, baleful, impious Troy !  the common grave
Of Europe's warriors and of Asia's brave !
Troy, whose vast ruin the sad ashes boasts
Of wisdom, valour, and unnumber'd hosts !
Troy, where my brother died, untimely torn
From the lone wretch whom he has left to mourn !
Alas !  his eyes are closed in lasting gloom !
Brother, our house lies with thee in the tomb ;
Thy friendship still my life with pleasures fed,
And all my pleasures now with thee are dead.
Not 'mid ancestral tombs for ages traced,
Nor with the urns of kindred ashes placed ;
But hateful Troy, Troy's melancholy plains
Hold in ungenial soil thy loved remains.
To Troy then hastening, the assembled band
Of Grecian youth had left their native land,

To burst on Paris with the din of arms,
To rouse him from th' adulteress matron's charms;
Nor let his wrong its lawless rapture shed
On days of quiet or a peaceful bed.

'Twas in that hour, that he, beloved too well,
Thine heart-dear spouse, Laodamia, fell;
And wild despair with overwhelming flow
Hurried thee down the deep abyss of woe.
Less deep that gulf described in Grecian lands,
Where Pheneus flows and high Cyllene stands,
Which pour'd the waste of waters through its drain,
And gave to man the firm and fertile plain.
Amphytrion's falsely-father'd son, they say,
Through the broad mountain clove its lofty way,
When, by a worthless lord's command employ'd,
His darts the birds of Stymphalus destroy'd:
'Twas for a throne in heaven his task he plied,
And blooming Hebe for his virgin bride.

How vast, how deep that gulf upon whose soil
A slaving god had spent a lengthen'd toil!
More vast the love that warm'd thy bridal vows;
More deep thy sorrow for thy plighted spouse.
Not to the sire so dear, when grey with years,
The late-born son an only daughter rears;
Who, soon as first he draws the vital air,
Named by his grandsire for his only heir,
Blasts the fond hopes that hungry kinsmen fed;
And drives like vultures from the hoary head.
Not e'en so much the tender sports of love
Please the soft partner of the snowy dove,
Who still with fire, to which her mate's is weak,
Plucks ceaseless kisses with a clinging beak.
(Never can love to manly breasts impart
The doting ardour of the female heart.)
With all their fires thy glowing passion vied,
When first the fair-hair'd warrior claim'd his bride.

Thus erst, thy bright compeer in love and charms,
Light of my life, the damsel sought my arms;

While Cupid, then in saffron vest array'd,
Hovering on sportive wing around her play'd.
What though, too warm to freeze in rigid truth,
Her love at times may bless some other youth ;
Well may her favourite uncomplaining bear
The stolen falsehoods of the modest fair.
Vex not your amorous lives with jealous pain,
Juno, (if such compare be not profane,)
Imperial Juno knew the lusts of Jove,
Still daily false, yet view'd him still with love.
Love, independent love, no care requires,
No chilling sanction of intrusive sires ;
For by no father's formal conduct brought,
No Syrian odours fill'd the home she sought :
But on that wondrous night, all nights above !
She gave at once the fullest gift of love ;
In that same night bestow'd, in that possess'd,
Warm from her lawful bed and husband's breast.
Enough that I that night of rapture pass'd,
Enough, had e'en that rapture been my last !

This gift of verse, 'tis all I can, I send
To pay the duties of a grateful friend :
This grateful verse shall keep thy name and praise
Known and revered through all succeeding days.
To thee the gods will every boon supply
Which Themis' self, in ages long gone by,
Whom never softness sway'd nor favour woo'd,
Heap'd on the wise, the pious, and the good.

Then, Manlius, blest be thou, and blest be she,
The fair, whose life is life and love to thee !
Blest be the lass, who, still of either fond,
Link'd love and friendship in a common bond :
Be e'en the mansion blest, whose walls contain'd
Our fervid sports in passion unrestrain'd ;
And he who made us friends, from whom hath grown
The highest solace that my days have known ;
And blest, more blest than all, that nymph divine,
Whose life alone can still give bliss to mine.    LAMB.

T

### LXIX.  TO RUFUS.

Nay, wonder not that no gay nymph will twine
In am'rous folds her tender frame with thine !
Nor think the costly vest, the gem's proud glare,
Proffer'd by thee, will ever tempt the fair !
A sorry tale they tell; that thou hast got
Under thy arms a vile and filthy goat:
Hence females fly; nor strange—for never, sure,
Can the sweet maid a beast in bed endure.
Then, Rufus, first that noxious pest destroy;
Or cease to wonder why the nymphs are coy.   Nott.


### LXX.  ON THE INCONSTANCY OF WOMAN'S LOVE.

My Fair says, she no spouse but me
Would wed, though Jove himself were he.
 She says it; but I deem
That what the fair to lovers swear
Should be inscribed upon the air,
 Or in the running stream.          Lamb.


### LXXI.  TO VERRO.

If gouty pangs, or a rank goatish smell,
Did ever with poor mortal justly dwell;
Thy rival, Virro, to console thy care,
Hath got of each disease an ample share:
For, when in hot embrace the lovers burn,
She's choked with stench, and he with gout is torn.
                                         Nott


### LXXII.  TO LESBIA.

#### ON HER FALSEHOOD.

To me alone, thou said'st, thy love was true,
And true should be, though Jove himself might woo.
I loved thee, Lesbia, not as rakes may prize
The favourite wanton who has pleased their eyes;
Mine was a tender glow, a purer zeal;
'Twas all the parent for the child can feel.

Thy common falsehood now, thyself I know ;
And though my frame with fiercer heat may glow,
Yet Lesbia's vile and worthless in my sight,
Compared with Lesbia once my heart's delight ;
Nor wonder passion's unrestrain'd excess
Makes me desire thee more, but love thee less.   LAMB.


## THE SAME.

THOU told'st me, in our days of love,
   That I had all that heart of thine ;
That ev'n to share the couch of Jove,
   Thou wouldst not, Lesbia, part from mine.

How purely wert thou worshipp'd then !
   Not with the vague and vulgar fires
Which Beauty wakes in soulless men,—
   But loved, as children by their sires.

That flattering dream, alas, is o'er ;—
   I know thee now—and though these eyes
Dote on thee wildly as before,
   Yet, ev'n in doting, I despise.

Yes, sorceress—mad as it may seem—
   With all thy craft, such spells adorn thee,
That passion ev'n outlives esteem,
   And I at once adore—and scorn thee.   MOORE.


## LXXIII. ON AN INGRATE.

CEASE, cease to toil for thanks, to merit well,
Or think that gratitude with man can dwell.
All are ungrateful.   Selfish sloth's the trade,
The only course by which we are repaid.
This hateful truth still more and more I rue,
Still more each day and hour I feel it true.

Alas for me ! whom no one hates so sore,
Whom no one angers, injures, tortures more,
Than he who owes me all man ever owes
To the first, best, and only friend he knows.   LAMB.

## LXXIV. ON GELLIUS.

GELLIUS had frequently been told,
His uncle used to rave and scold,
If any of his friends should be
Doing or talking wantonly:
He, to avoid reproof and strife,
Affects to flout his uncle's wife;
His uncle silent, and his friend
Thus made, Gellius had gain'd his end;
Who now this very uncle jeers,
And not one word of censure fears.   NOTT

## LXXV. TO LESBIA.

No fair was ever yet so dear
   As thou, my Lesbia, wert to me;
No faith was ever so sincere
   As that which bound my heart to thee.

Now even by thy frailties caught,
   So straitly is my will confined;
The tender duties it hath wrought
   So wholly have enslaved my mind;

Practise each virtue o'er and o'er,
   Or every vice in turn approve,
Nor that could make me love thee more,
   Nor this could make me cease to love.   LAMB

### THE SAME.

No nymph among the much-loved few
   Is loved as thou art loved by me:
No love was e'er so fond, so true,
   As my fond love, sweet maid, for thee!

Yes, e'en thy faults, bewitching dear!
   With such delights my soul possess,
That whether faithless or sincere,
   I cannot love thee more, nor less!   ANON.

## LXXVI. THE LOVER'S PETITION.

### TO HIMSELF.

If virtuous deeds, if honour ever fair,
    Pleasure the memory and console the mind ;
And faith preserved, and pious vows that ne'er
    Attested heaven to deceive mankind ;

Then great the bliss that waits your future day,
    From thy past passion for this thankless maid ;
For all that tenderest love could do or say
    By thee, Catullus, has been done and said.

'Twas vain ; false Lesbia's breast forgot it all.
    Why on this rack thy heart then longer stretch ?
Cast off, undauntedly, your slothful thrall,
    And cease, in spite of heaven, to be a wretch.

'Tis hard to lay long-cherish'd love aside ;
    'Tis hard at once.   But 'tis your only plan ;
'Tis all your hope.   This love must be defied ;
    Nor think you cannot, but assert you can.

Ye gods, if pity 's yours, if e'er ye raise
    The wretch who sinks by hovering death opprest,
Oh ! look on me.—If I have lived with praise,
    Root out this plague and fury from my breast ;

Which, like a torpor creeping through my frame,
    Have peace and pleasure from my heart displaced.
I ask not that she should return my flame,
    Or, what e'en ye could never give, be chaste :

I ask to have my life again mine own,
    Eased of the languid load that on me weighs.
Oh ! grant me this, ye gods ; with this alone
    Repay my piety, and bless my days.    Lamb.


## LXXVII. TO RUFUS.

Rufus, oh thou I deem'd my friend, on whom
    I love in vain and fruitless trust bestow'd.—

Fruitless, ah no ! for from that trust a doom
　　Of heaviest loss and sad misfortune flow'd.

Thus didst thou creep into my secret breast ;
　　And wasting thus my very heart with woe,
'Reft from me all that yet my life had bless'd,
　　And all the future bliss it hoped to know ?

Alas ! alas ! thou poison of my days !
　　Alas ! alas ! my easy friendship's pest !
And now thy noisome mouth 's foul dew bewrays
　　That purest fair's pure lip I oft have press'd.

Yet not unpunish'd shall thy falsehood go,
　　That thus destroys my love's ecstatic flame :
All ages foul and base thy life shall know,
　　And Fame, when doting, gossip of thy shame.  LAMB


## LXXVIII.  ON GALLUS.

Two brothers has Gallus : the one
　　Boasts a wife most seducingly fair ;
The other is blest with a son
　　As seducing in person and air.

Now Gallus, so weak, so gallant,
　　Would the beautiful stripling persuade
To make a bold push at his aunt,
　　And entice the sweet thing to his bed :

But Gallus must surely want thought ;
　　For, since married, methinks it should strike,
That nephews, so charmingly taught,
　　Will cornute every uncle alike.          NOTT


## LXXIX.  ON GELLIUS.

GELLIUS is handsome.—I agree.—
Yes, Lesbia would thy race and thee
　　For him, Catullus, spurn.
Yet he shall all my race devote
To sale, if but three men of note
　　His greeting will return.

Whom Rome abhors, her sons despise,
And pass with scorn-averted eyes,
   My anger ne'er can move.
I do not envy, cannot hate;
I grudge him, bought at such a rate,
   Not even Lesbia's love.     LAMB.

## LXXX. TO GELLIUS.

WHENCE can those lips, that far out-shamed the rose,
Assume a paleness like the wintry snows;
When from his home each morning Gellius flies,
Or when at two in summer noons he'll rise?
Fame whispers then, (but does she whisper right?)
" Too much thou revel'st in obscene delight."—
Fame whispers right; for thy parch'd lips must show
Thy lustful flame; nay, Virro tells it too.    NOTT.

## LXXXI. TO JUVENTIUS.

COULDST thou, in all the Roman race,
   No youth more pleasing see;
And could thy favour no one grace
   A worthier friend for thee,

Than one of that unhealthy crew
   From damp Pisaurus' vale?
The gilded statue's sallow hue
   Is never half so pale.

Is such a wretch so dearly prized
   By thy disgusting whim;
And must I be by thee despised,
   And also yield to him?

Thou canst not see this foul abuse,
   I fain would think, in kindness;
And for thee seek thy sole excuse
   In ignorance and blindness.    LAMB.

### THE SAME.

CAN none of all the Roman race
   Engage your heart? and shall alone

Be foided in your fond embrace
  One of Pisaurus' sickly town!

The wretch whom you so much prefer,
  Is sallow as a gilded bust:
But, O sweet fav'rite, have a care!
  You little know to whom you trust.   NOTT

### LXXXII. TO QUINTIUS.

QUINTIUS, if 'tis thy wish and will
  That I should owe my eyes to thee,
Or anything that's dearer still,
  If aught that's dearer there can be:

Then rob me not of that I prize,
  Of the dear form that is to me,
Oh! far, far dearer than my eyes,
  Or aught, if dearer aught there be.   LAMB.

### LXXXIII. ON LESBIA'S HUSBAND

LESBIA still loads me with abuse,
And when her husband's by, the goose
  O'erjoys to hear her flout me.
Dolt! were she mute, did she not deign
To speak my name, 't would then be plain
  She cared no jot about me.

But while she me for ever chides,
'Tis plain she thinks of none besides:
  Indifference never spent
On one despised such daily din;
And hot must be the flames within
  That need such constant vent.   LAMB.

### LXXXIV. ON ARRIUS.

WHEN Arrius would *commodious* say,
*Chommodious* always was his way;
And when *insidious* he would name,
Straight from his lips *hinsidivus* came:

Nay more, he thought, with that strong swell,
He spoke *hinsidious* wondrous well.
His uncle Liber, and his mother,
I doubt not, so address'd each other;
And that his grandsire, and grandame,
By female line, did just the same.

When Arrius was to Syria sent,
Each wearied ear became content:
But now no more these words displease,
Pronounced with neatness and with ease;
Of aspiration no one thought;
When sudden this dread news was brought,
That Arrius was return'd, and, strange!
Had dared th' Ionian sea to change;
For 'twas no more th' *Ionian* sea,
But the *Hionian*, from that day.          NOTT.

### LXXXV.  ON HIS OWN LOVE.

I HATE and love—ask why—I can't explain;
I feel 'tis so, and feel it racking pain.      LAMB.

#### THE SAME.

I LOVE thee and hate thee, but if I can tell
  The cause of my love and my hate, may I die!
I can feel it, alas! I can feel it too well,
  That I love thee and hate thee, but cannot tell why.
                                               MOORE.

### LXXXVI.  THE COMPARISON.
#### ON QUINTIA AND LESBIA.

THE crowd of beauteous Quintia prate:
To me she is but fair and straight;
  So far I can comply.
Those stated charms her form displays;
But still the full, the general praise
  Of beauteous I deny.

No grain of sprightliness or grace
In all her lofty form we trace.
  I Lesbia beauteous call:

Who, stealing from the lovely host
The separate charms each fair could boast,
    Herself united all.                    LAMB.


### THE SAME.

QUINTIA is beauteous in the million's eye :
    Yes—beauteous in particulars, I own ;
Fair-skinn'd, straight-shaped, tall-sized ; yet I deny
    A beauteous whole ; of *charmingness* there's none :
In all that height of figure there is not
A seasoning spice of that—I know not what ;
That piquant something, grace without a name :
But Lesbia's air is charming as her frame ;
Yes—Lesbia, beauteous in one graceful whole,
From all her sex their single graces stole.      ELTON.


### LXXXVIII.  TO GELLIUS.

TELL me, Gellius, what merits that fellow who'll itch
    For his mother and sisters ; and stript of his vest,
Waste the whole night with either, 'tis no matter which,
    Or the conjugal bliss of his uncle molest ?

Dost thou know the extent of his baseness, I say ?
    So enormous it is that great Tethys in vain,
With old Ocean, who fathers the Nymphs of the sea,
    Would attempt to wash out the indelible stain.

'Tis so great, 'tis a crime of such matchless offence,
    That the wretch of all wretches is scarce more to blame,
Who, deaf to the dictates of nature and sense,
    Lays his hand on himself, and bows down to his shame.
                                                    NOTT


### LXXXIX.  ON GELLIUS.

FROM Gellius' and his parent's guilt shall rise
A sage deep vers'd in Eastern sacrifice ;
For, as from Persian oracles we learn,
Of son and mother must the sage be born ;
Soon for the gods the solemn song he'll frame,
And cast the entrails in the mystic flame.      NOTT.

### XCI. TO GELLIUS.

GELLIUS, my hope, that thou wouldst faithful prove
To the rash trust of my unhappy love,
On no tried honesty nor truth relied,
No dread of infamy nor jealous pride.
But not from thee could my confided fair
Claim filial duty or fraternal care:
No incest heighten'd with its richer gust
The simple treachery of the broken trust.

Though I, 'twas true, from thee could justly claim
All that is due to friendship's holy name;
Still did I deem thy daring love for crime
Sought richer prey and trophies more sublime;
Nor such trite petty sin could aught impart
To suit the blacker relish of thy heart.

But I was fool'd.—Thy guilt can e'en descend
To spoil a female or betray a friend.
Thine avarice lets no sin that's offer'd go,
Still grasps the high, but ne'er neglects the low;
While amply gorged with crimes of highest price,
Still finds some pleasure in the smallest vice.     LAMB.

### XCII. UPON LESBIA'S ABUSE OF HIM.

LESBIA still rails at me when by,
Still does the same though far I fly;
Yet Lesbia loves me, or I'll die.
  You ask me how I tell:
How! why for ever do not I
Retort her words? yet let me die
  But I love Lesbia well.     LAMB.

### XCIII. AND XCIV. ON CÆSAR

So little I for Cæsar care,
  Whatever his complexion be,
That whether dark, or whether fair,
  I vow 'tis all the same to me!

His favourite so debauch'd is got,
  Yes, so debauch'd is his rank blood,
Folks say, he's like a kitchen pot
  That's cramm'd with ev'ry dainty food.   Nott.

## XCV. ON "SMYRNA;"

### A POEM WRITTEN BY CINNA.

Smyrna, my Cinna's poem, which nine years
His Muse hath labour'd, now at length appears;
While brisk Hortensius hath conceived, and done,
And given the world five thousand lines in one.
Far Atrax' waves will hear of Smyrna's name,
And latest ages still keep Smyrna's fame;
The while Volusius' Annals, soon forgot,
Shall wrap up herrings and in Padua rot.

The smaller labours of poetic art
Still please my feelings most and touch my heart;
But let the crowd's applauses still be cast
On long Antimachus and dull bombast.   Lamb.

### THE SAME.

Smyrna, my Cinna's little book, has ta'en
Its author nine years' labour of the brain,
When swift Hortensius has, in less than one,
Of fifty thousand lines a volume done.
But here's the difference: times unborn shall hear
Smyrna rehearsed with an attentive ear.
When vile Hortensius' short-lived work shall die,
Neglected by our ear and by our eye;
For nothing fit, though noisy and sublime,
But to wrap mack'rel with in mack'rel time.
Oh! let my verse be few, but great my pains;
None but the mob can like Antimachus's strains.

                           Anon

## XCVI. TO CALVUS.

### ON THE DEATH OF QUINTILIA.

Calvus, if any joy from mortal tears
  Can touch the feelings of the silent dead;

When dwells regret on loves of former years,
  Or weeps o'er friendships that have long been fled,

Oh! then far less will be Quintilia's woe
  At early death and fate's severe decree,
Than the pure pleasure she will feel to know
  How well, how truly she was loved by thee!    LAMB.

### THE SAME.

If e'er in human grief there breathe a spell
  To charm the silent tomb, and soothe the dead;
When soft regrets on past affections dwell,
  And o'er fond friendships lost, our tears are shed;
Sure, a less pang must touch Quintilia's shade
  While hov'ring o'er her sad, untimely bier,
Than keen-felt joy that spirit pure pervade,
  To witness that her Calvus held her dear.    ELTON.

### XCVII. ON ÆMILIUS.

By all that's sacred I declare
I'm doubtful which I should prefer;
Whether, Æmilius, I would choose
Thy odious mouth, to feast my nose,
Or that more odious part, which shame
Forbids me in my verse to name!
Neither is over-clean at best;
But if I must, I'd take the last;
It's toothless sure; whereas, you know
Your mouth has tusks a yard or so;
Has gums so full of holes and stink,
'Twas a worm-eaten chest you'd think;
And then its width! which to my mind
Brings some toil'd mule that's oft inclined
To stale, when, chafed by summer heats,
The brine's lax aperture dilates.
Yet to the nymphs this homely swain
Makes love, and of his form is vain:
Oh, worthier sure a lash to feel,
And work with asses at the mill!
Who'd kiss that wretch might kiss, I swear,
A pale-faced hangman you know where.    NOTT

### XCVIII. TO VETTIUS.

Whate'er is said that's rude and gross
To the most silly and verbose,
May well with meaning just and true
Be, foul-mouth'd Vettius, said to you.
Your rugged tongue might sound and whole
Lick e'en the ploughboy's filthy sole.

If all you know, 't would give you joy
To blast, to injure, and destroy,
But ope your mouth the wish to teach,
And no one can outlive the speech.      Lamb

### XCIX. THE PROMISE.

#### TO HIS LOVE.

While playfully sporting, I ventured to snatch
  A kiss from thy lips, dearest maid of my soul;
And all heaven's ambrosia itself could not match
  The ravishing sweetness of that which I stole.

Ah! 'twas not unpunish'd.—I suffer'd more pain
  Than the crucified wretch left to linger awhile.
For pardon I sued; but not tears could obtain
  One accent of kindness, one favouring smile.

You scornfully cleansed from the lip I'd possess'd
  Every trace, every feeling by mine left behind;
And wash'd it, as if by some profligate prest,
  The foulest in person and basest in mind:

You sought every method to banish my bliss,
  And Love the tormentor's rough duty embraced;
Till all its ambrosia was lost to the kiss,
  And 'twas bitter as bitterest hellebore's taste.

If this penance must follow each amorous slip,
  From such thefts I for ever an abstinence vow;
For not even the sweetness I taste on your lip
  Can repay me the anger that sits on your brow.      Lamb

## CI. THE RITES AT HIS BROTHER'S GRAVE.

BROTHER, I come o'er many seas and lands
   To the sad rite which pious love ordains,
To pay thee the last gift that death demands;
   And oft, though vain, invoke thy mute remains:
Since death has ravish'd half myself in thee,
O wretched brother, sadly torn from me!

And now ere fate our souls shall re-unite,
   To give me back all it hath snatch'd away,
Receive the gifts, our fathers' ancient rite
   To shades departed still was wont to pay;
Gifts wet with tears of heartfelt grief that tell,
And ever, brother, bless thee, and farewell!    LAMB.

### THE SAME.

SLOW pacing on, o'er many a land and sea,
Brother! I come to thy sad obsequy:
The last fond tribute to the dead impart,
And call thee, speechless ashes as thou art,
Alas, in vain! since fate has ravish'd thee,
E'en thee, thyself, poor brother! torn from me
By too severe a blow; let this be paid,
This rite of ancestry, to soothe thy shade;
Let this, all bathed in tears, my friendship tell,
And oh! for ever bless thee! and farewell!    ELTON.

### THE SAME.

O'ER many a realm, o'er many an ocean tost,
I come, my brother, to salute thy ghost!
Thus on thy tomb sad honour to bestow,
And vainly call the silent dust below.
Thou too art gone! Yes, thee I must resign,
My more than brother—ah! no longer mine.
The funeral rites to ancient Romans paid,
Duly I pay to thy lamented shade.
Take them—these tears their heart-felt homage tell;
And now—all hail for ever. and farewell!    HODGSON.

## CII INVITATION TO CONFIDENCE.

### TO CORNELIUS.

IF e'er friend dared a secret impart
    To the friend in whose faith he believed ;
Or in any affectionate heart
    Confided, and was not deceived :

Believe me, Cornelius, as just ;
    To secrecy's duties as true.
There needs but a friend who will trust
    To make me Harpocrates too.　　LAMB.

## CIII. THE ALTERNATIVE.

### TO SILO.

SILO, restore the sums I paid,
And lay aside the pander's trade
    To seek an honest name :
Then practise every coarse affront,
Be noisy, quarrelsome, and blunt ;
    And I will nothing blame.

But if you venal pass your days,
Then low obedience, servile praise,
    Must be your fitting mood.
A cheat and pander must not wear
Such rudeness as we scarce forbear
    To censure in the good.　　LAMB.

## CIV. TO SOME ONE,

### WHO SPREAD RUMOURS CONCERNING HIMSELF AND LESBIA.

DID you believe that I had cursed
    My heart, my life, my cherish'd fair ?
No cause inflamed my rage to burst ;
Or had I cause, the gravest, worst,
    My desperate love must still forbear.

But whence the tale I well conceive,
 For when with noise and wine elated,
When with your tavern host at eve,
Let one but talk and one believe,
 And any miracle's created.      LAMB.

## CV. ON MAMURRA.

Lo! Formian, in his daring flight,
 Would soar to Pimpla's tuneful brow;
But, with their pitchforks, from the height
 The Muses chuck him down below.      NOTT.

## CVI. ON AN AUCTIONEER.

WHEN along with a sly auctioneer
 Such a dainty young thing we behold,
To the world it must surely appear,
 That its beauty is meant to be sold.      NOTT.

## CVII. THE RECONCILIATION.

### TO LESBIA.

WHEN the first wish the bosom knows,
 But hope has never dared to plight,
Some unexpected hour bestows,
 How heartfelt is the mind's delight!

Thus grateful to my lovesick vow,
 Than all the wealthiest can acquire
More precious far, thus, Lesbia, thou
 Restor'st thyself to my desire.

Yes, thou restor'st thyself, my fair,
 When high my love, but hope how dark!
And this recorded day shall bear
 Of all my life the happiest mark.

I ask the prosperous crowd in vain
 For one possess'd of greater bliss:
Yes, challenge thought itself to feign
 A boon that blesses more than this.      LAMB.

U

### CVIII. TO COMINIUS.

If your foul age, which every vice defiles,
  Were doom'd, Cominius, by the people's law;
First your coarse tongue, that all the good reviles,
  Cut out, would glut the vulture's hungry maw;
The crow's black gorge your torn-out eyes digest;
Your entrails dogs devour, and wolves the rest.   Lamb

### CIX. LESBIA'S VOW OF CONSTANCY.

#### ADDRESSED TO HERSELF.

Dost thou, my life, a tender bond propose
  Of lasting truth and constant love's delights?
Gods grant, that truly from thy heart it flows,
  And nerve that heart to keep the faith it plights!

Thus let their hallow'd vows, their fond career
  Till both shall end, our lives and loves pursue;
And coming time through each succeeding year
  Find me as fond as now, and her as true.   Lamb.

#### THE SAME.

Say you, my life, that we shall ever love?
Oh! may no time the pleasing words disprove!
Heav'n to these words eternal truth impart;
Let her have breathed them from her inmost heart;
And through our lives to Lesbia's spirit grant
Firmness to keep this holy covenant.   Hodgson

### CX. TO AUFILENA.

I like girls, Aufilena, of consciences nice,
  For the favours they grant who are honestly paid;
But you, who have cheated, and taken the price
  Of the love you withhold, are an infamous jade.

'Tis an honest girl's part, what she 's promised, to do;
  'T were a modest one's not to have promised the deed:
But she who can jilt, while she pockets like you
  The money for favours she will not concede,

Commits a base fraud, which would shame and disgrace
The lowest and worst of the prostitute race.    LAMB.

### CXI. TO AUFILENA.

WITH only one fond spouse to live content,
    O Aufilena! best becomes the bride;
Yet, if thou art on prostitution bent,
    Go sin with those to whom thou'rt not allied;
But let no uncle share thy body's shame,
Nor raise up children thou must blush to name.    NOTT.

### CXII. ON NASO.

DOES greatness to that man belong,
    (And in thy own esteem, I know,
Thou'rt counted great,) who in lust's throng
    Descends to all that's vile and low?—
Naso, it does: for we behold in thee
Greatness, combined with lustful infamy.    NOTT.

### CXIII. THE GROWTH OF ADULTERY.

#### TO CINNA.

WHEN Pompey was Rome's Consul first,
'Twas but with two adulterers curst;
And, Cinna, when again he reign'd,
Those two, still unreform'd, remain'd.
But, ah! so skill'd their trade to teach,
A thousand then had sprung from each.

For easier much can love be grown
For others' wives than for our own.    LAMB.

### CXIV. TO MAMURRA.

#### ON HIS ESTATE.

JUSTLY, Mamurra, does your Formian land
The grateful epithet of rich command:
All rural wealth, all wholesome fruits abound,
And fish, and game, and plough'd and pasture ground.

Yet spite of all, how great your own distress,
Who squander three times more than you possess.
Rich then you are, if 'tis a name alone,
And means your farm's abundance, not your own.

LAMB

## CXV.　ON MENTULA.

FORMIANUS, that vile debauchee, is possest
Of a good thirty acres of meadow at least,
With some full forty more, all in arable lands;
Nay, whole oceans of fortune the letcher commands.
With the wealth of rich Crœsus his wealth surely vies,
So immensely extended his opulence lies:
His huge forests, his moors, with grove, pasture, and plain,
Would reach furthermost Scythia, or stretch o'er the main:
Yet this wretch, who such ample possessions can boast,
Is a blustering, bawdy poltroon at the most.　　　NOTT.

## CXVI.　TO GELLIUS.

GELLIUS, I oft in thought debated,
　　Whether I should the poem send
I from Callimachus translated,
　　For you to criticise and mend.

I hoped it might have soothed your hate,
　　And all your weak attempts have ended,
Poor fly! to sting my well-arm'd pate
　　By store of weapons well defended.

But vain I find is all my toil;
　　You will not to my wish incline.
So still my cloak your darts shall foil;
　　While you shall keenly smart with mine.　LAMB.

# THE VIGIL OF VENUS.

LET those love now, who never loved before;
And those who always loved, now love the more

The spring, the new, the warbling spring appears,
The youthful season of reviving years;
In spring the loves enkindle mutual heats,
The feather'd nation choose their tuneful mates,
The trees grow fruitful with descending rain,
And, drest in different greens, adorn the plain.
She comes; to-morrow beauty's empress roves
Through walks that winding run within the groves
She twines the shooting myrtle into bowers,
And ties their meeting tops with wreaths of flowers
Then, raised sublimely on her easy throne,
From nature's powerful dictates draws her own.

Let those love now, who never loved before;
And those who always loved, now love the more.

'Twas on that day which saw the teeming flood
Swell round, impregnate with celestial blood;
Wand'ring in circles stood the finny crew,
The rest was left a void expanse of blue;
Then parent ocean work'd with heaving throes,
And dripping wet the fair Dione rose.

Let those love now, who never loved before;
And those who always loved, now love the more.

She paints the purple year with varied show,
Tips the green gem, and makes the blossom glow.
She makes the turgid buds receive the breeze,
Expand to leaves and shade the naked trees.
When gath'ring damps the misty nights diffuse,
She sprinkles all the morn with balmy dews;

Bright trembling pearls depend at every spray,
And kept from falling, seem to fall away.
A glossy freshness hence the rose receives,
And blushes sweet through all her silken leaves;
(The drops descending through the silent night,
While stars serenely roll their golden light;)
Close till the morn her humid veil she holds;
Then deck'd with virgin pomp the flower unfolds.
Soon will the morning blush, ye maids, prepare;
In rosy garlands bind your flowing hair;
'Tis Venus' plant: the blood fair Venus shed,
O'er the gay beauty pour'd immortal red:
From love's soft kiss a sweet ambrosial smell
Was taught for ever on the leaves to dwell;
From gems, from flames, from orient rays of light,
The richest lustre makes her purple bright;
And she to-morrow weds; the sportive gale
Unties her zone; she bursts the verdant veil;
Through all her sweets the rifling lover flies,
And as he breathes, her glowing fires arise.

  Let those love now, who never loved before;
  And those who always loved, now love the more.

Now fair Dione to the myrtle grove
Sends the gay Nymphs, and sends her tender love.
And shall they venture? Is it safe to go,
While nymphs have hearts and Cupid wears a bow?
Yes, safely venture; 'tis his mother's will;
He walks unarm'd and undesiring ill;
His torch extinct, his quiver useless hung,
His arrows idle, and his bow unstrung.
And yet, ye nymphs, beware, his eyes have charms;
And love that's naked, still is love in arms.

  Let those love now, who never loved before;
  And those who always loved, now love the more.

From Venus' bower to Delia's lodge repairs
A virgin train complete with modest airs:
" Chaste Delia, grant our suit! oh shun the wood,
Nor stain this sacred lawn with savage blood.

Venus, O Delia, if she could persuade,
Would ask thy presence, might she ask a maid."
Here cheerful choirs for three auspicious nights
With songs prolong the pleasurable rites:
Her crowds in measures lightly decent move ;
Or seek by pairs the covert of the grove,
Where meeting greens for arbours arch above,
And mingling flowerets strew the scenes of love.
Here dancing Ceres shakes her golden sheaves ;
Here Bacchus revels, deckt with viny leaves ;
Here wit's enchanting god, in laurel crown'd,
Wakes all the ravish'd hours with silver sound.
Ye fields, ye forests, own Dione's reign,
And Delia, huntress Delia, shun the plain.

    Let those love now, who never loved before ;
    And those who always loved now love the more.

Gay with the bloom of all her opening year,
The Queen at Hybla bids her throne appear,
And there presides ; and there the fav'rite band,
Her smiling Graces, share the great command.
Now, beauteous Hybla ! dress thy flowery beds
With all the pride the lavish season sheds ;
Now all thy colours, all thy fragrance yield,
And rival Enna's aromatic field.
To fill the presence of the gentle court
From every quarter rural Nymphs resort,
From woods, from mountains, from these humble vales,
From waters curling with the wanton gales.
Pleased with the joyful train, the laughing Queen
In circles seats them round the bank of green ;
And, "lovely girls," she whispers, "guard your hearts ;
' My boy, though stript of arms, abounds in arts."

    Let those love now, who never loved before ;
    And those who always loved, now love the more.

Let tender grass in shaded alleys spread ;
Let early flowers erect their painted head ;
To-morrow's glory be to-morrow seen ;
That day old Ether wedded Earth in green.

The vernal father bade the spring appear,
In clouds he coupled to produce the year;
The sap descending o'er her bosom ran,
And all the various sorts of soul began
By wheels unknown to sight, by secret veins
Distilling life; the fruitful goddess reigns
Through all the lovely realms of native day,
Through all the circled land and circling sea;
With fertile seed she fill'd the pervious earth,
And ever fix'd the mystic ways of birth.

    Let those love now, who never loved before;
    And those who always loved, now love the more.

'Twas she, the parent, to the Latian shore
Through various dangers Troy's remainder bore.
She won Lavinia for her warlike son,
And winning her, the Latian empire won.
She gave to Mars the maid whose honour'd womb
Swell'd with the founder of immortal Rome.
Decoy'd by shows the Sabine dames she led,
And taught our vigorous youth the means to wed.
Hence sprung the Romans, hence the race divine
Through which great Cæsar draws his Julian line.

    Let those love now, who never loved before;
    And those who always loved, now love the more,

In rural seats the soul of pleasure reigns;
The love of Beauty fills the rural scenes;
Ev'n Love (if fame the truth of Love declare)
Drew first the breathings of a rural air,
Some pleasing meadow pregnant Beauty prest,
She laid her infant on its bowery breast;
From nature's sweets he supp'd the fragrant dew,
He smiled, he kiss'd them, and by kissing grew.

    Let those love now, who never loved before;
    And those who always loved, now love the more

Now bulls o'er stalks of broom extend their sides,
Secure of favours from their lowing brides.

Now stately rams their fleecy consorts lead,
Who bleating follow through the wand'ring shade.
And now the goddess bids the birds appear,
Raise all their music, and salute the year;
Then deep the swan begins, and deep the song
Runs o'er the water where he sails along;
While Philomela tunes a treble strain,
And from the poplar charms the list'ning plain.
We fancy love exprest at every note;
It melts, it warbles in her liquid throat.
Of barbarous Tereus she complains no more,
But sings for pleasure, as for grief before.
And still her graces rise, her airs extend,
And all is silence till the syren end.
How long in coming is my lovely spring?
And when shall I, and when the swallow sing?
Sweet Philomela, cease;—or here I sit,
And silent loose my rapturous hour of wit.
'Tis gone; the fit retires, the flames decay;
My tuneful Phœbus flies averse away.
His own Amyclæ thus, as stories run,
But once was silent, and that once undone.

Let those love now, who never loved before,
And those who always loved, now love the more.

PARNELL.

THE SAME.

[*First printed* 1651.]

Love he to-morrow, who loved never;
To-morrow, who hath loved, persever.

The spring appears, in which the earth
Receives a new harmonious birth;
When all things mutual love unites;
When birds perform their nuptial rites;
And fruitful by her watery lover,
Each grove its tresses doth recover.
Love's Queen to-morrow, in the shade,
Which by these verdant trees is made,

Their sprouting tops in wreaths shall bind
And myrtles into arbours wind;
To-morrow, raised on a high throne,
Dione shall her laws make known.

>   Love he to-morrow, who loved never;
>   To-morrow, who hath loved, persever.

Then the round ocean's foaming flood
Immingled with celestial blood,
'Mongst the blue purple of the main,
And horses whom two feet sustain,
Rising Dione did beget
With fruitful waters dropping wet.

>   Love he to-morrow, who loved never;
>   To-morrow, who hath loved, persever.

With flowery jewels everywhere
She paints the purple-colour'd year;
She, when the rising bud receives
Favonius' breath, thrusts forth the leaves,
The naked roof with these t' adorn;
She the transparent dew o' th' morn,
Which the thick air of night still uses
To leave behind, in rain diffuses;
These tears with orient brightness shine,
Whilst they with trembling weight decline
Whose every drop, into a small
Clear orb distill'd, sustains its fall.
Pregnant with these the bashful rose
Her purple blushes doth disclose.
The drops of falling dew that are
Shed in calm nights by every star,
She in her humid mantle holds,
And then her virgin leaves unfolds.
I' th' morn, by her command, each maid
With dewy roses is array'd;
Which from Cythera's crimson blood,
From the soft kisses Love bestow'd,
From jewels, from the radiant flame,
And the sun's purple lustre, came.

She to her spouse shall married be
To-morrow ; not ashamed that he
Should with a single knot untie
Her fiery garment's purple dye.

    Love he to-morrow, who loved never ;
    To-morrow, who hath loved, persever.

The goddess bade the nymphs remove
Unto the shady myrtle grove ;
The boy goes with the maids, yet none
Will trust, or think Love tame is grown,
If they perceive that anywhere
He arrows doth about him bear.
Go fearless, nymphs, for Love hath laid
Aside his arms, and tame is made.
His weapons by command resign'd,
Naked to go he is enjoin'd,
Lest he hurt any by his craft,
Either with flame, or bow, or shaft.
But yet take heed, young nymphs, beware
You trust him not, for Cupid's fair,
Lest by his beauty you be harm'd ;
Love naked is completely arm'd.

    Love he to-morrow, who loved never ;
    To-morrow, who hath loved, persever.

Fair Venus virgins sends to thee,
Indued with equal modesty :
One only thing we thee desire,
Chaste Delia, for a while retire ;
That the wide forest, that the wood,
May be unstain'd with savage blood.
She would with prayers herself attend thee,
But that she knew she could not bend thee ;
She would thyself to come have pray'd,
Did these delights beseem a maid.
Now might'st thou see with solemn rites
The Chorus celebrate three nights ;
'Mongst troops whom equal pleasure crowns,
To play and sport upon thy downs ;

'Mongst garlands made of various flowers,
'Mongst ever-verdant myrtle bowers.
Ceres nor Bacchus absent be,
Nor yet the poet's deity.
All night we wholly must employ
In vigils, and in songs of joy;
None but Dione must bear sway
Amongst the woods; Delia, give way.

   Love he to-morrow, who loved never;
   To-morrow, who hath loved, persever.

She the tribunal did command
Deck'd with Hyblæan flowers should stand;
She will in judgment sit; the Graces
On either side shall have their places;
Hybla, thy flowers pour forth, whate'er
Was brought thee by the welcome year;
Hybla, thy flowery garment spread,
Wide as is Enna's fruitful mead;
Maids of the country here will be;
Maids of the mountain come to see;
Hither resort all such as dwell
Either in grove, or wood, or well.
The wing'd boy's mother every one
Commands in order to sit down;
Charging the virgins that they must
In nothing Love, though naked, trust.

   Love he to-morrow, who loved never;
   To-morrow, who hath loved, persever.

Let the fresh covert of a shade
Be by these early flowers display'd,
To-morrow (which with sports and play
We keep) was Æther's wedding day;
When first the father of the spring
Did out of clouds the young year bring.
The husband Shower then courts his spouse
And in her sacred bosom flows,
That all which that vast body bred
By this defluxion may be fed:

Produced within, she all there sways
By a hid spirit, which by ways
Unknown diffused through soul and veins,
All things both governs and sustains.
Piercing through the unsounded sea,
And earth, and highest heaven, she
All places with her power doth fill,
Which through each part she doth distil;
And to the world the mystic ways
Of all production open lays.

   Love he to-morrow, who loved never;
   To-morrow, who hath loved, persever

She to the Latins did transfer
The Trojan nephews; and by her
Was the Laurentian virgin won,
And join'd in marriage to her son.
By her assistance did Mars gain
A votaress from Vesta's fane.
To marriage Romulus betray'd
The Sabine women, by her aid,
(Of Romans the wide-spreading stem,)
And in the long descent of them
In whom that offspring was dilated,
Cæsar her nephew she created.

   Love he to-morrow, who loved never;
   To-morrow, who hath loved, persever.

The fields are fruitful made by pleasure;
The fields are rich in Venus' treasure;
And Love, Dione's son, fame yields
For truth, his birth had in the fields;
As soon as born the field reliev'd him,
Into its bosom first receiv'd him;
She bred him from his infant hours
With the sweet kisses of the flowers.

   Love he to-morrow, who loved never;
   To-morrow, who hath loved, persever.

See how the bulls their sides distend,
And broom-stalks with the burthen bend:

Now every one doth safely lie
Confined within his marriage tie;
See, with their husbands here are laid
The bleating flocks beneath the shade.
The warbling birds on every tree
The goddess wills not silent be.
The vocal swans on every lake,
With their hoarse voice a harsh sound make;
And Tereus' hapless maid beneath
The poplar's shade her song doth breathe;
Such as might well persuade thee, love
Doth in those trembling accents move;
Not that the sister in those strains
Of the inhuman spouse complains.
We silent are whilst she doth sing,
How long in coming is my spring?
When will the time arrive, that I
May swallow-like my voice untie?
My muse for being silent flies me,
And Phœbus will no longer prize me:
So did Amiclæ once, whilst all
Silence observed, through, silence fall.

Love he to-morrow, who loved never;
To-morrow, who hath loved, persever.

                                    THOMAS STANLRY

# ELEGIES OF TIBULLUS.

## BOOK I.

### ELEGY I.

THE glittering ore let others vainly heap,
  O'er fertile vales extend th' enclosing mound;
With dread of neighb'ring foes forsake their sleep,
  And start aghast at every trumpet's sound.

Me humbler scenes delight, and calmer days;
  A tranquil life fair poverty secure!
Then boast, my hearth, a small but cheerful blaze,
  And, riches grasp who will, let me be poor.

Nor yet be hope a stranger to my door,
  But o'er my roof, bright goddess, still preside!
With many a bounteous autumn heap my floor,
  And swell my vats with must, a purple tide.

My tender vines I'll plant with early care,
  And choicest apples with a skilful hand;
Nor blush, a rustic, oft to guide the share,
  Or goad the tardy ox along the land.

Let me, a simple swain, with honest pride,
  If chance a lambkin from its dam should roam,
Or sportful kid, the little wanderer chide,
  And in my bosom bear exulting home.

Here Pales I bedew with milky showers,
  Lustrations yearly for my shepherd pay,
Revere each antique stone bedeck'd with flowers
  That bounds the field, or points the doubtful way

My grateful fruits, the earliest of the year,
    Before the rural god shall duly wait.
From Ceres' gifts I'll cull each browner ear,
    And hang a wheaten wreath before her gate.

The ruddy god shall save my fruit from stealth,
    And far away each little plunderer scare:
And you, the guardians once of ampler wealth,
    My household gods, shall still my off'rings share.

My num'rous herds that wanton'd o'er the mead
    The choicest fatling then could richly yield;
Now scarce I spare a little lamb to bleed
    A mighty victim for my scanty field.

And yet a lamb shall bleed, while, ranged around,
    The village youths shall stand in order meet,
With rustic hymns, ye gods, your praise resound,
    And future crops and future wines entreat.

Then come, ye powers, nor scorn my frugal board,
    Nor yet the gifts clean earthen bowls convey;
With these the first of men the gods adored,
    And form'd their simple shape of ductile clay.

My little flock, ye wolves, ye robbers, spare,
    Too mean a plunder to deserve your toil;
For wealthier herds the nightly theft prepare;
    There seek a nobler prey, and richer spoil.

For treasured wealth, nor stores of golden wheat,
    The hoard of frugal sires, I vainly call;
A little farm be mine, a cottage neat,
    And wonted couch where balmy sleep may fall.

"What joy to hear the tempest howl in vain,
    And clasp a fearful mistress to my breast;
Or lull'd to slumber by the beating rain,
    Secure and happy sink at last to rest."

These joys be mine!—O grant me only these,
    And give to others bags of shining gold,
Whose steely heart can brave the boist'rous seas,
    The storm wide-wasting, or the stiff'ning cold.

Content with little, I would rather stay
    Than spend long months amid the wat'ry waste;

In cooling shades elude the scorching ray,
  Beside some fountain's gliding waters placed.

Oh perish rather all that 's rich and rare,
  The diamond quarry, and the golden vein,
Than that my absence cost one precious tear,
  Or give some gentle maid a moment's pain.

With glittering spoils, Messala, gild thy dome,
  Be thine the noble task to lead the brave;
A lovely foe me captive holds at home,
  Chain'd to her scornful gate, a watchful slave.

Inglorious post!—and yet I heed not fame:
  Th' applause of crowds for Delia I'd resign:
To live with thee I'd bear the coward's name,
  Nor 'midst the scorn of nations once repine.

With thee to live I'd mock the ploughman's toil.
  Or on some lonely mountain tend my sheep;
At night I'd lay me on the flinty soil,
  And happy 'midst thy dear embraces sleep.

What drooping lover heeds the Tyrian bed,
  While the long night is pass'd with many a sigh;
Nor softest down with richest carpets spread,
  Nor whisp'ring rills can close the weeping eye.

Of threefold iron were his rugged frame,
  Who, when he might thy yielding heart obtain,
Could yet attend the calls of empty fame,
  Or follow arms in quest of sordid gain.

Unenvied let him drive the vanquish'd host,
  Through captive lands his conquering armies lead;
Unenvied wear the robe with gold emboss'd,
  And guide with solemn state his foaming steed.

Oh may I view thee with life's parting ray,
  And thy dear hand with dying ardour press:
Sure thou wilt weep—and on thy lover's clay,
  With breaking heart, print many a tender kiss

Sure thou wilt weep—and woes unutter'd feel,
  When on the pile thou seest thy lover laid!
For well I know, nor flint, nor ruthless steel,
  Can arm the breast of such a gentle maid.

x

From the sad pomp, what youth, what pitying fair,
　　Returning slow, can tender tears refrain?
O Delia, spare thy cheeks, thy tresses spare,
　　Nor give my ling'ring shade a world of pain.

But now while smiling hours the Fates bestow,
　　Let love, dear maid, our gentle hearts unite!
Soon death will come and strike the fatal blow;
　　Unseen his head, and veil'd in shades of night.

Soon creeping age will bow the lover's frame,
　　And tear the myrtle chaplet from his brow:
With hoary locks ill suits the youthful flame,
　　The soft persuasion, or the ardent vow.

Now the fair queen of gay desire is ours,
　　And lends our follies an indulgent smile:
'Tis lavish youth's t' enjoy the frolic hours,
　　The wanton revel and the midnight broil.

Your chief, my friends and fellow-soldiers, I
　　To these light wars will lead you boldly on:
Far hence, ye trumpets, sound, and banners fly;
　　To those who covet wounds and fame begone.

And bear them fame and wounds; and riches bear;
　　There are that fame and wounds and riches prize.
For me, while I possess one plenteous year,
　　I'll wealth and meagre want alike despise. GRAINGER

### THE SAME.

LET others raise enormous heaps of gold,
And by sure tenure numerous acres hold;
Whom daily fears of neighbouring foes affright,
While the shrill trumpet breaks their sleep at night.
Me let my easy poverty release
From anxious cares, in liberty and ease;
While my glad hearth with daily fires is bright,
And slumbers, undisturbed with cares, at night.
Still let the seasons crown my smiling field,
Of kindly fruits a plenteous harvest yield.
Still may the product of my loaded vine
Swell all my vessels with nectareous wine.

Myself th' industrious husbandman will be,
And set with ready hand the apple tree;
And in due season plant the tender vine;
Nor e'er the joys of solitude resign.
Nor shall I blush the rustic fork to wield,
Or goad the sluggish ox to plough the field;
Or in my arms to bear the straggling lamb,
Or tender kid, home to the mourning dam.
With rural rites my careful shepherd here
I'm used to lustrate each revolving year;
Propitious sacred Pales to retain,
I sprinkle milk upon the rising grain.
For still I worship wheresoe'er I see
An ancient stone, or remnant of a tree,
With flowery garlands crown'd in open field,
Or where three ways decisive limits yield.
The rural gods as offerings shall receive
The earliest fruit my loaded orchards give.
Thy temple gates, O Ceres, I 'll adorn
With auburn wreaths of ripen'd ears of corn.
And in my orchard let Priapus stand
With the dire sickle in his ruddy hand,
To scare the noxious birds from off my land.
And you, my household gods, shall have your due,
More spreading fields were once preserved by you.
The guardians once of large extended plains,
Now one small farm your kind protection gains.
A cow-calf then for numerous herds of kine
Fell a lustration to your powers divine.
A lambkin now at your bless'd altar dies,
Of narrow soil the mighty sacrifice.
A lambkin to your deities shall fall,
While round the rustic youths on you shall call.
"Good harvest and good vintage, oh! bestow!
Harvest and vintage to your smiles we owe.
Be present, O ye gods! nor yet disdain
To take the off'rings of a lowly swain,
Though such small earthen vessels them contain.
The swains of old in earthen bowls caroused,
E'er glittering gold or silver yet were used.

And you, ye thieves and wolves, my flock refrain
Your prey from larger herds you'll easier gain,
My father's wealth's below my just desire,
Or the full granaries of his potent sire.
A little crop my wishes will supply,
It is enough upon my couch to lie.
Let me on that my wearied limbs repose,
And give a toilsome grandeur to my foes.
On that reclined, how pleasing 'tis to hear
The winds inclement make tumultuous war,
Clasping within my arms my clinging fair!
Or when, by winter's cold congeal'd, the rain,
In rattling showers assaults my hut in vain.
Delia and I secure to slumbers haste,
Lull'd by the rocking storms and winter's blast
This be my fate; let riches be their share
Who can the fury of the billows dare,
And, patient of the weather, tempests bear.
My wishes move within a narrow bound,
Content at last with little I have found.
The tedious paths to wealth no more I'll stray,
My easy soul abhors that rugged way.
Beneath the shadow of some spreading tree,
From fear, from hope, from toil, from wishes free,
Upon the brink of a cool tumbling stream,
I shun the dog-star's fierce and sultry gleam.

Oh! perish rather, all ye glittering gold,
And jewels which fond mortals precious hold,
Than any tender she let fall a tear,
Struck, by the danger of my ways, with fear!
In thee, Messala, war has wondrous charms,
While land and sea are conquer'd by thy arms;
When as the crown of all thy glorious toils,
Thou seest thy house adorn'd with hostile spoils.
Bound with Love's fetters, here will I remain,
I cannot break soft beauty's lovely chain.
No lust of praise invades my peaceful breast,
Whilst thus with thee, my Delia, I am blest.
Of sloth and idleness I court the fame;
Thou art a solid good, that but a name.

If thou, my Delia, still with me remain,
To yoke the steers myself affords no pain.
I can, when thou art by, on lonely downs
Feed my own herds, secure from Delia's frowns.
While thee I can within my bosom keep,
I on the rugged ground can calmly sleep.
Of what avail are Tyrian beds of down,
When love averse will only give a frown?
The tedious night in tears will slowly move,
The joys of night we only owe to love.
'Tis not the down, nor yet the Tyrian loom,
Nor all the golden carpets of thy room,
Nor the soft murmurs of the water's fall,
Can to thy rescue gentle slumbers call.

How dull is he! more lumpish far than lead,
Who can have thee within his happy bed,
And yet would leave thee for the dire alarms
(In chase of spoils) of horrid martial arms:
Though his victorious troops subdue the foe,
And wait his nod where'er he please to go;
Though clad in silver, cover'd o'er with gold,
Upon his prancing horse, most graceful to behold.
Thee let me view when I resign my breath,
Thee let me grasp e'en in the pangs of death;
And press, with falt'ring hands, thy lovely arms,
In death my Delia still would have her charms.
You'd weep, my Delia, when you saw me die,
Beheld me on my bed expiring lie;
On my cold lips thy kisses thou wouldst fix,
While flowing tears with thy dear kisses mix.
Yes, you would weep, you would let fall a tear;
Those lovely eyes a drooping grief would wear.
I know thee well, all tenderness thou art,
Nor steel, nor stone, in thee have any part,
But love and soft compassion fill thy heart.
No, from my funeral no kind youth would go,
Nor tender virgin, ere their tears did flow.
Spare, spare my Manes, gentle Delia, spare
Thy lovely locks, thy bright, dishevell'd hair,
And violence to that dear face forbear.

    While fate permits, then let us join our loves,
Death with his gloomy brow too swiftly moves;
And feeble age steals on, when love will be
Indecent and in vain in thee and me.
With hoary hairs soft toys will not agree.
Now is the time bright Venus to enjoy,
And taste the pleasures of the wanton boy.
While youth is high, the pretty strifes of love,
Its war and peace, a sweet delight will move.
In this a soldier's merit I may claim,
And e'en a general's more exalted fame:
Far hence, ye ensigns! far, ye trumpets' sounds,
To those who court them bear your blood and wounds
Bear to the same the heaps of gold away,
For gold and fame I yield their sordid prey.
Pleased with my present store, securely wise,
Hunger and wealth I equally despise.          OTWAY.

### THE SAME.

LET others pile their yellow ingots high,
    And see their cultured acres round them spread;
While hostile borderers draw their anxious eye,
    And at the trumpet's blast their sleep is fled.

Me let my poverty to ease resign;
    While my bright hearth reflects its blazing cheer;
In season let me plant the pliant vine,
    And, with light hand, my swelling apples rear.

Hope, fail not thou! let earth her fruitage yield;
    Let the brimm'd vat flow red with virgin wine:
For still some lone bare stump that marks the field,
    Or antique cross-way stone, with flowers I twine,

In pious rite; and, when the year anew
    Matures the blossom on the budding spray,
I bear the peasant's god his grateful due,
    And firstling fruits upon his altar lay.

Still let thy temple's porch, O Ceres! wear
    The spiky garland from my harvest field;
And, 'midst my orchard, 'gainst the birds of air,
    His threatening hook let red Priapus wield.

Ye too, once guardians of a rich domain,
   Now of poor fields, domestic gods! be kind.
Then, for unnumber'd herds, a calf was slain;
   Now to your altars is a lamb consign'd.

The mighty victim of a scanty soil,
   A lamb alone shall bleed before your shrine;
While round it shout the youthful sons of toil,
   " Hail! grant the harvest! grant the generous wine!

Content with little, I no more would tread
   The lengthening road, but shun the summer day,
Where some o'er-branching tree might shade my head,
   And watch the murmuring rivulet glide away.

Nor could I blush to wield the rustic prong,
   The lingering oxen goad; or some stray lamb,
Embosom'd in my garment, bear along,
   Or kid forgotten by its heedless dam.

Spare my small flock! ye thieves and wolves, assail
   The wealthier cotes, that ampler booty hold;
Ne'er for my shepherd due lustrations fail;
   I soothe with milk the goddess of the fold.

Be present, deities! nor gifts disdain
   From homely board; nor cups with scorn survey,
Earthen, yet pure; for such the ancient swain
   Form'd for himself, and shaped of ductile clay.

I envy not my sires their golden heap;
   Their garners' floors with sheafy corn bespread;
Few sheaves suffice: enough, in easy sleep
   To lay my limbs upon th' accustom'd bed.

How sweet to hear, without, the howling blast,
   And strain a yielding mistress to my breast!
Or, when the gusty torrent's rush has past,
   Sink, lull'd by beating rains, to shelter'd rest!

Be this my lot; be his th' unenvied store,
   Who the drear storm endures, and raging sea;
Ah! perish emeralds and the golden ore,
   If the fond, anxious nymph must weep for me!

Messala! range the earth and main, that Rome
   May shine with trophies of the foes that fell;

But me a beauteous nymph enchains at home,
  At her hard door a sleepless sentinel.

I heed not praise, my Delia! while with thee;
  Sloth brand my name, so I thy sight behold;
Let me the oxen yoke; oh come with me!
  On desert mountains I will feed my fold.

And, while I press'd thee in my tender arms,
  Sweet were my slumber on the rugged ground:
What boots the purple couch, if cruel charms
  In wakeful tears the midnight hours have drown'd?

Not the soft plume can yield the limbs repose,
  Nor yet the broider'd covering soothe to sleep;
Not the calm streamlet that in murmurs flows,
  With sound oblivious o'er the eyelids creep.

Iron is he who might thy form possess,
  Yet flies to arms, and thirsts for plunder's gains;
What though his spear Cilician squadrons press,
  What though his tent be pitch'd on conquer'd plains?

In gold and silver mail conspicuous he
  May stride the steed, that, pawing, spurs the sand;
May I my last looks fondly bend on thee,
  And grasp thee with my dying, faltering hand!

And thou wilt weep when, cold, I press the bier,
  That soon shall on the flaming pyre be thrown;
And print the kiss, and mingle many a tear;
  Not thine a breast of steel, a heart of stone.

Yes—thou wilt weep.  No youth shall thence return
  With tearless eye, no virgin homeward wend:
But thou forbear to violate my urn,
  Spare thy soft cheeks, nor those loose tresses rend.

Now fate permits, now blend the sweet embrace:
  Death, cowl'd in darkness, creeps with stealing tread;
Ill suits with sluggish age love's sprightly grace,
  And murmur'd fondness with a hoary head.

The light amour be mine; the shiver'd door;
  The midnight fray; ye trumps and standards, hence!
Here is my camp; bleed they who thirst for ore:
  Wealth I despise in easy competence.          ELTON.

## PART OF THE SAME.

IRON were he, who, when he could possess
Thy charms, preferr'd renown to happiness.
Though deck'd with spoils, the guerdon of the brave,
O'er conquer'd lands he bids his banners wave.
Though captive monarchs throng his sounding car,
And bow beneath that thunderbolt of war.
I envy not the blood-stain'd hero's pride,
Content to feed my flocks at Delia's side.

If thou art with me, oh! how sweet my toil,
Though doom'd to turn for bread a thankless soil!
On the cold hill to lay my pensive head,
If thou art with me, oh! how soft my bed!
What joy remains, when gentle love has flown?
On downy pillows, wretched and alone,
Still through the night the sons of fortune weep,
Nor gold, nor blushing purple, brings them sleep;
Celestial music pours a fruitless strain,
Murmur soft airs and fountains flow in vain.

HODGSON.

## ELEGY II.

WITH wine, more wine, my recent pains deceive,
Till creeping slumber send a soft reprieve:
Asleep, take heed no whisper stirs the air,
For waked, my boy, I wake to heart-felt care.
Now is my Delia watch'd by ruthless spies,
And the gate, bolted, all access denies.
Relentless gate! may storms of wind and rain
With mingled violence avenge my pain!
May forky thunders, hurl'd by Jove's red hand,
Burst every bolt, and shatter every band!
Ah no! rage turns my brain; the curse recall;
On me, devoted, let the thunder fall!
Then recollect my many wreaths of yore,
How oft you've seen me weep, insensate door!
No longer then our interview delay,
And as you open let no noise betray.

In vain I plead!—dare then my Delia rise!
Love aids the dauntless, and will blind your spies!
Those who the godhead's soft behests obey,
Steal from their pillows unobserv'd away;
On tip-toe traverse unobserv'd the floor;
The key turn noiseless, and unfold the door:
In vain the jealous each precaution take,
Their speaking fingers assignations make.
Nor will the god impart to all his aid:
Love hates the fearful, hates the lazy maid;
But through sly windings and unpractis'd ways
His bold knight-errants to their wish conveys:
For those whom he with expectation fires
No ambush frightens, and no labour tires;
Sacred the dangers of the dark they dare,
No robbers stop them, and no bravoes scare.
Though wintry tempests howl, by love secure,
The howling tempest I with ease endure:
No watching hurts me, if my Delia smile,
Soft turn the gate, and beckon me the while.

She's mine.  Be blind, ye ramblers of the night
Lest angry Venus snatch your guilty sight:
The goddess bids her votaries' joys to be
From every casual interruption free:
With prying steps alarm us not, retire,
Nor glare your torches, nor our names inquire:
Or if ye know, deny, by heaven above,
Nor dare divulge the privacies of love.
From blood and seas vindictive Venus sprung,
And sure destruction waits the blabbing tongue!
Nay, should they prate, you, Delia, need not fear;
Your lord (a sorceress swore) should give no ear!
By potent spells she cleaves the sacred ground,
And shuddering spectres wildly roam around!
I've seen her tear the planets from the sky!
Seen lightning backward at her bidding fly!
She calls? from blazing pyres the corse descends,
And, re-enliven'd, clasps his wondering friends!
The friends she gathers with a magic yell,
Then with aspersions frights them back to hell!

She wills,—glad summer gilds the frozen pole!
She wills,—in summer wintry tempests roll!
She knows ('tis true) Medea's awful spell!
She knows to vanquish the fierce guards of hell!
To me she gave a charm for lovers meet,
("Spit thrice, my fair, and thrice the charm repeat.
Us in soft dalliance should your lord surprise,
By this imposed on he'd renounce his eyes!
But bless no rival, or th' affair is known;
This incantation me befriends alone.
Nor stopp'd she here; but swore, if I'd agree,
By charms or herbs to set thy lover free.
With dire lustrations she began the rite!
(Serenely shone the planet of the night,)
The magic gods she call'd with hellish sound,
A sable sacrifice distain'd the ground——
I stopp'd the spell: I must not, cannot part:
I begg'd her aid to gain a mutual heart.   GRAINGER.

THE SAME.

OH! give me wine, to heal my wounded breast,
And close my aching eyes in pleasant rest.
Let not a sound disturb the blissful bed,
Where love itself lies tranquil as the dead.
For cruel guards my weeping girl immure,
And heavy bolts her iron gate secure.
Gate of my rival! enemy to love!
May lightning blast thee, darted from above!
No, gentle gate, thou 'lt listen to my prayer,
Turn on thy noiseless hinge, and guide me to my fair,
And, if a lover's phrensy wish'd thee ill,
Heaven on himself avenge his guilty will.
Rather, kind gate, recall my suppliant hours,
And thy bright pillars hung with living flowers.
Thou too, my Delia, boldly brave thy guards—
Venus herself the dauntless pair rewards;
And helps the boy who jealous walls explores,
And helps the girl who opes forbidden doors!

To glide in silence from the downy bed,
To mount the staircase with a noiseless tread,

Hold the warm language of the varying eye,
And kiss by tokens when the fool is by—
Powers to the favour'd few by Venus given,
Betray the cuckold-making aid of heaven.
Such arts are theirs who fly from sluggard ease,
Cross the dark moor, and in the tempest freeze,
Till, safely nestling in their fair one's arms,
They feel the glowing change exalt her charms.

No lawless robber in my path shall rove,
For sacred is the messenger of love;
Nor storm nor howling rain shall cloud my road,
If Delia beckon to the dear abode;
Draw the soft bolt, and silently advise
My sounding footsteps with her fearful eyes,
With eager finger on her lip imprest,
Impatient brow, and quickly-beating breast.
Veil, veil your lamps, whoever travel nigh,
The thefts of Venus shun the curious eye.
Nor tread too loudly, nor inquire my name,
Nor to my face advance your taper's flame.
And ye, who chance to see, the sight forswear,
And vow by all the gods ye were not there.
The prating babbler shall confess with pain
That Venus issued from the savage main.
Nay, e'en your lord the tell-tale shall distrust,
And scorn the lying rumour of your lust.

So sang the witch, whose prophecy divine
Assured my hopes, and made thee wholly mine.
She draws the stars from heaven with influence strong
And turns the course of rapid streams by song;
Cleaves the firm ground, the dead with life inspires,
Bids rattling bones start forth from burial fires,
With magic yell the gathering ghosts commands,
Or purifies with milk their parting bands.
Wills she—the clouds of thunder disappear!
Wills she—dark whirlwinds overcast the sphere!
Sole mistress she of dire Medea's charms,
Her power alone the dogs of hell disarms.
A rhyme she framed, which if thou thrice rehearse
Thy lord shall yield such homage to the verse,

That not a tale his spies relate of me,
No, nor the hot embrace his eyes may see,
Shall win his faith—but if my rivals dare
To snatch the slightest favour from my fair,
Her jealous lord shall every theft perceive,
Know all he suffers, all he hears believe.

Shall I too trust the sorceress' potent art,
By herb, or song, to free my captive heart?
The lustral torches blazed at midnight hour,
Fell the black victim to each magic power,
And thus I pray'd—" Oh! cure me not of love!
But Delia's breast with mutual fondness move!
I would not wish for freedom from my pains,
Oh! what were life unless I wore her chains!"

HODGSON

### THE SAME.

WITH wine, more wine, deceive thy master's care,
  Till creeping slumber soothe his troubled breast;
Let not a whisper stir the silent air,
  If hapless love a while consent to rest.

Untoward guards beset my Cynthia's doors,
  And cruel locks th' imprison'd fair conceal.
May lightnings blast whom love in vain implores,
  And Jove's own thunder rive those bolts of steel.

Ah, gentle door, attend my humble call,
  Nor let thy sounding hinge our thefts betray;
So all my curses far from thee shall fall.
  We angry lovers mean not half we say.

Remember now the flowery wreaths I gave,
  When first I told thee of my bold desires;
Nor thou, O Cynthia, fear the watchful slave,
  Venus will favour what herself inspires.

She guides the youth who see not where they tread;
  She shows the virgin how to turn the door,
Softly to steal from off her silent bed,
  And not a step betray her on the floor.

The fearless lover wants no beam of light;
  The robber knows him, nor obstructs his way;
Sacred he wanders through the pathless night,
  Belongs to Venus, and can never stray.

I scorn the chilling wind and beating rain,
   Nor heed cold watchings on the dewy ground,
If all the hardships I for love sustain,
   With love's victorious joys at last be crown'd:

With sudden step let none our bliss surprise,
   Or check the freedom of secure delight—
Rash man, beware, and shut thy curious eyes,
   Lest angry Venus snatch their guilty sight.

But shouldst thou see, th' important secret hide,
   Though question'd by the powers of earth and heaven
The prating tongue shall love's revenge abide,
   Still sue for grace, and never be forgiven.

A wizard dame, the lover's ancient friend,
   With magic charm has deaft thy husband's ear;
At her command I saw the stars descend,
   And winged lightnings stop in mid career.

I saw her stamp and cleave the solid ground,
   While ghastly spectres round us wildly roam;
I saw them hearken to her potent sound,
   Till, scared at day, they sought their dreary home.

At her command the vigorous summer pines,
   And wintry clouds obscure the hopeful year;
At her strong bidding, gloomy winter shines,
   And vernal roses on the snows appear.

She gave these charms, which I on thee bestow;
   They dim the eye, and dull the jealous mind;
For me they make a husband nothing know,
   For me, and only me, they make him blind.

But what did most this faithful heart surprise,
   She boasted that her skill could set it free:
This faithful heart the boasted freedom flies;
   How could it venture to abandon thee?   HAMMOND.


## ELEGY III.

WHILE you, Messala, plough th' Ægean sea,
Oh sometimes kindly deign to think of me:
Me, hapless me, Phæacian shores detain,
Unknown, unpitied, and oppress'd with pain.

Yet spare me, death, ah spare me, and retire:
No weeping mother's here to light my pyre:
Here is no sister, with a sister's woe,
Rich Syrian odours on the pile to throw:
But chief, my soul's soft partner is not here,
Her locks to loose, and sorrow o'er my bier.

What though fair Delia my return implored,
Each fane frequented, and each god adored;
What though they bade me every peril brave,
And Fortune thrice auspicious omens gave;
All could not dry my tender Delia's tears,
Suppress her sighs, or calm her anxious fears;
E'en as I strove to minister relief,
Unconscious tears proclaim'd my heart-felt grief:
Urged still to go, a thousand shifts I made,
Birds now, now festivals my voyage stay'd:
Or, if I struck my foot against the door,
Straight I return'd, and wisdom was no more.
Forbid by Cupid, let no swain depart;
Cupid is vengeful, and will wring his heart.

What do your offerings now, my fair, avail?
Your Isis heeds not, and your cymbals fail!
What though array'd in sacred robes you stood,
Fled man's embrace, and sought the purest flood?
While this I write, I sensibly decay,—
" Assist me, Isis, drive my pains away:
That you can every mortal ill remove,
The numerous tablets in your temple prove:
So shall my Delia, veil'd in votive white,
Before your threshold sit for many a night;
And twice a day, her tresses all unbound,
Amid your votaries famed, your praises sound:
Safe to my household gods may I return,
And incense monthly on their altars burn."

How blest man liv'd in Saturn's golden days,
E'er distant climes were join'd by lengthen'd ways.
Secure the pine upon the mountain grew,
Nor yet o'er billows in the ocean flew;
Then every clime a wild abundance bore,
And man liv'd happy on his natal shore:

For then no steed to feel the bit was broke,
Then had no steer submitted to the yoke;
No house had gates, (blest times!) and, in the grounds
No scanty land-marks parcell'd out the bounds:
From every oak redundant honey ran,
And ewes spontaneous bore their milk to man:
No deathful arms were forged, no war was waged,
No rapine plunder'd, no ambition raged.
How changed, alas!   Now cruel Jove commands;
Gold fires the soul, and falchions arm our hands:
Each day, the main unnumber'd lives destroys;
And slaughter, daily, o'er her myriads joys.
Yet spare me, Jove, I ne'er disown'd thy sway,
I ne'er was perjur'd; spare me, Jove, I pray.

But, if the Sisters have pronounced my doom,
Inscribed be these upon my humble tomb.
"Lo! here inurn'd a youthful poet lies,
Far from his Delia, and his native skies!
Far from the lov'd Messala, whom to please
Tibullus follow'd over land and seas."

Then Love my ghost (for Love I still obey'd)
Will grateful usher to th' Elysian shade:
There joy and ceaseless revelry prevail;
There soothing music floats on every gale;
There painted warblers hop from spray to spray,
And, wildly-pleasing, swell the general lay:
There every hedge, untaught, with cassia blooms,
And scents the ambient air with rich perfumes:
There every mead a various plenty yields;
There lavish Flora paints the purple fields:
With ceaseless light a brighter Phœbus glows,
No sickness tortures, and no ocean flows;
But youths associate with the gentle fair,
And stung with pleasure to the shade repair:
With them Love wanders wheresoe'er they stray,
Provokes to rapture, and inflames the play:
But chief, the constant few, by death betray'd,
Reign, crown'd with myrtle, monarchs of the shade

Not so the wicked; far they drag their chains,
By black lakes sever'd from the blissful plains;

Those should they pass, impassable the gate
Where Cerberus howls, grim sentinel of fate.
There snake-hair'd fiends with whips patrol around,
Rack'd anguish bellows, and the deeps resound:
There he, who dared to tempt the queen of heaven,
Upon an ever-turning wheel is driven:
The Danaids there still strive huge casks to fill,
But strive in vain, the casks elude their skill:
There Pelops' sire, to quench his thirsty fires,
Still tries the flood, and still the flood retires:
There vultures tear the bow'ls, and drink the gore,
Of Tityus, stretch'd enormous on the shore.
Dread love, as vast as endless be their pain
Who tempt my fair, or wish a long campaign.

O let no rival your affections share,
Long as this bosom beats, my lovely fair!
Still on you let your prudent nurse attend;
She'll guard your honour, she's our common friend.
Her tales of love your sorrowings will allay,
And, in my absence, make my Delia gay:
Let her o'er all your virgin-train preside,
She'll praise th' industrious, and the lazy chide.
But see! on all enfeebling languors creep;
Their distaffs drop, they yawn, they nod, they sleep.
Then, if the destinies propitious prove,
Then will I rush, all passion, on my love:
My wish'd return no messenger shall tell,
I'll seem, my fair, as if from heaven I fell.
A soft confusion flushes all your charms,
Your graceful dishabille my bosom warms,
You, Delia, fly and clasp me in your arms.

For this surprise, ye powers of love, I pray,
Post on, Aurora, bring the rosy day.     GRAINGER.

### THE SAME.

How well they lived in Saturn's golden times,
Ere earth lay open to her farthest climes;
Ere hollow pine-trees mounted on the wave,
And to the wind their swelling canvass gave;
Or sailors, wand'ring to a world unknown,
Prest their deep bark with produce not their own.

No lordly bull then dragg'd the pond'rous wain,
Nor noble horse obey'd the slavish rein ;
No house was guarded by the jealous wall,
No selfish landmark robb'd the wealth of all.
Spontaneous oaks distill'd their honey'd dews,
Their milk was offer'd by the teeming ewes :
War had not yet his iron front display'd,
Nor savage craft contrived the murd'rous blade.
Danger and death pursue the thunderer's reign,
And cross, by countless paths, the land and main.
Oh ! spare me, Jove ! no perjured tongue is mine,
No impious curses hurl'd at names divine.
Yet, if my fated length of life is gone,
Be this inscription graved upon my stone,
" Here young Tibullus slumbers with the dead,
O'er earth and sea by loved Messala led."

But I, who living yield to gentle love,
Dying shall seek the blest Elysian grove.
There tuneful choirs o'er verdant meadows stray,
And dance and song delight th' immortal day ;
Uncultur'd cassia scents the teeming ground,
And od'rous roses flourish all around.
There many a tender girl and favour'd boy
Renew the wonted interchange of joy.
There roam the pairs of guiltless lovers dead,
With wreaths of myrtle on each youthful head.

But Guilt's pale dens lie hid in night profound,
Where sable floods rush horribly around ;
Their snake-crown'd heads the hissing Furies rear,
And the damn'd souls are hurried here and there ;
His scorpion jaws black Cerberus expands,
And at the brazen gate expecting stands !
There, on the rapid wheel is lust impaled,
Lust that the queen of heaven herself assail'd.
There Tityus, stretch'd at his enormous length,
Feeds the keen vulture with his bleeding strength.
There thirsting Tantalus, with eager eyes
And outstretch'd hands, pursues the stream that flies
There the false brides who shed their husbands' blood
Through hollow vessels pour the ceaseless flood.

There be the wretch who wishes me to rove,
In painful absence from my only love.

But rest for ever pure, my lovely bride,
Thy aged nurse still watching at thy side,
Telling sweet tales of seasons long gone by—
While, at their lamps, the circling damsels ply
The curious labours of the length'ning thread,
Or o'er the distaff bend their drowsy head.
Then, on a sudden, will thy lover come,
As if from heaven descending to his home:
No courier's speed my Delia shall prepare,
But in her chance undress I'll find the fair.
Then will she run these smiling eyes to meet,
Loose her dark locks, and bare her snowy feet.
Oh! with what joy I'll strain her to my breast,
While tears and tender murmurs speak the rest. ELTON.

## ELEGY IV.[1]

### POET.

So round my god may shady coverings bend,
No sun-beams scorch thy face, no snows offend!
Whence are the fair so proud to win thy heart,
Yet rude thy beard, and guiltless thou of art?
Naked thou stand'st, expos'd to wintry snows!
Naked thou stand'st when burning Sirius glows!
Thus I—and thus the garden-power replied,
A crooked sickle glittering by his side.

### PRIAPUS.

Take no repulse—at first what though they fly!
O'ercome at last, reluctance will comply.
The vine in time full ripen'd clusters bears,
And circling time brings back the rolling spheres:

---

[1] Those who understand the original, need not to be told the reasons which obliged the translator to alter and omit many passages of this Elegy; which, with some few others of the same stamp, were probably those parts of Tibullus, which made the pious Anthony Possevin apply to heaven in prayer, to preserve him from temptation whenever he purposed to read our poet.—GRAINGER.

In time soft rains through marble sap their way,
And time taught man to tame fierce beasts of prey.
Nor awed by conscience meanly dread to swear;
Love-oaths, unratified, wild tempests bear!
Banish then scruples, if you'd gain a heart;
Swear, swear by Pallas' locks, Diana's dart,
By all that's most rever'd—if they require:
Oaths bind not eager love, thank heaven's good sire!
Nor be too slow; your slowness you'll deplore;
Time posts; and, oh! youth's raptures soon are o'er:
Now forests bloom, and purple earth looks gay;
Bleak winter blows, and all her charms decay:
How soon the steed to age's stiffness yields,
So late a victor in th' Olympic fields?
I've seen the aged oft lament their fate,
That senseless they had learnt to live too late.
Ye partial gods, and can the snake renew
His youthful vigour and his burnish'd hue?
But youth and beauty past, is art in vain
To bring the coy deserters back again?

### POET.

Jove gives alone the powers of wit and wine,
In youth immortal, spite of years, to shine.

### PRIAPUS.

Yield prompt compliance to the maid's desires;
A prompt compliance fans the lover's fires:
Go pleased where'er she goes, though long the way,
Though the fierce dog-star dart his sultry ray;
Though painted Iris gird the bluish sky,
And sure portends that rattling storms are nigh:
Or, if the fair one pant for sylvan fame,
Gay drag the meshes and provoke the game:
Nay, should she choose to risk the driving gale,
Or steer, or row, or agile hand the sail:
No toil, though weak, though fearful, thou forbear;
No toils should tire you, and no dangers scare.
Occasion smiles, then snatch an ardent kiss;
The coy may struggle, but will grant the bliss:
The bliss obtain'd, the fictious struggle past,
Unbid, they'll clasp you in their arms at last.

POET.

Alas! in such degenerate days as these,
No more love's gentle wiles the beauteous please!
If poor, all gentle stratagems are vain!
The fair ones languish now alone for gain!
Oh may dishonour be the wretch's share,
Who first with hateful gold seduced the fair!

PRIAPUS.

Ye charming dames, prefer the tuneful choir,
Nor meanly barter heavenly charms for hire.
What cannot song? The purple locks that glow'd
On Nisus' head, harmonious song bestow'd!
What cannot strains? By tuneful strains alone
Fair iv'ry, Pelops, on thy shoulder shone!
While stars with nightly radiance gild the pole,
Earth boasts her oaks, or mighty waters roll,
The fair, whose beauty poets deign to praise,
Shall bloom uninjur'd in poetic lays:
While she who hears not when the Muses call,
But flies their fav'rites, gold's inglorious thrall!
Shall prove, believe the bard, or soon, or late,
A dread example of avenging fate!

Soft, flattering songs, the Cyprian queen approves:
And aids the suppliant swain with all her loves.

POET.

The god, no novice in th' intriguing trade,
This answer, Titius, to my question made:
But caution bids you fly th' insidious fair,
And paints the perils of their eyes and air;
Nor these alone devoted man subdue,
Devoted man their slightest actions woo.

Be cautious those who list—but ye who know
Desire's hot fever, and contempt's chill woe,
Me grateful praise—contempt shall pain no more;
But wish meet wish, instructed by my lore:
By various means, while others seek for fame,
Scorn'd love to counsel be my noblest aim.

Wide stands my gate for all—I rapt foresee
The time, when I Love's oracle shall be!
When round my seat shall press th' enamour'd throng
Attend my motions, and applaud my song.

Alas! my hopes are fled, my wiles are vain;
The fair I dote on treats me with disdain:
Yet spare me, charmer, your disdain betrays
To witty laughter my too boastful lays.     GRAINGER.

## ELEGY V.

OF late I boasted I could happy be,
Resume the man, and not my Delia see!
My boasts of manhood, boasts of bliss are vain;
Back to my bondage I return again!
And like a top am whirl'd, which boys, for sport,
Lash on the pavement of a level court!

What can atone, my fair, for crimes like these?
I'll bear with patience, use me as you please!
Yet, by Love's shafts, and by your braided hair,
By all the joys we stole, your suppliant spare.
When sickness dimm'd of late your radiant eyes,
My restless, fond petitions won the skies.
Thrice I with sulphur purified you round,
And thrice the rite, with songs, th' enchantress bound
The cake, by me thrice sprinkled, put to flight
The death-denouncing phantoms of the night:
And I nine times, in linen garbs array'd,
In silent night, nine times to Trivia pray'd.
What did I not?   Yet what reward have I?
You love another, your preserver fly!
He tastes the sweet effects of all my cares,
My fond lustrations, and my solemn prayers.

Are these the joys my madding fancy drew,
If young-eyed health restored your rosy hue?
I fondly thought, sweet maid, oh thought in vain!
With you to live a blithesome village swain.
When yellow Ceres asks the reaper's hand,
Delia (said I) will guard the reaper's band;

Delia will keep, when hinds unload the vine,
The choicest grapes for me, the richest wine:
My flocks she'll count, and oft will sweetly deign
To clasp some prattler of my menial train:
With pious care will load each rural shrine,
For ripen'd crops a golden sheaf assign,
Cates for my fold, rich clusters for my vine:
No, no domestic care shall touch my soul;
You, Delia, reign despotic o'er the whole;
And will Messala fly from pomp of state,
And deign to enter at my lowly gate?
The choicest fruitage that my trees afford
Delia will cull herself to deck the board;
And wondering, such transcendent worth to see,
The fruit present, thy blushing hand-maid she.

Such were the fond chimeras of my brain,
Which now the winds have wafted o'er the main.
O power of Love, whom still my soul obey'd,
What has my tongue against thy mother said?
Guiltless of ill, unmark'd with incest's stain,
I stole no garland from her holy fane:
For crimes like these I'd abject crawl the ground,
Kiss her dread threshold, and my forehead wound.

But ye who, falsely wise, deride my pains,
Beware; your hour approaches—love has chains.
I've known the young, who ridiculed his rage,
Love's humblest vassals when oppress'd with age:
Each art I've known them try to win the fair,
Smooth their hoarse voice, and dress their scanty hair:
I've known them, in the street, her maid detain;
And weeping, beg her to assist their pain.
At such preposterous love each school-boy sneers;
Shuns, as an omen; or pursues with fleers.

Why do you crush your slave, fair queen of joy?
Destroying me, your harvest you destroy!   GRAINGER.

## ELEGY VI.

WITH wine I strove to soothe my love-sick soul,
But vengeful Cupid dash'd with tears the bowl:

All mad with rage, to kinder nymphs I flew;
But vigour fled me, when I thought on you.
Balk'd of the rapture, from my arms they run,
Swear I'm devoted, and my converse shun!

By what dire witchcraft am I thus betray'd?
Your face and hair unnerve me, matchless maid:
Not more celestial look'd the sea-born fair,
Received by Peleus from her pearly chair.
A rich admirer his addresses paid,
And bribed my mistress by a beldam's aid.
From you my ruin, curst procuress, rose;
What imprecations shall avenge my woes?
May heaven, in pity to my sufferings, shed
Its keenest mischief on your plotting head!
The ghosts of those you robb'd of love's delight,
In horrid visions haunt your irksome night!
And, on the chimney, may the boding owl
Your rest disturb, and terrify your soul!
By famine stung, to churchyards may you run;
There feast on offals hungry wolves would shun!
Or howling frantic, in a tatter'd gown,
Fierce mastiffs bait you through each crowded town!

'Tis done! a lover's curse the gods approve;
But keenest vengeance fires the queen of love.
Leave then, my fair, the crafty, venal jade;
What passion yields not, when such foes invade?

Your hearts, ye fair, does modest merit claim?
Though small his fortunes, feed his gentle flame;
For genuine love's soft raptures would ye know?
These raptures merit can alone bestow;
The sons of opulence are folly's care,
But want's rough child is sense and honour's heir.

In vain we sing—the gate still bolted stands;
Come, vengeance, let us burst its sullen bands.
Learn, happy rival, by my wrongs to know
Your fate; since Fortune governs all below.

                                          GRAINGER

## ELEGY VII.

LOVE still invites me with a smiling eye !
Beneath his smiles what pains and anguish lie !
Yet since the gods, dread power, must yield to thee,
What laurels canst thou gain from conquering me ?
Me Delia loved ; but by thy subtle wiles,
The fair, in secret, on another smiles :
That my suspicion's false, 'tis true, she swears ;
And backs her imprecations with her tears !
False fair, your oaths and Syren tears refrain ;
Your Syren tears and oaths no credit gain ;
For when your lord suspected me of yore,
As much you wept, as many oaths you swore.

Yet wherefore blame I Love ? the blame is mine ;
I, wretched I, first taught her to design !
I first instructed her her spies to foil ;
Back on myself my wanton arts recoil :
Herbs of rare energy my skill supplied,
All marks of too-fond gallantry to hide !
More artful now, alone the wanton lies ;
And new pretexts her cozening brains devise.

Uncautious lord of a too cunning spouse !
Admittance grant me, she shall keep her vows !
Be warn'd, my friend, observe her when her tongue
Commends in wanton phrase the gay-dress'd young ;
Oh let her not her heaving bosom bare,
Exposed to every fop's immodest stare,
When leaning on the board, with flowing wine,
She seems to draw some inconsiderate line ;
Take heed, take heed, (I know the warning true,)
These random lines assign an interview.
Nor let your wife to fanes so frequent roam,
A modest wife's best temple is at home :
But if your prohibitions all are vain,
Give me the hint, I'll dodge her to the fane ;
What though the goddess snatch my curious sight,
I'll bring her wanton privacies to light.

Some gem she wore, I'd oft pretend to view
But squeez'd her fingers unperceiv'd of you :

Oft with full racy bowls I seal'd your eyes,
Water my bev'rage, and obtain'd the prize.
Yet since I tell, forgive the pranks I play'd,
Love prompted all, and Love must be obey'd!

  Nay, 'twas at me (be now the truth avow'd)
Your watchful mastiff used to bark so loud;
But now some other, with insidious wait,
Intent observes each creaking of your gate,
At which, whoever of the house appears,
Passing, the mien of quick despatch he wears;
But comes again the minute they remove,
And coughs, sure signal of impatient love!

  What boots, though marriage gave a wife so fair,
If careless you, or she eludes your care?
While men are artful, and your wife can feign,
Vain are your brazen bolts, your mastiffs vain.

  Cold to the raptures of the genial bed,
She lays the fault upon an aching head:
'Tis false; the wanton for some other sighs;
From this her coolness, this her aches arise.

  Then, then be warn'd, intrust her to my care;
Whips, chains I laugh at, if you grant my prayer.
" Hence from my ward, ye sparkish essenced beaus;
Illegal love oft springs from essenced clothes."
Where'er she walks, not distant I'll attend,
And guard your honour from the casual friend!
" Off, gallants, off: for so the gods ordain,
So the dread priestess in unerring strain!"
(When holy fury fires the frantic dame,
She mocks all torture, and exults in flame;
Her snow-white arms and heaving breast she tears;
And with the gushing gore Bellona smears;
Deep in her side she plants the glittering sword;
And the dread goddess prompts each fateful word.)
" Ye youths, beware, nor touch whom Cupid guards
Unpunish'd none attempt his gentle wards:
As my blood flows, and as these ashes fly,
Their wealth shall perish, and their manhood die."

  She menaced then the fair with dreadful pain;
E'en were you guilty, may her threats be vain:

Not on your own account; your mother's age,
Your worthy mother deprecates my rage:
When Love and Fortune smiled, her gentle aid
Oft me conducted to the blooming maid;
My footsteps, wakeful, from afar she knew,
Unbarr'd the gate, nor fear'd the nightly dew:
Half of my life's long thread I'd pleas'd resign,
My sweet conductress, could I lengthen thine!
Still, still, though much abus'd, I Delia prize;
She's still thy daughter, and enchants my eyes.

Yet though no coy cimarr invest the fair,
Nor vestal fillet bind her auburn hair;
Teach her what decent modesty requires,
To crown my fire, alone, with equal fires.
Me too confine; and if, in wanton praise
Of other maids, my tongue luxuriant strays,
Let thy suspicion then no limits know,
Insult me, spurn me, as thy greatest foe!
But if your jealousies are built in air,
And patient love your usage cannot bear;
What wrath may perpetrate, my soul alarms,
For wrath, I warn you, heeds not female charms.
Nor yet be chaste from mean unamorous fear;
Be still most modest when I am not near.

For those, whom neither wit nor worth secure,
Grow old, unpitied; palsied, worthless, poor;
Yet with each servile drudgery they strive,
To keep their being's wretchedness alive!
The gay regard their woe with laughing eyes;
Swear they deserve it, and absolve the skies!
Nor Venus less exults! " May such a fate,
(From heaven she prays) upon th' inconstant wait."

The same my wish! but oh may we two prove,
In age, a pattern of unalter'd love!     GRAINGER.

## ELEGY VIII.

" THIS day" (the Fates foretold in sacred song,
And singing drew the vital twine along)

" He comes, nor shall the gods the doom recall,
He comes, whose sword shall quell the rebel Gaul.
With all her laurels him shall Conquest crown,
And nations shudder at his awful frown ;
Smooth Atur, now that flows through peaceful lands,
Shall fly affrighted at his hostile bands."
'Tis done ! this prophecy Rome joys to see,
Far-famed Messala, now fulfill'd in thee :
Long triumphs ravish the spectators' eyes,
And fetter'd chieftains of enormous size :
An ivory car, with steeds as white as snow,
Sustains thy grandeur through the pompous show.

Some little share in those exploits I bore ;
Witness Tarbella, and the Santoigne shore ;
Witness the land where steals the silent Soane,
Where rush the Garonne, and th' impetuous Rhone ;
Where Loire, enamour'd of Carnutian bounds,
Leads his blue water through the yellow grounds.

Or shall his other acts adorn my theme ?—
Fair Cydnus, winding with a silver stream ?
Taurus, that in the clouds his forehead hides,
And rich Cilicia from the world divides ;
Taurus, from which unnumber'd rivers spring,
The savage seat of tempests, shall I sing ?
Why should I tell, how sacred through the skies
Of Syrian cities, the white pigeon flies ?
Why sing of Tyrian towers, which Neptune laves ;
Whence the first vessel, venturous, stemm'd the waves ?
How shall the bard the secret source explore,
Whence, father Nile, thou draw'st thy watery store ?
Thy fields ne'er importune for rain the sky,
Thou dost benignly all their wants supply :
As Egypt, Apis mourns in mystic lays,
She joins thy praises to Osiris' praise.

Osiris first contrived the crooked plough,
And pull'd ripe apples from the novice bough ;
He taught the swains the savage mould to wound.
And scatter'd seed-corn in th' unpractised ground.
He first with poles sustain'd the reptile vine,
And show'd its infant tendrils how to twine :

Its wanton shoots instructed man to shear,
Subdue their wildness, and mature the year:
Then too the ripen'd cluster first was trod;
Then in gay streams its cordial soul bestow'd;
This as swains quaff'd, spontaneous numbers came,
They praised the festal cask, and hymn'd thy name;
All ecstasy, to certain time they bound,
And beat in measured awkwardness the ground.
Gay bowls serene the wrinkled front of care;
Gay bowls the toil-oppressed swain repair!
And let the slave the laughing goblet drain;
He blithesome sings, though manacles enchain.

Thee sorrow flies, Osiris, god of wine;
But songs, enchanting Love, and dance are thine:
But flowers and ivy thy fair head surround,
And a loose saffron mantle sweeps the ground.
With purple robes invested, now you glow;
The shrine is shown, and flutes melodious blow:
Come then, my god, but come bedew'd with wine!
Attend the rites, and in the dance combine;
The rites and dances are to Genius due!
Benign Osiris, stand confess'd to view!
Rich unguents drop already from his hair,
His head and neck soft flowery garlands share!
O come, so shall my grateful incense rise,
And cates of honey meet thy laughing eyes!

On thee, Messala, ('tis my fervent prayer,)
May heaven bestow a wise, a warlike heir:
In whom, increased, paternal worth may shine,
Whose acts may add a lustre to thy line,
And transports give thee in thy life's decline.

But should the gods my fervent prayer deny,
Thy fame, my glorious friend, shall never die.
Long as (thy bounteous work) the well-made way
Shall its broad pavement to the sun display,
The bards of Alba shall in lofty rhyme
Transmit thy glory down the tide of time:
They sing from gratitude: nor less the clown
Whom love or business have detain'd in town

Till late, as home he safely plods along,
Thee chants, Messala, in his village song.

Blest morn, which still my grateful Muse shall sing,
Oft rise, and with you greater blessings bring.

GRAINGER

## ELEGY IX.

In vain would lovers hide their infant-smart
From me, a master in the amorous art;
I read their passion in their mien and eyes,
O'erhear their whispers, and explain their sighs.
This skill no Delphian oracles bestow'd,
No augurs taught me, and no victims show'd;
But Love my wrists with magic fillets bound,
Lash'd me, and lashing, mutter'd many a sound.
No more then, Marathus, indifference feign,
Else vengeful Venus will enhance your pain!

What now, sweet youth, avails your anxious care,
So oft to essence, oft to change your hair?
What though cosmetics all their aid supply,
And every artifice of dress you try?
She's not obliged to bredes, to gems, to clothes,
Her charms to nature Pholoe only owes.

What spells devote you? say, what philtres bind?
What midnight sorceress fascinates your mind?
Spells can seduce the corn from neighbouring plains!
The headlong serpent halts at magic strains!
And did not cymbals stop thy prone career,
A spell thee, Luna, from thy orb would tear!

Why do I magic for your passion blame,
Magic is useless to a perfect frame!
You squeez'd her hands, your arms around her threw,
Join'd lip to lip, and hence your passion grew.

Cease then, fair maid, to give your lover pain
Love hates the haughty, will avenge the swain.
See youth vermilions o'er his modest face!
Can riches equal such a boy's embrace?
Then ask no bribe—when age affects the gay,
Your every smile let hoary dotage pay;

But you your arms around the stripling throw,
And scorn the treasure monarchs can bestow.
But she who gives to age her charms for pay,
May her wealth perish and her bloom decay.
Then when impatience thrills in every vein,
May manhood shun her, and the young disdain.

Alas! when age has silver'd o'er the head,
And youth that feeds the lamp of love is fled,
In vain the toilette charms; 'tis vain to try,
Grey scanty locks with yellow nuts to die;
You strip the tell-tales vainly from their place,
And vainly strive to mend an aged face.

Then in thine eyes while youth triumphant glows,
And with his flowers thy cheeks, my fair one, sows,
Incline thine heart to love and gentle play,
Youth, youth has rapid wings, and flies away!
The fond old lover vilify, disdain;
What praise can crown you from a stripling's pain?
Spare then the lovely boy; his beauties die,
By no dire sickness sent him from the sky:
The gods are just; you, Pholoe, are to blame;
His sallow colour from your coyness came.

Oh, wretched youth! how oft, when absent you,
Groans rend his breast, and tears his cheeks bedew!
"Why dost thou rack me with contempt?" he cries,
"The willing ever can elude their spies.
Had you, oh had you felt what now I feel,
Venus would teach you from your spies to steal.
I can breathe low; can snatch the melting kiss,
And noiseless ravish Love's enchanting bliss;
At midnight I securely grope my way,
The floor tread noiseless, noiseless turn the key.
Poor fruitless skill! my skill if she despise,
And cruel from the bed of rapture flies.
Or if a promise haply I obtain,
That she will recompense at night my pain;
How am I duped! I wakeful listen round,
And think I hear her in each casual sound.
Perish the wiles of Love and arts of dress!
In russet weeds I'll shroud my wretchedness.

The wiles of Love and arts of dress are vain,
My fair to soften and admittance gain."

Youth, weep no more, your eyes are swoln with tears;
No more complain, for oh! she stops her ears.
The gods, I warn you, hate the haughty fair,
Reject their incense, and deny their prayer.
This youth, this Marathus, who wears your chains,
Late laugh'd at love, and ridiculed its pains!
Th' impatient lover in the street would stay!
Nor dreamt that vengeance would his crimes repay.
Now, now he moans his past misdeeds with tears,
A prey to love, and all its frantic fears:
Now he exclaims at female scorn and hate;
And from his soul abhors a bolted gate!

Like vengeance waits you, trust th' unerring Muse,
If still you're coy, and still access refuse!
Then how you'll wish, when old, contemn'd of all,
But vainly wish, these moments to recall!   GRAINGER.

## ELEGY X.[1]

WHY did you swear by all the powers above,
Yet never meant to crown my longing love?
Wretch, though at first the perjured deed you hide,
Wrath comes with certain, though with tardy stride;
Yet, yet, offended gods, my charmer spare!
Yet pardon the first fault of one so fair!

For gold the careful farmer ploughs the plain,
And joins his oxen to the cumbrous wain;
For gold, through seas that stormy winds obey,
By stars, the sailor steers his watery way.
Yet, gracious gods, this gold from man remove,
That wicked metal bribed the fair I love.

Soon shall you suffer greatly for your crime,
A weary wanderer in a foreign clime;

The translator has been obliged to use pretty much the same freedom
with this Elegy as with the fourth.  Had the other Elegies of Tibullus
been like these two, he had never taken the trouble of translating them.
But, as both in this version are new modelled, it is hoped that neither of
them can shock the most delicate modesty.

Your hair shall change, and boasted bloom decay,
By wintry tempests and the solar ray.

" Beware of gold," how oft did I advise !
" From tempting gold what mighty mischiefs rise !
Love's generous power," I said, "with ten-fold pain,
The wretch will rack, who sells her charms for gain.
Let torture all her cruelties exert,
Torture is pastime to a venal heart.

" Nor idly dream your gallantries to hide,
The gods are ever on the sufferer's side.
With sleep or wine o'ercome, so fate ordains,
You'll blab the secret of your impious gains."

Thus oft I warn'd you; this augments my shame;
My sighs, tears, homage, henceforth I disclaim.

" No wealth shall bribe my constancy," you swore;
" Be mine the bard," you sigh'd, " I crave no more:
Not all Campania shall my heart entice,
For thee Campania's autumns I despise.
Let Bacchus in Falernian vineyards stray,
Not Bacchus' vineyards shall my faith betray."

Such strong professions, in so soft a strain,
Might well deceive a captivated swain;
Such strong professions might aversion charm,
Slow doubt determine, and indifference warm.
Nay more, you wept, unpractised to betray,
I kiss'd your cheeks, and wiped the tears away.

But if I tempting gold unjustly blame,
And you have left me for another flame,
May he, like you, seem kind, like you, deceive,
And oh may you, like cheated me, believe.

Oft I by night the torch myself would bear,
That none our tender converse might o'erhear;
When least expected, oft some youth I led,
A youth all beauty, to the genial bed,
And tutor'd him your conquest to complete,
By soft enticements, and a fond deceit.

By these I foolish hoped to gain your love !
Who than Tibullus could more cautious prove ?

z

Fired with uncommon powers, I swept the lyre,
And sent you melting strains of soft desire.
The thought o'erspreads my face with conscious shame
Doom, doom them victims to the seas or flame.
No verse be theirs, who Love's soft fires profane,
And sell inestimable joys for gain.

But you who first the lovely maid decoy'd,
By each adulterer be your wife enjoy'd.
And when each youth has rifled all her charms,
May bed-gowns guard her from your loathed arms!
May she, oh may she like your sister prove,
As famed for drinking, far more famed for love!
'Tis true, the bottle is her chief delight,
She knows no better way to pass the night;
Your wife more knowing can the night improve,
To joys of Bacchus joins the joys of love.

Think'st thou for thee the toilette is her care?
For thee, that fillets bind her well-dress'd hair?
For thee, that Tyrian robes her charms enfold?
For thee, her arms are deck'd with burnish'd gold?
By these, some youth the wanton would entice,
For him she dresses, and for him she sighs;
To him she prostitutes, unawed by shame,
Your house, your pocket, and your injured fame:
Nor blame her conduct, say, ye young, what charms
Can beauty taste in gout and age's arms?

Less nice my fair one, she for money can
Caress a gouty, impotent old man;
O thou by generous Love too justly blamed!
All, all that Love could give, my passion claim'd.
Yet since thou couldst so mercenary prove,
The more deserving shall engross my love:
Then thou wilt weep when these adored you see;
Weep on, thy tears will transport give to me.
To Venus I'll suspend a golden shield,
With this inscription graved upon the field:

"Tibullus, freed at last from amorous woes,
This offering, Queen of Bliss, on thee bestows:
And humbly begs, that henceforth thou wilt guard
From such a passion thy devoted bard."     GRAINGER.

### ELEGY XI.

Who was the first that forged the deadly blade?
Of rugged steel his savage soul was made;
By him, his bloody flag ambition waved,
And grisly carnage through the battle raved.
Yet wherefore blame him? we're ourselves to blame;
Arms first were forged to kill the savage game:
Death-dealing battles were unknown of old;
Death-dealing battles took their rise from gold.
When beechen bowls on oaken tables stood,
When temperate acorns were our fathers' food,
The swain slept peaceful with his flocks around,
No trench was open'd and no fortress frown'd.

Oh had I lived in gentle days like these,
To love devoted and to home-felt ease;
Compell'd I had not been those arms to wear,
Nor had the trumpet forced me from the fair;
But now I'm dragg'd to war, perhaps my foe
E'en now prepares th' inevitable blow!

Come then, paternal gods, whose help I've known
From birth to manhood, still protect your own,
Nor blush, my gods, though carved of ancient wood,
So carved in our forefathers' times you stood;
And though in no proud temples you were praised,
Nor foreign incense on your altars blazed,
Yet white-robed faith conducted every swain,
Yet meek-eyed piety serened the plain;         [hair
While clustering grapes, or wheat-wreaths round your
Appeased your anger, and engaged your care:
Or dulcet cakes himself the farmer paid,
When crown'd his wishes by your powerful aid;
While his fair daughter brought with her from home
The luscious offering of a honey-comb:
If now you'll aid me in the hour of need,
Your care I'll recompense—a boar shall bleed.
In white array'd, I'll myrtle baskets bear,
And myrtle foliage round my temples wear:
In arms redoubtable let others shine,
By Mars protected mow the hostile line;

You let me please, my head with roses crown,
And every care in flowing goblets drown ;
Then when I'm joyous let the soldier tell,
What foes were captived and what leaders fell ;
Or on the board describe with flowing wine,
The furious onset and the flying line.
For reason whispers, Why will short-lived man
By war contract his too contracted span ?
Yet when he leaves the cheerful realms of light,
No laughing bowls, no harvests cheer the sight,
But howl the damn'd, the triple monster roars,
And Charon grumbles on the Stygian shores :
By fiery lakes the blasted phantoms yell,
Or shroud their anguish in the depths of hell.

In a thatch'd cottage happier he by far,
Who never hears of arms, of gold, or war.
His chaste embrace a numerous offspring crown,
He courts not fortune's smile, nor dreads her frown
While lenient baths at home his wife prepares,
He and his sons attend their fleecy cares.
As old, as poor, as peaceful may I be,
So guard my flocks, and such an offspring see.
Meantime, soft Peace, descend ; oh bless our plains !
Soft Peace to plough with oxen taught the swains.
Peace plants the orchard and matures the vine,
And first gay-laughing prest the ruddy wine ;
The father quaffs, deep quaff his joyous friends,
Yet to his son a well-stored vault descends.

Bright shine the ploughshare, our support and joy !
But rust, deep rust, the veteran's arms destroy !

The villager, (his sacred offerings paid
In the dark grove and consecrated shade,)
His wife and sons, now darkness parts the throng,
Drives home, and whistles as he reels along.
Then triumphs Venus ; then love-feuds prevail ;
The youth all jealous then the fair assail ;
Doors, windows fly, no deference they pay,
The chastest suffer in th' ungentle fray :
These beat their breasts and melt in moving tears ;
The lover weeps and blames his rage and fears ;

Love sits between, unmoved with tears and sighs,
And with incentives sly the feud supplies.

Ye youths, though stung with taunts, of blows beware;
They, they are impious, who can beat the fair:
If much provoked, or rend their silken zone,
Or on their tresses be your anger shown:
But if nor this your passion can appease,
Until the charmer weep, the charmer tease!
Blest anger, if the fair dissolves in tears!
Blest youth, her fondness undisguised appears!
But crush the wretch, O war, with all thy woes,
Who to rough usage adds the crime of blows.

Bland Peace, descend with plenty on our plains,
And bless with ease and laughing sport the swains.

GRAINGER.

# BOOK II.

### ELEGY I.

ATTEND! and favour! as our sires ordain,
The fields we lustrate, and the rising grain:
Come, Bacchus, and thy horns with grapes surround;
Come, Ceres, with thy wheaten garland crown'd;
This hallow'd day suspend each swain his toil,
Rest let the plough, and rest th' uncultured soil:
Unyoke the steer, his racks heap high with hay,
And deck with wreaths his honest front to-day.
Be all your thoughts to this grand work applied!
And lay, ye thrifty fair, your wool aside!
Hence I command you mortals from the rite,
Who spent in amorous blandishment the night,
The vernal powers in chastity delight.
But come, ye pure, in spotless garbs array'd!
For you the solemn festival is made;
Come! follow thrice the victim round the lands!
In running water purify your hands!

See! to the flames the willing victim come!
Ye swains with olive crown'd, be dumb! be dumb!
" From ills, O sylvan gods, our limits shield,
To-day we purge the farmer and the field;
Oh let no weeds destroy the rising grain;
By no fell prowler be the lambkin slain;
So shall the hind dread penury no more,
But gaily smiling o'er his plenteous store,
With liberal hand shall larger billets bring,
Heap the broad hearth, and hail the genial spring.
His numerous bond-slaves all in goodly rows,
With wicker huts your altars shall enclose.
That done, they'll cheerly laugh, and dance, and play,
And praise your goodness in their uncouth lay."

The gods assent! see! see! those entrails show
That heaven approves of what is done below!
Now quaff Falernian, let my Chian wine,
Pour'd from the cask, in massy goblets shine!
Drink deep, my friends; all, all, be madly gay,
'Twere irreligion not to reel to-day!
Health to Messala, every peasant toast,
And not a letter of his name be lost!

O come, my friend, whom Gallic triumphs grace,
Thou noblest splendour of an ancient race;
Thou whom the arts all emulously crown,
Sword of the state, and honour of the gown;
My theme is gratitude, inspire my lays!
Oh be my Genius! while I strive to praise
The rural deities, the rural plain,
The use of foodful corn they taught the swain.
They taught man first the social hut to raise,
And thatch it o'er with turf, or leafy sprays:
They first to tame the furious bull essay'd,
And on rude wheels the rolling carriage laid.
Man left his savage ways; the garden glow'd,
Fruits not their own admiring trees bestow'd,
While through the thirsty ground meandering runnels
    flow'd.
There bees of sweets despoil the breathing spring,
And to their cells the dulcet plunder bring.

The ploughman first to soothe the toilsome day,
Chanted in measur'd feet his sylvan lay:
And, seed-time o'er, he first in blithesome vein,
Piped to his household gods the hymning strain.
Then first the press with purple wine o'erran,
And cooling water made it fit for man.
The village lad first made a wreath of flowers
To deck in spring the tutelary powers:
Blest be the country, yearly there the plain
Yields, when the dog-star burns, the golden grain ;
Thence too thy chorus, Bacchus, first began,
The painted clown first laid the tragic plan.
A goat, the leader of the shaggy throng,
The village sent it, recompensed the song.
There too the sheep his woolly treasure wears ;
There too the swain his woolly treasure shears ;
This to the thirsty dame long work supplies ;
The distaff hence, and basket took their rise.
Hence too the various labours of the loom,
Thy praise, Minerva, and Arachne's doom !
Mid mountain herds Love first drew vital air,
Unknown to man, and man had nought to fear ;
'Gainst herds, his bow th' unskilful archer drew ;
Ah my pierced heart, an archer now too true !
Now herds may roam untouch'd, 'tis Cupid's joy,
The brave to vanquish, and to fix the coy.
The youth whose heart the soft emotion feels,
Nor sighs for wealth, nor waits at grandeur's heels ;
Age fired by Love is touch'd by shame no more,
But blabs its follies at the fair one's door !
Led by soft Love, the tender, trembling fair
Steals to her swain, and cheats suspicion's care,
With outstretched arms she wins her darkling way,
And tiptoe listens that no noise betray !

Ah wretched those on whom dread Cupid frowns !
How happy they whose mutual choice he crowns !
Will Love partake the banquet of the day ?
O come—but throw thy burning shafts away.

Ye swains, begin to mighty Love the song,
Your songs, ye swains, to mighty Love belong !

Breathe out aloud your wishes for my fold,
Your own soft vows in whispers may be told.
But hark! loud mirth and music fire the crowd—
Ye now may venture to request aloud!

    Pursue your sports; night mounts her curtain'd wain
The dancing stars compose her filial train;
Black muffled sleep steals on with silent pace,
And dreams flit last, imaginations race!   GRAINGER.


## ELEGY II.

RISE, happy morn, without a cloud arise!
This morn, Cornutus blest his mother's eyes!
Hence each unholy wish, each adverse sound,
As we his altar's hallow'd verge surround!
Let rich Arabian odours scent the skies,
And sacred incense from his altar rise;
Implored, thou tutelary god, descend!
And deck'd with flowery wreaths the rites attend!
Then as his brows with precious unguents flow,
Sweet sacred cakes and liberal wine bestow.

    O Genius, grant whate'er my friend desires;
The cake is scatter'd, and the flame aspires!
Ask then, my noble friend, whate'er you want:
What, silent still? your prayer the god will grant:
Uncovetous of rural wide domains,
You beg no woody hills, no cultured plains:
Not venal, you request no Eastern stores,
Where ruddy waters lave the gemmy shores:
Your wish I guess; you wish a beauteous spouse,
Joy of your joy, and faithful to your vows.
'Tis done! my friend! see nuptial Love appears!
See! in his hand a yellow zone he bears!
A yellow zone, that spite of years shall last,
And heighten fondness, e'en when beauty's past.

    With happy signs, great power, confirm our prayer,
With endless concord bless the married pair.
O grant, dread Genius, that a numerous race
Of beauteous infants crown their fond embrace:

Their beauteous infants round thy feet shall play,
And keep with custom'd rites this happy day.

GRAINGER.

### ELEGY III.

My fair, Cornutus, to the country's flown,
Oh how insipid is the city grown!
No taste have they for elegance refined,
No tender blossoms, who remain behind:
Now Cytherea glads the laughing plain,
And smiles and sports compose her sylvan train.
Now Cupid joys to learn the ploughman's phrase,
And clad a peasant, o'er the fallows strays.
Oh how the weighty prong I'll busy wield!
Should the fair wander to the labour'd field;
A farmer then, the crooked ploughshare hold,
Whilst the dull ox prepares the vigorous mould:
I'd not complain though Phœbus burnt the lands,
And painful blisters swell'd my tender hands.

Admetus' herds the fair Apollo drove,
In spite of med'cine's power, a prey to love;
Nor aught avail'd to soothe his amorous care,
His lyre of silver sound, or waving hair.
To quench their thirst the kine to streams he led,
And drove them from their pasture to the shed:
The milk to curdle, then, the fair he taught,
And from the cheese to strain the dulcet draught.
Oft, oft his virgin sister blush'd for shame,
As bearing lambkins o'er the field he came!
Oft would he sing the list'ning vales among,
Till lowing oxen broke the plaintive song.
To Delphi trembling, anxious chiefs repair,
But got no answer, Phœbus was not there.
Thy curling locks that charm'd a step-dame's eye,
A jealous step-dame now neglected fly!
To see thee, Phœbus, thus disfigured stray,
Who could discover the fair god of day?
Constrain'd by Cupid in a cot to pine,
Where was thy Delos, where thy Pythian shrine?

Thrice happy days, when Love almighty sway'd!
And openly the gods his will obey'd.
Now Love's soft power's become a common jest—
Yet those who feel his influence in their breast,
The prude's contempt, the wise man's sneer despise,
Nor would his chains forego to rule the skies.

Curst farm! that forced my Nemesis from town,
Blasts taint thy vines, and rains thy harvests drown.
Though hymns implore your aid, great god of wine!
Assist the lover, and neglect the vine;
To shades, unpunish'd, ne'er let beauty stray;
Not all your vintage can its absence pay!
Rather than harvest should the fair detain,
May rills and acorns feed th' unactive swain!
The swains of old no golden Ceres knew,
And yet how fervent was their love and true!
Their melting vows the Paphian queen approved,
And every valley witness'd how they loved.
Then lurk'd no spies to catch the willing maid;
Doorless each house; in vain no shepherd pray'd.
Once more, ye simple usages, obtain!
No—lead me, drive me to the cultur'd plain!
Enchain me, whip me, if the fair command;
Whipp'd and enchain'd I'll plough the stubborn land!
                                        GRAINGER.

## ELEGY IV.

CHAINS and a haughty fair I fearless view!
Hopes of paternal freedom, all adieu.
Ah, when will Love compassionate my woes?
In one sad tenour my existence flows:
Whether I kiss or bite the galling chain,
Alike my pleasure, and alike my pain.
I burn, I burn! oh banish my despair!
Oh ease my torture, too, too cruel fair:
Rather than feel such vast, such matchless woe,
I'd rise some rock o'erspread with endless snow;
Or frown a cliff on some disastrous shore,
Where ships are wreck'd, and tempests ever roar!

In pensive gloominess I pass the night,
Nor feel contentment at the dawn of light.
What though the god of verse my woes indite,
What though I soothing elegies can write,
No strains of elegy her pride control;
Gold is the passport to her venal soul.
I ask not of the Nine the epic lay;
Ye Nine! or aid my passion, or away.
I ask not to describe in lofty strain
The sun's eclipses, or the lunar wane;
To win admission to the haughty maid,
Alone I crave your elegiac aid;
But if she still contemns the tearful lay,
Ye and your elegies away, away!
In vain I ask, but gold ne'er asks in vain;
Then will I desolate the world for gain!
For gold, I'll impious plunder every shrine;
But chief, O Venus, will I plunder thine!
By thee compell'd I love a venal maid,
And quit for bloody fields my peaceful shade:
By thee compell'd I rob the hallow'd shrine,
Then chiefly Venus will I plunder thine!

Perish the man! whose curst industrious toil
Or finds the gem, or dyes the woolly spoil;
Hence, hence the sex's avarice arose,
And art with nature not enough bestows:
Hence the fierce dog was posted for a guard,
The fair grew venal, and their gates were barr'd.
But weighty presents vigilance o'ercome,
The gate bursts open, and the dog is dumb.

From venal charms, ye gods! what mischiefs flow!
The joy, how much o'erbalanced by the woe!
Hence, hence so few, sweet Love, frequent thy fane,
Hence impious slander loads thy guiltless reign.

But ye! who sell your heavenly charms for hire,
Your ill-got riches be consumed with fire!
May not one lover strive to quench the blaze,
But smile malicious as o'er all it preys!
And when ye die no gentle friend be near,
To catch your breath or shed a genuine tear!

Behind the corpse to march in solemn show,
Or Syrian odours on the pile bestow.

Far other fates attend the generous maid;
Though age and sickness bid her beauties fade
Still she's revered; and when death's easy call
Has freed her spirit from life's anxious thrall,
The pitying neighbours all her loss deplore,
And many a weeping friend besets the door;
While some old lover, touch'd with grateful woe,
Shall yearly garlands on her tomb bestow;
And home returning, thus the fair address,
"Light may the turf thy gentle bosom press."

'Tis truth; but what has truth with love to do?
Imperious Cupid, I submit to you!
To sell my father's seat should you command,
Adieu, my father's gods, my father's land!
From madding mares, whate'er of poison flows,
Or on the forehead of their offspring grows,
Whate'er Medea brew'd of baleful juice,
What noxious herbs Æmathian hills produce;
Of all, let Nemesis a draught compose,
Or mingle poisons, feller still than those;
If she but smile, the deadly cup I'll drain,
Forget her avarice, and exult in pain!     GRAINGER

### THE SAME.

I SEE my slavery, and a mistress near;
  Oh, freedom of my fathers! fare thee well!
A slavery wretched, and a chain severe,
  Nor Love remits the bonds that o'er me fell.

How have I then deserved consuming pain?
  Or for what sin am I of flames the prey?
I burn, ah me! I burn in every vein!
  Take, cruel girl, oh take thy torch away!

Oh! but to 'scape this agonizing heat,
  Might I a stone on icy mountains lie!
Stand a bleak rock by wreaking billows beat,
  And swept by madding whirlwinds of the sky!

Bitter the day, and ah! the nightly shade;
   And all my hours in venom'd stream have roll'd;
No elegies, no lays of Phœbus, aid;
   With hollow palm she craves the tinkling gold.

Away, ye Muses! if ye serve not Love:
   I, not to sing of battles, woo your strain;
How walks the bright-hair'd sun the heavens above,
   Or turns the full-orb'd moon her steeds again.

By verse I seek soft access to my fair;
   Away, ye Muses! with the useless lore;
Through blood and pillage I must gifts prepare;
   Or weep, thrown prostrate at her bolted door.

Suspended spoils I'll snatch from pompous fanes;
   But Venus first shall violated be;
She prompts the sacrilege, who forged the chains;
   And gave that nymph insatiable to me.

Perish the wretch! who culls the emerald green,
   Or paints the snowy fleece with Tyrian red!
Through filmy Coan robes her limbs are seen,
   And India's pearls gleam lucid from her head.

'Tis pamper'd avarice thus corrupts the fair;
   The key is turn'd; the mastiff guards the door:
The guard's disarm'd, if large the bribe you bear;
   The dog is hush'd; the key withstands no more.

Alas! that e'er a heavenly form should grace
   The nymph that pants with covetous desires!
Hence tears and clamorous brawls, and sore disgrace
   E'en to the name of love, that bliss inspires.

For thee, that shutt'st the lover from thy door,
   Foil'd by a price, the gilded hire of shame,
May tempests scatter this thy ill-got ore,
   Strewn on the winds, or melted in the flame.

May climbing fires thy mansion's roof devour,
   And youths gaze glad, nor throw the quenching wave;
May none bemoan thee at thy dying hour,
   None pay the mournful tribute to thy grave.

But she, unbribed, unbought, yet melting kind,
   May she a hundred years, unfading, bloom;

Be wept, while on the flaming pile reclined,
　　And yearly garlands twine her pillar'd tomb.

Some ancient lover, with his locks of grey,
　　Honouring the raptures that his youth had blest,
Shall hang the wreath, and slow-departing say,
　　" Sleep!—and may earth lie light upon thy breast!"

Truth prompts my tongue; but what can truth avail?
　　The love her laws prescribe must now be mine;
My ancestors' loved groves I set to sale—
　　My household gods, your title I resign!

Nay—Circe's juice, Medea's drugs, each plant
　　Of Thessaly, whence dews of poison fall;—
Let but my Nemesis' soft smile enchant,
　　Then let her mix the cup—I'll drink them all!　ELTON

## ELEGY V.

To hear our solemn vows, O Phœbus, deign!
A novel pontiff treads thy sacred fane:
Nor distant hear, dread power! 'tis Rome's request,
That with thy golden lyre thou stand'st confest:
Deign, mighty bard! to strike the vocal string,
And praise thy pontiff; we his praises sing:
Around thy brows triumphant laurels twine,
Thine altar visit, and thy rites divine:
New flush thy charms, new curl thy waving hair;
O come the god in vestment and in air!
When Saturn was dethroned, so crowned with bays,
So robed, thou sung'st th' almighty victor's praise.
What fate, from gods and man, has wrapt in night,
Prophetic flashes on thy mental sight:
From thee diviners learn their prescient lore,
On reeking bowels as they thoughtful pore:
The seer thou teachest the success of things,
As flies the bird, or feeds, or screams, or sings:
The Sibyl-leaves if Rome ne'er sought in vain,
Thou gav'st a meaning to the mystic strain:
Thy sacred influence may this pontiff know,
And as he reads them with the prophet glow.

When great Æneas snatch'd his aged sire,
And burning lares, from the Grecian fire,
She, she foretold this empire fix'd by fate,
And all the triumphs of the Roman state ;
Yet when he saw his Ilion wrapp'd in flame,
He scarce could credit the mysterious dame.

(Quirinus had not plann'd eternal Rome,
Nor had his brother met his early doom ;
Where now Jove's temple swells, low hamlets stood
And domes ascend, where heifers cropp'd their food.
Sprinkled with milk, Pan graced an oak's dun shade,
And scythe-arm'd Pales watch'd the mossy glade ;
For help from Pan, to Pan on every bough
Pipes hung, the grateful shepherd's vocal vow ;
Of reeds, still lessening, was the gift composed,
And friendly wax th' unequal junctures closed.
So where Velabrian streets like cities seem,
One little wherry plied the lazy stream,
O'er which the wealthy shepherd's favourite maid
Was to her swain, on holidays, convey'd ;
The swain, his truth of passion to declare,
Or lamb, or cheese, presented to the fair.)

### THE CUMÆAN SIBYL SPEAKS.

"Fierce brother of the power of soft desire,
Who fliest, with Trojan gods, the Grecian fire !
Now Jove assigns thee Laurentine abodes,
Those friendly plains invite thy banish'd gods !
There shall a nobler Troy herself applaud,
Admire her wanderings, and the Grecian fraud !
There thou from yonder sacred stream shalt rise
A god thyself, and mingle with the skies !
No more thy Phrygians for their country sigh,
See conquest o'er your shatter'd navy fly !
See the Rutulian tents, a mighty blaze !
Thou, Turnus ! soon shalt end thy hateful days !
The camp I see, Lavinium greets my view !
And Alba ! brave Ascanius ! built by you :
I see thee, Ilia ! leave the vestal fire,
And, clasp'd by Mars, in amorous bliss expire !

On Tiber's bank thy sacred robes I see,
And arms abandon'd, eager god! by thee.
Your hills crop fast, ye herds! while fate allows
Eternal Rome shall rise, where now ye browse:
Rome, that shall stretch her irresistless reign
Wherever Ceres views her golden grain;
Far as the east extends his purple ray,
And where the west shuts up the gates of day.
The truth I sing; so may the laurels prove
Safe food, and I be screen'd from guilty love."

Thus sung the sibyl, and address'd her prayer,
Phœbus! to thee, and madding, loosed her hair.
Nor, Phœbus! give him only these to know,
A further knowledge on thy priest bestow:
Let him interpret what thy fav'rite maid,
What Amalthea, what Mermessia said:
Let him interpret what Albuna bore
Through Tiber's waves, unwet, to Tiber's farthest shore

When stony tempests fell, when comets glared,
Intestine wars their oracles declared:
The sacred groves (our ancestors relate)
Foretold the changes of the Roman state:
To charge the clarion sounded in the sky,
Arms clash'd, blood ran, and warriors seem'd to die:
With monstrous prodigies the year began;
An annual darkness the whole globe o'erran;
Apollo, shorn of every beamy ray,
Oft strove, but strove in vain, to light the day:
The statues of the gods wept tepid tears;
And speaking oxen fill'd mankind with fears!

These were of old: no more, Apollo! frown,
But in the waves each adverse omen drown.
Oh! let thy bays in crackling flames ascend,
So shall the year with joy begin and end!
The bays give prosperous signs; rejoice, ye swains!
Propitious Ceres shall reward your pains.
With must the jolly rustic purpled o'er,
Shall squeeze rich clusters, which their tribute pour,
Till vats are wanting to contain their store.

Far hence, ye wolves! the mellow shepherds bring
Their gifts to Pales, and her praises sing.
Now, fired with wine, they solemn bonfires raise,
And leap, untimorous, through the strawy blaze!
From every cot unnumber'd children throng,
Frequent the dance, and louder raise the song:
And while in mirth the hours they thus employ,
At home the grandsire tends his little boy;
And in each feature pleased himself to trace,
Foretells his prattler will adorn the race.

The sylvan youth, their grateful homage paid,
Where plays some streamlet, seek th' embowering shade;
Or stretch'd on soft enamel'd meadows lie,
Where thickest umbrage cools the summer sky:
With roses, see! the sacred cup is crown'd,
Hark! music breathes her animating sound:
The couch of turf, and festal tables stand
Of turf, erected by each shepherd-hand;
And all well-pleased the votive feast prepare,
Each one his goblet and each one his share.
Now drunk, they blame their stars and curse the maid,
But sober, deprecate whate'er they said.

Perish thy shafts, Apollo! and thy bow!
If Love unarmed in our forests go.
Yet since he learn'd to wing th' unerring dart,
Much cause has man to curse his fatal art:
But most have I; the sun has wheel'd his round
Since first I felt the deadly festering wound;
Yet, yet I fondly, madly, wish to burn,
Abjure indifference, and at comfort spurn;
And though from Nemesis my Genius flows,
Her scarce I sing, so weighty are my woes!

O cruel Love! how joyous should I be,
Your arrows broke and torch extinct to see!
From you, my want of reverence to the skies!
From you, my woes and imprecations rise!
Yet I advise you, too relentless fair!
(As heaven protects the bards) a bard to spare!

E'en now, the pontiff claims my loftiest lay,
In triumph soon he'll mount the sacred way.

Then pictured towns shall show successful war,
And spoils and chiefs attend his ivory car:
Myself will bear the laurel in my hand,
And pleased, amid the pleased spectators stand.
While war-worn veterans, with laurels crown'd,
With Io-triumphs shake the streets around.
His father hails him as he rides along,
And entertains with pompous shows the throng.

O Phœbus! kindly deign to grant my prayer;
So may'st thou ever wave thy curled hair;
So ever may thy virgin-sister's name
Preserve the lustre of a spotless fame.  GRAINGER.

## ELEGY VI.

MACER campaigns; who now will thee obey,
O Love! if Macer dare forego thy sway?
Put on the crest, and grasp the burnish'd shield,
Pursue the base deserter to the field:
Or if to winds he gives the loosen'd sail,
Mount thou the deck, and risk the stormy gale:
To dare desert thy sweetly-pleasing pains,
For stormy seas, or sanguinary plains!
'Tis, Cupid! thine, the wanderer to reclaim,
Regain thy honour and avenge thy name!
If such thou spar'st, a soldier I will be,
The meanest soldier, and abandon thee.
Adieu, ye trifling loves! farewell, ye fair!
The trumpet charms me, I to camps repair;
The martial look, the martial garb assume,
And see the laurel on my forehead bloom!
My vaunts how vain! debarr'd the cruel maid,
The warrior softens, and my laurels fade.
Piqued to the soul, how frequent have I swore,
Her gate so servile to approach no more!
Unconscious what I did, I still return'd,
Was still denied access, and yet I burn'd!

Ye youths, whom Love commands with angry sway
Attend his wars, like me, and pleased obey.

This iron age approves his sway no more:
All fly to camps for gold, and gold adore:
Yet gold clothes kindred states in hostile arms
Hence blood and death, confusion and alarms!
Mankind, for lust of gold, at once defy
The naval combat, and the stormy sky!
The soldier hopes, by martial spoils, to gain
Flocks without number, and a rich domain:
His hopes obtain'd by every horrid crime,
He seeks for marble in each foreign clime:
A thousand yoke sustain the pillar'd freight,
And Rome, surprised, beholds th' enormous weight.
Let such with moles the furious deep enclose,
Where fish may swim unhurt, though winter blows:
Let flocks and villas call the spoiler lord!
And be the spoiler by the fair adored!
Let one we know, a whipp'd barbarian slave,
Live like a king, with kingly pride behave!
Be ours the joys of economic ease,
From bloody fields remote, and stormy seas!

In gold, alas! the venal fair delight!
Since beauty sighs for spoil, for spoil I'll fight!
In all my plunder Nemesis shall shine,
Yours be the profit, be the peril mine:
To deck your heav'nly charms the silk-worm dies,
Embroidery labours, and the shuttle flies!
For you be rifled ocean's pearly store!
To you Pactolus send his golden ore!
Ye Indians! blacken'd by the nearer sun,
Before her steps in splendid liveries run;
For you shall wealthy Tyre and Afric vie,
To yield the purple and the scarlet dye.    GRAINGER.


IMITATION OF PART OF THE SAME.


FEW are the maids that now on merit smile,
    On spoil and war is bent this iron age:
Yet pain and death attend on war and spoil,
    Unsated vengeance and remorseless rage.
                2 A 2

To purchase spoil, ev'n love itself is sold,
　　Her lover's heart is least Neæra's care,
And I through war must seek detested gold,
　　Not for myself, but for my venal fair:

That while she bends beneath the weight of dress,
　　The stiffen'd robe may spoil her easy mien:
And art mistaken make her beauty less,
　　While still it hides some graces better seen.

But if such toys can win her lovely smile,
　　Hers be the wealth of Tagus' golden sand,
Hers the bright gems that glow in India's soil,
　　Hers the black sons of Afric's sultry land.

To please her eye let every loom contend,
　　For her be rifled ocean's pearly bed.
But where, alas! would idle fancy tend,
　　And soothe with dreams a youthful poet's head?

HAMMOND

### ELEGY VII.

THOUSANDS in death would seek an end of woe,
But hope, deceitful hope! prevents the blow!
Hope plants the forest, and she sows the plain,
And feeds with future granaries the swain;
Hope snares the winged vagrants of the sky,
Hope cheats in reedy brooks the scaly fry;
By hope the fetter'd slave, the drudge of fate,
Sings, shakes his irons, and forgets his state;
Hope promised you, you haughty still deny;
Yield to the goddess, O my fair! comply.
Hope whisper'd me, "Give sorrow to the wind!
The haughty fair one shall at last be kind."
Yet, yet you treat me with the same disdain:
O let not hope's soft whispers prove in vain!

Untimely fate your sister snatch'd away;
Spare me, O spare me, by her shade I pray!
So shall my garlands deck her virgin-tomb;
So shall I weep, no hypocrite, her doom!
So may her grave with rising flowers be drest,
And the green turf lie lightly on her breast.

Ah me! will nought avail? the world I'll fly,
And, prostrate at her tomb, a suppliant sigh!
To her attentive ghost, of you complain;
Tell my long sorrowing, tell of your disdain.
Oft, when alive, in my behalf she spoke:
Your endless coyness must her shade provoke:
With ugly dreams she'll haunt your hour of rest,
And weep before you, an unwelcome guest!
Ghastly and pale as when besmear'd with blood,
Oh fatal fall! she pass'd the Stygian flood.

No more, my strains! your eyes with tears o'erflow,
This moving object renovates your woe:
You, you are guiltless! I your maid accuse;
You generous are! she, she has selfish views.
Nay, were you guilty, I'll no more complain;
One tear from you o'erpays a life of pain!
She, Phryne, promised to promote my vows:
She took, but never gave my billet-doux.
You're gone abroad, she confidently swears,
Oft when your sweet-toned voice salutes mine ears:
Or, when you promise to reward my pains,
That you're afraid, or indisposed, she feigns:
Then madding jealousy inflames my breast;
Then fancy represents a rival blest;
I wish thee, Phryne! then, a thousand woes;—
And if the gods with half my wishes close,
Phryne! a wretch of wretches thou shalt be,
And vainly beg of death to set thee free!  GRAINGER.

### THE SAME.

MANY by death their fatal ills would end,
Credulous hope does still their reign extend,
And promise wonders from the following day;
To-morrow's sun shines always bright and gay.
Hope feeds the husbandman, and soothes his toil;
Hope lends the seed-corn to the furrow'd soil,
That with a large increase the fertile field
May to his thirsty wishes golden harvests yield:
This to the snare the heedless birds betrays,
This to the hidden hook the finny race.

The galley-slave, bound fast in solid gyves,
From this a comfort in his woes derives;
Who, whilst his legs resound with clinking chains,
Tugs at the oar and sings amidst his pains.
Hope shows me Nemesis all soft and kind,
But still averse the froward nymph I find.
Let not the goddess of thy name appear,
Ah! cruel maid! less fierce and less severe,
Ah! spare my anguish and thy hate abate,
I beg this for thy sister's timeless fate.
Disturb not with thy cruelty her grave,
But with a speedy smile thy votary save.
She is my saint, I to her tomb will bear
My gifts and chaplets wet with many a tear;
Yes, to her tomb I'll fly, her suppliant prove,
And with her silent urn deplore my love:
She will not leave her client to his pain,
Nor let his tears for thee be ever vain.
I charge thee therefore in her name to prove
More swiftly kind to my complaining love.
Lest her neglected manes in the night
Thy conscious slumbers with sad dreams affright;
And stand before thee all besmear'd with blood,
As she fell downward to the Stygian flood.
But hold—that dismal story I'll forbear,
Lest I renew my fair one's anxious care;
I am not so much worth to call from her one tear,
Nor is it fit that tears should e'er disguise
The lustre of those dear loquacious eyes.
The bawd's my foe, and makes my vows all vain;
The tender maid would else my pain:
Phryne the bawd against me bars the door,
A bawd is still obdurate to the poor.
Within her secret bosom she conveys
The amorous billets for the man that pays.
Oft when the pleasing music of her voice
Alarms my heart with the approaching joys,
Though to the door the well-known accents come,
This cursed bawd will swear she's not at home.
And often when my soul is all on fire,
Summon'd by love, and swelling with desire,

E'en in the harbour all my joys are split,
The eager lover Phryne won't admit;
But with dissembled terror in her air,
Pretends that sudden pangs have seized my fair;
Or that some threaten'd danger must that night
Prorogue the promised moments of delight.
Oh! then my wounded soul in cares expires,
And feels new anguish from my jealous fires:
My pregnant fancy soon begets alarms,
And paints some happy lover in her arms;
Paints all the tumults of the ravish'd pair,
And all the several ways he grasps the fair.
Then fall my curses on thy destin'd head,
Detested Phryne! better thou wert dead,
Than that the gods but one of them should hear;
For all the racks that the most guilty fear,
Would be thy hated lot, thy cursed share.     OTWAY.

---

# BOOK III.

## ELEGY I

### POET.

THY calends, Mars! are come, from whence of old
The year's beginning our forefathers told:
Now various gifts through every house impart
The pleasing tokens of the friendly heart.
To my Neæra, tuneful virgins! say,
What shall I give, what honour shall I pay?
Dear, e'en if fickle; dearer, if my friend!
To the loved fair what present shall I send?

### MUSES.

Gold wins the venal, verse the lovely maid:
In your smooth numbers be her charms display'd,
On polish'd ivory let the sheets be roll'd,
Your name in signature, the edges gold.

No pumice spare to smooth each parchment scroll,
In a gay wrapper then secure the whole.
Thus to adorn your poems be your care;
And, thus adorn'd, transmit them to the fair.

POET.

Fair maids of Pindus! I your counsel praise:
As you advise me, I'll adorn my lays:
But by your streams, and by your shades, I pray,
Yourselves the volume to the fair convey.
O let it lowly at her feet be laid,
Ere the gilt wrapper or the edges fade;
Then let her tell me, if her flames decline,
If quite extinguish'd, or if still she's mine.
But first your graceful salutations paid,
In terms submissive thus address the maid:
"Chaste fair! the bard, who dotes upon your charms,
And once could clasp them in his nuptial arms,
This volume sends; and humbly hopes that you
With kind indulgence will the present view.
You, you! he prizes more, he vows, than life;
Still a loved sister, or again his wife.
But oh! may Hymen bless his virtuous fire,
And once more grant you to his fond desire!
Fix'd in this hope, he'll reach the dreary shore,
Where sense shall fail and memory be no more."

GRAINGER.

ELEGY II.

HARD was the first who ventured to divide
The youthful bridegroom and the tender bride:[1]

---

[1] *Hard was the first,* &c.] This sentiment is finely expressed by Hammond, El. ix.

I.

He who could first two gentle hearts unbind,
   And rob a lover of his weeping fair,
Hard was the man; but harder, in my mind,
   The lover still who died not of despair.

More hard the bridegroom who can bear the day
When force has torn his tender bride away.
Here too my patience, here my manhood fails ;
The brave grow dastards, when fierce grief assails ;
Die, die I must ! the truth I freely own ;
My life too burthensome a load is grown.
Then, when I flit a thin an empty shade,
When on the mournful pile my corse is laid,
With melting grief, with tresses loose and torn,
Wilt thou, Neæra ! for thy husband mourn ?
A parent's anguish will thy mother show,
For the lost youth, who lived, who died for you ?

But see the flames o'er all my body stray !
And now my shade ye call, and now ye pray.
In black array'd ; the flame forgets to soar ;
And now pure water on your hands ye pour ;
My loved remains next, gather'd in a heap,
With wine ye sprinkle, and in milk ye steep.
The moisture dried, within the urn ye lay
My bones, and to the monument convey.
Panchaian odours thither ye will bring,
And all the produce of an Eastern spring :
But what than Eastern springs I hold more dear,
Oh wet my ashes with a genuine tear !

## II.

With mean disguise let others nature hide,
 And mimic virtue with the paint of art ;
I scorn the cheat of reason's foolish pride,
 And boast the graceful weakness of my heart.

  *  *  *  *  *

Sad is my day, and sad my lingering night,
 When, wrapt in silent grief, I weep alone ;
Delia is lost ! and all my past delight
 Is now the source of unavailing moan.

What follows is an improvement on Tibullus :

Where is the wit, that heighten'd beauty's charms ?
 Where is the face, that fed my longing eyes ?
Where is the shape, that might have blest my arms ?
 Where all those hopes, relentless Fate denies ?

Thus, by you both lamented, let me die,
Be thus perform'd my mournful obsequy!
Then shall these lines, by some throng'd way, relate
The dear occasion of my dismal fate:
"Here lies poor Lygdamus; a lovely wife,
Torn from his arms, cut short his thread of life."

GRAINGER

### THE SAME.

AN iron soul had he who first could part
The tender lover from the tender fair;
But sure that youth had still a harder heart,
Who bore the loss, and died not of despair.

Not for endurance is my nature known;
Grief breaks the heart, the brave are vanquish'd too:
I blush to speak my shame, I blush to own,
Life, worn with sufferings, palls upon my view.

Then, when I change to flitting shade and air,
And dusky ashes my white bones bespread,
Before my pile, with long dishevell'd hair,
Bathed in her tears, let chaste Neæra tread.

But let her with her sorrowing mother come,
And one a son, and one a husband weep;
Call my departed soul, and bless my tomb,
And their pure hands in living waters steep.

Ungirded then collect whate'er was mine,
My ivory bones in sable vestment swathe;
First sprinkle with the mellow juice of wine,
Anon with snowy milk the relics bathe.

Absorb the moisture soft with linen veils,
And dry, repose them in a marble tomb;
With gums, whose incense dew'd Panchaia's gales,
Arabia's balm, and Syria's rich perfume.

With odours let remembrance mingle tears;
So, turn'd to dust, would I in peace be laid;
While the sad cause of death inscribed appears,
Thus, in graved characters of verse, display'd:

" The tomb of Lygdamus you here survey ;
    With love and anguish worn he pining sigh'd ;
He saw his spouse Neæra torn away,
    And, yielding to the sorrow, sank and died."   ELTON.


## ELEGY III.

WHY did I supplicate the powers divine ?
Why votive incense burn at every shrine ?
Not that I marble palaces might own,
To draw spectators, and to make me known ;
Not that my teams might plough new-purchas'd plains,
And bounteous autumn glad my countless swains :
I begg'd with you my youthful days to share,
I begg'd in age to clasp the lovely fair ;
And when my stated race of life was o'er,
I begg'd to pass alone the Stygian shore.

    Can treasured gold the tortured breast compose ?
Or plains, wide cultured, soothe the lover's woes ?
Can marble-pillar'd domes, the pride of art,
Secure from sorrow the possessor's heart ?
Not circling woods, resembling sacred groves,
Not Parian pavements, nor gay-gilt alcoves,
Not all the gems that load an Eastern shore,
Not whate'er else the greedy great adore,
Possess'd, can shield the owner's breast from woe,
Since fickle fortune governs all below :
Such toys, in little minds, may envy raise ;
Still little minds improper objects praise.
Poor let me be, for poverty can please
With you ; without you, crowns could give no ease.

    Shine forth, bright morn ! and every bliss impart,
Restore Neæra to my doting heart !
For if her glad return the gods deny,
If I solicit still in vain the sky,
Nor power, nor all the wealth this globe contains,
Can ever mitigate my heart-felt pains ;
Let others these enjoy ; be peace my lot,
Be mine Neæra, mine a humble cot !

Saturnia, grant thy suppliant's timid prayer!
And aid me, Venus! from thy pearly chair!

Yet, if the Sisters, who o'er fate preside,
My vows contemning, still detain my bride,
Cease, breast, to heave! cease, anxious blood, to flow!
Come, death! transport me to thy realms below.

GRAINGER.

### THE SAME.

WHY should my vows, Neæra! fill the sky,
  And the sweet incense blend with many a prayer?
Not forth to issue on the gazing eye
  From marble vestibule of mansion fair.

Not that unnumber'd steers may turn my field,
  And the kind earth its copious harvests lend:
But that with thee the joys of life may yield
  Their full satiety, till life has end.

And, when my days have measured out their light,
  And, naked, I must Lethe's bark survey;
I on thy breast may close my fading sight,
  And feel my dying age fall soft away.

For what avails the pile of massive gold?
  What the rich glebe by thousand oxen plough'd?
Roofs, that the Phrygian pillars vast uphold,
  Tænarian shafts, Carystian columns proud?

Mansions, whose groves might seem some temple's wood;
  The gilded cornice, or the marble floor?
Pearls glean'd from sands of Persia's ruddy flood,
  Sidon's red fleece, and all the crowd adore?

For envy clings to these: the crowd still gaze,
  Charm'd with false shows, and love with little skill:
Not wealth the cares of human souls allays,
  Since fortune shifts their happiness at will.

With thee, O sweet Neæra! want were bliss;
  Without thee I the gifts of kings disdain:
Oh clear the light! blest day, that brings me this;
  Thrice blest, that yields thee to my arms again!

If to my vows for this thy sweet return,
   Love's god, kind, listen, nor avert his ear;
Then Lydia's river, rolling gold, I'll spurn:
   Kingdoms and wealth of worlds shall poor appear.

Seek these who may: a frugal fare be mine:
   With my dear consort let me safely dwell:
Come, Juno! to my timid prayers incline!
   Come, Venus! wafted on thy scallop'd shell!

But, if the Sister Fates refuse my boon,
   Who draw the future day with swift-spun thread,
Hell to its gulfy rivers call me soon,
   To sluggish lurid lakes, where haunt the dead. ELTON.


## ELEGY IV.

LAST night's ill-boding dreams, ye gods, avert!
Nor plague, with portents, a poor lover's heart!
But why?  From prejudice our terrors rise;
Vain visions have no commerce with the skies:
Th' event of things the gods alone foresee,
And Tuscan priests foretell what they decree.
Dreams flit at midnight round the lover's head,
And timorous man alarm with idle dread:
And hence oblations to divert the woe,
Weak, superstitious minds on heaven bestow.
But since whate'er the gods foretell is true,
And man's oft warn'd, mysterious dreams! by you;
Dread Juno! make my nightly visions vain,
Vain make my boding fears, and calm my pain!
The blessed gods, you know, I ne'er reviled,
And nought iniquous e'er my heart defiled.

Now night had laved her coursers in the main,
And left to dewy dawn a doubtful reign;
Bland sleep, that from the couch of sorrow flies,
(The wretch's solace,) had not closed my eyes;
At last, when morn unbarr'd the gates of light,
A downy slumber shut my labouring sight:
A youth appear'd, with virgin laurel crown'd,
He moved majestic, and I heard the sound.

Such charms, such manly charms, were never seen,
As fired his eyes, and harmonized his mien;
His hair, in ringlets of an auburn hue,
Shed Syrian sweets, and o'er his shoulders flew;
As white as thine, fair Luna! was his skin,
So vein'd with azure, and as smoothly thin;
So soft a blush vermilion'd o'er his face,
As when a maid first melts in man's embrace;
Or when the fair with curious art unite
The purple amaranth and lily white.
A bloom like his, when tinged by autumn's pride,
Reddens the apple on the sunny side;
A Tyrian tunic to his ancles flow'd,          [show'd.
Which through its sirfled plaits his godlike beauties
A lyre, the present mulciber, bestow'd,
On his left arm with easy grandeur glow'd;
The peerless work of virgin gold was made
With ivory, gems, and tortoise interlaid;
O'er all the vocal strings his fingers stray,
The vocal strings his fingers glad obey,
And, harmonized, a sprightly prelude play:
But when he join'd the music of his tongue,
These soft, sad elegiac lays he sung:

" All hail, thou care of heaven! (a virtuous bard,
The god of wine, the Muses, I regard;)
But neither Bacchus nor the Thespian Nine,
The sacred will of destiny divine:
The secret book of destiny to see,
Heaven's awful sire has given alone to me;
And I, unerring god, to you explain
(Attend and credit) what the Fates ordain.

" She who is still your ever-constant care,
Dearer to you than sons to mothers are,
Whose beauties bloom in every soften'd line,
Her sex's envy, and the love of thine:
Not with more warmth is female fondness moved,
Not with more warmth are tenderest brides beloved.
For whom you hourly importune the sky,
For whom you wish to live, nor fear to die,

Whose form, when night has wrapt in black the pole,
Cheats in soft vision your enamour'd soul;
Neæra! whose bright charms your verse displays,
Seeks a new lover, and inconstant strays!
For thee no more with mutual warmth she burns,
But thy chaste house and chaste embrace she spurns.

"Oh cruel, perjured, false, intriguing sex!
Oh born with woes poor wretched man to vex!
Whoe'er has learn'd her lover to betray,
Her beauty perish, and her name decay!

"Yet, as the sex will change, avoid despair;
A patient homage may subdue the fair.
Fierce Love taught man to suffer, laugh at pain;
Fierce Love taught man, with joy, to drag the chain,
Fierce Love, nor vainly fabulous the tale,
Forced me, yes, forced me, to the lonely dale:
There I Admetus' snowy heifers drove,
Nor tuned my lyre, nor sung, absorb'd in love.
The favourite son of heaven's almighty sire,
Preferr'd a straw-pipe to his golden lyre.

"Though false the fair, though Love is wild, obey,
Or, youth, you know not Love's tyrannic sway.
In plaintive strains address the haughty fair;
The haughty soften at the voice of prayer.
If ever true my Delphian answers prove,
Bear this my message to the maid you love.

"Pride of your sex, and passion of the age!
No more let other men your love engage;
A bard on you the Delian god bestows,
This match alone can warrant your repose."

He sung. When Morpheus from my pillow flew,
And plunged me in substantial griefs anew.

Ah! who could think that thou hadst broke thy vows,
That thou, Neæra! sought'st another spouse?
Such horrid crimes as all mankind detest,
Could they, how could they, harbour in thy breast?

The ruthless deep, I know, was not thy sire;
Nor fierce Chimæra, belching floods of fire;
Nor didst thou from the triple monster spring,
Round whom a coil of kindred serpents cling;
Thou art not of the Libyan lion's seed,
Of barking Scylla's, nor Charybdis' breed;
Nor Afric's sands, nor Scythia gave thee birth;
But a compassionate, benignant earth.
No! thou, my fair! deriv'st thy noble race
From parents deck'd with every human grace.

Ye gods! avert the woes that haunt my mind,
And give the cruel phantoms to the wind.    GRAINGER

### THE SAME.

Now heaven forefend!—nor bring those dreams to light
That haunted the pale close of yesternight!
Away! far hence, ye false, vain shadows, fly!
Hope not to win my fond credulity:
From gods alone unerring warnings come,
When seers in entrails read the future doom.
Dreams, like the cheating shades of night, we find,
Play with false fears upon the timid mind.
Such midnight omens superstition sees,
Which crackling salt and holy meal appease.
But whether truth to others shadow'd seem
In the seer's warning, or the lying dream;
At least may Luna chase these fears in air,
Which my poor heart has ill deserved to bear:
If pure my conscience from crime's deepening dye,
Nor e'er my tongue blasphemed the powers on high.

Night now had measured heaven's cærulean steep
With sable steeds; her laved wheels touch'd the deep:
But sleep, that soothes the wretched, soothed not me;
Still from an anxious chamber prompt to flee:
Till, when the sun peep'd faint from eastern skies,
Late slumber settled on my languid eyes.
When lo! a youth was seen my floor to tread,
Chaste laurels nodding round his wreathed head.

No form so fair adorn'd the age of gold:
No form so fair could spring from human mould:
Loose o'er his tapering neck the ringlets flew,
That breathing myrtle dropp'd with Tyrian dew:
White as the moon did his complexion show,
And tinting crimson flush'd his skin of snow.
As virgin cheeks with tender blushes dyed,
When to the youth consents the yielded bride:
As girls with purple am'ranths lilies thread;
As apples pale catch autumn's streaky red.
A sweeping robe around his ankles trail'd;
His dazzling limbs the gorgeous vesture veil'd:
On his left side a harp suspended hung,
Of precious shell, with gold resplendent strung:
Soft, at his first approach, the chord he smote
With ivory quill, with sweet-breathed vocal note:
His fingers and his voice preluded clear,
Then sweet, but sad, his accents thrill'd my ear.
" Hail, care of heaven! the bard of spotless love
Apollo, Bacchus, and the Nine approve:
But ah! not Bacchus, not the Nine, have power
To read the shadows of the future hour:
To me the father gave the laws of doom,
The mystic volume of events to come.
What I, unerring prophet, tell, receive:
The god's true lips shall speak; do thou believe.
She whom thou dear hast held, and loved to prize,
Dear as a daughter in her mother's eyes;
Dear as the virgin when, with blushing charms,
She sinks within her panting bridegroom's arms;
For whom thy voice has wearied heaven with prayer;
For whom thy feverish days are cross'd with care;
And who, when sleep its umber'd mantle throws,
With nightly phantoms haunts thy vain repose:
She—fair Neæra—in thy verse divine,
Inconstant sighs for other arms than thine;
Far other wishes heave her sinful breast,
Nor in her chaste home is Neæra blest.
Ah, cruel sex! ah woman! faithless name!
Be every man-deceiver's portion, shame!

Yet may she bend; for mutable the race:
Do thou, still patient, stretch thy true embrace.
Fell Love has taught the hardest toils to dare:
Fell Love has taught e'en cruel stripes to bear:
I once Admetus' snowy heifers fed;
Not vain the tale in sportful fictions read:
No more my hand the harp sonorous play'd;
No more my voice responsive cadence made;
But on a flimsy oat I whisper'd love:
E'en I, Latona's son, the son of Jove.
Ah! youth! thou know'st not love! unless thou bear
A thorny pillow, an unfeeling fair.
Yet doubt not, nor despair; but soft complain:
Hard hearts at soft complaint have turn'd again.
If true my temple's oracles, now go:
This in my name let false Neæra know:
' Phœbus himself insures this marriage tie:
Here blest, no longer for another sigh.'"

He said: the idle slumber took its flight:
Ah! from such ills I turn my loathing sight:
I dare not think thy vows are vow'd from me;
That sins can harbour'd in thy bosom be:
For not from ocean's depths thy being came,
Nor fierce Chimæra breathed thee forth in flame:
Not hell's grim dog with viperous brood o'erhung,
Monster of triple head and triple tongue;
Not Scylla, twi-form'd maid, thy nature gave,
Around whose waist the dogs engendering rave;
No lioness produced thee in the wild,
Nor Syrt, nor Scythia, rear'd thee as its child.
But thine a polish'd and humane abode,
Where never cruelty its features show'd:
In thy mild mother all her sex we view,
Thine, amiablest of men, a father too.
Now, pray the gods! these dreams befall me fair!
Light may they vanish on the tepid air!        ELTON.


## ELEGY V.

WHILE you at Tuscan baths for pleasure stay,
(Too hot when Sirius darts his sultry ray,

Though now that purple spring adorns the trees.
Not Baia's more medicinal than these,)
Me harder fates attend, my youth decays ;
Yet spare, Persephone ! my blameless days :
With secret wickedness unstung my soul ;
I never mix'd, nor gave the baneful bowl ;
I ne'er the holy mysteries proclaim'd ;
I fired no temple, and no god defamed ;
Age has not snow'd my jetty locks with white,
Nor bent my body, nor decay'd my sight.
(When both the consuls fell, ah fatal morn !
Fatal to Roman freedom ! I was born.)
Apples unripe, what folly 'tis to pull,
Or crush the cluster ere the grapes are full !

Ye gloomy gods ! whom Acheron obeys,
Dispel my sickness, and prolong my days !
Ere to the shades my dreary steps I take,
Or ferry o'er th' irremeable lake,
Let me (with age when wrinkled all my face)
Tell ancient stories to my listening race.

Thrice five long days and nights consumed with fire,
(O soothe its rage !) I gradually expire ;
While you the Naiad of your fountain praise,
Or lave, or spend in gentle sport your days :
Yet, O my friends ! whate'er the Fates decree,
Joy guide your steps, and still remember me !

Meantime, to deprecate the fierce disease,
And hasten glad returns of vigorous ease,
Milk, mix'd with wine, O promise to bestow,
And sable victims, on the gods below.

GRAINGER.

## ELEGY VI.

### LOVER.[1]

COME, Bacchus, come ! so may the mystic vine
And verdant ivy round thy temples twine !
My pains, the anguish I endure, remove ;
Oft hast thou vanquish'd the fierce pangs of love.

[1] Grainger has taken needless liberties with this Elegy, and apologizes for
them as follows : " This poem, which is one continued struggle between

2 B 2

Haste, boy, with old Falernian crown the bowl,
In the gay cordial let me drench my soul.
Hence, gloomy care! I give you to the wind;
The god of fancy frolics in my mind!
My dear companions! favour my design,
Let's drown our senses all in rosy wine!

### COMPANION.

Those may the fair with practised guile abuse,
Who, sourly wise, the gay dispute refuse:
The jolly god can cheerfulness impart,
Enlarge the soul, and pour out all the heart.

### LOVER.

But Love the monsters of the wood can tame,
The wildest tigers own the powerful flame:
He bends the stubborn to his awful sway,
And melts insensibility away:
So wide the reign of Love!

### COMPANION.

Wine, wine, dear boy!
Can any here in empty goblets joy?
No, no! the god can never disapprove,
That those who praise him should a bumper love.
What terrors arm his brow? the goblet drain:
To be too sober is to be profane!
Her son, who mock'd his rites, Agave tore,
And furious scatter'd round the yelling shore!
Such fears be far from us, dread god of wine!
Thy rites we honour, we are wholly thine!
But let the sober wretch thy vengeance prove:

the powers of Love and Wine, but in which the latter triumphs over the former, the translator has thrown into a dialogue between the Lover and one
of his boon Companions. This gives it a more spirited air, but does not
entirely remove all its obscurities; and hence the translator has been led
to believe that it is imperfect; unless, with some judicious critics, it is
supposed that, as the author was agitated with a diversity of passions at
the time of his composing it, so the hyperbaton and disorderly connexion
was the result of judicious choice, and not the fault of imperfection.

LOVER.

Or her, whom all my sufferings cannot move !
—What pray'd I rashly for ? my madding prayer,
Ye winds ! disperse, unratified, in air :
For though, my love ! I'm blotted from your soul,
Serenely rise your days, serenely roll !

COMPANION.

The love-sick struggle past, again be gay :
Come, crown'd with roses, let's drink down the day !

LOVER.

Ah me ! loud-laughing mirth how hard to feign !
When doom'd a victim to Love's dreadful pain :
How forced the drunken catch, the smiling jest,
When black solicitude annoys the breast !

COMPANION.

Complaints, away ! the blithesome god of wine
Abhors to hear his genuine votaries whine.

*          *          *          *          *

LOVER.

You, Ariadne ! on a coast unknown,
The perjur'd Theseus wept, and wept alone ;
But learn'd Catullus in immortal strains
Has sung his baseness, and has wept your pains.

*          *          *          *          *
*          *          *          *          *

COMPANION.

Thrice happy they who hear experience call,
And shun the precipice where others fall.
When the fair clasps you to her breast, beware,
Nor trust her by her eyes although she swear ;
Not though, to drive suspicion from your breast,
Or love's soft queen, or Juno she attest :
No truth the women know ; their looks are lies.

LOVER.

Yet Jove connives at amorous perjuries.
Hence, serious thoughts ! then why do I complain ?
The fair are licensed by the gods to feign.

Yet would the guardian powers of gentle love,
This once indulgent to my wishes prove,
Each day we then should laugh, and talk, and toy,
And pass each night in hymeneal joy.
O let my passion fix thy faithless heart!
For still I love thee, faithless as thou art!
Bacchus the Naiad loves; then haste, my boy!
My wine to temper cooler streams employ.
What though the smiling board Neæra flies,
And in a rival's arms perfidious lies,
The live-long night, all sleepless, must I whine?
Not I—

### COMPANION.

Quick, servants! bring us stronger wine.

### LOVER.

Now Syrian odours scent the festal room,
Let rosy garlands on our foreheads bloom.   GRAINGER

### THE SAME.

AH me! how hard, the mask of joy to wear
And feign the jest, with thoughts of brooding care!
Ill suits the smile with looks that joy belie,
Or wine's gay wit with mental misery.
Fond wretch! what boots complaint? vile cares, away!
Know, father Bacchus hates the mournful lay.
So thou, O Cretan maid! didst once deplore
A perjured tongue, left lonely on the shore,
As skill'd Catullus tells, who paints in song
The ingrate Theseus, Ariadne's wrong.
Take warning, youths! oh blest! whoe'er shall know
The art to profit by another's woe!
Let not the hanging nymph's embrace deceive,
Nor protestations of base tongues believe:
Not though the traitress by her eyes may swear;
Her Juno, Venus; for no faith is there.
Jove laughs at lovers' perjuries; the gales
Of heaven disperse these light protesting tales.
Why, then, so oft the treacherous nymph arraign?
Begone sad words! begone the pensive strain!

How would I rest whole nights within thy bower!
And share whole days thy every waking hour!
Faithless! with undeserved disdain severe!
Faithless! yet faithless as thou art, most dear!
Bacchus the Naiad loves: quick—loitering slave!
Temper the mellow wine with Martian wave:
No—if the giddy nymph my board has fled,
And fickle sought some unknown lover's bed;
I will not through the night in sighings pine:
Boy! mix it pure: come—dash it strong with wine:
Nay—long ago the Syrian nard should breathe
Round my moist brow; and flowers my hair inwreath.

ELTON.

---

# BOOK IV.

## POEM I

### A PANEGYRIC TO MESSALA.

MESSALA, thee I sing, although thy name,
Thy well-known merit, and thy spreading fame
Startle me, lest I feebly should repeat
A verse inferior to desert so great;
But though unequal to the theme I raise,
Yet I'll attempt at least to sing thy praise:
I, the designer of an humble verse,
Since none with justice can thy praise rehearse,
Unless he had thy language to express,
And clothe thy mighty deeds with manly dress;
A task superior to my trifling skill,
Yet take (if the performance fails) the will;
Let that suffice, nor thou the gift refuse,
The humble tribute of an humble Muse.

    Thus Phœbus kind received with smiling cheer
The little gift the Cretan could prefer.
Thus Icarus, by his celestial guest,
Bacchus, was far preferr'd before the rest,
As those bright signals in the heavens declare,
Fair Virgo, and the scorching Syrian star:

Alcides, destined for unbounded power,
Oft visited the poor Molorchus' bower.
The gods above do not mean off'rings scorn,
Nor always claim the ox with gilded horn;
So may this humble verse, so small it be,
Come an accepted off'ring due to thee;
That I encouraged may, in time, repeat
A verse more worthy, and thy praise more great.

Others, inspired with a sublimer flame,
May sing the vast creation's wondrous frame;
And how the earth is press'd with air around,
And how the circling sea confines the ground;
And how the fluid body of the air
Is moved with constant motion here and there;
And lightly wafting upwards does aspire
To join the high and pure ethereal fire;
And lastly, how different those bodies lie
Enclosed with the vast concave of the sky.

But if my verse can well express thy praise,
Or (what's a desperate thought) can higher raise
Or if it cannot to thy name be just,
But sinks below thy worth, as sure it must;
Whatever thoughts are spread in every line,
Whate'er I sing, the votive verse be thine.

You, though your race illustriously are known,
Unsatisfied with honours handed down;
Still follow glory with a steady pace,
And emulate the greatness of your race;
Thus all those merits which your fathers knew,
Your sons may see again revived in you.

Nor shall an empty title hold thy fame,
But endless volumes shall record your name:
Crowds shall contend to have thy worth declared
The orator, historian, and the bard:
But may the task at length on me be laid,
That so my name may with thy deeds be read.

For who can greater cause for praises yield
Than you?   Or in the forum or the field,

With equal worth you claim a just renown,
Braced in the helmet, or the peaceful gown.
The spreading laurels lie in equal scales,
And neither pendent hemisphere prevails.

You, if the giddy vulgar rise to rage,
Appease their fury and their heat assuage.
Nor Pylus, nor could Ithaca contain
So great a worthy in their boasted train:
Nor Nestor, noted for his vast renown,
Nor great Ulysses of a little town;
Though one had seen three hundred suns go round
Their annual courses, and revive the ground;
The other all the cities did explore,
Where'er the farthest sea includes the shore.

He overcame the Thracians, fierce in arms,
Nor was subdued by Lotophagian charms.
He check'd the one-eyed monster's fell design,
Making him drunk with Maronean wine.
Æolian gales he carried o'er the sea,
And to the Lestrygonians took his way,
Rough race! o'er whom Antiphates was king,
Where cool Artacia spreads her limpid spring.
Circe's bewitching arts by him were known;
Circe! the powerful daughter of the Sun,
Who by her skill in magic simples knew
To change old Nature's forms to bodies new:
Then to Cimmerian caves he took his way,
Wherever Phœbus roused the lightsome day,
Whether above the earth, or underneath the sea.
He view'd the dark Plutonian coasts below,
There saw the demi-gods and heroes go,
Mingled among the spectres to and fro.
Secure his easy vessel sail'd along,
Unstopp'd by the alluring Syren's song:
Him steering 'twixt the jaws of death his course,
Nor Scylla could affright with rapid source;
Though dreadful and tremendously she raves,
Girt round with barking dogs beneath the waves:
Nor could Charybdis, with tempestuous sea,
Destroy his vessel in her usual way:

Nor when to heaven uprose the waves profound,
Nor when dividing they disclosed the ground:
Nor shall I pass great Jove's severe award,
Declared for Phœbus' violated herd:
Nor how at length he fair Calypso found,
Her generous love and hospitable ground:
Nor how Phæacia was the happy isle
That closed his journey and relieved his toil.

Now whether these were in the world we know,
Or fables feign them in some world below;
Let him his labour boast and hardy deed,
While you in moving eloquence exceed.

In you the ready skill of war is found,
How to intrench the camp and raise the ground;
And how against the adverse host oppose,
Defensive palisadoes placed in rows,
And where to lead the ditch and ground enclose;
And ere you pitch the camp, to choose that ground
Which does with pure refreshing springs abound.
Swift through your troops communications go,
Which are cut off before they reach the foe.
You various sports and active games devise,
To keep the troops in manly exercise.

What chief like you can toss the pond'rous spear?
Or send the flying arrow through the air?
Or throw the jav'lin with an arm so strong,
To cut the air and drive the clouds along?
Or who direct the fiery courser's will,
Or moderate the rein with greater skill?
Or ride th' extended race with swifter force,
Or wheel the circling ring and round repeated course?
Or who more ready heaves the shield in fight,
To guard the left side, or secure the right?
To ward with sure defence, or here, or there,
And take the fury of th' invading spear?

In time, when raging Mars with fury glows,
When ensigns ensigns face, and spears do spears oppose,
Then you in meet array the squadrons place,
And fix the battle with a threat'ning face,

Whether you join them in a solid square,
That equal sides compact the foes may dare;
Or into other forms the battle fling,
And lead the soldiers to a spreading wing;
That either may a mutual aid dispense,
And guard each other with a joint defence.

But let me not uncertain trophies raise,
For wars I sing, and wars confirm thy praise:
Witness the Illyrians taught the Roman sway,
The base Pannonian rebels to obey:
And Arupinum taken, which did yield
One born to arms, and constant in the field:
Poor and unknown, him whosoe'er had seen,
Unbroke with age, and e'en in winter green,
With less surprise would hear the story told
Of rev'rend Nestor's fame, three cent'ries old:
For though since first he had received his birth,
A hundred annual suns had warm'd the earth;
He springing in the saddle press'd the horse,
And fix'd, he sat him in the swiftest course:
An able vet'ran for the dusty plains,
And a just moderator of the reins.
Subdued by thee, when all their power was vain,
They bent their necks beneath the Roman chain.

But these shall not suffice to speak thy praise,
Actions to come shall greater honours raise;
For I have more surprising things in view,
From omens sure as e'er Melampus knew.
For on that day when you, sublimely great,
Was clothed in purple and enrobed in state,
The sun above the ocean raised his head,
And o'er the earth uncommon lustre spread:
The seas with swelling billows rise no more,
But roll'd their silent waters to the shore;
The struggling winds their noisy discord cease,
And every whisp'ring gale lay hush'd in peace.
No bird did through the air his journey steer,
Or shook his whistling pinions in the air:
No savage beasts were grazing in the shade;
But all stood silent at the vows you made.

Jove, in his chariot wafted through the air,
Left his Olympus to receive thy prayer;
And seem'd intent to bend a list'ning ear.
Th' assenting power to every word you said
Gave the majestic nod, and waved his head:
Sudden the shining altars seem'd more bright,
And shooting flames diffused a greater light.

The gods approve! begin the mighty deed,
For thee uncommon triumphs are decreed.
Not neighbouring Gallia shall confine thy course,
Nor vast Hispania with its savage force;
Nor wealthy confines which the Tyrians sow,
Nor where the Nile and great Choaspes flow;
Nor where swift Gyndes does the land divide,
The lasting proof of Cyrus' foolish pride;
Nor where the waters through their sulph'rous veins
Diffuse the heat to Arectæan plains;
Nor that vast land where Thomyris bore sway,
And swift Araxes rolls his rapid way;
Nor vile Padæans at the farthest east,
Who load their tables with a hateful feast;
Nor where the Hebrus spreads his golden sand,
Nor where the Tanais laves the Scythian land.

But why should I insist on these alone,
When thy vast conquest the whole world shall own:
For thee remains the distant British shore,
Unbent by Roman power, a conquest yet in store;
For thee remains the farthest torrid zone,
Regions remote, and countries yet unknown.

For air does this terraqueous globe surround,
And five divisions in the orb are found;
Two parts whereof in chilly regions lie,
Perpetual frosts, and an inclement sky.
The earth is there with darkness wrapp'd around,
And sullen night sits brooding o'er the ground:
No living waters there the earth divide,
Nor cheerful streams in pleasant wand'rings glide;
But everlasting ice the floods constrains,
And drifts of snow o'erspread the dreary plains;

There never did the sun diffuse a ray,
Or give the cheerful promise of a day.

The middle regions feel the scorching sun,
Whether he nearer brings our summer on;
Or when he does a swifter course display,
And wheels in circles short the wintry day:
Therefore the plough is never there in use,
No corn the fields, nor herbs the lands produce:
No god indulgent makes the fields his care,
Bacchus and Ceres never visit there.
No cattle there can graze the smoking ground;
There nothing that possesses life is found.

Between this freezing cold and scorching heat
Our temperate zone is placed, a happy seat:
To this opposed, a fellow climate lies,
The same meridian holds, and temperate skies.
Here first the stubborn steer to toil was broke,
And oxen bent their neck beneath the yoke.
Here vines were taught their flexile shoots to ease,
And hang their clusters on the neighbouring trees,
And annual harvest gave a large increase.
Here first the earth received the vexing plough,
And first the sea was raised with brazen prow:
Then by degrees at distance cities rise,
And swelling walls and towers divide the skies.

Therefore where'er by fame thy acts are hurl'd,
They shall be known by all in either world.
For me, I cannot so much praise rehearse,
Though Phœbus should himself inspire my verse.
But Valgius, he can swell a warrior's name;
Valgius, next Homer in eternal fame.
The works will not my leisure hours decay,
Though Fortune vexes me, as is her way.

For I could once command a stately seat,
Splendidly wealthy, and sublimely great:
And yellow harvests waving o'er the plain,
Seem'd to o'ercrowd my fields with golden grain.
When my unnumber'd flock of flocks were fled,
And o'er the hills in crowded herds were spread.

Sufficient for their lord my lambs did stray,
And too, too many for the beasts of prey;
But now of every pleasing view bereft,
Reflection on their loss is all I've left.
Fresh grief I feel, and still repeated cares,
Oft as I cast my eye on former years.

But though the Fates, with more severe decrees,
Shall fix a train of heavier woes than these,
Yet still unwearied with my misery,
The Muse shall never fail to sing of thee.

Nor will the Muse alone suffice to prove
How much I prize my friend, how much I love.
For thee I'd run the hazard of the sea,
And tempt the roughest of the waves for thee.
For thee I singly could whole troops oppose,
Or throw myself where flaming Ætna glows.

And while I think you but regard my name,
I neither wish the Lydian realms to claim,
Nor the vast honours of Gylippus' fame:
Nor would I ask Apollo to inspire
My Muse with Homer's strength and lasting fire;
If but this humble verse can pleasing be,
No time shall stop my tongue from praising thee.

And when I've suffer'd Fate's unalter'd doom,
Closed in the gloomy mansion of a tomb;
If death in time shall make his forceful rape,
Or I survive, though in a different shape;
If as a horse I beat the dusty plain,
Or in a bull's majestic form remain;
Or if I as a feather'd fowl appear,
And beat with flutt'ring wings the fluid air;
Or in a human form increase my days,
I'll always fill whole volumes with thy praise.   DART


POEM II.

THE EULOGY OF SULPICIA.

GREAT god of war! Sulpicia, lovely maid,
To grace your calends, is in pomp array'd.

If beauty warms you, quit th' ethereal height,
E'en Cytherea will indulge the sight:
But while you gaze o'er all her matchless charms,
Beware your hands should meanly drop your arms.
When Cupid would the gods with love surprise,
He lights his torches at her radiant eyes.
A secret grace her every act improves,
And pleasing follows wheresoe'er she moves:
If loose her hair upon her bosom plays,
Unnumber'd charms that negligence betrays:
Or if 'tis plaited with a labour'd care,
Alike the labour'd plaits become the fair.
Whether rich Tyrian robes her charms invest,
Or all in snowy white the nymph is drest,
All, all she graces, still supremely fair,
Still charms spectators with a fond despair.
A thousand dresses thus Vertumnus wears,
And beauteous equally in each appears.

The richest tints and deepest Tyrian hue,
To thee, O wondrous maid! are solely due:
To thee th' Arabian husbandman should bring
The spicy produce of his eastern spring:
Whatever gems the swarthy Indians boast,
Their shelly treasures, and their golden coast,
Alone thou merit'st!  Come, ye tuneful choir!
And come, bright Phœbus! with thy plausive lyre!
This solemn festival harmonious praise,
No theme so much deserves harmonious lays.

                                    GRAINGER.


THE SAME.

MARS! on thy calends, fair Sulpitia see,
Deck'd in her gay habiliments for thee.
Come—Venus will forgive: descend, if wise:
To view her beauties leave thyself the skies.
But oh beware! lest, gazing on her charms,
Fierce as thou art, thou drop thy shameful arms.
For from her eyes, when gods are Cupid's aim,
He lights two lamps, that burn with keenest flame.

In every act, and step, and motion seen,
Grace stealthy glides, and forms her easy mien:
Graceful her locks in loose disorder spread;
Graceful the smoother braid that binds her head:
She charms, when Tyrian purple folds her limbs;
She charms, when white her snowy drapery swims:
Thus blithe Vertumnus in th' Olympian hall
Shifts all his thousand shapes, and charms in all.
She only of her sex deserves the grain
Of wool twice dipp'd in Tyrus' crimson stain:
Hers to possess whate'er the Arab reaps
Of harvest shrubs, whence liquid fragrance weeps:
Whatever pearls the sable Indian's hand
Culls on his eastern ocean's ruddy sand.
Her on these calends, O ye Muses! sing:
Let thy shell'd harp, exulting Phœbus! ring:
The festal rite let future years prolong;
No nymph more worthy of your choral song. ELTON.


## POEM III.

### SULPICIA ON HER LOVER'S GOING TO THE CHASE.

WHETHER, fierce churning boars! in meads ye stray,
Or haunt the shady mountain's devious way;
Whet not your tusks, my loved Cerinthus spare!
Know, Cupid! I consign him to your care.
What madness 'tis, shagg'd tractless wilds to beat,
And wound with pointed thorns your tender feet:
Oh! why to savage beasts your charms oppose?
With toils and blood-hounds why their haunts enclose?
The lust of game decoys you far away;
Ye blood-hounds, perish, and ye toils, decay!

Yet, yet could I with loved Cerinthus rove
Through dreary deserts and the thorny grove;
The cumbrous meshes on my shoulders bear,
And dare the monsters with my barbed spear;
Could track the bounding stags through tainted grounds
Beat up their cover, and unchain the hounds:
But most to spread our artful toils I'd joy,
For while we watch'd them, I could clasp the boy!

Then, as entranced in amorous bliss we lay,
Mix'd soul with soul, and melted all away!
Snared in our nets, the boar might safe retire,
And owe his safety to our mutual fire.

Oh! without me ne'er taste the joys of love,
But a chaste hunter in my absence prove.
And oh! may boars the wanton fair destroy,
Who would Cerinthus to their arms decoy!
Yet, yet I dread!—Be sports your father's care;
But you, all passion! to my arms repair!    GRAINGER.

### THE SAME.

AH! spare, ye gentle boars, my lovely boy,
(From his dear arms you need not fear annoy,)
Whether through flowery meads you take your way,
Or o'er the shadowy pathless mountains stray.
Nor whet your tusks with fury to destroy;
Love is the guardian of my lovely boy:
The lust of hunting leads his feet astray,
And far from love directs his devious way.
Oh! perish all ye woods, ye yelping hounds,
Wound me no more with your detested sounds.
What strange fantastic notions fill that mind,
That in these sports can any pleasure find;
To set the woody hills around with toils,
With hands all torn to seek such worthless spoils!
Yet could I with my dear Cherinthus rove,
Through devious forests and the shady grove,
O'er mountains I the winding net would bear,
And chase with pleasure the swift-footed deer;
I would uncouple with these hands the hounds,
And fancy music in their deep-mouth'd sounds;
Then would the fields, then would the woods delight,
If in thy arms I lay, my love, my light,
Before the very toils, my charming boy,
Dissolved in pleasure, panting with the joy;
Though in the net, the boar might safe retire,
And not disturb our bliss with furious ire.
Then without me ne'er taste the sweets of love,
But a chaste hunter in my absence prove;

And may the ravenous beasts of prey destroy
Whatever she would clasp my lovely boy.
Then to thy parent quit the huntsman's charms,
And swiftly fly to thy Sulpitia's arms.      OTWAY.

### THE SAME.

OH savage boar ! where'er thy haunt is found,
  In champaign meads or mountain thickets deep,
Spare my dear youth ; nor whet thy fangs to wound ;
  May guardian Love the lover harmless keep.

Him far away the wandering chase has led :
  Wither all woods and perish every hound !
What frantic mood, the tangled net to spread,
  And sore his tender hands with brambles wound !

Where is the joy, to thread the forest lair,
  While with hook'd thorns thy snowy legs are fray'd ?
But if, Cherinthus, I thy wanderings share,
  Thy nets I'll trail through every mountain glade.

Myself will track the nimble roebuck's trace,
  And from the hound the iron leash remove :
Then woods will charm me, when in thy embrace
  The conscious nets behold me, oh my love !

Unharm'd the boar shall break the tangling snare,
  Lest our stolen hours of bliss impeded be :
But, far from me, soft Venus' joys forbear ;
  With Dian spread the nets, when far from me.

May she, that robs me of thy dear embrace,
  Fall to the woodland beasts, by peacemeal torn :
But to thy father leave the toilsome chase ;
  Fly to my arms, on wings of transport borne. ELTON

### POEM IV.

#### ON SULPICIA'S ILLNESS.

COME, Phœbus ! with your loosely floating hair,
Oh soothe her torture, and restore the fair !
Come, quickly come ! we supplicant implore,
Such charms your happy skill ne'er saved before !

Let not her frame consumptive pine away,
Her eyes grow languid, and her bloom decay;
Propitious come; and with you bring along
Each pain-subduing herb and soothing song;
Or real ills, or whate'er ills we fear,
To ocean's farthest verge let torrents bear.
Oh! rack no more, with harsh, unkind delays,
The youth, who ceaseless for her safety prays;
'Twixt love and rage his tortur'd soul is torn;
And now he prays, now treats the gods with scorn.

Take heart, fond youth; you have not vainly pray'd,
Still persevere to love th' enchanting maid:
Sulpicia is your own! for you she sighs,
And slights all other conquests of her eyes:
Dry then your tears; your tears would fitly flow
Did she on others her esteem bestow.

O come! what honour will be yours, to save
At once two lovers from the doleful grave?
Then both will emulous exalt your skill;
With grateful tablets both your temples fill;
Both heap with spicy gums your sacred fire;
Both sing your praises to th' harmonious lyre:
Your brother-gods will prize your healing powers.
Lament their attributes, and envy yours.   GRAINGER.


## POEM V.

### SULPICIA ON HER LOVER'S BIRTH-DAY.

WITH feasts I'll ever grace the sacred morn,
When my Cerinthus, lovely youth! was born.
At birth to you th' unerring Sisters sung
Unbounded empire o'er the gay and young:
But I, chief I! (if you my love repay,)
With rapture own your ever-pleasing sway.
This I conjure you, by your charming eyes,
Where love's soft god in wanton ambush lies!
This by your genius and the joys we stole,
Whose sweet remembrance still enchants my soul!

Great natal Genius! grant my heart's desire.
So shall I heap with costly gums your fire!
Whenever fancy paints me to the boy,
Let his breast pant with an impatient joy:
But if the libertine for others sigh,
(Which Love forbid!) O Love! your aid deny.
Nor, Love! be partial, let us both confess
The pleasing pain, or make my passion less.
But oh! much rather 'tis my soul's desire,
That both may feel an equal, endless fire.

In secret my Cerinthus begs the same,
But the youth blushes to confess his flame:
Assent, thou god! to whom his heart is known,
Whether he public ask, or secret own.     GRAINGER.


## POEM VI.

### TO SULPICIA'S JUNO.

ACCEPT, O natal queen! with placent air,
The incense offer'd by the learned fair.
She's robed in cheerful pomp, O power divine!
She's robed to decorate your matron shrine;
Such her pretence; but well her lover knows
Whence her gay look, and whence her finery flows.

Thou who dost o'er the nuptial bed preside,
Oh! let not envious night their joys divide,
But make the bridegroom amorous as the bride!
So shall they tally, matchless lovely pair!
A youth all transport, and a melting fair!
Then let no spies their secret haunts explore;
Teach them thy wiles, O Love! and guard the door.

Assent, chaste queen! in purple pomp appear;
Thrice wine is pour'd, and cakes await you, here.
Her mother tells her for what boon to pray;
Her heart denies it, though her lips obey.
She burns, that altar as the flames devour;
She burns, and slights the safety in her power.

So may the boy, whose chains you proudly wear,
Through youth the soft indulgent anguish bear;
And when old age has chill'd his every vein,
The dear remembrance may he still retain!

GRAINGER.

## POEM VII.

### SULPICIA'S AVOWAL.

LET other maids, whose eyes less prosperous prove,
Publish my weakness, and condemn my love.

Exult, my heart! at last the queen of joy,
  Won by the music of her votary's strain,
Leads to the couch of bliss herself the boy;
  And bids enjoyment thrill in every vein.

Last night entranced in ecstasy we lay,
And chid the quick, too quick return of day!
But stop, my hand! beware what loose you scrawl,
Lest into curious hands the billet fall.
No—the remembrance charms!—begone, grimace!
Matrons! be yours formality of face.
Know, with a youth of worth the night I spent,
And cannot, cannot for my soul, repent!   GRAINGER.

## POEM VIII.

### SULPICIA TO MESSALA.

AT last the natal odious morn draws nigh,
  When to your cold, cold villa I must go;
There, far, too far from my Cerinthus sigh:
  Oh why, Messala! will you plague me so?

Let studious mortals prize the sylvan scene,
  And ancient maidens hide them in the shade;
Green trees perpetually give me the spleen;
  For crowds, for joy, for Rome, Sulpicia's made!

Your too officious kindness gives me pain.
  How fall the hail-stones! hark! how howls the wind!
Then know, to grace your birth-day should I deign,
  My soul, my all, I leave at Rome behind.   GRAINGER.

## POEM IX.

### TIBULLUS TO MESSALA.

At last the fair's determin'd not to go:
  My lord! you know the whimsies of the sex.
Then let us gay carouse, let odours flow;
  Your mind no longer with her absence vex:
For, oh! consider, time incessant flies;
But every day's a birth-day to the wise!    GRAINGER.

## POEM X.

### SULPICIA TO CERINTHUS.

That I, descended of Patrician race,
With charms of fortune, and with charms of face,
Am so indifferent grown to you of late,
So little cared for, now excites no hate.
Rare taste, and worthy of a poet's brain,
  To prey on garbage, and a slave adore!
In such to find out charms, a bard must feign
  Beyond what fiction ever feign'd of yore.
Her friends may think Sulpicia is disgraced;
No! no! she honours your transcendent taste.
                                          GRAINGER.

## POEM XI.

### SULPICIA TO CERINTHUS.

On my account, to grief a ceaseless prey,
  Dost thou a sympathetic anguish prove?
I would not wish to live another day,
  If my recovery did not charm my love:
For what were life, and health, and bloom to me,
Were they displeasing, beauteous youth! to thee.
                                          GRAINGER.

## POEM XII.

### SULPICIA TO CERINTHUS.

IF from the bottom of my love-sick heart,
  Of last night's coyness I do not repent,
May I no more your tender anguish hear,
No longer see you shed th' impassion'd tear.

  You grasp'd my knees, and yet to let you part—
Oh night more happy with Cerinthus spent!
My flame with coyness to conceal I thought,
But this concealment was too dearly bought.

                                    GRAINGER.


## POEM XIII.

### TIBULLUS TO HIS MISTRESS.

To you my tongue eternal fealty swore,
  My lips the deed with conscious rapture own;
A fickle libertine I rove no more,
  You only please, and lovely seem alone.

The numerous beauties that gay Rome can boast,
  With you compared, are ugliness at best;
On me their bloom and practised smiles are lost,
  Drive then, my fair! suspicion from your breast.

Ah no! suspicion is the test of love:
  I too dread rivals, I'm suspicious grown;
Your charms the most insensate heart must move;
  Would you were beauteous in my eyes alone!

I want not man to envy my sweet fate,
  I little care that others think me blest;
Of happy conquests let the coxcomb prate;
  Vain-glorious vaunts the silent wise detest.

Supremely pleased with you, my heavenly fair!
  In any trackless desert I could dwell;
From our recess your smiles would banish care,
  Your eyes give lustre to the midnight cell.

For various converse I should long no more,
  The blithe, the moral, witty, and severe ;
Its various arts are hers whom I adore ;
  She can depress, exalt, instruct, and cheer.

Should mighty Jove send down from heaven a maid,
  With Venus' cestus zoned, my faith to try,
(So, as I truth declare, me Juno aid !)
  For you I'd scorn the charmer of the sky.

But hold ! you're mad to vow, unthinking fool.
  Her boundless sway you're mad to let her know :
Safe from alarms, she'll treat you as a tool—
  Ah, babbling tongue ! from thee what mischiefs flow !

Yet let her use me with neglect, disdain ;
  In all, subservient to her will I'll prove ;
Whate'er I feel, her slave I'll still remain ;
  Who shrinks from sorrow, cannot be in love !

Imperial Queen of Bliss ! with fetters bound,
  I'll sit me down before your holy fane ;
You kindly heal the constant lover's wound,
  Th' inconstant torture with increase of pain.
                                        GRAINGER.


                    THE SAME.

" NEVER shall woman's smile have power
    To win me from those gentle charms ! "
Thus swore I in that happy hour
    When Love first gave them to my arms.

And still alone thou charm'st my sight—
    Still, though our city proudly shine
With forms and faces fair and bright,
    I see none fair or bright but thine.

Would thou wert fair for only me,
    And couldst no heart but mine allure !
To all men else unpleasing be,
    So shall I feel my prize secure.

Oh love like mine ne'er wants the zest
  Of others' envy, others' praise;
But in its silence safely blest,
  Broods o'er a bliss it ne'er betrays.

Charm of my life! by whose sweet power
  All cares are hush'd, all ills subdued—
My light in ev'n the darkest hour,
  My crowd in deepest solitude!

No; not though heaven itself sent down
  Some maid of more than heavenly charms,
With bliss undreamt thy bard to crown,
  Would I for her forsake those arms.   MOORE.


THE SAME.

No second love shall e'er my heart surprise,
  This solemn league did first our passion bind:
Thou, only thou, canst please thy lover's eyes,
  Thy voice alone can soothe his troubled mind.

Oh that thy charms were only fair to me,
  Displease all others, and secure my rest,
No need of envy,—let me happy be,
  I little care that others know me blest.

With thee in gloomy deserts let me dwell,
  Where never human footstep mark'd the ground;
Thou, light of life, all darkness canst expel,
  And seem a world with solitude around.

I say too much—my heedless words restore,
  My tongue undoes me in this loving hour;
Thou know'st thy strength, and thence insulting more,
  Wilt make me feel the weight of all thy power.

Whate'er I feel, thy slave I will remain,
  Nor fly the burden I am form'd to bear;
In chains I'll sit me down at Venus' fane,
  She knows my wrongs, and will regard my prayer.
                                        HAMMOND

## POEM XIV.

FAME says, my mistress loves another swain;
    Would I were deaf, when Fame repeats the wrong!
All crimes to her imputed give me pain,
    Not change my love: Fame, stop your saucy tongue!

GRAINGER

## THE END.

# INDEX.

C. stands for Catullus; T. for Tibullus; V. for the Vigil of Venus. Roman numerals mark the number of the poem, Arabic that of the page.